BOUND

THE DEVIL'S DUE (BOOK 3)

EVA CHARLES

QUARRY ROAD PUBLISHING

Copyright © 2020 by Eva Charles

ALL RIGHTS RESERVED

No part of this book may be used or reproduced in any form whatsoever without express written permission from the author or publisher, except in the case of brief quotations embedded in critical articles and reviews.

This book is a work of fiction. Any references to historical events, real people, or real places are used fictitiously. All other names, characters, places, and incidents are products of the author's imagination. Any resemblance to actual events, places, organizations, or persons living or dead is entirely coincidental.

Trademark names appear throughout this book. In lieu of a trademark symbol with each occurrence of a trademark name, names are used in an editorial fashion with no intention of infringement of the respective owner's trademark.

- Cover by Murphy Rae
- Dawn Alexander, Evident Ink, Content Editor
- Nancy Smay, Evident Ink, Copy and Line Editor
- Virginia Tesi Carey, Proofreader
- Stephanie Taylor, Proofreader

For more information, contact eva@evacharles.com

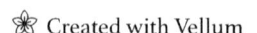

❈ Created with Vellum

To Sister Jackie who taught me so much, including that resources are scarce. Take only what you need. I think of you every time I reach for a napkin.

Perhaps this is the moment for which you have been created.

— ESTHER 4:14, THE BIBLE

A NOTE FROM EVA

*D*ear Readers and Friends,
    I suppose any romance book that includes a Catholic priest requires a note from the author. From the number of messages I've received, Bound is no exception.

Let me begin by saying, the priest could have been a rabbi, a minister, or any clergy, really, (although nothing is quite as scandalous as a naughty priest).

The story is not meant to cast aspersions on any particular religion, and certainly not the Catholics (note the dedication). It's that I spent years under the tutelage of the Sisters of the Sacred Heart, and then with the Jesuits—write what you know, they say. So I did.

Bound is a romantic suspense with dangerous men and dark elements. While our thresholds are different, there are dark facets to this story. I'm not kidding. If you have reservations about the content, please don't hesitate to contact me prior to reading.

For those who relish the kind of evil that lurks in shadowy corners, words that make your eyes bleed, and dirty sex, welcome back to Charleston!

Please note: While Bound can be read as a standalone, it is

the third book in The Devil's Due series and is best enjoyed after reading Depraved and Delivered. Bound has no cliffhanger.

Thank you for reading!

xoxo

Eva

PS. You're going to LOVE Smith!

1

SMITH

*G*ray Wilder's number lights up my dashboard for the fourth time today. I've dated stage-five clingers who were less annoying.

My first inclination is to disconnect Bluetooth, toss my phone out the window, and go grab a beer. But I don't. Gray's more than a client. He's pretty much family, and right now, he's needier than my three-year-old niece on the brink of a spectacular meltdown.

"What now?" My irritation emphasizes each word.

"Just checking that you're on your way."

Got to hand it to him, unlike his older brother, he lets my piss-poor attitude roll off his back. JD would have never let it pass.

"Do I blow off assignments? When I say I'm going to be somewhere, have you ever known me not to show up?"

"You weren't exactly thrilled about taking the meeting."

That's the understatement of the century.

"Well, I'm here. Parked across the street from Tallulah's, where I can see McKenna when she pulls into the lot."

"Okay. Good."

Gray's anxiety level is off the charts. Kate McKenna has been hanging around, asking too many questions, pestering him nonstop. If she discovers the truth about his club, Wildflower, it will be a disaster of epic proportions. I get it. But I'm not much of a hand-holder. I expect grown men to handle their shit like grown men.

"This is the *fourth* time you've called—not to mention all the texts. Can't you find a distraction? You own a goddamn sex club. You must know someone who'd be willing to entertain your dick for a few hours so you can leave me the hell alone."

"You're beginning to sound a lot like my brother. That's not a compliment. Maybe it's your dick that needs entertaining."

Not a terrible idea. But it'll have to wait until I'm finished intimidating a nosy little reporter.

I bang my forehead against the worn leather steering wheel while he drones on and on. "Just make sure you take care of this bullshit once and for all. I don't want to hear that reporter's name again after today."

I might work for Wilder Holdings, and it's one thing to take direction from the top, but regardless of how old Gray is, he'll always be JD's kid brother, and I'm not taking orders from him. At least not without giving him plenty of shit.

"I was chasing bad guys through the desert and into caves when you were still calling your pathetic hard-on a chubby. But if you think you can do a better job, by all means come on down because there are a million ways I'd rather spend a Sunday."

"Don't underestimate McKenna," Gray snaps. "She's tenacious. Worse than a rabid little dog."

I glance into the rearview mirror as a car with Massachusetts tags turns onto the quiet street. "Well, I'm a Pit Bull. I snack on little dogs and I don't give a flying fuck if they're rabid."

"What's got you so damn surly?"

Before I can answer, the beat-up Volvo pulls into the parking lot with a redhead at the wheel. *Showtime.* "If you've got something that can't wait, text me. Otherwise, let me do the job you pay me to do."

I disconnect the call and watch the woman exit the vehicle, lugging an enormous purse behind her. *Why do women saddle themselves with ridiculous accessories?* The thing probably weighs a ton. I could pack for six months in a bag half that size.

Kate McKenna presses the key fob without bothering to check if the lock engaged, and traipses through the near-deserted parking lot without once checking her surroundings. That kind of blatant disregard for safety usually drives me nuts, but today I plan to use it to my advantage.

From here, she's at least as good-looking as the photos splashed across social media. With all the filters people use, you never know what you're actually going to get when you finally meet them.

McKenna is so preoccupied, she trips over the uneven pavement. *Jesus.* What a disaster. She's damn lucky she didn't hit the ground face-first. Most people look around after they pull a stunt like that to see if anyone witnessed it. *Not her. She's too busy in her own head.* Too busy to notice me stalking her. Either she's reckless or too trusting. Maybe both. The two often go hand in hand. Getting rid of her should be a piece of cake.

Three years ago, I was extricating high-value hostages from the jungle in a corrupt, drug-infested South American country, and flushing terrorists out of caves in the Middle East and Africa. Now, I'm chasing a two-bit reporter out of a sleepy city in the South.

Fuck me.

I can't do this shit anymore. My fingers tighten around the wheel. *I just can't.* I need to talk to JD, and it can't wait any longer. He's not going to be happy, but it's the way it has to be—plain and simple. *If it's so simple, why is my damn gut burning like a sonofabitch?*

Red pauses in the middle of the lot to dig through that stupid purse. Her shoulders hunch forward while she rummages. She's not tiny, yet something about her seems small and vulnerable.

Big bad reporter. *Pfft.* She looks like a college kid. Nice ass, though. I'd like to sink my teeth into one of those tight little cheeks.

2

KATE

The phone rings as I trudge across the parking lot. It sounds shriller than usual, maybe because I'm on edge, or maybe it's an omen. *A bad omen.*

While I root around the bottom of my tote, a sense of dread slithers into my chest, twisting and contorting the muscles as it consumes me. *Please don't be Smith Sinclair canceling the interview. Please.*

It's only a matter of seconds before I locate the phone. But by then my hands are trembling, and I'm struggling to breathe.

When I peek at the screen, the breath caught in my chest escapes in a long dramatic whoosh. It's Colin, my editor at the Washington Sun. The second-to-last person in the entire universe I want to hear from right now, but at least it's not Sinclair. I pull my shoulders back and force myself to exude more confidence than I'm feeling. "Hello."

"Just checking in."

"I'm about to meet Sinclair. Can we talk later?"

"Kate, I know you believe in this story, but you're out of time." *Just checking in. Right.* "If the interview goes nowhere, I need you at your desk by noon tomorrow."

It's a solid fourteen hours from Charleston to DC without stops. I'd have to drive all night to be there by midday. But I don't remind Colin of this, because I have no intention of making the trip tonight, or tomorrow for that matter.

"You can always work the story on the side," he soothes, placating me as if I'm a disappointed child. I can almost feel him pat my head. "I've done all I can for now," he adds for good measure.

It's a lie, and we both know it. He's done all he's willing to do. *Work the story on the side. Right.* When I get back to DC, I'll be so inundated with fluff pieces there won't be a second to pursue any real stories. "Warren King's confirmation hearing is set to begin in less than a week. Supreme Court Justices have jobs for life. Once he's confirmed, it's too late."

"Listen, King wouldn't have been my pick, but the national press was holed up in Charleston for weeks talking to his neighbors, sifting through his trash, following every lead, just like you've been doing. And despite all the diligence, and all the hunches, what did they find? *Nada,*" he says when I don't respond.

"He's a member of a secret society. Some of those societies have ties to human trafficking. If it's all on the up-and-up, why all the secrecy?"

We've been having this same conversation for a week now. I'm tired of justifying myself, and the irritation in my voice is palpable, but Colin either doesn't hear it, or he doesn't care.

"St. Anslem's is not a secret," he explains with his patience on edge.

"But everything that happens inside is."

"Rumors. Unsubstantiated rumors."

"From sources with knowledge."

"Kate—" I picture him rolling his eyes and tapping that stupid Superman pen he loves on the edge of a yellow notepad. Patience is not Colin's strong suit, and I've tested it repeatedly with this assignment. "Aside from the local press, there's no one left in Charleston from a reputable media outlet."

"Big stories are unearthed by reporters who work hard and continue to dig long after everyone else has put down the shovel. I've heard you give that spiel dozens of times. Is it just an empty platitude?"

The silence on the other end of the phone is deafening. "It's time for you to come home. I'm sorry."

I stop short at the base of the stairs, squeezing the wrought iron railing. DC is *not* my home. *And it never will be.* It's just a place I landed when home was no longer a viable option. I don't say that to him because it sounds ungrateful. Colin hired me when my prospects were slim, and for that, I will always be indebted to him.

"I'm confident my meeting with Sinclair will yield fruit."

"It better be a truckload of fruit. Ripe fruit. As it is, I owe the Style editor a *huge* favor for borrowing you for three weeks during high season."

"You're fucking the Style editor, Colin."

"That just gives her more opportunities to call in the favor. All hands on deck for the Keaton wedding—I gave her my word."

I swallow a groan. "Gotta go."

"Call me after you talk to Sinclair. Good luck."

"Thanks." I hang up before he can say anything else. I don't need any more reminders of how high the stakes are for me. The Washington Sun has an international reputation. After what happened in Boston, I'm lucky to have this job, even if it is at the Style desk.

Ambassador Keaton's daughter's wedding. The fairy tale Washington so desperately needs to distract itself from President Wilder's assassination and the ugly politics that followed the requisite mourning period.

But the grief has just begun for me if I'm stuck covering that fiasco.

I can see it now. Miles of imported French tulle embroidered with fine gold filigree, bridesmaid dresses in an array of pastels better suited to Easter eggs than to the human form, and a multi-tiered cake artfully draped in fondant, with a crumb so dry, guests won't be able to choke it down. Like everything else in Washington, the nuptials will be encased in a glossy veneer, all for show. Where I'm from, we call that gloss bullshit.

This is not how my career as a journalist began, nor how I envisioned it unfolding. It's not that covering the lifestyles of the rich and famous isn't honest work. Most of the reporters who write for the society pages are talented and hardworking. It's just that the longer I'm covering socialites, the less likely it is I will ever be given an investigative assignment, and if that doesn't happen, I'll never be able to do right by my mother. Although that train veered off the track when I left Boston. *But what choice did I have?*

My stomach roils as I pull open the solid oak door to Tallulah's. Before stepping across the threshold, I take a deep breath and adjust the heavy tote on my shoulder. *Smith Sinclair, you better come through big for me.*

Inside I blink a few times while my eyes adjust to the low light. The place has a kitschy charm with dark paneled walls and wide-plank floors that give it an outdated vibe. There's a pleasant citrus scent in the air, but it's too light to fully mask the booze, sweat, and promise of sex that's seeped into the wood through the years. Tallulah's is a working man's bar where every tongue and groove has a story to tell. It reminds me of a neighborhood place not far from where I grew up, where off-duty cops would hang out after their shifts.

I'm early, but I skim the room for Sinclair. I've never laid eyes on him, but I've seen enough photographs to recognize his face.

There are only a handful of patrons in the place. A middle-aged man with an unkempt beard is working his way through a platter of fried chicken at the bar, and several stools down, three guys are watching a basketball game, hissing at the screen. *All men.* But no Sinclair.

I scan the perimeter of the room, taking note of the exits. It's a well-ingrained habit. Sources often want to meet in sketchy, out-of-the-way locations where they won't be seen snitching to a reporter. I'm always careful, but I always go to the story—*always*—regardless of how dangerous it appears. That's what good investigative journalism requires. *That's what my mother did.*

Tallulah's doesn't exactly feel shady, but it certainly doesn't seem like the kind of place anyone closely associated with the Wilders would frequent.

"Can I help you, miss?" the bartender asks, juicing a lime into a tall Mason jar. He doesn't stop squeezing to make eye contact.

"I'm meeting someone. I don't think he's here yet."

"You're welcome to wait. Sit wherever you'd like." He cocks his chin toward an area of the room with a few booths and a smattering of tables scattered haphazardly. He doesn't ask if I want something to drink while I wait. I haven't been in Charleston long, but it's unusual for a local to act like they can't be bothered. I glance at the half-bushel of limes still to be juiced. Maybe I caught him at a bad time.

"Thanks."

The seating area is situated within earshot of the bar. I eye the booth closest to the back wall where we'll have the most privacy. I want Sinclair to be comfortable talking because I need answers. *Lots of them.*

One of the guys at the end of the bar tips his River Dogs cap as I pass, and his friends greet me with a chorus of pleasantries. The thing about Charleston is that most everyone smiles and says hello. They wield that famous southern charm effortlessly, but despite their impeccable manners, they don't like outsiders. This makes it almost impossible to get any useful information from them. But I understand. I'm from Boston, and we don't like outsiders either. The difference is we don't bother with the pasted-on smiles and polite airs. We're just plain old-fashioned rude.

I approach the booth and set my tote on the bench facing the door, pulling out a small notebook with some questions I prioritized this morning. I don't know how much time Sinclair will give me, and I don't want the interview to end before I have answers to the most crucial questions.

While I'm digging through my bag, a man slides into the booth across from me—a behemoth with the neck of an offensive lineman and shoulders that span nearly two-thirds of the bench.

Sinclair just stares. His face is stern, and he says nothing, not even hello.

The images on the web don't do him justice. Sure, they capture his strong features and proud, muscular frame. A few even caught a devilish grin. But he's not grinning now. And he's much bigger, and *so* much more imposing in person. I catch myself gaping, mouth open like I'm on a fly-catching expedition. "Mr. Sinclair?"

"Smith." His gaze drills through me like I'm made of cheap drywall that crumbles easily. Sinclair was a Green Beret, and there is a great deal of speculation that he had been a member of the elite Delta Force, but since the US military won't officially confirm anything about that unit, I can't be certain.

"I'm Kate McKenna." I hold out my hand but he ignores it. It's a slap in the face that stings a bit, but I hold my temper and disregard the brazen slight. I don't have the luxury of slapping back. "I didn't see you come in."

His response is to assess me openly, the way a prizefighter sizes up an inferior opponent. It's unnerving, and instinctively I call up the location of the closest exit. Not that I'm going anywhere—I can't—he'd have to threaten me with a weapon for that to happen, and even then, I might not walk away. I'm not going back to DC empty-handed. Not this time. "Thank—thank you for meeting with me." *Dammit.* I sound as nervous as I feel.

"Don't thank me yet." His voice is deep and rich. There's a seductive quality about it, much like there was when we spoke on the phone last fall, after I had been assigned to do a feature story on Zack Wilder, the former President's youngest son. Even though I had hated the message Sinclair very clearly delivered at the time, something about his voice beckoned. I remember it clearly.

His voice might be intoxicating, but his glare is relentless, tracking my every movement as I tuck a loose curl behind my ear. "I won't take up too much of your time. I have some questions about Wildflower, the social club Gray Wilder runs."

"You want me to answer questions about the Wilders and their business holdings?" His expression is unreadable, but there's a sarcastic edge to his words.

I bob my head a few times, the butterflies swirling erratically in my empty stomach. The request sounds foolish and incredibly naïve coming from his mouth. "Mainly about Wildflower. I know you're in charge of security for all of Wilder Holdings and for the Wilders personally. I just have a few questions about Wildflower."
Stop rambling, Kate.

Sinclair purses his smooth full lips. I catch a small twitch at the corner of his mouth like he's fighting off an urge to laugh in my face. "What do you want to drink?" he asks, after leaving me hanging for several seconds.

What do you want to drink? Yes! He's planning to stay, at least a little while. "I'll have a beer. Whatever's on tap."

My hands unfurl as the tension begins to dissipate. I'll have a chance to get some information. How much, though, depends entirely on his cooperation. I'm at his mercy.

He wiggles two fingers at the bartender, who has abandoned his limes and is leaning over the bar eager to take our order. "Got any of those corn nuts today?"

"Made a fresh batch this morning."

"You're the man, Beau."

When Sinclair's done with the bartender, he shifts back to me. "Beer. And not a light beer where they've siphoned off all the flavor. I'm impressed, Mary Katherine McKenna."

Mary Katherine McKenna. It catches me by surprise. Mary Katherine is my baptismal name. It's on all my official documents, but I never use it. Aside from Nana, and Father Tierney, our parish priest, unless I'm in trouble, everyone calls me Kate. Everyone but Smith Sinclair, it seems.

I regard him carefully for a moment. He's testing. I need to turn the tables quickly, otherwise he'll have the upper hand for the entire interview, and I'll leave here with nothing.

I flash him a cheeky smile, hoping it doesn't look as fake as it feels. "I do what I can to impress the fairer sex, Mr. Sinclair. Thank you for noticing—" I raise my brow in a perfectly orchestrated attack, and let my smile fade quietly, "unless you're insinuating that I *should* be drinking light beer."

I don't have much of a flair for the dramatic, but that was an Oscar-winning performance. These days most men back far, far away from any comment they make to a woman that might be construed as demeaning. I don't know what he meant by it, and I don't really care. I just hope the act was enough to shake him up a bit.

He sits back comfortably, folding his large hands in front of him on the table, thumbs tapping against one another. His eyes wander from mine, raking over my jittery body, taking it all in—until he's satisfied. "I'd never suggest that to any woman. Even if it crossed my mind. But you should keep on doing whatever you're doing. It works for you."

Either Sinclair isn't most men, or the Academy Awards will have to wait. I'm guessing it's the former as I swallow to soothe a bone-dry mouth, then order my skin to *stop* tingling. *Damn him.* He's still winning.

Everything about him is unsettling. He's too big, too forward, too comfortable in his own skin, and he's taking up too damn much space in my head. At least it feels that way.

My face is overheated, and I'm not thinking straight. I need to come up with a new plan to win him over because the one I have isn't working. I should have known better. Yes, I expected him to be a brick wall I'd have to chip away at to get information, but I didn't expect him to have this kind of presence or to exert this kind of control—he wields control the way Thor wields his hammer: exacting and merciless.

Getting anything useful from Sinclair is going to be a challenge.

While I'm still trying to figure out the best way forward, he slaps one hand against the other, rubbing his palms together. "So, Mary Katherine, what exactly do you need in order to stop harassing the Wilders?"

My stomach coils into a tight ball. *Maybe an impossible challenge.* "Please call me Kate. When you call me Mary Katherine, I begin to worry I'm about to be punished."

There's a glimmer in his eyes. "No need to worry in that regard. When I'm ready to punish you, you'll know."

I can't believe he just said that. And I can't believe my brain is entertaining the countless ways he might punish me. But what really mortifies me is the unmistakable twinge of arousal between my legs. The kind that happens during a long, hot make-out session with someone who knows how to kiss. The kind of kissing that makes it impossible to stop, even when you know you should. I only hope my puckered nipples aren't visible through my thin shirt.

He starts to say more, but the bartender comes over with our beer and a bowl of corn nuts. "Thanks, Beau," Sinclair says. "I saw your daddy hauling firewood yesterday. Offered to give him a hand loading the truck, but he shook me off."

"Don't get me started on that stubborn old fool." Beau shakes his head. "The waitress will be here shortly. Holler if you need anything in the meantime."

"Carrie on tonight?" Sinclair asks, almost too casually. Beau glances over his shoulder with an easy grin that Sinclair returns.

For the record, he's still winning. He's now established that this is his place, and these are his people. It's a game for him. Like he's trying to psyche me out before the pissing contest starts. *Good luck, buddy.* I have an umbrella in my bag, and I'm not afraid of bodily fluids. I've been pissed on before. Shit on too, for that matter.

Focus, Kate. Focus. You need to regroup. Make a little small talk to warm him up. "How long have you been in Charleston?" I ask, sipping my beer.

"Three years." He grabs a fistful of corn nuts and nudges the bowl in my direction. "Why?"

I shrug, pull a single crispy nut from the container and devour it. Even if I wasn't starving, I can totally see how these salty little nuggets could become addictive. I try not to seem too greedy as I reach into the bowl for more and pop them into my mouth one after another.

Sinclair watches with great amusement as the punishing heat creeps up and sets my mouth on fire. I take a big swig of beer while the bastard sits across the table, smirking, those damn dimples winking at me.

"Go easy with those if you're not used to spicy food. Or even if you are. The burn sneaks up on you, and it can be brutal. Especially when the nuts are fresh." *He couldn't have mentioned this before I shoveled them into my mouth?*

I don't want to guzzle the beer or give him the satisfaction of watching me squirm. "I love spicy food," I announce brightly. He lifts his glass, but not before I spy that damn smirk again. I take a few more sips, but put down the beer when I realize it's not helping.

"Most people I've met here are exceedingly polite, but they

hold out-of-towners at arm's length." I manage to steer the conversation back to Charleston in a steady voice, as though the whole corn nut fiasco had never happened. "How long do you have to live here before the natives stop treating you like an outsider?"

"You thinking about making this home?" he asks, a big paw gripping the glass.

"No." The word comes out quickly. It's automatic. I don't need even a nanosecond to think about it. Boston's home. At least it used to be. And it will be again. *I hope.* I rub my hands up and down my arms to ward off a chill. "Just trying to figure this place out. It's somewhat of a mystery. There's something about the *Holy City* that makes me believe it's hiding dark secrets—like maybe it's not so *holy*."

I glance at him, hoping his expression will give something away. But he doesn't blink, so I prod some more. "Maybe because it's such an old city with a complicated history. Not sure. But I can't shake the feeling that the layers of charm are concealing a black heart."

"That attitude certainly isn't going to win you any friends in these parts. People from here take exceptional pride in the city, and they don't take kindly to strangers pointing out the flaws in their *complicated history*." He draws out each syllable, mocking me. "There are a lot of transplants in Charleston. Many more than the locals would like. Some of them will live out their entire lives here, and they'll always be outsiders."

"So what's your secret?"

"What makes you think I wasn't born and bred here?"

"Because you grew up at Fort Bragg." I did a little research too, and now that I'm beginning to settle in, the details are starting to come back to me.

"When I get to a new place, I adapt to the customs. People are generally proud of where they live, of who they are, and they don't take well to know-it-alls bringing their own ideas and customs to town—and trying to shove them down everybody's throat."

"That must have served you well in the military."

"*Ah.* Ms. McKenna did her homework." He rubs the back of his neck and smiles. It's not warm or sincere, and it fades before ever reaching his eyes.

"Ms. McKenna always does her homework." Unlike her mother, she's not talented or experienced enough to wing it.

"You're from Boston. I went to college there. They don't like outsiders, either. So don't act like you're experiencing culture shock." There's a sharpness to his voice. He expected me to research the Wilders, but it bothers him that I dug into his background too. The tables are finally turning in my favor, so I push a little more.

"You went to college in Cambridge," I say matter-of-factly. He cocks his head to the right, his lips thin and tight. "Harvard is in Cambridge. That's not Boston."

After what seems like an eternity, Sinclair leans across the table, heavily muscled forearms flat on the wooden surface. He's encroaching on my side of the booth, scowling. His beautiful face and sandy hair, gilded with the kind of highlights some women pay a fortune for, aren't doing a single thing to soften his appearance. If it weren't for the gold flecks in his eyes reflecting light, he could be easily mistaken for the kind of monster you wouldn't want to encounter in a dark alley. My heart is pounding again.

"Now that we've established you know my shoe size and how long my dick is, why don't you just tell me what the hell you want."

3

KATE

I see. He only likes to play if he's in control. Although his tone is rough and uncompromising, he doesn't raise his voice. He doesn't have to. Sinclair is attempting to intimidate me with his sheer size and vulgar language. If I allow it, I'm finished.

I sit up taller and force myself to lean toward him, gripping the bench for support. "I want to know about Wildflower." My mouth is pasty and the words get stuck in my throat. They emerge desperate and weak, and just like that, my attempt to project some authority falls flat—in a dazzling fashion. It's all over his face. His jaw is slack, and the glow of victory shines brightly in his eyes. But he doesn't rub my nose in it. *Not yet.*

"It's a social club," he responds coolly, checking his phone.

"A men's club?"

Sinclair slides the phone back into his pocket and takes a drink. "Don't waste my time with questions you already know the answers to. Most of the social clubs and societies in Charleston were founded by men. You already know this."

"The older clubs, but Wildflower hasn't been around that

long." He peers at me over his glass, but doesn't respond. I need to know if it's truly a men's club. Historically, it's the all-male clubs that close their eyes to, or even support, human trafficking. "Does the club have female members?"

"Women have all the privileges of belonging that men do."

He's dancing around the question. *But why?* "What kind of privileges?"

Sinclair takes a handful of corn nuts, tossing a few into his mouth, chewing and swallowing like they don't have the devil's spice sprinkled all over them. "The spa, tennis courts, gym, dining," he finally answers.

This is like pulling teeth from a lightly sedated bear. I need to move slowly, with razor sharp precision. One wrong move and he'll bite my head off and run into the woods. "Anything else?" I ask cautiously. I'm careful not to chase him away—or to get bitten.

"I'm sure there are other perks, like the sweet swag bag members get for joining, but I can't remember every little thing. I'm not much of a detail man."

"I don't believe that." It comes out as an accusation. And in a way it is—I don't believe him. But calling him a liar won't help my case, so I smile sweetly to temper the impact of the words.

The waitress comes over, Carrie I assume, and Sinclair chats her up. It's small talk, with some friendly banter but no real flirting. He doesn't bother to introduce us. I doubt it's an oversight. I doubt he does anything that's not calculated.

"I see you've almost finished off those nuts. Still hungry?" she asks, just at the moment I've decided to introduce myself.

"I—" I don't get to finish my introduction or to answer her question about food. Not that it matters. She isn't talking to me.

"We'll have two burgers, medium rare. One with a side of fries. The other with onion rings." *Two burgers?* He has an enormous appetite. *Probably in all things.* I adjust my butt on the seat to quiet a small zing between my legs. *Wait. We'll have two burgers? He ordered for me without bothering to ask what I wanted? Of all the overbearing, misogynistic—I'm going to stab him before this interview is over. And no one will blame me.*

"Cheese?" the waitress asks Sinclair. He glances across the table as though it just occurred to him I'm still here and might have an opinion about what I eat.

"Pepper Jack on the one with the onion rings," he instructs the waitress when I don't immediately chime in. "Something mild on the other." I'm sure his little smirk is meant for me. "I'll take a refill, please," he tips his mug, "and bring Miss McKenna one when you bring the burgers."

She flashes him a warm, pretty smile. "Anything else?"

"That's all for now. Thank you, ma'am."

I need his cooperation, but being a doormat hasn't worked very well so far, and I'm tired of playing the part. Besides, I have a feeling Smith Sinclair might be the kind of man who appreciates a little push back. Some men are like that.

"I wasn't planning on having dinner, but when I do, I normally order for myself. I've been choosing my own food for years now. I'm quite good at it."

Sinclair pushes his shoulder blades into the back of the faded vinyl bench. I have his *complete* attention now. It's more than I bargained for, and I will myself not to color under the scrutiny. "I always prefer a brat to a princess." He tips his head, rubbing a single thumb over the stubble along his jaw. "Especially one who turns pink without much effort. If you weren't so dead set on sticking your nose into Wilder business, we could be friends. *Good* friends."

The word *good* skitters across my skin, leaving tiny raised bumps in its wake. His eyes have mine in a tight hold. I want to look away, but I don't. I can't. Because even though my body is responding like this is the best foreplay it's experienced in years,

I'm here to do a job. I have to take the power back. *Back? Did you ever have it?*

I'm screwed. I need answers from him, but I have no idea how to get them. None.

"The menu's limited," he continues, drumming those long, thick fingers on the table, "as in, there isn't one. They have burgers and fried chicken. Don't tell me you wanted a salad." His tone is chock-full of innuendo. *What a jerk.*

"I might have preferred a salad. And I don't appreciate the little digs about my weight."

"Nobody orders salad here. If they're foolish enough to make that mistake, the cook tosses some of the lettuce, tomato, and onion they use for burgers on a plate. You'd stick out like an outsider. I did you a favor. And I already told you that you have a nice body. Maybe not in so many words." He hasn't released my eyes, and I'll be damned if I look away first. "For a reporter, you don't seem to read between the lines very well. Or be much of a listener."

I bite back the snarky remark on the tip of my tongue. "I don't eat cheeseburgers."

"Religious thing?"

"No."

"Lactose intolerant?"

I dig my fingers into my thighs so I don't reach across the table and throat punch him. "No."

"Then you're good. Just scrape off the cheese if you don't like it."

"And I don't need another beer." *Oh, God.* I sound like a whiny teenager, without a shred of dignity.

"The one you're sipping from like it's a rare vintage of champagne will be piss-warm before the food gets here, if it isn't already."

I'd like to dump my piss-warm beer over his head. *Keaton wedding, Easter egg dresses, dry cake—and most important of all, my mother's legacy.* These are the reasons Smith Sinclair isn't mopping beer off his gorgeous face.

I gather my composure and force myself to speak in a pleasant, upbeat tone. "Tell me about your relationship with the Wilders. You went to college with JD, right?"

"That is *never* happening. Next question."

It's only a matter of minutes before I begin pulling out my hair in clumps. I'm going to lay it all out for him. It might be perceived as a desperate move, but it's worked for me at times. And at this stage, I have nothing to lose. "Look, do us both a favor. I need some answers, and you want to be done with me. Just throw a little something my way and I'll be out of your hair forever. I don't care about the Wilders. I'm interested in the broader topic of Charleston's history with men's clubs and societies, and Warren King's relationship to them. My job depends on it."

While I plead my case, my voice cracks. It's a small fracture, so tiny, I doubt he notices. But I hear it, loud and clear. I'm ashamed at what a beggar I've become, but it doesn't stop me from continuing to grovel. "Please."

He assesses me carefully, the same way I'm assessing him. Just when I think he's about to give me something, the waitress approaches the table with our food. "Eat your burger. We'll talk after," he says, when Carrie walks away.

Arghhh! I've been successful because people open up to me. Even when they know I'm a reporter, they tell me things, confide in me in ways they probably shouldn't. I'm approachable and compassionate. I listen. Most people are desperate to talk. They just need someone to listen, because nobody really listens. Instead they're making lists in their heads, thinking about what comes next, how they can bring the conversation back around to them, deciding what they're going to prepare for dinner, or if it's a good time to ask if they can bring home a puppy. I don't do any of that. I know how to be present. How to listen empathetically. It's my greatest strength, and it's always worked for me—until Charleston.

Sinclair grabs a handful of fries from my plate. "Thought we'd share," he says in response to what I'm sure is a horrified look on my face. "Help yourself to all the onion rings you want. Just leave me a few."

He's taking food off my plate without bothering to ask, like we're animals in a barnyard. Oh. My. God.

I grew up with three older brothers, and all my life there have been cops—mostly men who worked for my dad—in and out of our house. Men with the manners of vultures are not a foreign concept to me. Although my standards don't approach Emily Post's, I just met this guy who's foraging from my plate, and his familiarity is obnoxious. I'm starting to wonder if dealing with him is worth *any* story.

Relax. Just relax. He's trying to get under your skin so you give up in frustration. This is exactly what he wants.

"Why did you leave the Boston Sentinel?" he asks, still grazing from my plate.

I shrug, and give him my standard response to the question. "It was time to move on." I don't even flinch as the well-rehearsed fib falls off my tongue.

"*Huh.* I read you eavesdropped and stole classified information from your father. That's how you became an overnight success."

It's a punch square to the gut. A clean slash into the armor I've carefully constructed, and the gasp of pain escapes before I can stop it.

Sinclair bites into his burger, pretending he's not gauging my reaction—not witnessing the acute distress or the gore spilling from the gaping wound. The bastard just sits there waiting to see if he landed the knockout blow.

I glare across the table without really seeing him, until I can pull myself together. I want to grab my tote and swing at his head before I run out of Tallulah's and back to DC, but I will not let this man take everything I've worked for. Everything I want for myself—and for my mother. I will not let him win. Not without a fight.

"That is not true." I answer definitively, in a strong voice, even though my insides are trembling as I cut the burger in two. I lift the top half of the bun to scrape the cheese off, but decide it's not worth the effort. "I started working at the paper when I was sixteen. I worked hard for any success I had there. None of it happened overnight."

"But the rest is true?" Smith asks, taking a couple onion rings off his plate, and depositing them on mine.

"None of it's true." I don't owe him a damn thing, certainly not an explanation, but if I share, maybe it will encourage him to speak more candidly too. "I left because my father deserves the police commissioner's job, and as long as I'm there investigating stories, I'm a convenient weapon for his detractors to use against him. I couldn't have that."

Sinclair doesn't say anything, but I feel his eyes on me while I mindlessly rearrange French fries on my plate. My appetite has disappeared.

"Everything I read sounded like bullshit." He takes a fry off my plate, drags it through a puddle of ketchup on his, and offers it to me. I shake my head. But he won't be denied. He touches it to my lips, and when my tongue darts out to catch a gob of ketchup, he slips the fry inside. It's an intimate gesture, but feels more conciliatory than sexual.

"People who want my father to have the job don't believe a word of it, and people who want the other guy to have it are sure it's all true," I tell him after I finish chewing.

"How about your colleagues at the paper?"

My colleagues were the least of my problems. "Most everyone knew it was a lie. But the few who were sure I was sleeping with my editor to get plum assignments had something new to gossip about."

"Were you?"

"Was I what?"

"Fucking your editor?"

I look him straight in the eye. "Of course not."

"How about your father? Did he believe you?"

My stomach ties itself into a painful knot. Sinclair's probing has disturbed the scab in my heart. It's still not quite healed. Maybe it will never be. *Mary Katherine, I want to believe you. But how else would you have gotten this information?* How else, indeed? Certainly not by skills or smarts. Or talent. Those possibilities didn't seem to resonate with him.

"My father believed me." *Eventually.* At least I think he did.

"That's not very convincing, Mary Katherine. Are you going to eat the other half of your burger?"

I shake my head, and push the plate toward him. "Help yourself."

"So you went to Washington to prove everybody wrong, to show them that you really are a talented reporter who didn't need to steal information from Daddy to publish a great story. But you got stuck on the society pages, and that's how you ended up chasing the Wilders."

Prick. Just when I feel like he has some measure of empathy, he's a total prick. *Again.* "I don't know how many times I have to say it. The Wilders are an inconsequential piece of what I'm after."

"Sure they are," he says with a smug tone, before finishing what's left of my burger in three bites.

"As I said earlier, Warren King is my focus. Wildflower is a logical place to begin." *And every other alley I've gone down is dark.* I take a sip of beer to fortify myself. "Tell me something about the club. How many members?"

"Not sure."

"Let's make a deal. I'll tell you all about why I left the Sentinel and went to Washington, every ugly detail, if you tell me a few things about Wildflower." I offer it up like it's a treasure, but it's not much of a deal. I've already shared the highlights, and there's no way I would ever tell him how terribly my family treated me, or how heartbroken I was over the whole sordid mess.

"I don't deal, Kate. Dealing is for people who have run out of ways to get what they want. I don't care why you left the Sentinel and went to DC. I was baiting you. And let's be clear, if I did care to know, I could find the answers with or without your cooperation."

My heart hammers against my chest wall, the way it does when you realize you're trapped with nowhere to go. When you've played all your pieces, and there's no way you can win because your opponent is always two steps ahead, shrewder, stronger, and just better at the game. *There will be other opportunities, Kate, with players who weren't trained as special operatives. He's out of your league. He'd be out of anyone's league.*

Just when I've decided to hoist the white flag and surrender to a lifetime of covering weddings and galas, he takes pity. Or maybe he's enjoying the game and he's not ready for it to be over—not ready to stop torturing me quite yet. He reels me back in with a measly crumb, so he can toy with me for a little while longer. And I allow it—that's what desperate people do.

"I don't have the exact membership numbers." He shrugs a shoulder. "There's a substantial buy-in, because there are numerous amenities. But I'm not an expert on the club."

That's a lie. *Another lie.* He knows plenty. He could help me, if he wanted. Somehow, I need to win his trust. Or distract him so he talks unwittingly. *But how?* I need to buy a little time to think. "Where's the ladies' room?" I ask, laying my napkin neatly on the table beside my plate.

"To the right of the entrance where you came in. There's a narrow hall. Second door on the left."

I excuse myself, anxious for a few minutes away from him.

The bathroom is tired, but spotless, with a couple stalls I don't need. I turn on the faucet and examine my face in the mirror while soaping my hands. I'm not beautiful, certainly not in a classic sense, but I have a thick mane of red hair that people of both sexes are drawn to as though it holds some kind of magical power. For most of my life it's been a blessing and a curse. Mostly a curse.

I bend forward at the waist and flip my hair over my head. Brushing it this way always makes it fall fuller over my shoulders. After applying two coats of fresh lip gloss, I tug on my collar until it's standing almost straight up, framing my neck attractively. I stare at my prim and proper image in the streaky glass. Maybe loosening another button on my shirt would make me look less uptight, and more approachable. Less like this is an interview, and more like ... *Like what, Kate?*

I'm the only person here. There's no harm in trying it. If it's too revealing, I'll rebutton the damn thing.

With shaky hands, I free the pearl disc from the tiny slit, and examine myself from all sides. There's no visible cleavage. This is exactly how I would wear the outfit to go out with friends for the evening, or on a date. I might even undo an additional button for a night out.

What's the big deal?

It's not as though I would ever exchange sex for a story. I wouldn't do that, not even for the woman who gave up her career, her family, her very life—for me. I will do almost anything to earn my mother the Pulitzer she justly deserves, even if it means stashing my dignity and pride while I deal with Sinclair. I can do that for her. It's so little compared to what she gave up for me. But sex is where I draw the line.

Is it, Kate? Are you sure about that? For a second, I catch a fifteen-year-old in the glass. She was willing to trade sex. I turn away from the glare of the mirror, shoving the thoughts back into the dark corners of my memory. *This is different.*

I won't have sex with him. But Sinclair can think whatever he wants as long as he gives me useful information.

When I finish justifying my questionable choices, I take a deep breath and head back to the table.

4

KATE

"Okay," I say in an optimistic voice as I slide into the booth. "Just tell me one teeny tiny thing about the clientele at Wildflower."

The lines on Sinclair's forehead become more prominent as his eyes flit from my freshly polished lips to the deep vee of my neckline. There's nothing to see, but still, I feel exposed.

I misjudged this—misjudged myself—*misjudged him*. My face is hot, and I'm sure it's a lovely shade of I-am-a-moron red. It seems ridiculous now, plotting to distract a former special forces operative with some lip gloss and a low neckline, like I'm some glamorous *femme fatale*. The embarrassment is scathing. My mother would have never stooped to such tactics to get a story, and until now, I never have.

It would be painfully obvious if I rebuttoned my shirt here at the table, so instead, I tug at the neckline discreetly, pulling the edges closed.

Sinclair was more responsive when I laid out my dilemma for him. I should try it again. Begging is less shameful than a come-on, even a fake one. "There must be something you can give me," I plead. "I need this story. I already told you I'd give up something in return. There must be something I have that you want. Anything."

"*Anything?*" His brown eyes have scores of gold flecks that should make them warm and inviting. But they're not. They're cool and calculating.

I hadn't meant it to sound like an open invitation, but the breathy plea came out all wrong. And God help me, I don't disabuse him of any assumptions, although I do choose my words cautiously. "I'll *tell* you anything."

Sinclair says nothing, and his face gives nothing away. We sit in silence playing a cat and mouse game. If animals played mind games, that is. While I'm still trying to read him, he slides both feet on either side of mine. He doesn't say excuse me, or offer anything resembling an apology, because it's not a mistake, and he's not sorry.

I'm a hair over five-eight, and I wear a size nine shoe, but his feet dwarf mine. The inner sole of each foot presses the outer sole of mine, dragging my legs together slowly, trapping them with my thighs crushed against one another. The sensitive skin chafes as the pressure between my legs mounts.

His jaw is set firmly, with the occasional tick popping under the scruff. Each time it happens, a shiver runs down my spine, making it almost impossible to sit still. I can't escape it. Just like I can't escape the oppressive heat radiating from across the table, creating bright streaks of jagged lightning that electrify my pussy.

"Do you want to see Wildflower?" His voice is thick and rough, like a man who has sex on the brain.

"*Wildflower? See Wildflower?*" *Wildflower*. The intensity of the moment fades. I forget all about the overwhelming sexual tension and throw all good sense out the window. This might be the break I need. There might be some small insight to be gleaned that can help me tie Warren King to Charleston's seamier side. At least something that will allow Colin to let me stay on the story. "You would take me there?" I'm practically salivating.

"Off the record."

Sinclair frees my feet, and I inch my legs apart, releasing the exquisite pressure that bloomed there. There's no time for sexy games right now. "Of course. Whatever you want."

He rakes his teeth over a full bottom lip. It's an excruciating slow movement—raw and primal. I shouldn't have said *whatever you want*—I certainly don't mean it, and I'm through playing. He's too male, and there's been a shift. I can feel it. All of a sudden, teasing feels too risky.

Sinclair motions for the check, then props his elbows on the table, cracking his knuckles. It's the only sound between us. I would give anything to know what he's thinking. *Maybe he's having second thoughts.* We need to get out of here now, before he changes his mind. I don't relax until Carrie approaches with the check. But even then, Sinclair seems broody and far away.

I reach into the tote for my wallet. "Let's split it."

"No." He drags the shot glass with the check out of my reach.

"You're a source. I don't feel comfortable with you buying me dinner."

He gazes at me, sliding the pad of an index finger over his right temple. "I don't feel comfortable splitting the check."

What? "You're kidding."

"No," he says, taking a few bills from his wallet. "I'm not. And right now, my comfort is more important than yours. Don't you agree, Kate?"

There's nothing unethical about me letting him buy me dinner. It's just not my practice. "Fine. I'll make an exception this one time." Just like that, once again today, I'm trading my principles for the story. I'm not proud of any of it.

He narrows his eyes, capturing mine, and holding them steady. His gaze is piercing. "You've put up with my shit for an hour and a half. It hasn't been easy for you. Once or twice, I thought sure you were going to haul off and punch me in the face." He pauses for a breath, or maybe for effect. "You must really want this story."

I shove my wallet back into the tote without responding. He's not looking for an answer, just gauging my reaction. I feel the weight of his stare while I reposition my bag, which doesn't need repositioning, on the bench. It seems lighter. I peek in and push a few things aside to have a better look. My heart drops into my stomach. *It's not here.* My gun is gone. And my phone. *Did I have them in the bathroom?* I try to remember. *Yes.* I definitely did.

"Looking for these?" Sinclair places the small handgun and the phone in the center of the table, between us.

How the hell did he get them? He removed the gun from a holster attached to the inside of my bag—without me knowing. I'm seeing black spots in front of me. "How? When—when did you take them?"

"I'm a man of many talents, Miss McKenna."

Maybe I didn't have my bag with me in the ladies' room. I'm not sure, anymore. "You rummaged through my purse while I was in the bathroom?"

"Come on. You really think I went through your purse while you were in the bathroom? What fun would that have been? Any two-year-old could have done that."

I had the tote with me because I brushed my hair and reapplied lip gloss. It was heavy when I lifted it off the vanity in the bathroom. I'm sure of it. The butterflies have returned, but they're quickly chased away by a raging storm. "When did you take them?" I demand.

"While I was offering you a visit to Wildflower."

I remember him reaching under the table. I thought maybe he was scratching his leg, or picking up something he dropped. It was just a matter of seconds—*right*? The truth is I didn't think much of it at the time—all I could think about was getting access to Wildflower.

"It was like taking candy from a baby."

Original. I ignore him and his stupid smirk and reach for my things.

"You will not take possession of your phone or your weapon until I've tucked you back into your car after our visit to Wildflower."

My eyes dart between him and my gun. *Tell him to go to hell. Grab your things and leave.* But I don't. I've come too far to walk away now. "I can't agree to that."

He shrugs. "That's the way it has to be. I hold them, and you get to see Wildflower. If you don't like it," he nudges my belongings toward me, "take your gun and your phone, and go home."

"I thought you didn't deal?"

"It's not a deal. It's an ultimatum."

I don't understand why I'm considering his terms. I know it's a bad idea. Although, if he took my gun from my purse while it was sitting next to me—if he can do that—my gun and phone won't offer much protection, anyway.

I'm rationalizing, and I know it.

Keep your eye on the prize, Kate.

I blow out a breath. He was a highly decorated special forces operative. An officer in the military. His father was the head of the Joint Chiefs of Staff during the last administration. He went to Harvard. He has sisters and a mother. *Ted Bundy didn't have sisters, right? Or was his sister his mother? Stop, Kate. Stop.*

"Okay." The word is weighted with hesitation. "But I want to text a friend."

"Which friend?"

"Fiona. She's a friend from Boston." Colin knows who I'm with, but Sinclair doesn't know that. I want him to see me tell Fiona that I'm with him. Besides, if something happens, I'd rather have Fiona on Sinclair's tail than Colin. If Smith Sinclair thinks I'm a pain in the ass, he needs to meet Fiona in mama-bear mode.

"What are you going to tell her?"

"That I'm on assignment meeting with a man named Smith Sinclair."

"What if I say no?"

I don't respond because we both know the answer to this. Add it to the list of things I'm not proud of.

He hesitates for a long minute, considering my request, or maybe he just wants to watch me squirm. "Go ahead. Text her. But nothing about Wildflower. That's off the record."

After I send the text, I place my phone in his outstretched hand. "You're not going to rape and murder me, are you?"

Sinclair freezes, glowering down at me. "No. Just rape you and leave you to live with the consequences." The ugly words fall like acid on my unprotected skin. "Are you actually stupid enough to trust my answer to that question?"

No. But it would give me a moment's comfort. A little reassurance from him might trick my brain into sending an all-clear signal so that my heart stops pounding. A heart attack now would be such poor timing.

5

KATE

It's a twenty-minute drive to Wildflower. During the car ride I don't mention the Wilders. Instead, I pepper Sinclair with questions about himself and his family, personal questions, most of which he answers with astounding brevity. I also tell him about my family. While I don't *really* believe he's going to hurt me, I still make an effort to humanize myself, and to remind him he's human too.

He's quiet, with his eyes on the road while I brag about my brothers, all proud Marines, Sean still in the Corps, and Liam who died when his unit was ambushed in the desert. I also tell him about my oldest brother, Tommy, a former Marine who is now a Boston cop.

What I don't mention is the complicated relationship I have with my family, how depression sank its poisonous fangs into my soul when Liam died, or that Tommy has never forgiven me for my mother's death. I do talk about Nana, who lived downstairs until she wandered off in the middle of the night and we had to put her in a home. How she was a stubborn, God-fearing Irish woman who went to Mass every morning at St. Claire's. I explain how Nana always found peace inside a Catholic church and comfort in the rituals, just as I do.

I prattle on and on, because no matter how much I kid myself, I'm nervous, and this is what I do when I'm nervous. Some people clam up. I don't shut up. Sometimes it's a chatty inner monologue, other times, like now, it's a severe case of verbal diarrhea. "What about you?" I ask. "Do you believe in God?"

Long seconds pass before he answers. "I'm not a churchgoer. But yes, I believe in God—although I've had moments of serious doubt."

I'm startled by the frank honesty. It's not an off-the-cuff answer. It's thoughtful and feels sincere. I don't trust people who say they've never once questioned their faith. How could you not?

Sinclair rests his elbow on the console between us. "I'm sorry about your brother. The desert has taken too many good people." His voice is gentle, but heavy, like the desert has stolen much from him too.

Despite the way he's behaved in the past two hours, there's plenty to like about him, and I've barely scratched the surface. Maybe we could be friends if the circumstances were different—maybe more than friends. I cast aside the foolish thought quickly. "Are you close to your sisters?"

"Very close," he answers, pulling into a parking lot enclosed by a tall fence, sandwiched between two rows of dense, manicured hedges. It's not only aesthetically pleasing, it affords absolute privacy to anyone in the lot.

Sinclair nods at the attendant who raises the remote arm so we can continue inside. I feel all the excitement of a child who has just arrived at the amusement park. I'm surprised I'm not bouncing on the seat. Wildflower might not hold all my answers, but it's a piece of the puzzle. I'm sure of it.

As we drive around to the back of the building, I try to commit even the smallest details to memory. It's often those seemingly insignificant facts that breathe life into a story and make it believable.

Sinclair stops at a cobblestone ramp, where he lowers the window and enters a code. A steel door opens and we proceed into an underground lot. *This is unusual.* Charleston floods frequently, so there are no underground parking lots, and few basements in this part of the city. *At least that's what I've been told.* It's too expensive to create the kind of barriers that can keep water out. Although cost is probably never a consideration for the Wilders.

Sinclair parks between a covered motorcycle and an expensive-looking sports car. There's no sign of water damage on the exterior walls, and the floor is pristine. The garage spans the entire width, but not the length, of the building. *There must be a basement beyond the interior wall.*

"It's deserted."

He nods. "Closed on Sundays, except in the winter." I don't know what I expected. It's not as though he was going to whisk me around the club, introducing me to one prominent member after another. Still, I'm a bit disappointed that it's so desolate.

"It must have cost a pretty penny to install an underground garage," I observe out loud, hoping he'll nibble.

"The Wilders have means." So much for my casual observation. He's back to the dismissive tone he used with me at the bar.

Sinclair doesn't say much beyond *watch your step*, as he leads me to a back entrance and into an elevator. Before I step inside and the doors close, I scan the garage one more time, taking note of the exits.

The elevator doors open into a wide hall with plush Persian rugs laid over gleaming wood floors. Elaborate molding and still life paintings grace the walls. Not the kind with gracious bouquets in antique urns, but crude bowls overflowing with fruit and nuts, and trussed game flanked by decanters of fortified wine. My eyes stop on a painting of a helpless lamb, legs bound, so lifelike it causes a twinge of melancholy. But the lamb doesn't appear despondent. There's a serenity about it, as though it's willingly accepted its fate. A sacrifice or a meal? Perhaps both.

As we make our way down the hall, there appear to be four doors, two on the left and two on the right, each lacquered in a navy gloss and outfitted with polished brass trim. Near each door there is a narrow marble table with a gooseneck lamp, where packages can be left or where one might rest a grocery bag while fiddling with a key. It all screams old money, like Ralph Lauren or one of his protégés hand-selected the decor.

I silently follow Sinclair to a door on the right, the one farthest from the elevator. He presses a few buttons on the keypad, and when the lock clicks, he pushes the door open and gestures for me to go inside.

I hesitate briefly before walking past him into the apartment. My arm grazes his abdomen as I pass. It's a solid mass, harder than I expected. The brief contact sends currents scrambling haywire through me.

Sinclair is hot and dangerous with all that muscle, and even with everything going on, it's enticing. I hate to admit it, but it's true.

My pussy is awake and all atwitter, and for long seconds, I contemplate how I might respond if he makes a move. How it might feel to be pinned under that massive body, his cock hard and insistent, his warm mouth feeding on my needy skin. *Kate! You'll say thanks, but no thanks, and hope he respects it.*

The door clicks shut behind me. The echo is deafening. I should be afraid. It's the last thought that registers as I proceed into the sparsely furnished apartment.

It's an open floor plan with soaring ceilings, more modern than the hall. I scan the rooms slowly, soaking up the details. It looks and smells like the housekeeper just left. There is not a single thing out of place—no socks strewn about, not a glass in the sink, nor are there any personal items anywhere to be seen—

not a photograph or anything resembling a memento—not even a decorative sofa cushion that might hint of his style. It's devoid of character, faceless, and I can't imagine having anything in common with the person who lives here. Even my lady parts have stilled.

"Is this your place?"

"It's a place I crash from time to time."

Crash. I'm sure it's a euphemism for have sex. If you're not married, and you don't live with your parents, why do you need a place to crash? *Why?* There's something about this city, its people, so many secrets and unspoken truths. Although I have to admit, I'm oddly relieved that he doesn't actually live here. "Do you share the apartment?"

"Like a roommate?"

"Yeah."

"*No.* Why would I want a roommate?"

Because this place has no soul, but it looks like it costs a fortune. And you don't actually live here. "Who else lives in the building?"

"I'm allowing you to infringe on my privacy, but you will not violate anyone else's privacy while you're here."

Hmmm. We'll see. "Is the club downstairs?"

"Dining room is on the first floor. The spa and gym are on the second floor. There's office space on the third and storage. Want some water?"

I nod, and he reaches into the refrigerator and lobs me a bottle of artisan water. I glance at the label. Someone else must do the shopping, because I can't picture him putting a case of this into a cart. "What's in the basement?"

I watch for a reaction, but he only shrugs. "Vermin. Although it's exterminated frequently."

I'm anxious to see the club, including the *vermin* in the basement, but he doesn't seem to be in any hurry. I hope he doesn't think bringing me to this sterile apartment is going to satisfy my curiosity. "It's getting late. Are you going to show me around?"

"I haven't decided yet."

My heart skips a full beat. *You fucker.* "I thought that's why we came?" I manage to keep my voice even and calm, without a hint of emotion, but my body is growing heavy with the possibility that this might be another dead end.

"I thought we came because you had questions."

"I do have questions."

He tosses his head back, guzzling every drop of the fancy-pants water without stopping for a breath. I watch, mesmerized by the ripples in his throat. When it's empty, he crushes the bottle in one hand. The crinkling plastic startles me, even as I watch him do it.

While I'm still regaining my poise, he drops the flattened plastic into a recycling bin under the counter, then strides toward me, inching closer until there's little daylight between us. I lift my chin cautiously, until our eyes lock.

Without a single word between us, he seizes control. I feel the floor beneath me shift as the universe tilts in his direction. My toes curl into the soft suede foot bed inside my sandals.

It's warm in the apartment. *Stifling.* A sheen is forming on the back of my neck.

Sinclair takes hold of a small section of my hair, twirling it around a finger. When he releases it, the soft curl bounces off my cheek. "I love redheads," he murmurs in a low seductive voice. "Is it true their pain threshold is higher?" His nimble fingers find my hair again, combing roughly through the strands. Just before he reaches the ends, he furls his hand and tugs firmly. "Is it, Kate?" My mouth falls open, but I can't form words. "Do you enjoy having your hair pulled?"

I hate having my hair pulled. At least that's what I always thought. But the tugging called my body to attention, put every nerve on high alert. And yes, I did enjoy it—all of it. But I especially enjoyed the way my scalp and pussy tingled in sync, as though they were engaging in an erotic dance for my pleasure alone. I'm still enjoying it. Although I have no intention of telling him that. I shake my head in response.

His eyes are dark slits. "Liar," he murmurs, a breath away from my temple.

The warm sensation caresses my skin. It's a stark contrast to the cruel word, *liar*. Is that what it would be like with him? Cruelty swathed in a tender caress? Would I enjoy that, too? *Oh, God.*

My throat is parched. My brain thick with fog. I'm aroused. And confused. With every circuit misfiring.

"How badly do you want those answers?" He hooks a thumb under my chin, forcing me to meet his gaze. "What are willing to do to get them?"

His last question jolts me out of my *he-is-hot-as-sin* and *I want to melt in the fires of hell* trance. "You're kidding?" I pant softly.

He smirks. It's a menacing little smirk. "I'm not kidding. If I'm going to answer your questions, you're going to make it worth my time. Or at least make it interesting. It's not too much to ask, is it, Kate?" He stands inches from me, his voice sultry and rich when he says my name.

I don't move. I can't. My heart is pounding. It's all I hear. That, and the small voice of reason nearly obscured by his chiseled features and strong hands. *Go, Kate. Now! While you can,* it shouts. But I don't. My feet are stuck to the floor, and there's nowhere to go, anyway. I can't get out of this place without the codes, and he could overtake me easily if I run. My eyes dart around the room looking for an escape. I should at least make some effort to leave.

"Relax. We won't do anything you don't want to do."

His voice has lost the perilous edge, but I'm not convinced he's any less dangerous. Or maybe I'm not sure that I need much convincing to do whatever it is he has in mind.

He steps away, and pulls out two ladder-back chairs from the table, arranging them about six or seven feet apart, facing each other. "I'm going to give you back your gun. We're going to leave it right here, within your easy reach." He places the gun on a table, near me, within arm's reach. "That should help you relax so we can play a little game. Do you like games?"

I glance at the gun. "What—what kind of game?"

"Ever play strip poker?"

Why am I still here? Because this is your chance to get the information you need to write a Pulitzer-winning story. She died less fearful than you are right now, Kate. Suck it up.

I shake my head. "No."

"You can ask me questions. Whatever you want. And I'll answer them. For every question I answer, you'll remove an article of clothing."

My mouth is dry. I swallow some water while he watches, like I'm an exotic sheep on display at the petting zoo.

"Start with anything you'd like. Lady's choice." I take another sip of water and screw back on the cap, tightening until the plastic cuts into my fingers. "When you're out of clothes, if you still have questions left, we'll come up with a different game. That's up to you. We won't do anything you're not comfortable with. The gun is your insurance policy. But I promise you won't need it. I won't hurt you—unless that's what you like."

I won't hurt you—unless that's what you like. I bat the thought away quickly.

He wants me to take off my clothes for the story. Those are his terms.

I bite down on my bottom lip so hard it stings. Once I'm undressed, once I agree to go that far, all bets are off. Why should I believe he'll stop, if I ask? There have to be some assurances. I lift my chin. "How do I know you won't force me—you won't hurt me?"

"Because I just gave you my word."

His word. Is that enough? "And you'll take off your clothes when I answer a question?" I'm not sure why I ask this, or even whether I want it to happen. My head is spinning, and I'm stalling trying to figure out a strategy where I can win.

"I don't barter with my clothes," he answers plainly, in the strong voice of a man who holds all the cards. Every single one. "I only take them off when I'm good and ready."

6

KATE

I'm not sure what to do. A part of me wants to demand he take me back to my car, but it's overshadowed by the part that wants to see this through. I might not have another chance. And I'm pretty confident he won't hurt me. I don't know why, exactly, but I am. I can stop at any time. I just need to stay one step ahead of him.

"Have a seat," he instructs. "You'll be more comfortable while we play."

I look at him pointedly. "I haven't decided if I want to play your little game."

"Yes, you have."

"You need humbling."

He smirks. "And you're going to handle that?"

God, he's obnoxious.

I've never played strip poker, but I've played poker. A lot of poker. The next best thing to a winning hand is a stone-cold bluff. I smile at him with all the bravado I can muster, which is a considerable task because I still don't have a cogent plan. "I need my notebook." If I'm going to humiliate myself by giving up my clothes, I don't want this to be a waste. Right now, I can only remember bits and pieces of what I prepared.

I retrieve my questions, and sit up tall, clutching the notebook to my chest. *You've got this, Kate.*

"I'm ready." I say it with my head high and an abundance of confidence. But it's a sham. I'm not at all ready. Maybe I'll ask just a few questions, that way I won't have to actually give up any of my clothes. It's not much of an attack plan, but it's all I've got.

He's drumming two fingers on his thigh, right above the knee. Otherwise, he seems relaxed. "I'm waiting."

I draw a breath and say a small prayer. "Wildflower membership is kept under tight wraps. Give me the name of one prominent member."

Sinclair hesitates. Maybe I shouldn't have started with that question, but there's no easing in slowly, if I plan on keeping my clothes. I don't have a single question to waste. "Just so you know, I'm not taking anything off if you tell me Larry Jones, Suzie Smith's grandfather from down the block. I need the name of a prominent Charlestonian who belongs—and it can't be one of the Wilders."

"One, and only one." He digs his teeth into his bottom lip and releases it with a snarl. "Jordan Hayward."

"The Governor?" I choke out. This little tidbit, in and of itself, is worth all the anxiety I had about playing the game.

He smiles. It's not a quick, easy grin, but rather the slow, lazy slide of a satisfied tomcat who's been on the prowl all night. At first, I think he's smiling because I'm wide-eyed at his jaw-dropping response. But that's not the reason.

"Yes," he responds without hesitation this time. "And that's two questions. You owe me two articles of clothing." Sinclair pauses briefly to enjoy my surprise. "Take them off and bring them to me."

I peer at him across the floor, preparing a solid argument, but decide against it. Arguing will make me seem weak and whiny.

And there's no way he'll give in. I'll gain nothing. *I need to be more careful before opening my mouth.*

My face and neck are burning, the mottled pink skin winking at him, as I slip off my sandals, and cross the room with all the dignity I can garner. I plop the shoes into his waiting hand with more force than necessary.

He's still delighting in my mistake, and it takes every ounce of self-control I have not to grab a sandal and whack him over the head with it.

When I get back to my seat, I take a quick peek at my notepad until I find the right question, and then I take a couple of minutes to think it through. He's wily, and will seize upon any advantage. I can't afford another unforced error.

"For someone with so many questions, it's taking you a long time to ask one." I ignore his snarky remark. I'll ask when I'm good and ready.

When I'm fully prepared, I look up and meet his gaze. "For how long has Wildflower been hosting sex parties?" I frame the question as if I have some basis of knowledge. I don't. There are hushed whispers of hedonistic sex fueled by drugs and alcohol, but I haven't been able to get anyone to confirm a thing. It's important information because Warren King might not be a current member, but he was an early investor in the club.

"Sounds like you're pretty confident about the parties. Are you sure you want to waste a question on it?"

Why is he pretending to be helpful after just demanding two pieces of clothing, in what was a total prick move? He's not. He's manipulating. I pause for a few seconds, but I can't come up with a motive. "I'm sure."

"Since it opened its doors." He holds out his hand. I get up and drop my watch into it, while he observes intently, his eyes never straying from me.

I'm beginning to understand why he arranged the chairs some distance apart. It requires me to get up and go over to him, hand him my discarded things, and walk back in disgrace. I feel the blister of the brand on my back each time I retreat, but I'm getting the answers I need, so I force myself to quietly endure the humiliation.

Sinclair deposits my watch on the table beside him, using great care not to scratch the crystal.

I planned to stop the game after a few questions, but he's talking, so I ask several more, until all I have left to give him is the shirt covering my undergarments, and the undergarments themselves.

My stomach churns with an array of emotion coated in a viscous bile. But I've come this far, and he's given me useful information. It might be enough to convince Colin to let me stay another week or two, maybe longer. I'm so close.

I take a deep breath. "What type of illicit drugs are used during the parties?"

He tips his head, and for a few seconds, I'm sure he's going to end the game. But he doesn't. "This is off the record." It's not a question, but I nod my acquiescence. He swallows hard. The knot in his throat bobs twice before he speaks. "Drugs are a membership perk. Members pick their poison. To each their own."

It's more than just rumor.

Sinclair leans back, legs out in front of him, hand outstretched. Waiting.

This is the moment of truth.

I search his face for mercy, but he's aloof and callous. There will be no leniency.

Slowly and carefully, my clumsy fingers untether each button, painfully aware that I'm wearing a turquoise bra from a big box discount store, one that's old and a little stretched out. My face flushes when I remember the panties I put on after my shower. They were a gift from Fiona when the accusations about me stealing information from the police department first began.

They have a smiley emoji on the back, with the words *kiss my ass* ... *Oh God*.

I'm not a woman who has a chest full of sexy underwear from Agent Provocateur. I have two kinds of underwear: clean and dirty. I have no idea why I care about any of this right now, but it's one of the errant thoughts swimming in my head while I slip the shirt off my shoulders and bring it to Sinclair, imagining his mocking thoughts when he gets a good look at my ridiculous underpants.

I glance at him. His gaze is all-knowing. It's as if he's able to bore into the depths of my soul and read every emotion I'm experiencing, so he can play it expertly.

He winds his long fingers around mine as I lay my shirt in his open palm. He squeezes, making it impossible for me to pull back my hand. My cheeks blaze as his eyes flicker over my bare skin, scorching the flesh everywhere they touch.

He's aroused and making no effort to hide it. I follow the outline of his cock against his leg. It grows longer and thicker from the attention. I avert my eyes, ignoring the ache between my legs, focusing on my racing pulse instead. The beats are coming too fast to count.

"Look at me," he demands, squeezing my fingers more tightly.

Without a second thought, I immediately obey, as though I've been a follower all my life.

There is something ruthless about him as he moves his hand from mine with a slow, deliberate slide. His fingers are nimble and strong, and he wields them masterfully.

When he's finished, I lower my gaze and go back to my seat, painfully aware that nearly every inch of flesh, every imperfection on my body, is on display for him.

Breathe, Kate. Breathe. Think about why you're doing this.

I don't remember meeting my mother, of course. But I've spent so much of my life combing through hers, gobbling up every detail from those who knew her, rereading everything she ever wrote until I know it by heart, and I never tire of admiring the photographs of her. I've been such a conscientious student that it sometimes feels as though I did know her. I see her face in front of me now. Her young, beautiful face—she never had the opportunity to develop the furrows and lines of a long life.

"Kate." I blink a few times. Sinclair's voice startles me. It's so out of place in my mother's story—at least it was until now.

"Are you done?" he asks.

It doesn't matter that I never planned on it getting this far. I'm like an addict, the more he feeds me, the more I need.

After drawing a breath, I wrap my icy fingers around the seat, and summon some of the grit my Boston neighborhood is famous for. *He's nothing more than a pawn*, I tell myself—a means to an end. Besides, he's a total jerk. *So what if he sees me naked?* It's not like I'm planning on having sex with him. I'll get my story then leave. We'll never see each other again. Two more questions, and I'll be done with him forever.

I repeat this several times while I decide which are the most important of the many questions I have left to ask. I cling to the seat, and choose two that will force the White House to reevaluate King's nomination. "How often do members participate in ritualized sex?"

"All the time."

The answer comes quickly. *Too quickly.* I feel the flush crawling, spiky limbs spreading like a cancer over my pale skin.

Bra or panties? Which do I give up first? If we were having sex, it would be the bra. Second base before third. Or is it first? I don't know, and it doesn't matter. My feverish brain continues sputtering nonsense—the inner babblings of a fool.

I have misgivings, but I'm not a coward or a cheater. *Just pull the bra off quick, like a bandage. Don't think about it. Then ask the question about sex trafficking, get dressed and get out.* My arms reach behind me, but before my fingers get anywhere near the hooks, Sinclair's voice booms.

"What the fuck is wrong with you?" he barks, stalking toward me with my clothes in hand. "Put your goddamn clothes back on."

It takes me several seconds to wrap my head around what's happening, and even then, I'm not exactly sure. He drops my things into my lap, towering above me. I feel the anger vibrating from him. Or maybe it's disgust. I begin to shrink inward, getting smaller and smaller until he finally steps back.

"Do you think that gun sitting there is going to help you without these?" He takes the bullets out of his pocket and dumps them on the table beside the gun. I see the shells, but they barely register. "And even if the bullets were in it, do you think you would be any match against me? I could wrest that gun from your hand without any effort. But that would have never happened, because I wouldn't give you the chance to get anywhere near it."

My stomach seizes as the realization hits. It's stark and bitter, and the pain is agonizing. I'm going to vomit. I cover my mouth with my wrist and focus on taking even breaths. "Nothing you told me was true, was it?"

"Of course not. My job is to protect the privacy of club members and the owners. Did you think I would trade my loyalty to see your tits?"

I squeeze my eyes shut. I was so desperate for information, I allowed myself to be played. Of course, they were all lies. A part of me knew it was a real risk all along, but I so wanted it to be different, I refused to consider it seriously. The tears are forming. Tears of anger and humiliation. Tears of a woman who is fresh out of time.

"The bathroom is the first door on the left. Get dressed."

I'm not just shaking inside, my hands are trembling, too. I hug my clothes to my chest, wrapping my arms across my body, gripping the clammy skin tightly to stop the shaking.

"I should call your cop brother and have him come get you and take you home to your father. But I won't, because they have enough on their plates without worrying about a little girl who is stupid enough to get herself caught in this kind of trap. I could have easily raped and killed you, disposed of your body in such a way that no one would ever discover it." He pounds his fist on the table, rattling my watch and jewelry. "And you knew that, but you decided chasing the story was more important than living to write it."

Call my cop brother. It's *déjà vu*. It can't be happening again. It's not possible.

I'm embarrassed, but I'm also so angry now, I can hardly see straight. "For your information, I assessed the risk. I knew you wouldn't hurt me."

"Bullshit. You were pale and scared. Fidgeting and yapping nonstop in the car on the way over here. You had no way of knowing what I would do."

I march right up to him. He's taller than me, but I stand on tiptoe and do my best to get in his face. "I'm an adult. Stop lecturing me like I'm an irresponsible teenager. I have a right to take my clothes off for whomever I want to take them off for. My brothers and my father don't get to make those decisions for me. I gave you a lot of slack today because I needed the story. But I was just a problem to be disposed of—like stinky trash."

I'm shaking uncontrollably. Tears that I have no intention of letting fall are threatening, but I will have my say. This bastard is going to hear everything. "Did it ever once occur to you, just once, that I'm a human being? That I'm only trying to do my job? No, of course not, because you're a first-class jerk—no, you're a complete asshole without a drop of honor or decency to your name. I'm sure you and your friends the Wilders will have a good laugh about this."

Without a single thought, I pull off my panties and fling them in his face. "Here's a little souvenir for you. Something to remind you of how despicably you treated me."

7

SMITH

Somehow, I find the decency not to check out her ass while she stomps off. After she slams the bathroom door, I pick up her panties off the floor and stuff them into her bag.

I can be a dick. But I'm normally not a hothead, and I rarely let anyone get that far under my skin. When I act like an asshole, it's usually calculated to make someone nervous, but inside I'm fully in control. Although, lately I've been flying off the handle left and right, and none of it's been an act.

Then today, when that woman showed up—that kid—with her damn smiley face underpants, and behaved in ways that put her safety at risk, I wanted to toss her over my lap and slap some sense into that tight round ass—*while I fingered her. Fuck.*

As I'm putting the chairs back, my phone vibrates with a text, but I don't bother to look. It's probably Gray wondering where the hell I am. Our plan was to meet at JD's place after I took care of Kate McKenna. *I took care of her all right. Used a damn nuclear bomb when a small hand grenade would have done the job.*

If some asshole pulled the shit on one of my sisters that I just pulled on her, I'd fillet them like a tuna and throw their guts overboard for the smaller fish to feed on.

She got the brunt of my pent-up frustration. Sure, she's a pain in the ass, but she didn't deserve to be humiliated to that extreme. *I'm better than that.*

The bathroom door creaks, and Kate comes into the living room, messy red hair spilling over her shoulders. One look at her swollen washed-out eyes and I feel like a total shit.

When she arrived at Tallulah's, her eyes were a vivid green with deep copper specks at the center, alive with expression—they hid nothing. But right now, they're so lifeless, I can't read them. *Anger? Disappointment? Sadness? Disgust?* Part of me wants her to feel all those things, and pull her tail between her legs and scoot back to DC, or Boston, or wherever she came from, and leave the Wilders the hell alone. Leave me the hell alone. Another part ... I don't let myself think about what that part wants, because that part is always looking for trouble, and I refuse to let it rule my life.

"If you give me back my phone and let me out of here, I'll call an Uber back to my car."

There's no fucking way she's calling an Uber. It's dark and the parking lot is empty, and I suspect the one where her car is parked is empty too. She doesn't pay attention to her surroundings even when she's not all shaken up.

"Here's your gun. The bullets are back in the chamber. And the safety's on. Do you know how to use that thing? I mean really know how to use it?"

She glares at me. "I would be happy to show you if you'd like." Her voice is strong and she doesn't sound as beaten as she looks. Frankly, I'm relieved by the sarcasm.

"Listen, I might have gone too far—"

"You think?"

I ignore the snark. "I agreed to the meeting to get rid of you. But it became clear you weren't going anywhere fast. I wanted to see how far you'd go to get the story—how important it was to you, and how big of a pain in the ass you were going to be. Then I started to get pissed off that you were careless about your safety. That you'd risk your life—for bullshit."

There's fire in her eyes—just a small spark, but it's there. "It might seem like—"

"I take it back. It's bullshit to me, but clearly important to you. I'm telling you this, though, nothing is worth the risk of enduring what I could have easily done to you. *Nothing.*"

She stands tall, flipping her hair over a shoulder. "You don't get an opinion about the decisions I make regarding my life. You don't even know me. I'm not an idiot. I checked you out. I knew you were a highly-trained operative. I knew full well you could've overpowered me. But I didn't believe you would."

You have no idea what I'm capable of, what I've done. If you did, you wouldn't sleep tonight. "You're not a mind reader. How could you possibly know what I might do? How?"

"Because I make a living based on intuition and then follow the facts. I'll admit, I was desperate and might have taken more risk than I would ordinarily. But we both know damn well the risk was tiny."

I'm still pissed off. But I don't argue the point, because I would never hurt her. She didn't read the situation wrong. "I'll show you around if you still want to see the club." I won't allow her to see anything that will peak her interest, but I want to give her something. I just do. "Then you can see for yourself that nothing here is worth taking your clothes off over. When we're through, I'll take you back to your car."

She glares at me. "I'll decide what's worth taking my clothes off over."

Christ, she's a pain in the ass. "Do you want to see the place or not?"

Thin lines appear, etching the smooth skin between her

brows. I'm pleased to see she's being cautious. "Are there any strings attached?"

"One."

"Forget it." She dismisses me with a wave of the hand, checks her weapon, and secures it in the holster inside her bag. She handles the gun properly, which also makes me feel a little better. But she still has no clue what an easy mark she is—young and pretty, *real pretty*, and as she hoists that stupid bag onto her shoulder, I'm still not entirely convinced the gun isn't just for show.

"The next time you're chasing a story, I want you to remember how easily things could have gone bad today." Her body tenses. It looks like I'm about to have my balls handed to me, but I don't give a shit. She's going to hear me out. "Next time, remember how much I struggled not to pull you onto my lap when you handed me your shirt. You saw the evidence—couldn't drag your eyes away." I glance at the smooth, creamy skin along her throat, my eyes lingering where it meets that defiant little chin. "Don't make it easy for fuckers like me. Remember today. That's my one string."

She swallows hard, blinking a dozen times in rapid succession, trying to digest what I just told her. It's all true, and I don't give a damn if she knows it. I didn't touch her, and I won't. In my line of work, the very last thing I need is a nosy reporter in my bed, but that doesn't mean I wasn't tempted. I wait for her to haul off and take a swing at my head, but she doesn't.

"Are you going to stand there all night and tell me what a fucker you are, as if I didn't already know, or are you going to show me the spa?"

I crack a smile. God, would I like to toss this woman over my shoulder and chain her to my bed for a week. "Yeah. I'll show you the spa. But while we're speaking freely, that ridiculous purse you carry—it's bigger than you. It looks like it weighs a ton. Makes it easy for someone to grab you, and less likely you could get away."

"I'm going to pretend you didn't just comment on my purse."

She showed a little spunk at Tallulah's, but mostly she was reined in tight, and after we left the bar she was too nervous to give me any lip. She doesn't have much to lose right now, and it appears Kate McKenna is done taking my crap.

I like this side of her. I like it a lot.

"The floor right below is the spa and gym. Let's start there and make our way down. I have an appointment and I'm already running late, so we might not get to everything, but you'll have a good feel for the place by the time we're through."

There is not one thing I show her that would raise a single suspicion. The kinky shit is on the lower level, and there are a few things in the apartment we just left. But she didn't see any of it.

"I'm sorry your visit didn't give you any leads."

"What about the basement?"

"I already told you that there wasn't much of a basement."

"Underground garage that takes up a small portion of the building. It was pristine. It doesn't make sense that someone would go to all that expense to park a couple dozen vehicles."

She's looking for a reaction from me that she's not going to get. "You're not dressed for the basement."

"What does that mean?"

"It means if you're going to crawl around with the vermin, you need to be appropriately dressed. That skirt and those shoes won't cut it."

"I already got plenty dirty today. I'm not afraid of a little more filth." That was a jab squarely at me.

I check my watch, not that I have any intention of taking her to the basement, but I want her to believe I'm considering it. "I don't have time. And I'm telling you—the answers to the secret societies you're researching are not at Wildflower."

"Then where are they?"

"I don't know." I really don't. "Some of what you insinuated, ritualized sex and nefarious secret societies, sound a little far-fetched for buttoned-up Charleston. But I suspect if there are secrets, it's because someone wants it that way. Poking the bear is rarely a good idea."

Kate glares at me over her shoulder, and my cock comes alive at her fiery green eyes. "Far-fetched?"

She's smart, too young, and hot as hell with that hand on her hip. I want to cancel my meeting and fuck her into next week—fuck all the sass out of her until she can't form a single intelligible word. But I don't take marching orders from my dick. Nothing good ever comes of that. "You should go back to Boston. It's your home. You should have never let the bastards drive you out."

"I can't right now." Maybe not, but she looks like she'd drop everything in a hot minute and head north if she could.

"I meant what I said about trumped-up accusations."

"How do you know they're not true? My behavior upstairs should be enough to convince you that I'd stop at nothing for a story."

"I just know. Gut feeling. Instinct. Call it what you will."

She tilts her head. "Why is it okay for you to trust your instincts about me, but it's not okay for me to trust mine about you?"

Because I'm highly trained commando and have spent years of my life in hellholes. But I don't tell her that. "I appreciate a person with goals and dreams. I hope you reach all of yours. Watch your back, Mary Katherine McKenna. You're a beautiful woman, and the world is filled with monsters, the likes of which you couldn't even begin to fathom."

"You're patronizing me."

"Nope. I'm just saying, don't take your clothes off for men who don't deserve it. Make them earn the privilege. I respect my sisters. They're capable adults, but that's exactly what I tell them all the time."

"Do they listen?"

"No. They do whatever the hell they want. Same as you."

8

KATE

*S*inclair drops me at my car and waits while I start the engine and get situated. I take the phone out of my bag, turn on the ringer, and place it on the console. The light flickers with messages, but with Sinclair still waiting, I don't take the time to check them.

I glance out the window and nod to let him know I'm all set. I don't know why I smile at him. It's just a small polite smile, maybe out of habit, or maybe to say thanks for waiting. Not that he deserves any thanks from me.

Sinclair lifts his chin in acknowledgment, but he doesn't go anywhere. No, he's not the kind of guy that would leave a woman in an empty parking lot after dark. Although his chivalrous behavior now is completely at odds with that little stunt from earlier.

When he pulls out of the lot behind me, I begin to wonder if he's planning on following me to the small motel that's been my home for the last few weeks, but at the top of the street, he turns in the opposite direction.

I'm embarrassed to admit, even to myself, that I'm a little disappointed. It's been that kind of evening, with so many highs and lows I still don't know if I'm coming or going. So many emotions—anger, relief, sadness, surprise, shame, and arousal—one poured on top of another, swirling and overlapping, creating a disturbing canvas, dark and erotic, with nary a glimmer of light to be found.

My phone chimes. I glance at the screen before answering. "Hey. I was about to call you."

"That was a weird message. I started to get worried when you didn't respond to my texts. I want all the details on Smith Sinclair."

Fiona has been my best friend since the day she wet her pants in kindergarten during circle time. Later that morning on the playground, Brett Nash called her Missy Pissy in front of the older kids. Everyone laughed. I was furious and kicked him in the shin so hard he cried like a baby. Everyone laughed then, too. I had to sit in the principal's office until lunchtime, but it was worth it.

"He's just a source for the Warren King story. I'll tell you about him in a minute. First, tell me about the boys." *Maybe by then my thoughts and emotions will stop swirling, and I'll be able to explain Smith Sinclair in a way that makes some sense to both of us.*

"The little monsters are finally asleep. Brett and his dad took them to a Sox game this afternoon, and they spent more time in the bathroom and at the concession stand than in their seats. I told Brett five was too young to sit through a baseball game." Yes, that Brett. He went from a toad to a prince. It took forever, and it wasn't pretty, but that kind of evolution can't be rushed.

"So what happened with Sinclair?"

"Nothing." I'm still not ready to talk about Sinclair, even to Fiona. "I didn't get anything helpful out of him. I have to go back to DC tomorrow."

"You don't have to. You can choose to go back, but you don't have to. You can stay in Charleston or go anywhere you want."

Anywhere I want. Does that include—I know the answer, but I ask anyway. "Is it too soon to go back—home?"

"I didn't mean Boston," she says tersely. The finality leaves me smarting. Fiona doesn't want me back in Boston. Every time I visit, she worries I'm not going to leave. Even though she misses me, and I know she does, she believes my family is toxic—believes it with every fiber of her being. "There's nothing good here for you, Katydid."

There's more for me there than anywhere else in the world. Before they accused me of stealing information from the police department, I was happy in Boston. *Wasn't I?* I clutch the steering wheel tightly. "You're there. And my godsons. And my dad, and now my brother Tommy. I miss you."

With the air between us still heavy with unspoken thoughts and feelings, I pull the car up to the entrance of the dingy motel and turn off the engine. I glance at the rundown building. The dim lighting hides the layers of grime on the siding, but does nothing to improve the depressing façade or to ease my loneliness.

"We're at the Cape from the end of June through the third week in July, but I'll come to visit as soon as I can string a few days together, after that—wherever you are. Brett's perfectly capable of managing the kids, and my mom and mother-in-law will be happy to help out while he's at work. It'll give the Nanas a perfect opportunity to check for dust bunnies under the beds and try to reverse the effects of my inept mothering before the twins grow up to be miscreants."

I dig a water bottle out of my bag while we joke about the Nanas. It's all in jest, but there's more than a grain of truth behind the humor. Fi is a wonderful mother, but she does things her way, making both her mother and Brett's crazy. I laugh so hard while she mimics her mother that I spray a mouthful of water all over the dashboard. For a few minutes I forget about Pulitzer prizes, the Keaton wedding, and Smith Sinclair. And I forget about how lonely I am, so far from home.

"When I got your text, I googled Sinclair. Impressive. All that muscle and those dimples—my ovaries nearly exploded. Damn he's *hot*."

I shiver, remembering his warm breath on my skin, *Do you like to have your hair pulled, Kate? I shake my head. Liar.*

"I didn't see much of the dimples today. He brought his A game—as in, he was a total asshole."

"What happened?"

What happened? Where do I begin? It's Fiona, just say it. I sigh. "He tricked me into taking my clothes off."

"Wait. *What?*"

I'm nearly drowning in shame—no, it's more like embarrassment. Not because I gave him my clothes, although that's a small part, but because I allowed him to make a complete fool of me, with nothing to show for it. Absolutely nothing. I take a breath and blow it out loudly.

"We played this game—for every question he answered, I had to take off a piece of clothing—everything he told me was a lie." The last part of the admission is so soft it's barely audible. I wonder if she's thinking about what happened in the frat house. It's crossed my mind a dozen times since the bathroom at Tallulah's.

"You took off your clothes for a stranger to get information for a story?"

Leave it to Fi to distill my stupidity into one clipped sentence. Plain English, and not the British kind, prettied up with a charming accent. "Yeah."

"You let him play you?"

I chew on my thumb, trying to contain a fresh wave of embarrassment. "Yeah."

"*Kate.*" She says my name gently, but I hear the small rebuke, laced with disappointment and pity. The pity is the worst.

Her tone makes me defensive, and for a few brief seconds I stop feeling sorry for myself. "Don't get all judgy-judgy on me."

Fiona sighs. "I'm not. Lord knows I've taken my clothes off for a stranger or three, with nothing but a chaffed vag to show for it." Water is running in the background and I hear the clang of metal against metal. I imagine her standing at the sink in her cheerful kitchen, enjoying a glass of wine while she does dinner dishes, and I'm more homesick than ever. "It just doesn't sound like you," she adds softly.

It's not like me, but I'm grateful for the validation, and relieved. I was beginning to have second thoughts about myself. "I needed the information, otherwise I'm back in DC covering silly stories." I hesitate, taking a second to come to terms with my future. "I don't think I can face that life again." She doesn't say anything. "I know there's a story here, Fi. An important story. I can't explain it, but I can feel it. It's pulling at me."

"If that pull is guilt about your mother, then maybe you should leave. But if you really believe there's a story in Charleston worth pursuing, then stay."

This is complicated and can't be distilled into black and white choices. There are too many variables. Fiona knows this, but she's pushing my buttons. Or maybe I'm too wound up to see my circumstances as clearly as she does.

"It's not that simple. If I stay, I'll be walking away from a prestigious news outlet and a paycheck. There will be no second chances. Those jobs are impossible to come by." I sound whiny and helpless, even to my own ears.

"I'm beginning to think you don't *really* believe what your gut is telling you. Or maybe you don't want the story bad enough. You're not normally a coward." *Unless my family is involved*—she doesn't say it, but that's what she's thinking. Fiona might have spared me on that front, but make no mistake, I'm getting a dose of tough love right now, like only Fi can deliver it. I suppose I need it, but that doesn't make it any more pleasant.

She's right. I'm not a coward, but I hate to disappoint—especially my dad. *What will he say if I quit my job on a hunch? Nothing supportive.* "It would be irresponsible to walk away from a good-paying job without any real prospects."

"Don't give me that shit. You're twenty-seven years old. You have no responsibilities but to yourself. This is the time to take risks." The water's off and it's quiet now. "Whatever you decide, I'm behind you one hundred percent." I hear Brett's voice in the background, calling her to come upstairs.

"I should let you go."

"Follow your heart, Katydid," she adds softly, before we hang up.

I should have stopped for a bottle of wine. I desperately need something to take the edge off so I can sleep, but now that I'm in my room, I don't feel like going back out. Fourteen long hours in the car tomorrow, and every second of it promises to be unpleasant.

After I text Colin to let him know I'll be back tomorrow evening, I turn off my phone. I don't want a response, or worse yet, to talk to him if he calls. He won't gloat. That's not his style, but I'm not ready for a heavy conversation with him. Nowhere near ready.

I'm still not sure whether I'll stay in DC, or if it will be a quick trip to pack up my belongings before returning to Charleston. Fi gave me plenty to think about, and I'll have lots of time to chew on it during the drive. Either way, Colin deserves a face-to-face conversation.

I glance at the clock on the nightstand before pulling out my pajamas from under the pillow. I'm still so keyed up that I'll be tossing and turning half the night. *Maybe a bath will help me relax.*

After wiping out the tub, I turn on the spigot, making minor adjustments until the water is the perfect temperature. I toss my clothes on an empty chair and twist my hair into a high ponytail, clipping it to the top of my head. It takes forever to dry, so I don't want it to get wet.

I grab my iPad and scroll through the playlist. I'm in the mood for a little Lady Antebellum tonight. I lay the tablet on the counter and turn off all the bathroom lights except for the small nightlight I purchased at the drugstore when I first arrived.

Mostly pleased with the mood in the room, I lower myself into the bath. The tub isn't cavernous and there are no pulsing jets, but the warm water does its job nicely, penetrating my tight muscles until they begin to melt. Even without a tub full of bubbles, or a scented bath bomb, this feels heavenly.

"Need You Now" starts to play, and I lean back against the cool porcelain and let my eyelids flutter closed. The music is soothing—until the lyrics begin to seep into my subconscious, and all I can see is Smith Sinclair. The man who was a complete ass to me today. That's not entirely true—and therein lies the problem.

In between being an insufferable jerk, there were moments that he touched my soul. When he talked about how the desert had stolen so much, my heart clenched, and then there were times, one or two, where I had to stop myself from tearing off his clothes and rubbing my body against his. *You saw the evidence—Oh, yes, I did.* I had to tear my eyes away from his swelling cock.

I spread my legs, letting the warm water lap against my pussy.

There was also that whole overprotective thing he had going on. I don't know what to make of it. On one hand, I hated the patronizing attitude, on the other, I was tempted by it. I might have grown up surrounded by men, but I've never felt very protected.

I push away the sadness threatening to ruin my bath. I've learned to protect myself—physically and emotionally—that's all that's important. Girls who grow up believing a knight in shining armor will ride in and save them often die in the tower. Life isn't a fairy tale.

Despite Sinclair's concern, my gun is not just for show. While my friends were getting pedicures with their mothers, or scouring the mall for sales, I spent weekends at the range with my dad. My emotional armor, however, isn't always as robust as it needs to be, and there are gashes and pings denting the surface. But it's resilient. Like me.

Since Smith Sinclair is hellbent on infiltrating my thoughts, I might as well give him a little help. After drying my hands, I reach for my iPad and open my research folder. I pull up an image of him at President Wilder's funeral. He's somber, in a dark suit perfectly tailored to his large frame. The jacket cinches at the waist, falling effortlessly over those powerful hips. Fi is right—he's hot—everything about him screams sin in these photos. *In person, too.*

I dredge up the photos, one after another, lingering, as I soak in the details of each frame. My favorite is one where he's standing at the helm of a listing sailboat, glancing over his shoulder with a playful grin. It's as though he's sharing a joke with someone behind him—maybe JD, or maybe he's with a group of friends. His dimples are on full display for the camera. My mouth waters at the contours of his back and shoulders, chiseled out of a deep bronze stone. The photo must have been taken a while ago. His muscular frame hasn't changed, but his hair is longer now.

While I'm admiring Sinclair, secretly wishing I had an opportunity to experience the broad grin and playful side of him, my hand slips between my legs. I ogle him one last time, and set my iPad back on the counter, away from the water.

I tease my clit, massaging in a way that usually gets me off quickly. But I want more than a tepid orgasm with pleasant ripples. I want something that will leave me limp and exhausted. *What I really want is Sinclair.*

I drain most of the water out of the tub and lie back on my elbows, hooking one leg over the edge of the tub, and bracing the other against the tile wall. My legs are spread wide, with my tingling pussy positioned directly under the spigot. I reach between my legs and turn on the water, fiddling until the temperature is perfect. With a few tiny moves, I adjust my bottom so that the water trickles directly over my clit. My head falls back and my eyes shutter when the stream hits the swollen hood, caressing gently but relentlessly. The throbbing builds slowly, deep within my core.

My hands slide to my breasts, circling the heated skin, teasing each puckered nipple, pulling and pinching until the throb between my legs is merciless. But I don't want to come yet. I want to draw out the pleasure for as long as possible. I concentrate on the way my skin feels. I absorb each tiny prickle. I listen intently as my breath comes in short quick pants.

The music plays somewhere in the background. There is not a single thought of hard to dry hair. Smith's enormous hands are on me, warm and strong, demanding all my focus as they explore every inch of flesh. When he reaches my thighs, his fingers glide over the smooth skin in long strokes, nudging my knees further and further apart with each sweep, until I'm fully open to him.

He gazes at me, hungry and demanding, slipping his fingers into my wet pussy. My inner walls caress them, and he growls his approval while lowering his head to taste me. The long, lush strokes of his tongue entwine with the silky water in one exquisite sensation.

My clit is throbbing, and I need more.

I nudge the handle with my big toe, forcing the water pressure higher, and return my leg to the wall, curling my toes into the slick tile.

Oh. My. God. *Yes.* I squirm against the slippery tub, arching my back as the pulsing water bounces off my pussy, stinging my sensitive clit. I can't hold off any longer. I grip the edge of the tub, clinging tightly as my hips begin an erratic buck.

Do you enjoy having your hair pulled? Smith's breath is hot against my temple. His cock is impossibly thick and impatient as it pushes into me.

My womb clenches into a tight fist, and a tortured groan emerges as the waves crash over me. I writhe and buck against the smooth porcelain, struggling to escape the deliciously cruel stream beating on my tender folds.

I lie spent in the empty tub, the beat of the music competing with my thumping heart. My limbs are so heavy, I can't move. And I can't keep my eyes open. No matter how hard I fight, I begin to drift.

Follow your heart, Katydid.

9

SMITH

I pause outside the door to JD's study to get my head on straight. Gray is already here, and his non-stop speculation about what's holding me up is setting my teeth on edge. I'm sure it's also driving his brother nuts. JD can be a huge pain in the ass too, but in a different way, and we've known each other so long that I'm used to his brand of bullshit.

Both men look up when I walk in and park my ass in a chair in front of the desk. "Hey."

"How did it go?" Gray asks tentatively, as if bracing for bad news.

"She's after Warren King. Just chasing her tail. She didn't get what she wanted from me. I guarantee she'll be gone before midweek." The revelation comes with a small pang of regret. Not that I'm sorry she'll be out of my hair, but that my brief time with her might have been better spent. I would have liked—

"Did she say that?" Gray demands, interrupting thoughts that I shouldn't be thinking. I shake my head. "Then how can you be so sure?"

I stretch out my legs and lean back in the chair, resting my elbows on the thin arms, and look straight ahead as I casually drop the bomb. "I took her to Wildflower."

"What?" Gray barks from the edge of his seat. "You did what?" I knew taking her to the club would freak him out, but I've seen corpses with more color in their cheeks. "Tell me you did not take her downstairs."

"You need to calm the fuck down."

JD hasn't said one damn word since I walked in, but he's peering at me from across the desk, quietly biding time. Sometimes it's hard to believe these two emerged from the same womb. "And don't talk to me like I'm an idiot," I add. "You had every opportunity to take the meeting with her, but you wanted me to do it. So I did—my way." Granted it might have been better if my way had involved a more light-handed approach, but that's water under the bridge.

Gray turns to his brother. "Don't you have a fucking thing to say about this?"

That might as well have been a rhetorical question for all the response it received. But JD's glare is now on his brother, and I'm relieved to have it off me. He sees too much sometimes, and I don't need that kind of scrutiny right now.

"We call it a social club," Gray spits out, as he moves closer to me, "but you do know it's a goddamn sex club, right?" Sarcastic bastard. A vein throbs in his neck as he looms over me. He better not get one inch closer or I'm going to grab him by the throat and compress that bulging vein with my thumb. "What the hell were you thinking?"

"Listen up, asshole. I am not your Sub. You want answers, put the Dom back in the box, and shut your trap, otherwise you're getting shit."

Gray snarls before taking a few steps back. He leans against the window frame, hands clasped behind his head.

"It's not like McKenna didn't know exactly where Wildflower was located. Sometimes giving up something small is a better deterrent than anything else. I let her see the restaurant, the spa, and the gym. She walked through the empty ballroom, and got a peek into the office space. All of it off the record, and designed that way to make her feel I was doing her a big favor. I'm not some fly-by-the-seat-of-my-pants chump. McKenna got nothing."

Gray can't stand still. He's wearing down the rug on one side of the desk, still agitated, but more measured. "She got something."

"She got shit."

"Are you going to keep an eye on her to make sure she stops snooping?"

Sure. I don't mind candy I can't eat dangling in front of me. I'm a masochistic sonofabitch like that. "We'll keep an eye on her, but I'm telling you, she's at the motel packing. McKenna's not interested in the club. She wants information on Warren King. His confirmation hearing is in a week and then this will all be over."

"A week is a long time for a reporter to be hanging around asking questions."

I slap the heels of my hands against the wooden arms of the chair. "*Jesus*. You are some kind of thick. I just got through telling you, *twice*, she's not going to be here a week."

"King hasn't been a member of the club for almost twenty years. He got out shortly after investing. I don't even know how she found out about the connection."

"Maybe she doesn't know about the connection." Even as I say it, I'm not sure. I don't know what she knows about King's relationship to Wildflower. We never got that far. I'm just trying to get Gray to chill.

"She wouldn't be asking questions if she didn't know something."

"She didn't bring it up. And trust me, she's not shy." The image of her in the middle of a world-class temper tantrum, whipping off those stupid panties and throwing them at me, pops into my mind and settles there. I already regret not checking out her ass as she marched off.

Gray's phone beeps, and he curses softly. "I've got to go. Are you sure you have this covered?"

"I'm all over it."

He places both hands flat on his brother's desk. "Thanks for all your input, JD. Your concern for Wildflower is touching."

JD sits back in his chair, glowering at his younger brother. "I'm not your Sub either, princess. So watch your tone."

Gray stalks out, mumbling something that sounds like *fuckers*.

When he's gone, JD reaches for his phone. "I know you didn't take her downstairs, but did you take her upstairs?"

Fucking JD. There's not a human being on earth that can read me better. "It's not what you think."

"She a real redhead?" He turns his phone so I can see Kate's face.

Something about seeing him with her picture in his hand makes me want to jump over the desk and choke him. "Fuck you. You have a wife and a kid. Don't you think it's time to stop stalking women?"

He holds up both hands in mock surrender. "Just wanted to get a look at her. See if I'd have to give you hazardous duty pay for keeping a close eye on her. But from the look of her, it seems like you might need to pay me."

I'd like to wipe that stupid smirk off his face. "You're enjoying this aren't you?"

His leans back, and chews on the knuckle of his index finger, his fucking lips twitching. "Immensely."

"You're an asshole." I snatch one of the baby's stuffed animals from the corner of his desk and whip it at him with everything I've got. He catches the baby chick as it bounces off his chest.

"I'm well aware," he drawls, studying me carefully. "Why did you take her upstairs?"

He expects me to say I wanted to fuck her. But that's not true.

Not really. That came after we were already in the apartment. "I wanted to see how badly she wanted the story." I shrug, brushing a thread from my pant leg.

"And?"

"She wants it bad."

JD sits forward, elbows on the desk, the fingers of his left hand pressed against the right. He takes a moment to search my face before he speaks. "You didn't."

"Of course not. I toyed with her, but put an end to it long before it got out of hand." *But not before I made her take off her clothes and cry.* I keep this information to myself, not that JD's a choirboy, but it feels wrong to share it.

"Really? Because from the way you're acting, it seems to me like it might have gotten out of hand. Like it might still be out of hand."

"I didn't touch her. She's young. I was on a fishing expedition. That's all."

"Fishing. Of course." He picks up a stack of papers off the desk and tosses them aside. "How young?"

"Mid-twenties." *Too young for my eclectic tastes.*

"That's not too young to cast a rod into."

No, but in this case, young has nothing to do with age. "Why are we talking about this?"

"Because she's a reporter. Maybe you didn't stick your dick into her, but you wanted it. And you're still thinking about it."

"You're a goddamn mind reader now? Well, tell me what else is on my mind."

"I have no idea, but I have a feeling you're about to tell me."

He just handed me my opening. We need to have this discussion, and now. But the guilt I'm shouldering is heavy. "Mind if I get a drink?"

"Help yourself. Although I'm not sure why you're asking."

I pour us each a couple fingers of whiskey and hand him a glass. I'm going to tell him, but I want the vibe in the room to change. I don't want this conversation to be flippant or laced with our usual sarcasm.

I sit down and sip my bourbon, appreciating the small burn in the back of my throat after the first drops trickle down.

"Now that you've set the mood and calmed your pretty little tits with my good bourbon, I'll give you the bad news. I'm not fucking you, no matter how much you beg."

I laugh. It comes all the way from my belly, and the corner of JD's mouth curls in response. He's a sonofabitch. *The best kind of sonofabitch.* I've never had a better friend.

"I appreciate you hiring me when I wasn't sure where my life was headed," I begin from the heart, because I remember how out of sorts—how lost—I felt after the surgery, after I left my unit. JD was there. I didn't say much, and neither did he. But he listened carefully to the few words I spoke, and to the silence. He called bullshit when necessary. Stood beside me while I healed and then gave me a job to do. A *real* job. Not some bullshit task to keep me busy like the military had planned. "I can't tell you how much I appreciated it at the time. Still do."

He rubs his hands over his face. "*Jesus Christ.* You sound like a teenage girl telling some pimply-faced bastard he's going home with blue balls. Spit it out."

I hesitate for a few seconds. I've thought about this moment often in the last month, considered the words carefully, but still, they don't come easy. "I'm ready to move on. I need more in my life. With your father gone, there are fewer safety concerns. You no longer need the kind of security I can offer."

He runs his knuckles across an unshaven jaw. "You're leaving?"

There's a catch in his voice that's rarely there. I suck in a breath and blow it out. "Don't want to. I'm hoping you let me hang around and grow the business from here. Do some high-level tracking—maybe some search and rescue—pick-up a government contract, here and there." I shrug. "The details are still up in the air. But there's a lot I can do remotely—even manage teams from here. Not much different from some of the work I did in the military, but I'll be my own guy. I have skills I could be using more effectively."

"Do it."

Do it. Things with JD are rarely simple. I expected some pushback. Some kind of negotiation. "That's it. Do it?"

"It's not exactly a secret that protecting me isn't your life's dream. You've been an irascible motherfucker lately."

I crack a smile. In all the times I thought about how unsatisfied I had become with the work, I didn't once consider that anyone else might have noticed. "You're pretty observant for a self-absorbed cocksucker."

"*Cocksucker.* In your dreams." He props an elbow on the arm of the chair. "I want to be an investor."

I should have expected this. "You don't need to do that. I'm not going to start big. I might not have the kind of money you do, but I have a pile of loose change hanging around."

"What you're describing is going to cost a pretty penny. I know what I'm talking about. Equipment, insurance, you name it, it all costs money. More than you think. You need investors."

I know he doesn't mean anything by it, but the offer nicks my pride. "I didn't come to you for money."

"Didn't think you did." He pauses for a few seconds, bouncing a pencil eraser off the desk. "I'd like us to be in business together. I'm happy to be a mostly silent partner." I catch the twinkle in his eyes and quietly shake my head. He might be a man of few words, but nothing about him is silent.

"You're going to do good things," he continues. "I'd like Wilder Holdings to be a part of it. I'd like to be a part of it."

I look up from my empty glass. "Mostly silent?"

He nods, swirling the whiskey around the tumbler in his hand.

"I'd like that, too," I say, after a few seconds pass. And I would.

He's smart and has much more experience running a business than I have, and most importantly, I trust him implicitly.

JD gets up and goes over to the bar, bringing back a bottle of Pappy's and two fresh glasses. He pours us each some whiskey. "Special occasions," he says, "call for my man, Pappy." He touches my glass with his, before sitting his ass on the edge of the desk a few feet away from me.

"What's going to happen with the security here?" he asks.

I've thought through every contingency carefully. Now to see if he'll go for it. "I don't want to give that up." He visibly relaxes, but I haven't lobbed the grenade yet. "Thought I'd put Rafe in charge of security here."

He freezes. His expression, like his words, is dead serious. "I don't want him off Gabrielle's security team. Rafe and Gus look out for her and the baby like they're their own."

"Wouldn't want to take them off, either. That's never been the plan."

JD nods, and his frown eases. "Do you plan on using any of your current team in the new venture?"

"Aside from me, Delilah is the most highly trained member of the team. She's the only one with the kind of skills that can be useful in what I'm thinking about. But there won't be any changes for a while. It's going to take some time before we hammer it all out, and it's up and running in a way that I'm comfortable bidding on contracts."

"Delilah. I can live with that." He lifts his glass in my direction. "Cheers."

10

KATE

While it took less than two hours to pack my furnished room in DC, mop the floor, and wipe up the bathroom, it's ten days before I'm back in Charleston, and two weeks before my job begins. So much has happened in the interim.

Warren King's confirmation hearing has been delayed until after Congress returns from their summer recess. I learned this little piece of news while driving through the Blue Ridge Mountains on the way back to DC. It cemented my decision to leave the paper.

Hearings are delayed for a myriad of reasons, big and small. It happens all the time. Maybe they found something concerning in King's background, or it could be a political calculation by the White House, or perhaps some Senator has a burr up his ass. It could be that simple. Nothing in the announcement provided any clue, and I parsed each word carefully.

It's only unusual because it means that when the Supreme Court begins its October term, they'll be down a justice—bad for the country, but the timing works in my favor. By October, the

Boston Police Commissioner's job will be long-filled, and I can go home again.

With the hearing delayed, there was no real urgency to get back to Charleston, except for a nagging pull that I still can't quite explain. So I stuck around to cover the Keaton wedding. My colleagues appreciated the help, and it eased my conscience not to leave them short-handed for the event.

The wedding was as godawful as I anticipated. When the mother-of-the-bride *accidentally* spilled an entire glass of red wine in the lap of the father-of-the-bride's mistress, I reminded myself that it was the last society event I would *ever* have to cover. It made the air kisses and the never-ending parade of lavender tulle more tolerable.

The extra time in DC also gave me an opportunity to find an affordable sublet in Charleston, and a part-time job at the library working with women who are homeless because of domestic violence, sex-trafficking, and poverty. It's not only meaningful work, but it will give me ample time to work on the King story, and it pays enough that I shouldn't need to dig into my savings.

I'm sure Smith Sinclair and his buddies will be thrilled that I'm back in town. I wonder what Sinclair will have up his sleeve for me? Whatever it is, I'll be prepared this time. *Maybe.*

Sinclair has been a regular in my naughty fantasies since our little encounter at Wildflower. I thought about him often while I was in DC—when I got bored with all the Keaton nonsense, and also, alone in my bed in the dark, with the soft hum of the Lelo in the background. The orgasms were epic. But I'm paying the price now. Since being back in Charleston, I'm constantly looking over my shoulder, wondering if he'll appear out of nowhere. I still can't decide if I would enjoy bumping into him casually. I wish I could say *no*, but I'm not sure.

Today is my first official day of work. I'm both nervous and excited as I add the finishing touches to the bulletin board in my office, that also doubles as a classroom, tucked behind the stacks in the library. This is where I'll be helping women put together resumes, fill out applications and forms, and provide advocacy, when necessary, along with holding ESL classes twice a week.

When I turn to grab a stapler from the table, there's a man in the doorway, preparing to knock on the open door. *A priest.* The white collar is a dead giveaway. His quiet presence startles me. It's not that I'm a stranger to priests—my childhood home abuts St. Claire's Church, and I spent a lot of time there soaking up Father Tierney's friendship. It's just—I must have been deep in my own little world because I didn't hear him approach.

"Hel—hello," I stammer. He smiles kindly. Even with a shock of dark hair, he has the look of an Irishman. A handsome, strapping Irishman is how Nana would have described him. I can almost hear the lilt in her voice, *Could have had any woman, but he chose Christ.*

"I'm sorry. I didn't mean to startle you." He steps inside and holds out his hand. "I'm Father Creighton. But most everyone calls me Father Jesse. You must be Kate."

How does he know my name? "Kate, yes. I'm Kate." I take his hand. It's large and warm, with a firm handshake. "Mary Katherine McKenna. But most everyone calls me Kate." I sound ridiculous, almost sheepish, as though he overheard me daydreaming about my Lelo and the mind-blowing orgasms.

"Mary Katherine. Lovely name for a lovely woman." He looks at me with nothing but kindness, but still, I feel a small blush from his careful scrutiny which seems to go on a tad too long.

"When I was in last week, Lucinda at the front desk told me you'd be taking over for Stacey while she's on maternity leave, and I wanted to drop these off, and to meet you."

He hands me a stack of cards—they look like business cards with the photo of a stately church printed on the front. "At Saint Mary Magdalene's, St. Maggie's—that's what most everyone calls her—" his bright blue eyes twinkle in a boyish manner, "we welcome everyone, but we have a special mission to serve women who are struggling, spiritually or worldly."

I glance at the cards. St. Maggie's is a gothic style structure, while St. Claire's in Boston is a Romanesque Revival. They're both grand, and quite beautiful from the outside, boasting tall tapering spires topped with Latin crosses.

"We have clothing and non-perishable food items—and God, of course." I look up from the cards, to the corner of his mouth curled at the corny joke. I smile, too. Father Tierney is also fond of dad jokes, but he's significantly older than Father Jesse, so the jokes don't seem quite so lame coming from him.

"I guess you could say we supplement the work you're doing here," he adds. "We also have connections that can assist women with things like an apartment or household items."

"That sounds fabulous. I'm new in town and have no connections."

"You have me now, and I have connections with the very best." It's an odd thing for a priest to say, and when I don't respond, he points toward the heavens and grins. I laugh softly when I finally get the joke.

Lame jokes aside, I like him. He's the most down-to-earth, approachable person I've met in Charleston. Maybe he wouldn't mind giving me some guidance. I'm totally confident about putting together resumes and filling out forms, but I've never worked with women at risk—with anyone at risk, and I've been a little worried about saying—or doing—something that might be insensitive or retraumatizing.

"I volunteered at a neighborhood soup kitchen in Boston and helped with clothing drives at our church, but I was never the one in charge. I know the women who come here for assistance are quite vulnerable. Is there anything you think I should know that might help me with my work here?"

He thinks for a minute, not breaking eye contact. "It can be trying, on many levels. Just remember that you are doing God's work, and you'll be fine. After spending only a few minutes with you—I can see you have a kind way about you and great empathy in your heart. You're perfect."

I'm not accustomed to such effusive praise and I'm a bit embarrassed. I glance to the side in an effort to deflect the glare of the spotlight. Father Jesse doesn't say anything more, but he studies me, again, this time with a faraway look, as though his mind is elsewhere. When the spaciness goes on for too long, it becomes a bit disconcerting, and I begin to wonder if he's having a seizure. It sounds silly, but a little girl who I babysat one summer suffered from a seizure disorder. She'd just stare into space—she was there, but not really. It felt just like this.

"Is everything okay?" I prod gently, so as not to alarm him.

He shakes his head with small movements, as though he's gently clearing the cobwebs. "Yes. Yes. I apologize for staring." He sighs. "It's that you remind of someone. But I can't quite put my finger on it. It's maddening." His brow is crinkled, and his expression seems—I don't know—agitated. Not angry—but as though there is upheaval happening inside him.

"Perhaps it's my hair?" I offer, hoping to lighten the mood. "There are so few redheads that people are always sure they've met me before."

"Yes. But that's not it." After another few awkward moments of chit chat, with him trying not to stare, his expression softens, and I see the glimmer of recognition in his eyes. "Your face has the serenity of a young Magdalene." His tone is hushed, almost reverent. "You resemble the images we have of her. It's uncanny, really. I don't know why I didn't notice it when I first came in." He wets his lips. "Perhaps I did," he adds, mostly to himself.

"Oh." That's a little strange. But I brush it off. I've had enough experience with priests to know they don't always think on the same level as the rest of us whose lives aren't steeped in philosophy, theology, and mysticism.

"Of course, we're not sure how she actually appeared. Instagram wasn't available back then." He cocks his head and smiles. "I made you uncomfortable. I'm sorry."

I shake my head. "You didn't." It's just a small fib. Lying to a priest might be bad, but it would be terribly rude for me to say otherwise.

His eyes stray from my face while he bends to pick up a pushpin from the floor. "Don't want anyone to step on this." He places the lime green pin carefully in the center of the table, where it won't accidentally roll off. "You're new in town?"

The change of subject isn't exactly seamless, but I'm glad to be talking about something besides how much I resemble a saint who lived at the time of Christ. "I arrived a few days ago, but I was here for three weeks last month too."

"If you're still looking for a church, I hope you'll give us a chance. We do a Sunday potluck after Mass. I'd love to say it's well-attended and you'll meet lots of people your age, but fewer than a dozen parishioners show up regularly, and they are mostly old enough to be your grandparents. But I can promise you'll be well fed." He sticks a hand casually into his trouser pocket before continuing. "Sometimes we get one of the women from the classes here, who needs a good meal or a friend."

I shift my weight from one foot to another, preparing to confess that I haven't stepped foot inside a church while in Charleston.

"I haven't found a church," I say softly, lowering my gaze. *Or even looked for one.*

Father Jesse rests a comforting hand on my shoulder. "Don't worry, your secret is safe with me," he whispers, with a wink so quirky and sweet, it charms me. "We're on Albert's Island. The bus runs from downtown a few times a day. You can almost always catch a ride back downtown with a parishioner. Not many people actually live on the island."

"I have a car."

His face lights up. "Then I can count on seeing you?" Even if I wanted to, I don't have the heart to say no.

And why not check out St. Maggie's? I would love to be part of a spiritual community again. I miss the feeling of belonging to something bigger than me, and Father Jesse has been more welcoming than anyone else I've met here. "I'd love to come. Should I bring something to the lunch?"

"Not this time."

"Mary Katherine." I look up to find Smith Sinclair striding into the room. Even with all the time I spent looking over my shoulder waiting for him to appear out of nowhere, I'm still surprised to see him standing here. It feels out of place, somehow, all wrong. Like I'm a five-year-old who just bumped into her kindergarten teacher at Target. He doesn't belong here.

I'm speechless, but I can't stop gawking. He looks delicious, in a faded, cadet blue T-shirt stretched over his chest and shoulders, the soft fabric barely corralling his biceps. *I hope priests are oblivious to the heady scent of pheromones that emanate from the aroused female body.*

"Father." He nods. "I don't think we've met. I'm Smith Sinclair."

"Father Creighton, from St. Maggie's."

"On Albert's Island."

"That's right." The two men size each other up. It must be a genetic thing with men. Even someone as evolved as a priest can't help himself.

Father Jesse turns to me. "I need to get back to the island. Please give out the cards."

"I will."

"I look forward to seeing you on Sunday. Perhaps your friend,

Mr. Sinclair, would like to join us for Mass." Father Jesse doesn't glance at Smith, even as he speaks about him.

Sinclair doesn't say a word in response. *Thankfully, because there is no way I'm taking him to church with me. The last thing I need is Sinclair intruding on what I hope will become my spiritual oasis.*

"Thank you for stopping by, Father. I'll see you on Sunday. But if I have any questions, or need a connection, you might hear from me sooner." After sharing the private little joke, I smile at him, and he chuckles softly.

I hold out my hand, and he takes it in both of his in a friendly gesture. "My door is always open for you, Kate." He lets go of me and turns to the man whose muscular ass fills out his worn blue jeans nicely. "Mr. Sinclair, good to meet you." Sinclair gives him a small curt nod of acknowledgment, but doesn't return the pleasantry.

I watch Father Jesse walk out the door and disappear behind the stacks. When I turn back around, Sinclair is sitting in *my* seat at the small table, like he owns the place. It's irritating, and my pheromones dry up.

"Why are you here?" I grab the to-do list he's eyeing and turn it over, quickly scanning the table to make sure there's nothing in his line of vision that he shouldn't see. I'd call him a nosy bastard, but I'd do the same thing in his shoes.

"I need some help polishing my resume," he says with a straight face. I scowl at him. "Be nice, Mary Katherine. I don't think the good Father is even out of the building yet. What do you think makes a man want to be a Catholic priest? Give up all his worldly possessions, his sexuality, and devote his life to a God that we're not even sure exists?"

"It's considered a great honor."

He raises his brow. "*Really?*"

"*Really.*" I hitch my thumb, signaling for him to get up. "You're in my seat."

"I'm not staying long." He glances pointedly at each available chair around the table. "Explain why it's such an honor to become a priest."

"After I explain, do you promise to leave?"

He smirks. "Very shortly after. Has anyone mentioned that your southern charm is sorely lacking?"

I sigh and sit diagonally across the table from him. "Becoming a priest is a special calling, directly from God, and having a priest in the family is a special blessing from God." I explain like I'm a catechism teacher and he's a bored fifth grader. "There are many Irish families, Catholic families, I suppose, but I can only speak for the Irish, who dream of having a priest in the family." Sinclair picks up the errant pushpin off the table and twirls it between his fingers while he listens. "But only the smartest, most reflective boys are sent to the seminary."

"That's old school stuff. I don't believe there's much honor in joining the priesthood anymore."

"Maybe not everywhere, but where I'm from, there is still much honor in becoming a priest and it's still a great blessing bestowed on families." The sex abuse scandal that I'm sure he's hinting at is a well-deserved black eye on the institution of the church. It involved so many innocent children, far too many, but it did not involve *all* priests. Not by a long shot. It grates on me when I hear people speak in sweeping generalities about the travesty. "Since you're not Catholic, maybe you should keep your uninformed opinion about the priesthood to yourself."

He tosses the pin aside, and gazes at me until my skin begins to tingle. "He likes you."

"Who?"

Sinclair lifts a purple pen out of my pencil holder, clicking it on and off a few times before replacing it. Then he takes out another pen, and another. I try to ignore it, but having him paw at my things is driving me crazy. "The Father," he answers matter-of-factly, while toying with my favorite orange pen.

"He's a priest. He likes everyone, even you."

"Something off about the way he looked at you—for a priest." I snatch the pen holder away from him, stashing it well out of his reach. "What do you want?"

Sinclair peers at me, his eyes narrowing. "I stopped by to say hello. I didn't expect to see you back in Charleston."

Stopped by to say hello, my ass. "Well, you've said hello, and now it's time for you to go. I have a lot of things to do before my class this evening."

"I'll be keeping my eye on you. And you ... will stay away from the Wilders."

"You know, your southern charm could use a little shine, too." I flash him a saccharine smile. "I already told you I have no interest in the Wilders."

"And I already told you I don't believe you. You took off your clothes to get a story. Any fool could have seen that wasn't your normal way of operating. That tells me you're looking for a big story. No bigger story in Charleston than the Wilders. And there's sure as hell no other story here worth leaving your paper for."

When he mentions my clothes, I dig my fingernails into my thighs to control my temper. He's trying to get a rise out of me, but I'll be damned if I give it to him. I'm so indignant it takes almost a full minute before it registers that he already knows I've left the paper.

"Life around here must be pretty dull if you have nothing to do but monitor my every move. Maybe the Wilders are paying you too much. Or maybe it's time to leave Charleston and find something to do that holds your interest so you don't need to be skulking around, puffing out your chest and growling at reporters trying to do their jobs."

His lips are pursed in a tight little line, and he's all but snarling. I plucked a nerve. For once, just once with him, I feel like I'm the one in control. Even in my fantasies, he's in charge.

"I can't imagine a man like you would be satisfied for long

doting on the rich and famous. I know just how you feel. That's exactly why I left the paper." His eyes are dark slits. He's pissed. *Good.* Now maybe he'll leave me alone—not just in the real world, but in my fantasy world, too. *Although, there's probably no harm in him making an occasional appearance there.*

Sinclair glowers at me, but today, I'm not squirming. The library is a public place with people milling about on every floor. Besides, I don't want anything from him. I'm done in that regard.

"Don't fuck with me, Kate. It's not a game you want to play. You won't win, and next time, you might lose more than your clothes."

"I have no interest in playing *any* game with you, Sinclair. But just like I decide when to take off my clothes, I decide what games I'm playing and who I'm playing them with."

He leans across the table and taps the edge of my wrist a couple times. "You keep up that line of thinking. See where it gets you." With one last snarl, he gets up and strides toward the door without even a goodbye. When he gets to the doorway, he turns abruptly. "That priest wants to fuck you."

I slap a hand over my eyes, covering them completely. He sounds like a jealous boyfriend, but that's not what this is about. This is pure, unadulterated manipulation. Psychological warfare.

"I can't say if he'll act on it. But he wants it."

"You're ridiculous."

With just a few strides, he's back, both hands flat on the table, leaning over me. "You believe whatever you want to believe. Faith is a highly personal thing." His eyes are ablaze, and I look away to avoid the singe. "But behind that starched white collar is a man. He's got the same capacity for good and evil as any other man. Same base needs—food, sleep, and sex. I've been all over the world, never seen any difference among men in that regard." He pauses for a few seconds, the silence vibrating in the room. "You'd be surprised what men do in the name of God."

Sinclair is trying to shake me up, to keep me away from the

comfort of the church and any friends I might make there. It'll be easier to chase me out of town if I'm alone and isolated.

I look down at my laptop and scroll through some documents, searching for nothing in particular. He doesn't say another word, but I feel his eyes penetrating—his shadow looming large. I don't breathe again until he's gone.

11

KATE

As I drive over the causeway to Albert's Island, the overgrown trees in the distance catch my eye—Live Oaks, draped with Spanish moss. They're all over Charleston, and for a girl from New England unaccustomed to them, they're a bit spooky. They remind me of a scene straight out of a horror flick.

The island is surrounded by swampland with vegetation and murky water on all sides. Albert's Island is a small landmass that holds St. Maggie's and a few houses that belong to the church—at least according to Google maps.

I follow a narrow dirt road a short distance, weaving to avoid the brush. It's not even summer yet, and the thorny shrubs have already taken over. I can't imagine this road will be passable in July if the bushes aren't tamed.

When I reach the clearing, St. Maggie's is directly in front of me—a Gothic marvel constructed almost entirely of stone with an ornate cross jutting into the heavens. More than a dozen armed gargoyles with misshapen features are perched along the roof, guarding the castle, perhaps from the devil, or maybe from other fallen angels. Regardless, it's a grand piece of architecture, out here on a lonely island. Striking, yet haunting, even in the bright sunlight.

There are a couple dozen cars in the parking lot—nothing particularly fancy or showy. I walk around to the front entrance and climb the steep granite stairs. At the top, I turn to survey the area. It's so close to the bustling city, yet so desolate.

A gentle breeze carries the familiar scent of brackish water. *The ocean.* It's the one thing about Charleston that always feels welcoming—that, and hopefully St. Maggie's.

When I step inside the vestibule, Father Jesse is there, dressed in traditional green vestments, greeting a couple who appear to be in their late sixties. Father Tierney always stood in the back of St. Claire's before mass began too.

While waiting my turn to say hello, I notice an opulent font, with cherubs carved from honed marble, along the back. The stone has worn smooth over time, giving it an elegant patina. I quietly admire its beauty before dipping my fingers into the holy water, reciting the silent prayer as I make the sign of the cross.

"Kate." Father Jesse approaches me and takes both my hands in his.

"Good morning, Father."

"I'm so glad you came. I wasn't sure you would. But I'm a man of great faith." He squeezes my fingers firmly before letting go. "I hope you're planning on joining us for lunch."

I wasn't sure if I would stay. My plan had been to scope out the situation, and decide after Mass. But I don't have anywhere else to go, and it will be hard to leave without making up a lie. I don't want to lie to a priest while standing in a church—not even a small fib to spare his feelings. If God doesn't punish me for that, surely Karma will. "I would love to stay for lunch and meet some of the parishioners. If it's still okay?"

His features soften. "More than okay." The processional hymn begins, filling the church with joyful sounds. "That's my cue." He winks, that charming quirky wink, and smiles. He has an easy boyish smile that bathes his features in a sweet innocence, and he's not shy about using it. "We'll talk more after Mass." Father Jesse motions for me to go inside and waits until I'm situated before proceeding up the grand aisle.

The liturgy is achingly familiar. When I close my eyes, I could be back in Boston, sitting in a pew at St. Claire's. The ritual of Catholic Mass is predictable, rarely deviating from the traditional, always providing comfort and a sense of grounding.

The church has always been my anchor, even when I strayed from its teachings. I feel protected inside the hallowed walls—physically, emotionally, and spiritually safe. I guess you could say it's coded into my DNA. Or perhaps it's the love and affection that Father Tierney showed me growing up. The times he babysat when no one else wanted the chore, snuck me Kit Kats and Hershey Kisses, or let me choose one item from the collection of donated clothes. I spent a great deal of time with him as a child. There was much solitude, but also much joy there. And it was safe. A kind of safe that I rarely felt growing up. Something beyond physical safety.

When it's time for communion, I hesitate. At St. Claire's, congregants are welcome to participate in communion, even if they haven't received the Sacrament of Reconciliation, or Confession as it is still sometimes called, as long as they are in a state of grace. Father Tierney interpreted grace broadly, but I'm unsure about the custom here, so I remain in the pew, kneeling while Father Jesse administers Communion. Once or twice, I'm sure he glances at me, although it might just be my conscience needling. It's been a long time since I've confessed my sins to a priest.

After the final blessing, Father Jesse makes his way down the aisle, and waits at the top of the landing outside, chatting amicably and inviting congregants to lunch. From his expression, I imagine that some of the conversations are more serious than others. He touches many of the people he talks with, gently—a hand on a shoulder, or on an arm, perhaps giving support or consoling. He's genuine and kind, and his way makes it feel like this is a place I want to return to.

"So, what did you think?" Father Jesse sneaks up behind me while I'm preoccupied with the intricate scrolls of the iron handrail. "Did the sermon bore you to tears? Is that why we can't entice anyone under forty to leave their warm bed and attend Sunday Mass?"

I smile broadly. There is something about him that catches me by surprise because it feels so ordinary. As though he's just another guy. Maybe it's because he's young. My experience is mainly with older clergy. "I enjoyed the sermon. It was fresh and filled with hope."

"Really?"

I nod and smile.

"Let me change, and I'll give you a tour of the grounds while we walk over to lunch. You can tell me what you enjoyed about my ramblings." He grins. "I'll be quick. It'll give you a few minutes to think of something polite to say." He squeezes my elbow in a friendly gesture, and he's gone.

I stand in the center of the church captivated by the sunlight streaming in through the stained glass, the diffuse light bathing the face of Jesus hanging on the cross. Like everything else, it's a magnificent rendition of the crucifixion. It's difficult to imagine that a church so poorly attended can manage the upkeep of a building this size.

"Let's go out this way," Father Jesse calls from the front. "It's a short cut."

"The church is stunning. I can't believe the craftsmanship that went into building it."

"It's a replica of a European Cathedral, or rather a collection of ideas that a generous benefactor brought back with him from his travels through Europe. He had the church constructed, and left his fortune to St. Maggie's in the form of an endowment that we still use to sustain the property."

"Wow. That is generous. Did he have a connection to St. Magdalene?"

He chuckles. "Apparently, he had a fondness for whores—that's the story, anyway. But I don't believe it. Magdalene has had a complex history with the church—but during that particular man's lifetime, she wasn't believed to be a whore. That came much later."

I've never heard a priest use the word whore so freely. While I'm deciding how I feel about it, we approach a building with a tall tower behind the church. "There are a couple small houses on the property," Father Jesse tells me, pointing down a small unpaved lane. "The church secretary and her son live in one, and Silas, the groundskeeper, in the other. Be mindful around him."

"Why is that?" I ask when he doesn't explain.

"He spent time in prison for rape. It was a long time ago. That's all I can say. This building holds the rectory," he continues, "the church office, and the common space. It's where I live."

"The turret is spectacular." So spectacular that I forget all about Silas. "It reminds me of something out of a fairy tale—a tower where princesses would hide away." As soon as the foolishness is out of my mouth, I feel ridiculous.

He smiles. "*Ah*. So you're a fan of fairy tales."

My face is warm, and I'm happy we're walking so he doesn't see the flush across my cheeks. "Not really. But occasionally I do indulge my inner girl."

"Nothing wrong with that. But I'm afraid there's never been royalty to speak of on Albert's Island. It's unlikely princesses were ever jailed here—sinners perhaps. Although we can't know for sure who's been hidden away in the turret as a sacrifice to God. Or during war and rebellion," he adds quickly.

"It was used as a prison?"

"I was joking." He shrugs. "But who knows. The tower is the only reinforced area in the rectory. It's where priests safely counted money from the Sunday collection plate, back when the pews were full. Although I think the idea of keeping sinners locked there is much more interesting, and princesses more interesting still."

I smile. "Are there historical records?"

"Fire destroyed much of the early history. There's little left, but you're welcome to comb through it if you're interested. Let's go inside so that lunch can get started. They refuse to eat until I arrive."

He opens the door for me and I follow behind to a large hall where some people are seated, and others mill around. There is a buffet table set up against the sidewall, across from a bank of windows, laden with more food than this group could eat in a week. It makes me a little sad, imagining women old enough to be my grandmother waking up at the crack of dawn to prepare food no one will eat.

"Let me introduce you to Virginia, the church secretary. She's not much older than you, and I think you'll like her." Father Jesse beckons Virginia over. "Virginia Bennett, meet Kate McKenna. She's new to Charleston, and I persuaded her to make the trip over by bribing her with lunch."

She holds out a small hand. "It's a pleasure to meet you, Kate." But I'm not sure it is. Her face is tense and her smile forced. Before I can say anything, Father Jesse is pulled away by a man wearing suspenders, and Virginia and I are left alone. After we chat for a few minutes, I realize she thinks I'm from the women's shelter.

"I don't live at the shelter. I work with women from the shelter, at the library."

"That's wonderful," she says, her brow unfurling. "There was a time when I was pregnant with Petey, that I could have used that kind of help. God bless you."

Working with the homeless women is my opportunity to do some research on Warren King. It's not as altruistic as she made it out to be, and I'm embarrassed enough to set her straight. "I'm happy to be working with women from the shelter, but I'm actually a journalist, in town to do a little research."

"That's interesting. What about, dear?" It's odd to hear her call me dear. She's probably only a few years older than I am, although she seems older. "The Charleston societies." Virginia freezes with a look on her face like she's sucking on a lemon. Clearly another Charleston native who believes it's impolite to dig into local business. "Nothing too intrusive," I assure her.

"Maybe you can help us with our newsletter—you being a journalist and all. I keep telling Father Jesse we need to spruce it up, maybe put it online if we're ever going to attract young people. But he doesn't have the time."

That was so random. She's nervous—I say random things when I'm nervous too.

A young man wanders over to us, and hands Virginia his tie without saying a word. "This is my son, Petey. Petey this is Miss Kate. She works at the library."

"I love the library," he says in a childlike voice. "We get books there. You have pretty hair." He grabs a fistful of my hair. "It's red like the devil."

"Petey!" Virginia admonishes. He lets go of my hair immediately. "Do not touch anyone's hair. You need to apologize to Miss Kate. Right now. Jesus is watching." There's something harsh about the way she chides him. It's not so much about what she says, but her tone.

"I'm sorry," he says, staring at the floor.

Petey is clearly mentally disabled in some way, and I don't want him to feel the shame of having disappointed his mother, or me, or Jesus for that matter. "It's okay, Petey. People like to touch my hair because of the color. There aren't too many redheads around, so they like to see if my hair feels different than their hair. It doesn't feel different though, does it?"

He shakes his head. "Can I touch it again?"

"Petey! No, you may not touch her hair again."

Virginia speaks in a raised voice that brings Father Jesse over. He peers at her, until she explains. "Petey's taken with Kate's red hair. He touched her." She lowers her head, much the way Petey did.

"I saw that," he responds, before turning to me. "Did you know Mary Magdalene was a redhead? At least that's how she was depicted in drawings."

"I was trying to persuade Kate to help modernize our newsletter," Virginia pipes up. There's something a bit off about her affect, or maybe she just has poor conversational skills. "We need to get with the times, Father, or we'll be the ones left to close the doors."

"The bulletin, Virginia."

"The bulletin," she repeats softly, lowering her eyes, again. "I better go supervise Petey's lunch." She hurries away in the direction of her son without another word.

"How old is Petey?" I ask.

"Sixteen. Almost the same age Virginia was when she gave birth to him. It hasn't been easy, but she's a wonderful mother, and takes great care of him. He's gotten to be a handful now that he's hit puberty. If you're going to be coming over to help us with the bulletin, you should be aware that he is—that he's unpredictable. Keep your wits about you when he's around." He looks directly at me. "I don't want anything to happen to you." His attention goes back to Petey. "Virginia insists he's harmless, but you have the right to know."

It sounds a bit dire, or maybe I seem fragile. "I have older brothers. I'm used to a bit of rough and tumble. I'm sure I'll be fine, but thank you for letting me know."

"I noticed that you're too polite to tell me that you haven't actually agreed to help with the bulletin."

I don't really need another job to cut into my research time, although a church bulletin shouldn't be that difficult to overhaul.

"I have a lot going on, but I would be happy to help, if you don't need it done in a hurry."

"I'm not sure that I need it done at all, but Virginia keeps nagging, and I'm willing to indulge her on this. Perhaps you can take a look at our back issues and give me your opinion. You're young and smart, just the kind of person we're seeking to entice."

"I'm not sure how smart I am, but I'm always happy to offer an opinion."

"Great. Maybe one evening after work you can come by for supper. Mondays are the best night because I have all these leftovers to eat. Trust me, you don't want to eat food I prepare." He quirks his brow. "Are you free tomorrow?"

Tomorrow? "I have a meeting at the library tomorrow, but next Monday will work."

"Good. We can confirm at Mass next week." He pauses. "That was presumptuous of me. There's no expectation that you attend Mass here. You might prefer another church. I'm sorry."

"Please don't apologize. I planned on attending next Sunday. I enjoyed the Mass today. It felt right." He stares at me, much the same way that he did in the library when I worried he was having a seizure. "Father?"

"Yes. I'm sorry. I have a lot on my mind. We should help ourselves to lunch while the food is still warm."

12

KATE

It's Friday evening and I'm relaxing on Miss Macy's porch with my laptop open, plotting the weekend's research while treating myself to a plate of shrimp and grits and a chilled rosé. Miss Macy's is known for smooth creamy grits, inexpensive wine, and free Wi-Fi. It's my kind of place.

Today is my twenty-eighth birthday. Bittersweet as always.

My family never celebrates with me because it reminds them too much of my mother. Except for my brother, Liam. Growing up, he was the only one who wished me a happy birthday, and bought me a present from money he had saved from shoveling snow. When he was older, he would take me out for a banana split at Brigham's, or sneak me an éclair from an elegant bakery downtown. While he was alive, even when he was stationed in the desert, he always remembered my birthday. I don't know if it seemed disloyal to my mom, or to the others, but he wanted it to remain our secret. I never betrayed him, not even to Fiona.

It wasn't as bad as it sounds. We celebrated my birthday every year in class during elementary school. Chocolate cupcakes with buttercream from Rita's Bakery would somehow materialize each year. Back then, I pretended it was my dad who would sneak the goodies in, but I'm an adult now, and I know better. I've nagged Rita for years to tell me who placed the orders, but her lips are sealed. I still don't know.

When we were teenagers, Fiona always made a huge deal of my birthday. We celebrated with friends and vodka pilfered from our parents' stashes. She never forgets me, and today was no different.

The day started with Fiona and the boys FaceTiming me to sing a loud, off-key rendition of "Happy Birthday." Their love and joy radiated off the screen as they promised there were more surprises in store. They were bursting with secrets, and Fiona had to finally shoo them away before they blabbed about the surprises.

She had an eight-layer chocolate cake delivered to the library, along with a huge basket of lilacs, and when I arrived home, there was a package waiting for me. I teared up as I carefully undid Fiona's exquisite wrapping, and lifted the gorgeous shirt from the box—a sexy off-the-shoulder style with a lace-up front and delicate hand embroidery, from a boutique on Newbury Street, near where she works. Fiona has always been better at dressing me than I am at dressing myself.

I wore my new shirt to my birthday dinner. Who cares if I'm eating alone and no one besides the waitstaff at Miss Macy's will see it? I see it, and it makes me feel pretty and loved. *That's what's important.*

Alone, or with friends, I've learned to commemorate my birthday in some way each year. To celebrate my life, because it's worth celebrating. My guidance counselor told me that the year I graduated from high school.

Aside from church, I have no weekend plans, just two full days to devote to research, and trying to put together the pieces I've already gathered. I still don't know why the King hearings were postponed, but I do have more information about him, although no smoking gun.

Lucinda, who volunteers at the library, is chatty, and she doesn't care that I'm not from Charleston. Apparently when she was younger, she was a *striking redhead too,* and has decided we were meant to be good friends.

She makes it her business to fill in the gaps—to teach me things I don't understand about the city or its people. Lucinda swears King was a dog back in the day, scouring Charleston after dark for a little tail. Those are her words, not mine.

While she acknowledges they exist and that there are secrets, she doesn't make much of the exclusive societies. She also doesn't have much use for the Wilders, except for Gabrielle, JD's wife. Says she's the only one who doesn't have her nose so high in the air that she can't say hello. Although Lucinda did confess if she were younger, she'd like to wrap her legs around Gray and let him take her for a ride—*on his motorcycle, you naughty girl,* she added when I began giggling.

I sense someone approaching the table, and look up with a smile, assuming it's the waitress with the cornbread I ordered. My smile fades when Sinclair pulls out an empty chair and sits down across the small table from me, our knees almost grazing.

I'm speechless. I open and close my mouth a few times to say something, but the synapses don't begin to fire on all cylinders until he speaks. "Nice night to have supper outside. Perfect weather and no bugs. We don't get enough evenings like this."

"This has to stop. You're always creeping around in the shadows. I can't even get a meal in peace. What are you doing here?"

"You're never going to get anyone to tell you a damn thing if you don't develop some manners. *Good* manners. It's like you were raised by Yankees, or some other gnarly creatures."

His tone is chiding, but his eyes have the glimmer of fun. Too bad I'm not in the mood for Sinclair's kind of fun tonight.

"Hello, Mr. Sinclair. It's a lovely evening, isn't it? What are you doing here?"

He shakes his head. "I came for the shrimp and grits, same as you." Sinclair hesitates, looks around, then leans across the table and whispers conspiratorially. "Please tell me you ordered the shrimp and grits."

"It's none of your business. And I don't believe you're here for the food."

"Believe it."

"Smithie," a woman cries, as she steps onto the porch with a starched apron tied around her generous hips. Her chestnut hair, dotted with silver, is coiled into a neat bun. She's beaming as she approaches the table. Sinclair gets up, takes the glass out of her hand, and gives her a bear hug, squeezing until her heels are off the ground. "I'm off at ten," she tells him. "If you get rid of this pretty little thing sittin' here, I'll see what I can do about ditchin' my husband."

Sinclair's immediate response is a loud boisterous laugh that echoes from every corner of the porch. "You, darlin', are more woman than even I can handle."

"You always know how to make an old lady feel good," she says, before pointing at the tumbler Sinclair took from her hand. "Jasper's workin' up some new concoction now that the weather's warming up, said to bring some out for you to try."

Sinclair sits back down, and takes a sip, and then another before he offers an opinion. "Tell him he's got a winner here."

"Praise the Lord! He's been tinkering with that damn drink all week. I'm sick of hearing about it." The woman reties her apron. "The usual?" she asks Sinclair.

"Yes, ma'am." His attention shifts momentarily to me. "Have you ordered?"

I nod. "Right before you sat down."

"Would you mind holding back Miss Kate's order some, so we can have our supper together?"

Really? Presumptuous bastard. I would kick him under the table, but he's too close for me to get up the momentum to make it hurt. "And can we get some of that jalapeno cornbread you bake up, please?" he asks. "I dream about that buttery crumb all the time."

"You watch yourself, Miss," she warns. "This man is a shameless flirt. No tellin' where his charm might lead you."

I stop myself from saying something snarky about him. Instead, I give her a warm smile. "He keeps me on my toes, that's for sure." Being pleasant isn't normally so difficult for me—unless Sinclair is around.

"Is that Missy Macy?" I ask when the woman walks back inside.

He shakes his head. "That's Miss Jolene, Jasper's wife. They own the place. He cooks and she bakes. They make everything from scratch. Miss Macy was Jasper's old hound."

How does the man know the details of everyone's life? And why do people adore him? Even Lucinda said she'd let him keep his slippers under her bed.

"Taste this," he says handing me the old-fashioned glass. I shake my head. "Come on. Jasper will appreciate a woman's point of view."

"A woman's point of view?"

"Yeah. You're a woman. We established that the first time we met, right?" *God, he's insufferable.* "Whiskey's a man's drink."

"A man's drink?" I glare at him across the table.

"Stop acting like I'm some kind of Neanderthal. Men drink all sorts of liquor, as do women. But my experience is men tend to drink whiskey more often, and although I know plenty of women who are whiskey drinkers, they tend to lean more toward clear spirits or wine." His gaze shifts to my glass of rosé. "I bet that's your experience, too."

I don't answer him, because he's right, *of course*. And it's *so* annoying. I take a taste of the drink and immediately give it back, trying not to make a sour face. "It's not bad ..."

"But?"

I smile sheepishly. "It's a little too whiskey-ish for me." His head falls back and he roars. I laugh, too. The bubbling laughter begins small and quiet, but gets louder as it floats out of my chest and into the open air. We laugh for what feels like a long time. Every time one of us stops, we catch the other's eye and we start again. My annoyance drifts away with the laughter. And as much as I hate to admit it, at this moment, I'm kind of glad he showed up.

We semi-compose ourselves when the waitress brings over Sinclair's bourbon and two kinds of cornbread. I avoid the bread with the jalapeños. I'm not falling for that again.

"Miss Macy's is a well-kept secret among the locals. How did you find it?"

"Lucinda from the library told me about it. She's a wealth of information on all things Charleston, and she doesn't mind sharing what she knows with me."

"Lucinda McCrae?"

I nod.

"She's a fixture in town. Speaks her mind, even when it would be better for everybody if she kept her mouth shut. You must be pretty special if she's takin' a liking to you."

"You've lived here three years. How do you know Lucinda's life story?"

He shrugs, breaking off a piece of pepper-studded cornbread and placing it on my plate. "When I started working for the Wilders it became my business to know Charleston—every inch of the landscape, every corner of the city, the players and the spectators. Why don't you put away your computer?"

"I'm sorry?"

"We're having supper. Put away the computer—it's the polite thing to do when someone is sitting with you."

"I didn't invite you to have dinner with me. You just sat down."

"You didn't tell me to leave, either."

Despite my better judgment, I close the laptop and store it in my bag.

"Taste this," he says, bringing a bite-size piece of cornbread to my mouth. My lips are sealed tight as I eye it suspiciously. "It's got just a small kick to it—mostly flavor. Nothing like the corn nuts."

I gaze at him for a few seconds, but look away before I eat from his fingers. The bread is delicious and being fed like this makes it seem almost decadent, but when his thumb catches a stray crumb from my lip, and he sucks it into his mouth—it's downright sinful.

I'm a bundle of nerves. That's what he does to me. Tonight it's the kind of nerves that take over when you're with an attractive man and you're not sure what's going to happen next—or even what you want to happen. I take a sip of wine to calm myself, and steer the mood back to a place that's more comfortable for me. "Do you just randomly go around and sit with any unaccompanied diner or only women?"

"It's part of my daily act of kindness."

The small throbbing between my legs continues, but it isn't enough to throw me completely. "How did you know I was here?"

"I thought I made it pretty clear that I'd be following you."

My jaw tightens. "You actually follow me from place to place?" The prospect of this total lack of privacy is unnerving. And infuriating.

He shakes his head, and butters a piece of cornbread, taking his sweet time before answering my question. "No. I don't have time for that. I have a newbie who's been tasked with the honor of keeping track of you. But we're not monitoring you that closely. Not yet, anyway."

I pull out my wallet and place a few bills under the edge of my bread plate to cover the dinner I haven't yet eaten, and gather my things. He places a heavy paw on my wrist. "Where you goin'?"

"I wanted a quiet night to myself. I don't need this." I pull my hand back, but he doesn't let go.

"Maybe you can ply me with booze and get me to talk." One side of his mouth curls. "You're not going to get me to spill my guts about the Wilders, but maybe there are other things about Charleston I can help you with."

"Stop manipulating. It's not going to work this time."

Sinclair tips his head from side-to-side as though he's weighing something. "You're right. I'm manipulating. That's a fair characterization."

"Why would you bother?"

"I want to have supper with you." I'm not sure which of us seems the most surprised by his revelation. The difference is, I don't believe it.

Right. "You want to have supper with me. Why?"

He takes a sip of bourbon. "It gives me a chance to see what you're up to ... and ... it allows me ... to have ... supper with you." The words emerge in fits and spurts, a bit tortured, like a tooth that cracked into a half dozen pieces while the dentist was attempting an extraction.

"Why?" I don't care if I sound like a parrot who has been taught only one word. I want the answer to that question.

He shrugs, rubbing his thumb in small circles on the inside of my wrist that he's still clutching.

"Here we are," the waitress announces brightly. "Careful, the plates are hot." Sinclair lets go of my wrist and pulls his arm back so she can put down the food.

"Why?" I probe, when she's gone. "Why do you want to have dinner with me?"

He wets his lips with the bourbon before draining the tumbler. "I like you," he says simply, his eyes focused on mine. "And it's your birthday. You shouldn't spend it alone."

"What?" How does he know it's my birthday? *They've been monitoring your every move. He already said as much.* The throbbing between my legs has migrated due north, and my head feels like it's seconds from exploding. I sip some water and swallow deliberately, asking myself over and over why I'm still sitting here.

"And you're a bit of an enigma," he mutters. "There are things about you I don't understand. I like puzzles." He pauses for a moment. "Why did you agree to that stupid game in the apartment?"

"I wanted the story."

He pins me with his eyes. "Bullshit."

"Maybe I was hoping you'd take off your clothes, too." I smooth the napkin on my lap, avoiding his eyes.

"The bullshit is piling up. How about a little truth before we drown in the stench?"

13

KATE

I take a bite of my dinner with Sinclair still studying me like I'm a lab experiment. I don't like being on this side of the probe.

His fixed stare is relentless. It's probably some kind of special operative tactic to get people to talk. It's not going to work. Although I suppose there's no harm in telling him a little something, so I can eat in peace. "I'm chasing the Pulitzer Prize," I throw out casually, before taking another bite of food. "It's awarded to honor exceptional—"

"I know what it is," he responds gruffly.

"This is delicious. You should eat before it gets cold."

"And ..."

Oh, for the love of God. "And the King story has a lot of promise." I hear the frustration in my voice and wonder if he hears it too. "It could earn me at least a nomination."

Sinclair still hasn't taken a single bite of food. He's fixated on me, as if waiting for some kind of grand declaration of truth.

"I realize it's something you don't understand. But it's important to me." I peer into his rich brown eyes, until I reach the soulless bottom. It's a place I've never been—not even at the apartment. He's ruthless. At least he can be. For the first time, I see a flash of danger in him.

But is he a danger to me?

I put down my fork to pull a thin wrap from my bag and drape it over my exposed shoulders while he watches quietly. "I want the prize." I shrug. "It's the truth."

And it is. I'm chasing a Pulitzer. Not the one that was rightfully my mother's. Nothing can change that. But I'm chasing it just the same so that I can at least make sure she gets some of the recognition she deserves. I don't tell him that part. It's none of his business.

His eyes still haven't wavered, but I keep shoveling in the savory grits, each mouthful accompanied by a bite of succulent shrimp, ignoring the scrutiny as best I can.

I've wolfed down a healthy portion of my grits and a generous square of cornbread by the time he picks up his fork and points it toward my half-empty plate. "I hope you're planning on saving room for dessert. Miss Jolene's chess pie is legendary."

I raise my brow. "Remind me why I didn't leave earlier?"

"Because I'm an enigma, too. And I don't know whether you like puzzles, but you're curious by nature, and you do like answers."

I'm drawn to him because he's an enigma. *Is it that simple?* I watch him take a forkful of food, scooping up the grits with a bite of shrimp, just like I've been doing. *I don't know.* It's hard to tell what draws me to him because I've muddied the waters. I've enjoyed at least a dozen orgasms with his name on my lips, and still more where he featured prominently. Most of them were mind-blowing orgasms that tore through my body and left me comatose. It makes it hard to hate him.

I should have been more disciplined. *It might not have mattered.* Maybe I was attracted to him even before I had a single one of those orgasms. Maybe it happened when he slid into the booth across from me at Tallulah's, or at the apartment when his rock-hard cock dared me to stroke it. Maybe it happened last year when he told me, in *that* voice, that he'd personally escort me off the property and out of the state if I tried to get anywhere near Zack Wilder. *Or maybe I'm attracted to assholes.* History certainly bears that out.

We finish dinner without attacking one another like rogue chimpanzees in the monkey house, and without any more scathing self-analysis on my part. I tell him about Fiona and the boys FaceTiming with me at the crack of dawn, how they were dying to spill the birthday secrets, and he tells me about his nieces. All five. He jokes that he'd do anything for a nephew, but the glow on his face gives him away. He adores them and couldn't care less that they're girls. I'm sure of it.

As I watch him with his guard down, I know exactly why I stayed for dinner.

Shortly after our plates are cleared, Miss Jolene appears with an enormous slice of chess pie, dusted with powdered sugar. There's a single slim candle atop the pie. The flame flickers gently as she sets the plate in front of me. Jasper's with her and the waitstaff, too. They sing "Happy Birthday" with everyone on the porch joining in.

My brain is slogging, the cogs turning slowly through the muck. The revelers seem far away, as though I'm a bystander at my own party, watching safely from the distance.

I'm overwhelmed. My eyelashes are wet, splashing a drop or two onto my cheeks every time I blink. I glance at Sinclair. He's not singing but has a look of concern. "Make a wish and blow out the candle," he urges as they sing the last note. And I do, to whoops and cheers.

Before the smoke dissipates, everyone disappears, and the porch diners go back to their own conversations. Now it's just us.

"Thank you," I whisper.

"You don't look all that thankful. You look a little pasty. All I said to Jolene was to send over an extra big piece of pie because I was still hungry and it was your birthday. I should have known she'd make a fuss. I take it you don't like a fuss?"

"No, it's not that. It surprised—I didn't expect—"

"I thought the Taurus loved to be the center of attention?"

God, even that smug little smirk is panty melting. "So you're an expert on astrological signs, too. Do you use them to profile?"

"Hell, no." He shakes his head. "I'm a Taurus too."

"Oh." I sit up tall. "When's your birthday?"

"Next month." He swipes one of the fat blackberries garnishing the dessert plate and pops it into his mouth. "Will you take a bite of that pie, already, so I can have some? I'm drooling over here."

We finish the pie and linger over the after-dinner drinks Jasper sent to the table. It's dark now, with a waning moon and a smattering of stars across the sky. The porch is dark too, just the small votives and a few strands of jazzy lights twinkling overhead. Almost every table is empty, but I can't recall a single person getting up to leave.

I sip the strawberry cordial. The burn at the back of my tongue is dulled by the sweet macerated strawberries at the bottom of the glass. I have a suspicion this is potent stuff masquerading as a genteel concoction you might find at a ladies' tea.

All and all, it's been a nice evening. Better than I expected when I reserved a table for one.

I twist my fingers in the silence and wet my lips carefully, stealing a quick glance at him so as not to get caught. But I'm not quick enough to evade his sharp eyes. "I played the stupid game —took the risk—because I was desperate for information." As I talk, I focus on the beads of sweat forming on the water glass. They grow fatter and fatter, jiggling before sliding down the side and puddling on the placemat.

"The King story is important," I continue, with a heavy heart. "Not just for the country. I am chasing a Pulitzer—not for me, but for my mother." I live with this every day. It's a central part of who I am. But only a handful of people know, and I'm not sure why I'm sharing something so deeply personal with Sinclair, but I don't stop. "Right before she got sick, she spent a year investigating the foster care system in Boston. After she died, the story was written from her notes, but she was never given any credit for her work. Not a mention."

Sinclair rubs the back of his fingers over an unshaven jaw. "What happened with your mother?" he asks cautiously, like he knows the answer might break me.

"You don't know?" I thought he had researched everything about me. That there were few surprises left.

He shakes his head. "Only that she was a reporter who died of a rare cancer not long after you were born." The candlelight has softened his features, casting a gauzy shadow on his cheek.

"A very rare cancer. She didn't get the treatment she needed because she was pregnant—with me." The last part trails off, as though I'm embarrassed to say it out loud. And it crosses my mind, as it always does, that I will be judged unworthy of such a sacrifice. I certainly don't blame anyone for considering the question. It's human nature, and there have been plenty of times when I questioned my own worthiness. My fingers find the napkin in my lap, and I caress it gently, trying to soothe myself with the starched cotton.

"She was a devout Catholic and didn't believe in abortion," I continue. "I'm not entirely sure, but I think Father Tierney, our parish priest, assured her that God would forgive her if she chose abortion. But she had always wanted a daughter."

I rest my elbows on the table, bringing my clasped hands to my mouth. Sinclair is watching me. I feel it, but I can't face him right now. "The treatment might have saved her life, or at least prolonged it."

My mouth is dry, and the last couple of words stick to my

tacky tongue. I take a small sip of water and compose myself before continuing. "She chose my life over hers."

For a long minute it feels like everyone, and everything in the restaurant—maybe all over Charleston, has fallen dark and silent. The circumstances surrounding her death are not a secret. I've talked about it before, just not in some time. And rarely with someone who didn't know her, or me, well.

"That's some gift," he says with the utmost of care. His voice is a tender embrace, cloaking me in warmth. I don't hear any judgment. "It must sit heavily on your shoulders."

I gaze at him, fighting back the tears. The world turns slowly, but forever forward, while I struggle to keep up. It's almost as though he's stolen my very breath with his words.

He's the first person who has ever said anything like that to me. Well-meaning people always say, *she must have really loved you*. And she did. *She must have been an incredible woman.* She was. But no one, no matter how kind, has ever said that her decision, her gift, is a burden. *My burden.* Not even the psychologist who I talked to when my teenage thoughts went to dark scary places suggested it. No one. And I've never said it out loud—not even to Fiona, because even to my own ears, it sounds selfish and ungrateful to harbor those feelings. So instead, I keep them buried in a small bleak corner of my heart.

A tear escapes, and I whisk it off my face with a quick swipe of the hand.

"That's exactly how it feels sometimes." I try not to let my mind wander too far into the shadows. It's not safe there. "Only I don't feel it on my shoulders." My voice is wobbly. "The weight is here." My hand finds its way to my chest, rubbing out the ache. "It makes it hard to breathe at times. Although not so much anymore." I glance at him. "How did you know?"

"I'm a soldier." He intertwines his fingers and bends them until the knuckles crack. "Was. Always will be, I guess." There's muted laughter from inside, a background din reminding me we're not alone. "On the battlefield," he continues, "men bravely stand and take a bullet, or throw themselves on a landmine, or in front of a grenade. They give their lives selflessly so others can live."

Smith regards me with a profound sorrow that I'm certain lives inside his soul, concealed by the clever sarcasm and humor, obscured by the dimpled smile. "They leave families and friends behind. They go someplace we don't understand—we don't even know if it exists. It's the ultimate sacrifice." His voice is grave and raw. "That gift comes with tremendous guilt for the recipient, and a weight so heavy not all men are able to shoulder it. I'm sure it's unbearable at times." He gives me a small sad smile. "You've done good, Kate. She'd be proud of you."

I bury the sniffling in the back of my hand. "How about you? Do you carry it?"

Smith shakes his head. "Not that burden. But I carry other kinds of guilt. We all do. It's human nature." He drains his drink and tosses the napkin on the table. "Come on, let's get out of here and let them clean up. It's been a long day for Jolene and Jasper, and first thing tomorrow, they start all over again."

He pulls out his wallet, and places some cash on the table, folded under a glass. "Don't even think about it," he growls before I can offer to split it.

We don't have the check. I look around for the waitress, but she's inside. "How do you know that's enough?"

"Jasper will put it on my tab if I'm short. But it's enough." I glance at the bills more carefully this time. It's enough. *More than enough.*

"Where are you parked?" he asks.

"I walked. I guess your guy wasn't tailing me that closely."

Smith shakes his head. "It's a nice night. I'll walk you home."

"You don't need to walk me home. I can find my way. It's not that late, and there are still plenty of people on the street."

"I'm walking you home. It'll give me a chance to hear your thoughts about King. I want to help you with the story."

He's going to help me because I told him about my mother. I stop dead in my tracks. Isn't that what I want—what I've been hoping for since we met? *Yes.* But his words are a slap in the face. *I hate pity.* Hate it more than anything. And even though I need the help, defensiveness takes over, and I clap back. "I don't need your pity. And you don't need to help me because you feel sorry for me—because it's my fault my mother died."

Sinclair grabs my arm and drags me off the porch, to the side of the building where there is a thick row of flowering bushes. No one from the restaurant can hear us. His face is screwed up in a way I can't read. "First, your mother died because of cancer." His tone is cold and uncompromising.

As I stand here captive, the perfume of the night jasmine quickly becomes too much. I cough to dislodge the tickle in the back of my throat, and wait for what comes next.

"Second, you're a strong, smart woman. You have a lot going for you. Why the fuck would I pity you?" He squeezes my arm above the elbow as if to make his point. "Helping you ensures that you stay away from the Wilders, and it gets you what you need. The way I see it, it's a win-win."

It's not about pity. It's not even about me. It's about helping the Wilders. *Of course.* I feel foolish. And maybe a tad disappointed. While I'm brushing off my ego, his eyes shift to where his hand is still clutching my arm. He releases the grip abruptly, as though my flesh is suddenly scalding. "Do you want the help or not?" he asks like he doesn't give a damn if I say yes or no.

I swallow my pride and grovel. "Yes. I'll take whatever help you can give me."

Sinclair doesn't say anything, but he takes my arm again, this time gripping gently below the elbow. He examines it, running two fingers over the cool skin. It takes me a minute to realize that he thinks he might have marked me.

I don't see a red spot, but it's dark, and he has the better angle. "I'm fair. I bruise easily. It's nothing."

"When a man puts his hand on you like I just did—without your consent—it's not nothing." He releases my arm. "But it doesn't look like it's going to bruise."

Smith motions toward the sidewalk, and we head in the direction of my house.

"Thank you for offering to help," I say when the silence becomes awkward. "I should have been more gracious. It's just that I hate pity—from anyone. And thank you for dinner. I don't think it's fair that you always pick up the check, but I know you hate to let a woman pay for your food." I'm on a spectacular ramble.

He snickers, but it's not mean-spirited. "I was just trying to get a rise out of you that day. I don't really care who pays for the food as long as I get to eat."

"I'm not entirely sure I believe you. Sounds like hyperbole to me."

We stop at the crosswalk a block from Miss Macy's, waiting for the light to turn green. He takes out his phone. "It is early," he says. "You up for a nightcap and a game of pool at Tallulah's?"

I freeze in the middle of the sidewalk. "You know I play pool?"

"Should I?" He slides the phone back into his pocket.

"No! You shouldn't. But it seems like you know everything else about me," my hands are gesturing wildly, "and you brought up pool, so—"

"You shoot pool?" The way he asks is so disarming, it lowers my blood pressure instantly.

"I can handle a stick," I answer haughtily.

His mouth curls. It's a smug, sexy curl that's irresistible. "Is that so?"

"It is."

"Sounds like a challenge, Miss McKenna."

"Put up or shut up, Sinclair."

14

SMITH

*T*allulah's is crowded. I shepherd Kate to an empty spot at the bar and wrangle a stool for her, but she doesn't sit.

"This is the waitress station," she explains, like I'm an idiot.

"*Yeah?*"

"Do you know how obnoxious it is when customers sit in the waitress station? It makes an already difficult job harder." She drags the stool away from the bar, but I grab the wooden leg with my foot and yank it back. I'm rewarded with a sharp look when she realizes that she's not taking that thing anywhere.

"There's one waitress on." I point to the other side of the bar where Carrie is emptying a tray of empty glasses. "She's working from the other station. This one's never used because it's too far from the tables."

She assesses the situation for a few seconds before sliding her gorgeous ass onto the stool.

"Protecting the waitresses. Such a good girl," I murmur. It's meant to tease—a harmless tease, but the joke's on me, because my dick jumps when I say it. "You okay with a beer, or you want to stick with wine?"

"Maybe I want a girlie vodka drink." She's trying hard not to smile, but her face, and those fiery green eyes hide very little.

"That strawberry cordial Jasper makes,"—it's not for everyone's ears, so I lower my head so I don't have to raise my voice to be heard over the music—"that's moonshine, baby." When I stand back, her eyes are like saucers. "It has a way of sneaking up on you long after you expect it. I'd go easy for now. But you're the boss."

"I'll have whatever's on tap."

Beau comes over and sticks out his hand, and I take it. "What'll it be?" he asks.

"Wet and cold," I answer. "Something in a bottle."

"Got just the thing." He pops the top off a couple pale ales and brings them over. "You want to start a tab?"

I nod, and point to the top of Kate's head. "And her money's no good tonight. I don't care how much she begs. It's her birthday."

Kate swats my arm away from her. "My money is just as good as his. Maybe better."

Beau puts up his hands and walks away, but he doesn't spare me the shit-eating grin. "Work it out between you," he tosses over his shoulder. "I don't get paid to referee."

"Why did you do that?" she demands while I'm putting my credit card back.

"Do what?"

"Tell him my money is no good. You paid for dinner. I want to buy the drinks."

"It's your birthday. Your money's no good on your birthday. It's a rule. Everybody knows that."

"A rule?"

Jesus she's mouthy. And begging for a kiss. Something rough and demanding to shut her up. *Or maybe that's what I want.*

"Yeah. A rule." I brush a hand over her cheek. "Eyelash." It's a good excuse for letting my fingers wander over her skin. And she allows it, without complaint.

"I'm a practical man. You just left your paper and moved here. I doubt that job at the library pays much." I shrug. "I'm doing pretty well. I have enough to share—no strings attached," I assure her. "When the tables turn, as they always do, you can buy me all the whiskey in the joint. I won't complain."

Her wheels are turning. They're always turning. It must be something to live inside that head. "Thank you," she says softly. It's heartfelt and humble, and it makes me wonder why a woman with a father and three older brothers is grateful for crumbs. Like I said, it must be something to live inside her head.

I hand her a beer. "Bottles tonight. Easier to manage while we're playing. I'm not letting you back out on the bet."

"Don't you worry. I want that game. But I don't recall making any bets."

I put my beer behind her on the bar. "You think of something while I go tell those guys playing now that we're next. Make it something you're prepared to lose."

There are a lot of lies guys tell themselves, especially when it comes to women. *I don't want her in my bed*, is the bullshit I'm currently peddling. *That* cannot happen. I have a job, and she's a target. And a reporter—not an inconsequential fact. So yeah, I want to taste that pussy, *want it bad*, but I won't be surrendering to my base desires. I have more discipline than that.

As I make my way back to the bar, some asshole is chatting her up. I don't spare him a glance, but place a hand on her thigh, as I reach over her for my beer. When I turn around, the little fucker is still standing there. *I might not be able to have her, buddy, but you sure as hell won't be laying a stubby finger on her.*

I inch closer to him. He's probably six inches shorter, and I must outweigh him by at least seventy pounds. Most guys have a look they use to warn off the enemy without coming to blows. I have several that I've perfected, and I use my best one on this little bitch.

"I-I think my friends are leaving," he stammers, stepping out of my reach. The guy's smarter than he looks.

"Smooth, Sinclair," Kate quips after he slithers away. "He's cute. I kind of liked him."

The not-at-all thinly veiled tweak rolls off my back, although the ride is bumpy. "Tell me more about your mother." I take a pull of beer to take the focus off her, and let the question settle.

Her chest moves up and down more rapidly than normal. "She's been gone for my entire life. I never knew her."

"She was an investigative reporter, like you?"

Kate nods. "I worked for the same paper in Boston where she did. But she was very talented. Naturally talented. I don't have that kind of talent."

"Don't sell yourself short." She looks up at me, through thick dark lashes, and takes a long pull of beer. I can't look away from her mouth, her full lips on the long neck of the bottle. I am *so* screwed. *Fuck.*

I'm saved by a guy in a grey T-shirt waving his hand in the air from the pool corner, signaling the table's free. Not a moment too soon. I can use a distraction.

———

Distraction. *Right.* Just what I need, Kate bent over the table, wiggling her hips while taking shot after shot, or batting those long eyelashes at me while I'm trying to focus on taking one. Every time I move so that my eyes aren't in line with her ass, I'm treated to the top of her creamy tits. I almost let her win, just to stop the torture. But I'm not that guy. In the end, I beat her both games. Although she's a pretty damn good player.

"So what did I win?" I ask after we hand off the sticks to the group waiting.

"You don't have to dance with me." Her bottom lip is out in an exaggerated pout.

I throw my head back and roar. "*Sweet Jesus.* My guardian angel must be on tonight." She shoves my arm, and I laugh some more as we go back to the bar.

The place is starting to clear out, and we don't have to shout to be heard. I order more beer, and Beau brings them over with a couple shots and a salt shaker. "Happy birthday," he says, "on the house."

Kate's face lights up slowly. "Thank you." She's so grateful, you'd think he just plunked down shots of Pappy's. When he walks away to serve another customer, she sniffs the drink. "Tequila?"

I nod. "The lime and the saltshaker are giveaways."

She sniffs it again.

"Ever done a shot of tequila?"

She shakes her head.

"Wet the back of your hand, like this, and put a little salt on it. Then lick off the salt and tip your head back. Take it all down at once, like any other shot." I throw back the shot. "And then shove the lime in your mouth, real quick."

She eyes the glass.

"You don't have to do the shot."

"No. I want to," she says, bringing her hand to her mouth. When she licks the skin with her wet pink tongue, I feel it in my groin, but I don't look away. Within seconds she's sucking on the lime, grimacing, and trying not to laugh at the same time. She's adorable. I reach out and sweep her to my chest, placing a kiss at the top of her head. Harmless gesture—normally—something I might do with Gabby, or any female friend. But it's not harmless with Kate. *And I fucking know this.* But I did it anyway—*without thinking. Goddammit.*

I plunk the bottle on the bar harder than necessary. "It's getting late. We should go."

"I haven't finished my beer. And—and—"

"And what?"

She looks up at me through her lashes. "I was hoping, maybe, I could still have that dance."

"You lost. That ain't happening."

"It's my birthday," she turns over her phone, "for ten more minutes."

"I don't dance."

"Not even a slow dance?" she asks, after throwing me a *you're a lying sack of shit* look.

"You mean slow, like at a high school dance, where we shuffle our feet without moving much, but my over-eager cock presses into you at every opportunity—that kind?"

"That very kind. Although the cock thing is an add-on I don't need." She tips her head and gives me a small smile. It's flirty with a hint of impertinence. The kind of smile you like to see from a woman when she gazes up at you from her knees.

"*Please*," she begs, dragging her fingers through her hair in seductive slow motion.

Jesus.

I put out my hand reluctantly, and she takes it, dragging me to the dance floor. "Don't blame me if your feet are all banged up when the music stops."

We start with one of my hands on her back, and the other hand holding hers. It's all civilized and innocent—until she lets go of my hand and wraps both arms around my neck.

This was a mistake.

Now I have a free hand with nothing to keep it out of trouble, so I rest it low on her back, pushing the heel into the sexy hollow. She sighs softly, lowering her head to my shoulder. I feel her warm breath on my skin as she melts into me. She's so relaxed, I'm practically the only thing holding her up. "You're drunk, Kate."

"A little," she murmurs. "It's my birthday."

She's warm and soft, and her hair smells like the sun-drenched Mediterranean. That first breath that fills your lungs when you step off the transport for a few days of much-needed leave. Where you breathe sandless air, refuel the tank, and tend to your dick. *I need to get my mind out from between her legs.*

"I didn't follow you to Miss Macy's," I confess. "I was having lunch with my guys there on Wednesday when you called to make a reservation." She lifts her head, searching my face with those innocent eyes. "No one ever calls to reserve a table, and Jasper was all hopped up about it. I knew it was you."

"How?"

I shrug. "Just knew, but I asked anyway. Sure enough. I wasn't planning on showing up." Although it crossed my mind once or twice. "But Josh, the guy who's been making sure you don't get into trouble, mentioned it was your birthday when he signed out this afternoon—I decided to join you."

"Why? I still don't know why."

I tighten my hold on her. "Yes, you do."

She rests her head back on my shoulder. The shirt she's wearing is so thin, I can feel her skin under my fingers, yielding gently, supple and creamy, a blank canvas waiting to be marked.

When the song ends, I pull away abruptly, because I'm a grown man with little control over his dick right now, and this isn't a high school dance.

"One more," she murmurs, clinging to my shoulders.

I place my hands firmly on her upper arms, trying not to let the smooth skin distract me. "Kate. My guys are monitoring you. You're a target. This," my finger gestures back and forth across the dance floor, "doesn't change that."

"I know," she says softly, without a twinge of regret in her voice. "One more. Then we can go."

I don't say a goddamn thing. Nothing. I just surrender to the moment. Let my hands slide over her round ass, cupping the curves while I soak up her scent. I want to fuck her. Bend her over, and plow into her until she's babbling. I want to feel her clit swell and harden on my tongue. I want to coat her throat with my cum.

"I love this song," she says, oblivious to my filthy thoughts—thoughts that don't involve anything resembling love. "Do you know it?"

I don't know. I haven't been paying attention. When I listen, I recognize the band. Lady Antebellum. "I've heard it."

"It won a Grammy. I think." She tucks her cheek into the crook of my neck. Her lips are almost grazing my skin. "Do you want to know a secret?"

I smile and pull her closer. "Sure. Is it a secret about you?" She lifts her head and nods, chewing on her plump lower lip.

"The last time we were here. When I went back to the hotel—I was confused, and agitated, or something. I don't know—aroused, I guess." She buries her face in my chest, like a shy little girl.

"Is that the secret?" I stroke the back of her head, my fingertips learning the contours of her scalp. She shakes her head. "Come on, don't be like that. You promised me a secret. I was expecting something good."

"I—I." She's smiling, but even in the dim light, I can see the top of her cheeks are bright pink. "This song came on while I was in the bathtub—and I touched myself—while I was thinking about you."

I push back the groan and say the stupidest thing any man who needs to keep his dick in his pants has ever said. "Tell me about how you touched yourself—in the bathtub. I want to know —everything." I drag my thumb over her cheek. "Was it filled with water?"

"I let most of it out. Then spread my legs and hooked them over the side." Her face is back in my chest. "I let the water run on my—"

I tug her hair back, just enough so she's forced to look at me.

"On your pussy? You let the water beat on your sweet pussy." I'm seconds away from tearing off her panties and burying my face in her cunt. But my words are measured, and my tone reserved. More reserved than I would normally use in this kind of conversation with an attractive woman. I don't care how many times she's gotten off under a faucet, she's inexperienced and I don't want to scare her. But I do want her to keep talking. To tell me more dirty secrets.

"I can't believe I just told you that."

I brush her hair back off her face. "I think you wanted me to know." She shakes her head vigorously, and rests it against me while we continue to dance. "I won't tell anyone, Kate." My hand glides up and down her back. "Your secrets are safe with me. All of them."

I'm convinced she wanted me to know. She's not so drunk she'd blab something like that. She's had just enough to give her a boost of courage, to make her all warm and fuzzy—and horny. I'm horny, too. I haven't had that much to drink, but I don't need booze to get me there.

While I'm trying to think about something, *anything*, besides about how hard my dick is, she reaches up to kiss me. But my training kicks in. It's automatic, and happens so fast, it's jarring. I press a finger to her lips to stop her. "We can't. We just can't."

15

KATE

By the time we leave Tallulah's the temperature has dropped, and there's a sobering breeze from the ocean. I can't believe I told Smith about the bathtub. *Is he right? Did I want him to know?* I'll have to unpack that later, or tomorrow when I'm thinking more clearly.

The drive to my place is quiet, but not awkward. I still have a decent buzz, so I'm nowhere near as embarrassed as I should be. Besides, Smith took the whole thing in stride, as though women confess their masturbation rituals to him all the time. *What did you do last night?* Nothing much. Laundry, watched a movie, polished my toenails, and got off in the bathtub fantasizing about your giant cock.

The twitch of shame is beginning as we pull up in front of my apartment, but it doesn't stop me from wondering if he'll kiss me goodnight. *Why, Kate—why do you wonder? He made it pretty clear that there would be no kissing.*

"What exactly do you want my help with?" A small panic ensues while I wrack my brain—I have absolutely no idea what he's talking about. "The story, Kate. What do you need from me?"

Oh. The story, yes. "I want to know about the St. Anslem's Society. King is a member. And I still haven't figured out why his hearing was postponed. But you probably won't be able to help with that."

"I'll talk to a few people. See what I can turn up," he says, his hand on the door handle. "Wait. I'll come around."

"You don't need to. I can make it inside. I've sobered up—since the dance floor." I smile through a flutter of embarrassment.

"Will you just wait?" His tone is clipped, but I ignore it, and wait for him to come around to open my door, because I know he expects it, and—because I know it will please him. *Where did that come from?*

We bide our time at the base of the porch steps, neither of us anxious to say goodnight. "Go inside," he says finally, cocking his head toward the front door. "And lock up behind you."

I want him to kiss me.

"This is a transitional neighborhood," he continues, clearly not reading my thoughts. "Not unsafe, but not exactly safe either."

"I have a gun, remember?"

"Do you actually know how to use it?" He asks it in such a way that maybe I don't want to kiss him anymore.

"I come from a family of cops and Marines. When other girls were having a girls' day out with their mothers, I was at the range with my father."

"My sisters come from a family of soldiers, but there's only one I'd trust to shoot straight. Make sure you carry that gun when you walk around at night."

"Anything else, sir?"

His lips part, and the flame in his eyes dances dangerously. Without warning, he grabs my hand and we duck into a narrow alley on the side of my house where my neighbor sometimes parks. Before I can adjust to the dim light, my body is pressed against the building. The stone is rough and uneven on my back, but still warm from the day's heat.

"You," he says gruffly. "You've been a tease all night. Do you know what happens to cock teases?"

He towers over me, one hand on the brick, the other still on my hip. *I have a pretty good idea, but I want to hear you say it.* I shake my head, clinging to his eyes. "Tell me."

Smith lowers his mouth, stopping inches from mine, and pounds a fist on the brick wall just above my head.

I hear the rumble of desire, before the eruption, and slide both hands to his chest. The reverberations are powerful, and my fingers tremble where they rest. But I don't wait passively while fate decides. I dig in and roll the tips over the dense muscles working the tempest loose with the skill of a trained masseuse.

"Fuck it," he growls, and his lips capture mine.

The first swipe is kind—soft, smooth lips that warm gently. But the tenderness is fleeting, and even though I've surrendered, it's a rough capture. His teeth sink into my bottom lip until I cry out, arching into him.

But there is no reprieve.

A strong hand slides through my hair, fisting the long strands possessively. My head falls back, exposing a large swathe of my neck to the cool air. I shiver when his tongue connects with the flesh, blazing an upward path.

His teeth scraping.

His tongue laving.

His hot breath raising an exquisite prickle on my scalp. The sensations are too much. I want to squirm. I *need* to squirm, but his hold is firm—there's no escape, not even when he bites into the tendon at the base of my throat.

A moan escapes into the thick sultry air. It's loud and frantic, pleading for more.

"Open your eyes," he demands in a raspy voice. "Don't hide from me." My eyelashes are still fluttering when his large calloused hands skirt under my blouse, kneading my breasts, while rolling the sensitive nipples between his fingers. Like his kiss, it begins gently, but as I sway into him, nudging his cock, his touch grows hungrier. Before I know what's happening, my bra is hanging loose and his hot mouth is on my nipple, sucking and coaxing, until it's long and hard.

"Let's go inside," I pant.

"Can't," he murmurs, his lips merely grazing my breast. For a harrowing few seconds, I fear he's going to stop—that I broke the spell, but his mouth finds the other nipple, working it with his tongue until the pleasure is almost unbearable.

"Are you wet, Kate?" He whispers in a voice that ensures if my panties weren't already soaked, they would be now.

Before I can form an answer, my skirt is gathered haphazardly above my thighs, and his fingers are on my panties, impatiently shoving the satin gusset aside. I part my legs to give him better access—to offer him full and complete access to my most intimate parts. It's sheer instinct, but his mouth curls against my neck at the shameless acquiescence. I want him. *And I don't give a damn if he knows*. Right now, the clawing ache is much too great for false modesty.

His face is buried in my neck. His lips cajoling small shivers from overheated skin. I cling to him as his fingers glide over my slick folds.

The groan comes from deep within his chest. Lusty, strangled sounds, scraping his throat as they emerge. The throb between my legs grows louder. "*Kate*. You are so wet," he murmurs, his nose brushing mine.

I feel the pulse of desire radiating from him. Thick and luscious droplets suspended in the air until I catch them on my tongue.

"Do you know how easy it would be for my cock to slide into your tight little pussy right now? Would you like that? Would you scream for me?"

I gasp softly. I've never been with a dirty talker, and I'm not sure how I feel about his filthy words, but there's no time to process. He slides a thick finger over my slippery clit, and pushes it inside. I gasp, louder this time, and he murmurs something I don't understand. All I know is the tightening in my belly and the zings of pleasure between my legs.

I clamp down, hugging his finger with my inner walls, but before I've had anywhere near enough, he wrenches his hand away.

No! I want to scream, *No!* But I don't normally talk during sex, clean or dirty. At least I never have. And I've always been too shy to ask directly for what I need.

While I'm still quietly grieving the loss of his finger, he lowers himself to his haunches, tugging my underpants to my ankles. "I can smell you, Kate." He runs his nose through my slit, the tip teasing my swollen clit. "You're musky and sweet. It's making me so damn hard."

"What are you doing?" My voice is as wobbly as my knees.

"You're horny as fuck, and I'm doing my part to conserve water."

"Bastard," I mutter, pressing my shoulders into the wall to stay upright, while he lifts my feet one at a time, and takes my panties.

He stands slowly. His fingers grazing the sensitive skin on the inside of my thighs as he rises. My back arcs off the wall as his fingertips sweep upward. The anticipation is a tortured bliss, but when he reaches the apex, he pulls his hands away. *Arghh! I can't take much more.*

"These are mine," he mutters, stuffing my underwear into his pocket.

I watch him, letting my breath come under control. "Are you going to look at them when you touch yourself?" I lift my chin and ask brazenly, as though I'm an expert on such things.

He snickers, securing my hands to the wall, just above my head. He pins me in place with his hips, his cock between us, swollen and hard. It's everything I crave right now.

"I don't touch myself, princess. I fuck my fist. Hard," he whispers coarsely, a breath from my temple. "That's what I'm going to do tonight after I leave you. Look at me." I gather the courage and raise my eyes. "And while I do, I'm going to think about your sexy little moans and tortured gasps. I'm going to let your scent fill me while I cum all over the sheets, pretending it's your ass, your tits, your tight little cunt. And then I'm going to do it again, and again, and again, until I'm too wrung out to think about you anymore." He caresses my entrance with two calloused fingertips, before sliding them inside me. I gasp into his mouth when he curls both fingers against the sensitive flesh, circling the rough spot in the silky walls.

His tongue is smooth and wet, licking into my mouth and exploring it thoroughly. When he grinds the heel of his palm into my grateful clit, I allow myself to explore his mouth with abandon too.

I don't think about where I am or what I'm doing. The sensations have staged a coup, and I have surrendered any good sense, and welcomed the captors with open arms. I'm nothing more than an achy ball of need, at their mercy.

"That's it, darlin'," he encourages, as I rock into his hand. "Tonight, you can take what you want." His teeth rouse my skin while his greedy mouth feeds on my throat, taking as it pleases. "Enjoy it, because next time, I'm going to hold you down, and you'll take what I give you."

I shudder at the threat, mewling my appreciation for his long fingers twisting inside me, pushing me closer to the edge. "I think you need more, Kate. Just one more." His tone is sweet—syrupy almost, and I'm a wet needy mess when he slides his hand out. It's for a brief time, *so* brief, but I want to snatch it back and hold the palm against my pussy until I come. But before I can make the desperate move, he pushes three fingers inside, filling me completely.

I press my mouth to his shoulder, to quiet myself. My legs

quiver and I clench his back, digging my fingernails into the corded muscle. I shutter my eyes and hump him—letting the pleasure cascade over me like a celestial shower against the midnight sky.

Smith tips his head back just before I topple over the edge. "Open those gorgeous green eyes," he demands, and with great effort, I force the lids open.

He watches me come undone—coal eyes peeking through thick lashes as I writhe and pant. It's too intimate. I'm too exposed. I squeeze my eyes tight as I buck against him, pulling out the last bits of pleasure like an insatiable whore.

His lips rest on my forehead as I quiet, but his fingers don't still. They continue to stroke the tender slippery skin until the meekest of pulses plays itself out.

"Don't hide from me, princess." He touches a slick index finger to my lips. "Open," he instructs and pushes into my mouth. "Suck," he demands, and I do, while he slides the thick finger over my tongue, occasionally letting it slip far enough back that I nearly gag.

I taste myself on his skin. It's a heady combination, salty, but sweeter than I expect. Before I can be too appalled, he steals his hand away, sucking the other two fingers he pleasured me with into his mouth until they're clean. "Now, I know how you taste," he says, each word rough and desperate.

I feel lost, and he must sense it, because he pulls me into his chest and runs a soothing hand over me like I'm a skittish pet, sprinkling small tender kisses on my hair. I'm not sure how long we stay like that, but it's the regret in his voice that yanks me from the safe haven where I've been resting. "It's late. You should go inside."

The short distance from the alley to my door is long and awkward, the air dense and heavy with thoughts that neither of us dare to vocalize. It's suffocating.

Without a kiss goodnight, or any other recognition of shared intimacy, Smith waits at the bottom of the stoop while I climb the porch stairs and unlock the door. I'm impatient to get inside so I can breathe again, but my clumsy hands don't cooperate and it takes longer than it should to escape.

"Kate." I freeze at the bellow from the sidewalk, my shoulders hunched forward, gripping the house key so tightly, the bitings notch my finger. "For the record, I planned on helping you before your mother's death ever came up."

I grasp the doorknob and glance over my shoulder. His arms crossed over a massive chest, pad the space between us. Despite what happened in the alley, the culmination of an evening filled with flirtatious innuendo, the nod to our undeniable attraction, despite all this, the distance separating us has never been greater than it is right now. It's palpable and scathing, and not entirely unexpected—at least it shouldn't come as a surprise. *That's what happens when girls mistake lust for love, Kate. You know this.* I do.

"Take some Tylenol or Advil before you go to bed," he instructs from the safety of the curb. "And have a big glass of water with it."

"I'm sober."

"I know. But when you wake up tomorrow and remember that you rode my fingers all the way home, in the alley next to your house, your head is going to pound like a sonofabitch. Better to stay ahead of it. Go inside."

"You're an asshole," I mutter, pushing the door open.

"You'd do well to remember that."

16

SMITH

"What do you know about St. Anslem's?" I ask, as JD tosses me a water bottle from the fridge at Sweetgrass. We just finished a brutal morning run. Brutal because I was up half the night making good on my promise to Kate. But it didn't help. I woke still thinking about her soft mouth, and that tight little pussy choking my fingers.

"The society?"

"Yeah." I'm sweating like a pig and use the bottom of my T-shirt to wipe the moisture off my face.

"It's as old as dirt. They do some charitable work. A lot of prominent Charlestonians are members. It's mostly a way to keep families insulated from the riff-raff." He unscrews the cap and takes a swig of water. "There are all sorts of rules."

"Like what?"

"Women with big sticks up their asses are only allowed to marry men with equally big sticks up their asses." He grabs a wad of paper towels to dry the back of his neck and tosses me the roll. "Although many of the men who belong don't seem to be all that picky about where they shove their sticks. Some of them are members of Wildflower too."

"Your family never belonged?"

JD shakes his head. "No. My grandfather wasn't a fan of inbreeding. Probably should have been, then maybe my mother might still be alive." He stares out the window into the abyss. Even a manicured backyard and an ocean view can't fill that void. "My father would have done anything to join, but he didn't have the right pedigree."

"Warren King's a member."

"I'm sure."

"Do you know what's holding up his confirmation hearings?"

JD throws me a sharp look. "No," he says pointedly, while assembling the ingredients for protein shakes.

"Will you do me a favor?"

"I'm listening," he says, measuring some protein powder and tossing it into the blender with a banana, some water, and ice.

"Can you find out why the hearings were postponed?"

JD throws his head back and groans. "This is about that reporter?"

The whirr of the blender is loud, and I act like I don't hear the question. "What about that priest at St. Magdalene's? Do you know anything about him?"

"I don't know shit about any priests. The closest I've gotten to one was when Gracie was baptized, and that was enough to last me a lifetime. Pious bastards. All hypocrites as far as I'm concerned." He pours a little of the shake into a glass and takes a taste before filling both tall glasses.

"What about the church?"

"It's not much anymore. It's the polar opposite of St. Anslem's. Nobody wants in. They'd be dead and buried if their survival depended on membership. But they had a wealthy benefactor who left enough money to keep the church running in perpetuity." He hands me a shake. "You looking for God, or is this about the reporter, too?"

"I told her I'd help her figure some things out." He stares at me from several feet away, expressionless. "The sooner she has the answers she wants, the quicker we'll get her out of town."

"You must think I'm a moron."

"JD—"

"No. Don't fucking JD me. I don't care where you stick your dick as long as you keep it away from my wife, and that reporter away from my family."

"Where are you sticking your dick, Smith, that's got my husband all hot and bothered on this lovely morning?" Gabby saunters into the kitchen and over to the coffeepot without sparing us a glance.

JD shoots me a warning while her back is turned. A warning I don't need. There's no way I'm having this discussion with her. I try to shield Gabby from the seamy side of Charleston almost as much as JD does. And I don't normally talk to her about women—at least I don't like to encourage that line of discussion. She, on the other hand, brings it up at every opportunity. "How's my favorite Wilder?"

"Don't try to change the subject." She curls into her husband's side, and he wraps a protective arm around her. It's effortless. At least they make it look that way. "Is there a woman in your life that I should know about?" *God help me.*

"Not a woman. A reporter," JD responds curtly.

"Tell me about her." JD stiffens at her words. I see it from here. Gabby brings the mug to her lips without giving anything away, but I'm sure she notices it, too. Damn woman never misses anything.

"Nothing to tell," I say nonchalantly, trying to cover for JD's blunder. "She's digging around for a story on Charleston societies, trying to connect them to Warren King."

"That doesn't sound like it has anything to do with us. So what's the problem?" She tips her face toward JD.

"We don't like reporters."

"We don't?"

JD scowls at me over her head, without uttering a single word. He can be difficult, but he's smart enough to know when to hold his tongue around his wife. She might not be very big, but she punches well above her weight class.

"That seems very ungracious of us. Maybe we need to rethink our values." She pokes JD's thigh. "And by we, I mean you."

"My values, like my opinion of reporters, don't need rethinking."

She twists away from him. "I don't agree. What if Gracie grows up and wants to be a journalist? Would we not like her?"

"Don't be ridiculous. No daughter of mine is ever going to be a journalist."

Now that was just a dumb thing to say. He deserves that ball-shrinking glare she gives him, before shifting her attention to me. "What's your friend's name?"

"She's not my friend."

"The reporter. What's her name?"

"Kate."

"*Kate.* I wonder if it's short for Katherine or Kathleen." She's not wondering a damn thing. She's baiting and watching. "Beautiful name. Strong and regal. I'd like to meet her some time. You should bring her by Sweetgrass for supper. Soon. Maybe next week," she says, almost to herself.

"He's not bringing her over for supper. He just got through saying that nothing is going on between them. And it's not going to, because pussy makes a man stupid, and Smith is already stupid enough." JD's pissed. I almost feel sorry for him, but he's the one who stiffened up when she started probing. He sold us out, and now he's paying the price. *Better him than me.*

"You know," she says, in a voice dripping with sugar, "if that truly is the case, I have an idea that will make you a whole lot smarter. And you're going to just *love* the new sheets on the spare room bed." She pats his wrist. "Gracie was calling for her Da when I came downstairs. I'm sure she's up there waiting to throw her chubby little arms around your neck."

"This discussion is finished," he barks, storming out. "I don't want to hear another goddamn word about any reporter coming to supper."

"Well," she says after he's gone. "I suspect he'd like it to be finished with me, but I'm sure you'll be getting an earful."

I clutch the edge of the marble island behind me, plotting my escape.

"You like her."

"Not particularly."

"Really? Because I thought I saw a gooey look on your face when you told me her name."

I scoff, white-knuckling the countertop.

"Don't worry, your balls won't shrink into miniature nuggets. The gooeyness lasted just a quick second." She's smirking, like a woman holding the goods. She knows I like Kate, something I'm not prepared to admit, even to myself.

"And JD wouldn't be so annoyed if *Kate* was just the flavor of the day." She pauses, glancing past me. "I can continue to build an airtight case, but I like that countertop, and you're squeezing so hard, I'm worried a piece is going to break off in your hand. Marble is a soft stone, you know."

I loosen my death grip on the stupid counter. "It doesn't matter what I feel. I'm not taking up with her. JD's absolutely right about reporters."

"So it's okay for him to be happy, but it's not okay for you? You're actually going to let him dictate who you date?" She pours herself another cup of coffee. "Want some?" she asks over her shoulder.

"I'm all set. It's getting late, and I need to grab a shower."

"I admire your loyalty. How you always stand tall beside him. It's one of the things I love most about you. But allowing him to run your love life is ridiculous."

"It's not about my loyalty to him. That's just a small piece of the equation. I'm developing the business, and secrecy is going to become even more important than ever. She's an investigative reporter. She chases stories. In my line of work, there will always be a big story. One that some believe the public has a right to know about. I can only be effective if I work covertly. I can't save lives if my tactics are broadcast through a megaphone."

She studies me for what feels like an eternity, her hands wrapped around the coffee mug. "Those are just details," she says softly. "Don't let the details get in the way of love."

"Love? You're ridiculous. I barely know the woman—we haven't even—"

"Details, Smith. They're just details to be worked out. Life's too short to shut the door on something good before you even enjoy it. Some people believe there are countless human beings in this world to fall in love with. I'm not one of those people. Sure, there are plenty who might do, but I believe the universe assigns us each one soul mate."

"That might be the way it is for you, but it's not like that for everyone." I guzzle my shake. The damn thing sat too long, and it goes down like cardboard.

"I'll give you that. But how do you know your experience won't be the same as mine? Maybe there's only one person out there that's right for you. What if Kate is that person, and you dismiss her before you've had the chance to find out? Are you willing to risk it?"

This is such a load of crap. I can't believe I'm standing here listening to it. I rinse my glass and set it into the dishwasher. "I need to go. I'll see you later."

She grabs my arm as I pass. "Easy is for those whose appetites are satisfied with milquetoast. It's not for people like us." She plants a kiss on my cheek, and releases me. "Bring Kate to supper on Friday. Lally will make something special."

"Never happening," I toss over my shoulder before the screen door slams behind me.

17

KATE

*I*t's eight-fifteen. Fiona's on her way to work. Now's a good time to call and confess last night's sins. *Oh God.* I pull the covers over my head and groan into the wrinkled linen.

In the alley.

I need a thorough postmortem on last night, and the voices inside my head are too complicit to give me an unvarnished opinion. And they're too judgmental—especially this morning. I need to talk to Fiona. I only wish it was over a cup of coffee, instead of across the miles.

"Hey, birthday girl!" Fi says brightly, picking up on the first ring. "Did you have a nice dinner?"

"You made my birthday perfect, like you always do. I don't know what I would do without you, Fifi."

"Yeah, yeah, yeah. Tell me about your birthday dinner. I'm doing Keto until I can fit into a bathing suit without looking like some seasoned pork stuffed into a casing. I need to live vicariously through you until then. What did you eat?"

"Shrimp and grits, and chess pie for dessert. It had a bajillion carbs and about two bajillion calories. We'll have some when you visit. But I don't advise coming to Charleston on a diet."

"I'm working on that visit."

"And you don't look like a sausage. I hate when you say things like that. Plus, diets that restrict healthy foods aren't good for you."

"Talk to me about it again when you're five-two, and your body has been stretched to capacity carrying twins. What else is going on?"

What else, indeed. I rest a hand on my forehead, shading my eyes as though she can see me through the phone. "Remember Smith Sinclair?"

"The guy with the please-fuck-me-now-muscles and ovary-splitting dimples?"

"*Mmhm.* He showed up at the restaurant last night and sat down at my table. He knew it was my birthday."

"And?"

"Oh God, Fi. I don't know. He was his usual self, but in between being a complete jerk, he was a nice guy, trying to make my birthday special, too. I think so, anyway."

"Did you have sex?"

"What makes you think that?"

"Because I can hear the *I'm sorry—not sorry* in your voice. Well?"

I take a breath and let it out slowly. "We made out in the alley near my house, and he took off my underpants and fingered me." No reason to spare her the lewd facts. She might as well have the full technicolor picture if she's going to help with the autopsy. "I humped his hand like a bitch in heat until I came all over it."

"Birthday sex with a big fat orgasm. Well, aren't you all grown up?"

"It wasn't sex. It was just—"

"Sex. Own it, baby. You have a thing for him."

I do. I'm afraid I do.

I throw the covers off and dangle my feet over the side of the mattress, before asking the question that's been gnawing at my soul since I crawled into bed last night. "I need to ask you something, and I need you to answer me truthfully, even if you think I'll end up in a fetal position for the rest of the day."

"*Mmhm.*"

"Promise me, Fi."

"I never lie to you, Katydid. Ask." If only it were so simple.

"Sinclair is hard to read. But he's not a nice guy—that's not exactly true. I can't put my finger on it, but something about him is dangerous. And you're right. I am attracted to him. So attracted, it's embarrassing. That whole thing in the alley—I'd do it again right now, in broad daylight with my neighbors watching out the window."

"It must have been good." She sighs. "Is he dangerous because you let yourself go around him? Because that can be a good kind of danger. Especially for you. You need more of that in your life."

I drag a ragged breath into my lungs, and home in on my struggle. "Is this like when I was fifteen? Is it the same thing all over again? Because it feels like it." My voice fades, leaving a long trail of regret and sadness in its wake.

"You know—letting guys take advantage of me." It pains me to dredge up the ugly events of the past, but I do it bravely, because if I want answers, that's what's required. "Pass me around, because I'm so desperate for a little affection? Sinclair is an asshole. He says it himself."

"I don't know Sinclair, but I do know what happened with those guys—they were college boys and you were a teenager," she says pointedly. "They were scum. They deserved to have their asses kicked all over town and I would have done it myself if they ever came near you again. Especially that Ryan." She spits out the ringleader's name in a tone one would reserve for Satan. "You're a woman now. You're allowed to have sex with whoever you want, as often as you want, wherever you want—no apologies."

"That's what I keep telling myself. But it rings hollow, like I'm justifying self-destructive behavior. It's not about the sex so much, it's, it's just that I've been so lonely, and feeling sorry for myself, and Sinclair is ... sin on a stick, and he makes me feel pretty, and desirable, and safe. But it's not real. I just want it to be. This is exactly what happened before. I'm walking into the trap again, only this time, my eyes are wide open."

"Listen to me," she says in a voice that dares me to defy her. "What happened with those guys—I meant every word I said about them. But it wasn't as big of a deal as your family made it out to be, and it sure as hell wasn't your fault. None of it. Teenage girls are vulnerable. You weren't special in that way. Dragging you to St. Claire's in the middle of the night so you could confess to Father Tierney—that was bullshit."

"Tommy didn't know what to do."

"So he treated you like you needed to have an emergency exorcism performed?"

"He meant well." I don't know why I defend him. Nothing I say will ever change Fiona's mind about him. And he doesn't deserve my empathy. It's taken me twenty-eight years to come to terms with this, but I'm still not ready to share it outside my head.

"Tommy is an asshole with anger management problems," she huffs. "I'm not telling you anything you don't know. He's a hair shy of exploding all over the place. Don't get me started on how he's allowed to carry a gun."

The rage simmers inside, but never comes to a full boil. No one besides Fi is allowed to talk about my family this way. *No one.* But even coming from her, it stings. I should know better than to discuss them with her—especially Tommy.

"Jesus, Fi. I didn't know you felt so strongly about what happened that night." We haven't talked about it since it happened. I did my punishment and buried the whole sordid mess while it still had a pulse. But when you bury something alive, no matter how deep the grave, it eventually comes back to haunt you.

"I'm an adult now," she explains, "and I see it differently—

more clearly. They shamed you—all of them. What teenage girl wants to have to tell a priest that she let four boys fondle her?" *And that she was seconds from giving them each a blow job, and more, if the police hadn't come by and broken up the party.* She spares me that part. "I don't care if Father Tierney was decent about it. Your family made you feel ashamed. Tommy that night, and then your father and Sean."

"It was so I would learn a lesson. Shame is a powerful teacher."

"Shame is a bully's weapon, wielded by the ignorant and the impotent. They missed an opportunity to show you kindness and compassion—and the love that you deserved. I'll never forgive them for that."

By them, she doesn't mean Father Tierney. He showed me plenty of kindness and love growing up. Fiona knows this. She means my family. My father and my brothers. I don't want to think about it anymore. "Can we leave the Norman Rockwell memories for another time, and get back to Sinclair?"

She sighs, long and deep into the silence, letting her thoughts unfurl and stretch, smoothing the rough edges into palatable words. Fiona is rarely careless with me. I stare at a speck on the ceiling while I wait, following closely as it shimmies into the light fixture.

"This is what I think about Sinclair. Men are men. Even the good ones are assholes. It's a fundamental part of the Y chromosome." I picture her gathering her long chestnut hair in one hand and draping it neatly over her shoulder. "It sounds like he showed some restraint last night—unless there's something you're not telling me."

"No." *I would have happily reciprocated.* "He didn't expect a thing."

"Take it slow. Enjoy him, if that's what you want, just don't give your heart away unless it's in a fair trade. I'm pulling into the salon and the valet is heading this way. The Oribe rep is coming this afternoon. I'll see if I can get you some samples."

"I love that shampoo. It smells *so* good." I catch myself smiling for the first time since last night. "And I love you Fi, with all my heart."

"I'll call you on my way home so I can bitch about how clients need to learn to take their make-up off at night if they want clear, poreless skin. I'm not a damn miracle worker. Answer your phone."

I toss the phone on the bed beside me, and it rings as soon as it hits the sheets. Fi must have forgotten to tell me something. We do this dance all the time.

"What did you forget?" I ask before she can get a word out.

"Kate. It's your father."

My heart begins to pound. He never calls unless he has something to say. Maybe he has news about the promotion. "Hi, Dad. I thought you were Fi calling me back."

"How's my little girl?"

"Things are good." Without thinking, I start to tell him about my birthday dinner, but I stop myself just in time. "How are things with you?"

"Same shit, different day."

"Anything on the commissioner's job?"

"Not yet. They're dragging their feet. I'm beginning to think it's in the bag for Moniz. We'll see. Either way, I should hear something soon."

"Good. You've been on pins and needles about this for too long. I'm planning on coming home for Father's Day. It's still weeks away, but it's something for me to look forward to. I haven't seen you since Christmas, and I wouldn't mind sleeping in my bed for a night or two."

"Bed's gone, Kate."

Gone? I don't understand. "What happened?"

"We had to move it to make a craft room."

All sorts of things flitted through my mind when he said my bed was gone. Flood, fire, ant infestation, all of it, but it never occurred to me that he got rid of it.

"Craft room? You've started crafting?"

"Not me." He chuckles like it's the most preposterous thing he's ever heard. "Joyce. She's crafty. Makes beautiful things. She's really spiffed up the house with her handiwork."

"Joyce is decorating our house?" Joyce who worked at the local bank while I was in high school. She was the branch manager, I think. The last time I saw her was on New Year's Eve, with her arm linked through my father's. They were headed to a house party across town. "I didn't realize it had gotten serious."

"With you gone, the house was too empty, and everyone kept telling me it would do me good to settle down again. You know I can't cook, and I hate to clean."

Most people would just hire a housekeeper if that's all they wanted. "Is she living in the house?"

"Yeah. Tommy still stays here every once in a while. And this is Sean's home when he's on leave. It made sense to use your old room. Joyce loved the pretty green color. Said it felt like the most feminine room in the house."

Of course. My room that I spent an entire month redecorating after my father begged me not to move out after college. I painted it floor to ceiling, every windowpane, every inch of molding, even in the closet. Then I installed white wrought iron shelves in just the right spot, so I could see all my treasures from the bed. I used money I'd saved to buy some sheer curtains and a new comforter, that matched the freshly painted walls.

"What did you do with all my stuff?" And Mom's things that I found hidden in the attic when I was fourteen.

"Joyce boxed it up, and Tommy put it in the cellar." *Great.* I'm sure he just dumped it all down there in a heap.

"I hope he put it on something so that it doesn't get wet when the cellar takes water."

"I'll ask him. Listen, I was wondering where you left that recipe book. The one your mother made before she died?"

"You need the recipe book?"

"Joyce is a master crafter, but she's not much of a cook. Thought she might be able to make some decent suppers if she had a straightforward guide."

"I have it with me." *Thank God.*

"Send it, would you, honey?"

"Sure." But not the original. Those are my mother's recipes—in her handwriting. Her family recipes. My family recipes. Joyce isn't getting the original. I'll make a copy at the library on Monday. "Dad, why didn't you tell me?"

"This is still my house, and I can use whatever room I want for whatever I want." He's defensive about giving my room to Joyce. It's strangely comforting.

"Not about my room." *Although that would have been nice.* "About Joyce. It sounds like things are serious with her."

"No man likes to talk to his daughter about the women he keeps company with." He's gruff and dismissive, but I don't stop.

"I know, but—"

"I've been alone for a long time, little girl. I've sacrificed plenty for something that wasn't my fault."

For something that was my fault. He doesn't have to say the words—the implication is crystal clear. It always is.

"I'm glad you have someone." And I am. "I worry about you being alone. I didn't mean to suggest otherwise. I'm just homesick and it gets the better of me sometimes."

"Don't worry about it. You've always been one to speak and act before you think. Got that from your mother's side. That, and your pretty green eyes and burnt-red hair. Joyce is staying at the house—but she'll never be your mother. Not a day goes by that I don't miss her."

My heart splinters, creating millions of tiny new fractures each time he talks about how much he loved my mother, and about the grief he's carried for all these years. "I know how hard it's been for you, Dad. I'm so sorry."

I'm not sure why I apologize. Maybe it's because I'm sorry he lost the love of his life too soon. Maybe I'm sorry for the choice she made—the one that changed my father's life, my brothers' lives, and devastated our family. I'm not sure anymore. I've been apologizing for so long, it's just a habit now.

We say goodbye after I promise to send the recipe book first thing next week.

I lie back down on the air mattress I've been sleeping on since I moved into this temporary apartment. *My room is gone.* I suppose that's what parents do after their children leave home. They turn the space into something practical. It's a natural progression—nothing personal.

I spend a long time making excuses, and I don't dwell on the fact that my father never said *you can stay in the den while you're home, or in the front parlor that we never use. I can't wait to see you.* He never said anything resembling that. I don't dwell on it because it hurts my heart.

18

KATE

I ring the bell at the rectory entrance and adjust my tote bag on my shoulder while waiting for someone to answer the door. This is such a vast structure in the middle of a tiny island. It must be lonely out here, especially in the winter.

The lock clicks, and the wooden door creaks open. "Kate," Father Jesse says warmly. "So good to see you."

"Hello, Father."

"Come in, please." He holds the screen door open for me. "Can I take your bag, or would you prefer to keep it?"

"I'll hold onto it. I have a notebook inside so I can jot down your ideas for the new bulletin."

"My living quarters are upstairs. I usually spend most of my off-duty time there. But we can have supper down here in the public space, if you prefer. I don't want you to be uncomfortable."

I smile. "Upstairs is fine."

"I was hoping you'd say that." He beckons with his head. "Follow me."

While Father Jesse leads me to the stairs, I can't help but mull over the contrast between him and Sinclair. One considers my comfort, and the other wants to make me as uncomfortable as possible, or at least keep me off kilter. And it's not just this. The differences between them are so stark, it's as though they come from different species.

"How are things going at the library?" he asks over his shoulder.

"Pretty well. I have a steady stream of clients who come in for help with job applications, or for some general advice about banking and utilities. I think some of them are just happy to have somewhere to be besides the shelter, and it doesn't hurt that Lucinda keeps a tin stocked with goodies in my office."

"We all deserve a treat now and then," he says as we reach the second-floor landing. There's a substantial door at the top, not a heavy-duty outside door, but more like something that would close off a bedroom from the rest of the house. It's unlocked.

"Here we are," he says, pushing the door open. "I suppose I could make this place a whole lot homier, but it suits my simple needs."

The apartment is cozy and neat as a pin. A simple wooden cross hangs on the wall above a console table in the entranceway, but the walls and surfaces are not otherwise cluttered with religious symbols. Nana had more crosses and virgins on display than Father Jesse.

"Let's go into the kitchen," he says. "I didn't want to put the oven on until I checked to see if you would be comfortable up here. But it shouldn't be too long. Are you hungry?"

"I am, but not so hungry that I can't wait a bit."

The eat-in kitchen is painted a cheery yellow, with a nautical themed valance dressing the window above the sink and matching cushions on the chairs.

"Can I get you a glass of wine?" he asks, turning on the stove.

Wine? I must hesitate for a second too long before answering. "Priests have an ancient, celebrated relationship with wine," Father Jesse quips. "We partake regularly, and not simply for ritual. It's allowed," he whispers in my direction, and I laugh.

When I was young, I sometimes had dinner with Father Tierney in the rectory, and during Lent and Christmas there was often a visiting priest in residence who would join us, but there was no wine, or private upstairs apartments, and there was only one kitchen on the first floor that everyone used.

Father Jesse pours us each a glass of ruby-tinted wine, and carefully removes a towel draped over the cheeseboard. My mouth waters at the wedge of cheddar and the delicate crackers sprinkled with poppy seeds accompanying it. A bunch of plump red grapes sits in the center of the small wooden board rounding out the selection.

"I know that I should preheat the oven, but I don't always follow the directions to the letter. Don't tell anyone or they might stop leaving me food." He wags his finger, giving me a lopsided grin.

"A rebel," I tease back.

He chuckles, placing a shallow casserole tented with foil into the oven. "I hope you like chicken pot pie."

"That wouldn't be the chicken pot pie that Bertha Clemmons made, would it?"

"The very same. I overheard you telling her how much you loved it. I was hoping you weren't just being polite."

"It was delicious. I had a second helping, larger than my first."

"Good. I put the extra one she brought aside, before Virginia could freeze it. Supper will be ready in about half an hour. Why don't we sit in the sunroom, have a little snack, and discuss the bulletin? Then, with that out of the way, we can enjoy a pleasant meal." He hands me a few paper napkins, and we take our wine and cheese into a lovely glass-enclosed solarium overlooking the distant ocean.

"Quite a view, isn't it?" he asks, placing the tray on a small table between us.

"It is." The outlying view is spectacular, but the area closer to the back of the rectory is overgrown and a bit eerie. From here, it looks almost as though the turret juts out over the swampland, but it's unlikely that it was actually constructed so close to the water. I read, somewhere, that storms have caused land erosion on all the sea islands, in some cases, putting structures at risk. That's probably what happened here. "Is the swamp deep?"

"Yes. But how deep depends on the tide and how much rain we've had."

Father Jesse slices a generous portion of cheese and lays it on a thin cracker before offering it to me. I take a quick bite, catching the crumbs in a napkin, and pull out my notebook.

"I'm at somewhat of a disadvantage because I'm new to the congregation. Tell me what you're thinking about for the bulletin. What kind of tone would you like it to convey?"

He separates a small cluster of grapes from the larger bunch and places them on a napkin. "I'm not exactly sure," he says, leaning back in his chair. "Something that offers hope. I want people to know about the kind of help we can offer them, but I don't like the idea of bragging, or calling too much attention to ourselves. I like that we're humble—that we perform good deeds quietly without seeking praise."

"I think it's a fabulous tone to set. We'll come up with something that's newsy with plenty of practical information, but without any kind of boasting. How does that sound?"

"It sounds like a tall order, even for a smart woman."

I smile shyly and help myself to a cracker and some cheese. "It's a fine line. We'll parse it carefully. It will mean several drafts, and honest, open communication between us. Virginia can help too."

"You are a ray of sunshine. I spend too much time around naysayers who are experts on why we *can't* do things. Your can-do attitude is refreshing. St. Maggie's is lucky to have you. As am I," he adds softly.

I feel the bloom on my cheeks and shift the subject away from me. "You mentioned a printed version when we last spoke. Do you have a subscriber list? Emailing would be much less expensive. There's little cost involved unless you're sending thousands of newsletters—I mean bulletins."

"Most of our congregants are older. Many of them don't get their information from the web. And the people we need to reach most, like the women you work with, don't have access to computers."

"Maybe we can do both. It would be easy to put the bulletin online. It can go right onto the church website, and we can print some copies to distribute to places like the library, the hospital emergency room, and leave some in the church as well."

"That's perfect."

The timer buzzes. "I think that's our signal that we've done enough work for the evening. Let me feed you."

Father Jesse moves around the kitchen with a graceful ease, not wasting a single step as he sets the table. "Can I help with something?" I ask.

"Sit," he says, pointing to a chair facing away from the stove. "You're my guest this evening. Let me serve you."

I try to imagine Sinclair preparing a meal—serving me—but despite my best efforts, the image is filmy with fuzzy edges, until my mind wanders to the dim alley. But I don't allow myself to linger there. Not now.

"I'm not much of a cook," Father Jesse says, dishing out the pot pie. "Although I can make a few simple things." He sets a pure white china plate on the placemat in front of me dotted with a few peas and a slice of carrot peeping out from under the well-browned crust. "My mother died when I was a toddler, and my father a few years later. My grandmother was sickly, so I often had to fend for myself at suppertime. But it was mostly cold cuts stuffed between slices of store-bought bread and boxed macaroni and cheese. You know, the kind with bright orange powder."

I nod. "I'm sorry. It must have been difficult growing up without either of your parents. Do you have siblings?"

"Only child. It was a bit lonely at times, but good practice for the solitude of the priesthood. Tell me about your family."

My fork stills midair. "I also lost my mother when I was very young. I never knew her. But I've tried to piece together her life, so that I have something to hold onto."

"God's plan isn't always apparent to us, but He always has one. When we're grieving, our hearts are often too closed off, but if we open them to Him, He will provide us ample comfort in our hour of need."

"I grew up hearing that she was in a better place. I hold onto that, especially when I'm missing her."

"One day you'll be together again, for all of eternity." He pats my arm gently. His fingers are warm and smooth. "Do you have siblings?"

"Three brothers—two who are living, and one who died while serving in the Marines."

"Are you close to them?"

"I was very close to Liam, who passed away, but not as close to the other two. They're somewhat older, and mostly think of me as an annoying little sister."

"I highly doubt that you've ever annoyed anyone."

I stare down at the plate, spearing a piece of tender chicken with my fork.

"You never told me what brought you to Charleston."

"I originally came to learn more about Warren King. But my interests have expanded beyond him, and now I'm trying to learn more about Charleston's societies and men's clubs. But everyone has been rather close-mouthed."

"The secrecy is part of the allure—it always has been, and probably always will be. In the church, too. I understand the confirmation hearings for Judge King might not happen until the fall."

"Do you know him?"

"Only in passing. But I did recently hear he's fallen ill."

"Oh? Perhaps that's why the hearings have been delayed." He doesn't respond, and I can't come up with another question on the spot that doesn't sound too pushy.

"And what about Smith Sinclair?" he asks. "Couldn't get him to join us for Mass?"

"We—we—I don't know how to describe our relationship," I answer sheepishly. "We're friends, I guess. It's an unlikely friendship. Charleston is not a very welcoming place. Or maybe, not terribly welcoming to journalists."

"Not just journalists. Priests too, but they eventually open their arms wide. It does take time, and it doesn't hurt to develop some thick skin while you wait for them to come around. Did you have any pets growing up?"

Pets? His transitions are often so clumsy. But now that I've had a chance to know him better, they seem less like a lack of conversational skills, and more like another charming quirk.

I shake my head. "No. I always wanted a dog, but my father didn't need anything else to take care of."

"You can get one now."

"I've thought about it, but they require a lot of attention and some stability. I don't think it's the right time in my life for a dog."

"A pet turtle then, perhaps. They're rather independent, although they're not much fun to play with." Father Jesse pours us each more wine and offers me a second helping of the chicken pie.

"It's delicious, but I've had enough, thank you."

After replacing the cork on the bottle, he sits back in his chair, swirling the wine around the balloon glass. "I'd like to ask you something, but please stop me if I'm overstepping." I nod solemnly, wondering what he has in mind. "I noticed that on both Sundays you attended Mass, you haven't received communion—although you've looked wistfully at the chalice."

I release a breath that I had apparently been holding. "I wasn't sure—at St. Claire's," I begin inelegantly. "At my parish in

Boston, congregants are welcome to receive communion so long as they are in a state of grace. I know that some parishes interpret, well, everything, more liberally than others. I wasn't sure about St. Maggie's, and I didn't want to do anything improper."

"*Ah*, I see." He clasps his hands together, elbows on the table. "Here at St. Maggie's, we are family. I want you to feel comfortable to ask me anything. But you can also ask Virginia, if you prefer. She's been with me for so long that she usually knows what I'm thinking, before I'm even thinking it."

He reaches for some bread and breaks off a crusty end. "I encourage everyone to partake in Reconciliation, because it's freeing—good for the soul, so to speak. I don't worry too much about parishioners being in a state of grace—I leave those decisions to God and their individual consciences. But of course, I offer spiritual guidance when asked. I highly doubt there's anything you've done that would remove you from grace." He dips the bread into a bit of creamy sauce left on the plate and pops it into his mouth.

Friday night against the brick wall in the alley with Sinclair comes immediately to mind. Premarital sex is definitely a mortal sin, but I keep this to myself.

"I'd be honored to hear your confession—although I prefer to think of it as reconciliation. St. Maggie's has a lovely reconciliation room downstairs overlooking the garden. We offer the sacrament with or without a privacy screen."

Honored? "Yes. I'd like that." I say it to please, but I'm not at all sure I would like it.

"I'm glad you're considering reconciliation because there seems to be something weighing heavily on you. Can I tempt you with dessert?" he asks, clearing my plate.

"Thank you, but it's getting late, and the road off the island is still new to me. I should probably go before it gets too dark."

"On the island, we enjoy the solace dark provides, but it takes getting used to. Before you go, I have a gift for you."

"A gift?" *A gift?*

"It's actually more of a regift. I hope that doesn't offend you."

"No of course not." I smile. "I've regifted once or twice myself."

He leaves the kitchen and returns with a large rectangular box that appears heavy.

"A well-meaning congregant brought this to me." He sets what appears to be a box holding a television on the table. "I played with the thing for hours—even read the instructions twice, but I can't make heads or tails of it." He shrugs. "It's a smart TV. Ever hear of it?"

I press my lips together, trying not to laugh. For someone who isn't even forty, he knows little about technology. "Yes. They connect to Wi-Fi and you can watch shows with subscriptions, like Netflix."

"I'm afraid this television is smarter than I am."

I chuckle. "You can use it like a regular TV. It doesn't have to be connected to the internet."

"I don't watch much TV, and the small one I have more than meets my needs. Do you have Wi-Fi at your place?"

"Yes."

"You would do me a great act of kindness by taking it off my hands." He glances at me and bursts out laughing. "*Please take this damn thing. Do with it what you will, just get it out of here.* Not much in the way of an offering, is it?"

"I would be happy to take the TV. I don't have one. I watch movies on my laptop now. This would be a big improvement over that."

"Good!" he cries, so loud the lusty echo surely resonates beyond the walls. "I can't tell you how much you've pleased me, Kate. Let me carry it out to your car."

19

KATE

"Kate?" a lovely dark-haired woman with warm brown eyes asks tentatively from the doorway of my library office. She's familiar, but I can't immediately place her. I glance at the designer purse she's carrying and the diamond on her finger. She certainly doesn't appear as though she's without resources.

"Yes." I stand and walk around the table as she enters the room. "May I help you?"

"I'm Gabby Duval." Her entire face lights up when she smiles. "Actually, Gabby Duval Wilder." That's how I recognize her—from the media coverage of President Wilder's funeral, and photographs splashed all over the local news. She's a bit of a celebrity in town. *But why is she here?* "I don't think I'll ever get used to saying that," she adds.

"It's nice to meet you, Mrs. Wilder." I extend my hand. "How can I help you?"

"Call me Gabby, please," she says, her perfectly manicured hand grasping mine firmly.

"Gabby." She's quite beautiful up close. Not like a fashion

model, but like a woman with good genes who wears sunscreen faithfully and washes her make-up off carefully every night. Fiona would appreciate her flawless skin.

"I'm here for two reasons," she says. "Let's do a little business first."

Okay. "Would you like to sit?" I gesture toward the mismatched chairs around the table. They seem childish and unpolished compared to her. If she notices, she doesn't let on.

"I only have a few minutes, but I would love to sit. I've been running around all day, and these shoes are every bit as uncomfortable as they look." I glance down at her strappy sandals, casual, but modern, like her outfit.

As she sits, it occurs to me that I should offer her something to drink—that it would not only be polite, but expected. Sinclair's right. My southern charm is lacking. "Would you like some water, or a cookie?" I sound more like an idiot than a gracious host, but she doesn't seem to notice.

"That depends. Is it a sugar cookie?"

"Snickerdoodle."

She side-eyes the tin at the end of the table. "I better not. I've already had two cookies today. And an orange-glazed scone," she adds with an impertinent grin. "But thank you."

We settle in across from one another, and I wait on pins and needles while she pulls a folder from a large leather satchel. I hope she's not doing her husband's bidding and here to chase me out of town.

"I recently started an after-school program for girls, Georgie's Place," she explains, sliding a bold fuchsia folder toward me. "While all girls are welcome at the center, I'm particularly interested in creating a safe space for vulnerable girls, and an atmosphere that builds them up and helps them imagine a promising future for themselves."

Her words hit close to home, and for a few seconds, I wonder if she knows about my history. *No, that makes no sense. She couldn't possibly know anything about me.*

"I'm lining up speakers to come in and talk to the girls formally, and informally, about career choices," she continues. "To introduce them to an array of possibilities and make their worlds a little bigger. I would love if you would come by the center and talk to them about journalism—about what you do. I'm sure most of those little girls have never met a journalist."

My fingers unfurl as I relax. "I would be happy to speak to the girls. Maybe I can bring some pens and notepads with me. Depending on how many girls there are," I add.

"That would be wonderful." She smiles. "We can help with the supplies."

"When were you thinking you might like to have me come in?" Between my work at the library, the King investigation, and the church bulletin, I'm not even sure where I'll find the time. But it sounds like a great program and I want to be a part of it.

"The after-school coordinator will email you with some proposed dates. Do you have a card?"

"Yes." I take one of the simple business cards the library had made for me off the miniature easel and hand it to her.

"I'm also always trying to find volunteers with an hour or two a week to spare. There's a vetting process, but I hope you'll consider it." She pauses for a breath, studying me while I study her. "I've managed to twist a lot of arms—women of all ages— many the same age as we are, so in addition to doing angel's work, it will be a nice opportunity for you to make friends. I know how hard it can be to break into the Charleston scene when you don't know anyone. I grew up here, but when I came back after being away for several years, it was even hard for me."

I tuck a curl behind my ear. "I would love to help in any way I can. Having a chance to meet other women my age is a bonus."

"You just made my day," she says, tapping her hand on the

bright pink folder. "There's information about the center inside, as well as my contact information, and a form for a criminal records check, if you're interested in a regular volunteer stint."

"Thank you. I'll read through it this evening." *Tell her about what you do. There are so many similarities.* "I work with homeless women here," I begin hesitantly. "If you meet anyone through Georgie's Place that could use some supportive services, this is a sampling of what we provide." I hand her a list of what we offer.

She takes it and scans the list quickly. "This is a nice complement to what we do. Together we could be a formidable team." She smiles broadly and slides the paper into her bag. "Now, for the next item of business. You should know upfront that I won't take no for an answer, unless you have an audience with the queen on that very day. Then *maybe*, I'll let you slide."

I shift in my seat. There is absolutely nothing snobby or off-putting about Gabrielle Wilder. She couldn't be nicer, but there is something about the way she speaks that I'm not used to, and it has me mesmerized. It's an unhurried cadence with an enchanting combination of clever prose and a lyrical accent that floats from her perfectly shaped mouth. I might be developing a serious girl-crush.

"It's Smith's birthday next week and we're having a party for him," she says with her hands clasped on the table. "Just a few friends. I want you to join us at Sweetgrass."

Wait. What? How does she know Smith and I—are friends? "I don't know," I say, averting my eyes.

"Smith speaks fondly of you. He'll love you to be there."

It was him. He told her about us. What did he say? Clearly nothing too awful or she wouldn't be here. "Does he know about the party?"

"No. It's a surprise. Not a jump out from behind the drapes and yell surprise kind of surprise. Although he might get a kick out of that." She smiles impishly. "He's been invited to supper. He just doesn't know that there will be some extra people joining us, and a big coconut cake piled with boiled icing for dessert. The man will eat anything that doesn't move, but that's his favorite."

"I-I'm not sure he would appreciate me crashing his birthday party."

"You've been officially invited. That's not crashing." She stands and gathers her things. "I've heard a lot about you from Smith, and from my husband. There is absolutely no doubt in my mind that Smith likes you—very much. I'll see you a week from Friday at seven. It's casual. Just give the guards at the gate your name. You'll be on the list of approved visitors. It was nice meeting you, Kate," she says warmly, before turning toward the door.

"Gabby?" She stops and pivots.

"Smith, your husband, and Gray Wilder ... you should know ... they want me to leave Charleston. I-I don't think they—especially your husband—would want me at your home."

She takes several steps toward me and drops her bag on the table with a hand propped on top. "I don't believe for a minute that Smith wants you to go anywhere. I'm sure he's given you that impression. I can't explain the male courting rituals, except to say they don't advance much past sixth grade," she says, rolling her eyes. "I invited a *friend* of Gray's, too. He'll have plenty on his plate that evening, and it won't have a thing to do with you. So check him off your list of concerns. As for my husband—don't spend a single second worrying about him."

I swallow some of the anxiety that's been building since she issued the invitation. "Your husband doesn't seem like the kind of man whose bark is worse than his bite."

Gabby arches a well-groomed brow, and her eyes grow wide and serious. "Oh, his bite is venomous. If you tangle with him, you better have the correct anecdote handy. But trust me. He will be on his best behavior that evening—although that's not saying much." She lifts the satchel off the table and onto her shoulder. "Should I send a car for you? It might make it easier."

"No." I shake my head. "Thank you. I can find my way."

"Good," she gushes, with a toothy grin that makes her eyes sparkle.

Oh, Kate, what on earth did you just agree to?

20

SMITH

"What?" I bark into the phone.

"You go first, darlin'," JD drawls, "because it sounds like someone stepped on your fragile little feelings, or is it that the menstrual cramps are particularly bad this month?"

"I don't need your shit right now."

"What happened?"

"Nothing happened. I've been on the damn phone all morning negotiating prices and delivery time for the new equipment." There is almost nothing I hate more than being stuck in my office for hours trying to reason with morons.

"The heat-sensing devices and night-vision goggles are on back order," I continue, whacking the desk with a yellow pad filled with notes. "Because those stupid fuckers who think they're going to fight off the United States military from bunkers in the backyard have eaten up all the inventory, not to mention driven the cost sky-high."

"What now?"

"They add us to the list and we wait. Six months, maybe longer."

"How much to get to the top of the list?"

"Too much," I mutter. "The computer equipment is more important."

"That's not what I asked." *Damn JD.* Once he gets something in his head, he can never let it go.

"I thought you were going to be a silent partner? That's what we agreed on."

"You know there are jackasses all over the Carolinas that are less stubborn than you. Use the damn money I transferred into the account."

"I'm planning on it. But I don't want to drain the account at this stage in the operation. Things are going to come up that we'll need that money for, including a hefty insurance bond when the first contract comes through."

"So? We'll transfer more."

"No."

"Alright. Let's talk about something else before I'm so pissed off, I have to drive over to your office and slap some sense into your thick skull. I have information on King."

"I'm listening."

"There's a rumor being floated that he's sick. Smart people don't believe it. They think that it might be an excuse so that when they pull his nomination, he can still keep his current judgeship."

It takes a moment for the pieces to fall together. "If that's true, that means whatever the White House dug up has legs. Otherwise, King's people wouldn't be worried that he'd lose his judgeship. Those are lifetime appointments."

"Yep."

"What do you think?"

"The information comes from a source that doesn't trade in gossip. I'm inclined to believe there's at least some truth behind it."

"Any sense of what it is?"

"Not really. But King fucked anything with a pussy back in the day. One source tells me he wouldn't be at all surprised if this involved a woman."

"Thanks. I appreciate you asking around."

"I guess this means that reporter is going to be staying in Charleston."

I don't like his tone. "You could cut her a break."

"I could, but I won't. She's trouble, Smith. I feel it in my bones."

We hang up without any more discussion about Kate. When JD's thinking clearly, his instincts are solid, but he can't think straight when it involves her. Not after she tried to do a story on Zack last year. JD protects his brothers fiercely, but when it comes to Zack, who is helpless, JD is a bear and wouldn't hesitate to kill to protect him. No different than he feels about his wife and daughter.

My instincts are more than solid. They're well-honed and battle-tested. But my dick has gotten in the way and compromised my judgment where Kate's concerned. It's inexcusable and demonstrates a total lack of discipline on my part—at least that's what General Sinclair would say. And he'd be right.

The bottom line is I don't entirely trust her either. Can't afford it. As much as I want to let my guard down around her, I simply can't. It's always possible she's using me to get closer to the Wilders. Everyone wants a piece of them. It started even before their father became a presidential nominee. Three young guys, filthy rich, and powerful. Even with the old man dead, they're irresistible to the media.

I can't let my dick take the lead on this. I just can't. But I can give her the information on King. That, I can do.

―

I stroll past the circulation desk where Lucinda McCrae is checking out a book for a woman with a young child strapped on her back. "Can't bring drinks into the library," she chides, like I'm a schoolboy.

"I'm taking it up to Kate McKenna. Going straight to her room. Won't be anywhere near a book." I don't stop and wait for permission.

"Next time," she calls after me, "I take my coffee with a big dollop of cream and no sugar. I'm sweet enough."

I pause on the bottom rung, turning my head to look at her. She has a damn sassy twinkle in her eyes that makes me grin. I'm sure every story about the woman is true. "I'll remember that for next time, Miss McCrae."

"I'm counting on it, Mr. Sinclair. I hope you have an appointment to see Miss McKenna," she says, when I'm halfway up the stairs. "She's a busy young lady who doesn't have time to entertain everything that blows up from the street."

I should be annoyed by the crack, but I'm not. For some reason Lucinda McCrae has made it her business to watch out for Kate and that's fine by me.

When I get to the top, I snake my way through the stacks to Kate's office, standing in the doorway to watch her for a few seconds before I barge in. Her elbow is propped on the table, and she's twisting a hunk of hair around her hand, sharp eyes trained on the computer screen.

Shit. She's gorgeous. There's nothing more I want than those long legs wrapped around my waist, heels digging into my bare ass. *That's enough. This kind of thinking is not helping your judgment.*

I stow the not-for-prime-time thoughts, and stride into the room, kicking the door shut behind me. "Hey."

"Hey, yourself." Not sure the broad smile is for me or for the coffee she's eyeing longingly, but either way, it's all good. "I didn't expect you for another twenty minutes."

"Light traffic." I place the cup on the table in front of her.

"Thank you. Must be some news, if you have to shut the door."

I grunt and plunk my ass in the chair across from her. "There's a rumor that King's sick, and that's why the hearing's been delayed."

"I heard that," she murmurs, prying off the lid, and blowing on the coffee before taking a sip.

"There are people who believe it's a ruse. That King's camp leaked the lies, so when the White House pulls the nomination, no one will start digging for the reasons why, and he can keep his federal judgeship."

"Why doesn't the White House just pull his name if they're not planning on proceeding with him?" She fidgets with a pen while her mind churns. "Why would they want to be complicit in a lie that doesn't benefit them?"

"I doubt they do. But they won't pull it before they have another nominee. It will make them seem disorganized and inept."

"And this White House always does everything it can to avoid that look," she says. "It plays right into King's hands."

I nod. Whatever is happening with King isn't good for the country, but to be honest, all I can think about right now is how relieved I am that the story isn't dead, because when it comes down to it, I don't want her to leave Charleston. *Not yet.* It might not make me very patriotic, but it makes me very human. I'm a civilian, and I get to choose human now, but not without the pinch of conscience.

"Why would he be afraid of losing his current job?" she continues. "That makes no sense." Her brow furrows tightly. "Unless—"

"They're pulling the nomination because of some scandal he's involved with," I respond before she can finish.

"It would have to be something serious to force him out of his current position. Do you have any ideas?"

"No."

She disappears somewhere deep inside her head. "Do you know Judge Sorlin?" she asks, tapping a finger mindlessly on the bow of her lip.

Judge Sorlin? I wrack my brain, but I can't come up with anything. "Never heard of him. Who is he?"

"Lucinda told me that he was King's mentor back in the day. Carefully groomed King to be what he is today. He's in a nursing home with dementia. His only daughter lives in Richmond. Maybe I should talk to him."

"A demented judge doesn't sound like he'll be much help to you."

"I don't know. My grandmother had dementia. Not every second is confused. She had lucid periods. Depends what stage he's in."

I can see where this is going—into a big dead end. Maybe I can grease the wheels, make her life a little easier. *Why? Why do you want to do that?* I ignore common sense. Why not, when it come to her, I'm on a roll in that regard. "How are you going to get in to talk to him?"

"Unless it's different here, you'd be surprised how easy it is to walk into a nursing home. They're short-staffed, so nobody bothers you, especially if you look like you could be family, and act like you know where you're going."

"That's reassuring," I say dryly. "Do you want me to go with you?"

"No. It's too late to go today. He's likely to be more confused as the sun sets. I'll go tomorrow, mid-morning. I think it might be less overwhelming for him if it's just me."

I wonder for a minute if there's another reason she doesn't want me to go. Maybe she doesn't trust me anymore than I trust her. Probably smart. Although I'd never betray her—at least I don't think so.

"Be careful." I'm not sure why I feel the need to warn her. But something about this whole King mess is beginning to eat at me, and it doesn't have a thing to do with Wildflower.

21

KATE

After I meet with Judge Sorlin, I have back-to-back appointments at the library, and then a literacy class. There's scarcely a minute to visit the restroom.

It's past seven by the time I lock my office door and head downstairs to let them know I'm leaving. Before I make it to the circulation desk, a man wearing a sheriff's uniform approaches me. "Mary Katherine McKenna?" the deputy asks.

"Yes."

He hands me a sealed envelope. "It's self-explanatory. But there's a number inside to call if you have questions. Have a nice evening."

My hands tremble as I tear open the flap and pull out the paperwork. I read each word carefully. It's a temporary restraining order, issued by a judge in Charleston County. It states that I am to have no contact with Judge Sorlin, and that I am ordered to stay away from the nursing home. A hearing on the merits has been scheduled for ten days from today. I read it through twice more before sitting on the bench just inside the main door, where I read it again. It's intimidating with its formal language and judicial seal.

Someone doesn't want me talking to Judge Sorlin. Maybe he does know something. He might, but if today was any indication, it's unlikely he'll ever be able to tell me. Maybe it's just that someone doesn't want to risk that I'll upset him. Maybe it's that simple.

I'm not sure what to do. I no longer have an editor or colleagues. After a couple minutes stewing, I still have nothing.

I could talk to Smith. There's really no one else to turn to for guidance. Do I really want him to know about this? When I can't think of one good reason why not, I text him.

Kate: *Do you have a few minutes?*
Smith: *What's going on?*
Kate: *I was just served with a judicial order to stay away from Judge Sorlin.*
Smith: *I'll meet you at your place in an hour.*

By the time I get home, shower, and tidy up the house a bit, Smith is at my door with a pizza large enough to feed a family of four and a six-pack of a hoppy beer we both like.

"I hope you like cheese on your pizza," he says, with a cocky half-smile, "because I know you don't like it on burgers." I shove his arm playfully and take the box, setting it on the counter while I get out plates.

"As long as it's not covered in anchovies, I'm happy. I don't have beer glasses. How about these?" I hold up one of the tall etched tumblers that was in the cupboard when I moved in.

"Don't bother dirtying glasses on my account. The bottle's fine." He uses the opener from his keyring to pry off the cap from two bottles and stashes the rest in the fridge. "Let me see the restraining order."

I hand Smith the paperwork, watching him closely while he reads. As usual, his face gives little away. "It's signed by a judge," he says, folding the order carefully and stuffing it back into the envelope.

I'm not sure what he means. "It's a court order. I would expect a judge to have signed it."

"In Charleston County, restraining orders are normally issued by magistrates and usually only after two incidences of harassment. Have you visited Sorlin before?" I shake my head. "Contacted him?"

"No. I just showed up."

"Whoever sought the order had access, otherwise it's unlikely they would have ever gotten near a judge. How did you know what room he was in?"

"Lucinda. They're old friends and she brings him lunch a couple times a month. She gave me his room number when she suggested I pay him a visit."

"When was that?"

"More than a week ago."

"Did she know you went to see him today?"

"No. She was off today and had left yesterday by the time I decided to go." I'm starting to feel like he's accusing Lucinda of setting me up. It's ridiculous. "Lucinda didn't sic a judge on me."

He nods, and takes a swig from the bottle. "Probably not. Let's eat. I need a couple minutes to think." I would prefer to figure it out first, then eat. But I'm grateful he's helping, so I keep my mouth shut.

"The pizza smells great." I flip open the box, and there's a slice missing. "What happened here?" He side-eyes me, but doesn't respond. "Does Fazio's make a special-shaped pie they sell at a discount? Or did a big rat walk away with a slice?"

His lips twitch madly, as he tries to hold back a smile. "Don't give me that shit. I left plenty. I was starving."

"Then let's feed you before you waste away to nothing and I'm somehow blamed for it." I hand him a plate with a slice of pizza.

"Put another one on there," he says, "I'm a growing boy."

Gabby was right. The man will probably eat anything that doesn't move. I wonder what they'll serve at the party to go along with his favorite coconut cake? *The party.* What if Gabby's wrong and Smith doesn't want me there? I told her I would go, but I could email her with an excuse. There's still time to beg out.

"Where's the TV?" Smith asks.

"The TV?"

"The basketball playoffs begin tonight," he explains sheepishly. "I'll keep it on mute. I just want to keep track of the score."

"Right." I've never met a single male who only keeps the TV on during a game to keep an eye on the score. They say it, but it always ends up with them yelling things at the TV from the couch. At least that's the way it always went down at my house growing up. But I don't mind watching the game. Like most Bostonians, I'm a huge sports fan.

"Come on," Smith begs shamelessly, flashing a dimpled grin that would melt the polar caps. He knows it, too. "I have a small wager on the game."

In the bedroom. Ugh. "Follow me."

On our way to find the TV, he peeks inside the oddly furnished living room. There are a couple of end tables and a coffee table in the room, along with a standing lamp, but nowhere to sit.

"Where's the sofa?"

"I don't have one. This house belongs to a professor at the University. She put her upholstered furniture in storage before she left town for the summer. The only items she kept in the house can be wiped off easily or cleaned when she returns."

"You should've told her you like to get off in the bathtub, so you won't make anything dirty."

I glare at him over my shoulder to hide the embarrassment. I'll never live it down. That's what I get for telling him. "Do you want to watch the game, or give me decorating tips?"

"What I want is to see if the Lakers are winning," he says as we get to the bedroom. "Wait. Is that an air mattress?"

"Yes. Mattresses are upholstered. They definitely can't be wiped off."

"You're fucking kidding me. She took the bed? But she left that ugly-ass rug? That's made of fabric, too."

"The rug is mine, thank you very much." I grab the remote from the bedside table and sit on the floor cross-legged with my food.

"You sleep on that thing? I'm not sure it will hold my weight."

I do sleep on it, and I do other things on it too—*while I fantasize about you.* But today, I'm not liquored up and horny, so I have the presence of mind not to share any of it with him.

"Weight capacity is not a problem, because you're not sleeping on it. And you're not lounging on it with that pizza, either. Sit your butt on my ugly-ass rug or go get yourself a kitchen chair."

"*Pft.* Why don't you buy a mattress, so you'll have something decent to sleep on?"

"I'm not sure I'll be in Charleston long enough to justify the purchase." The words stir uneasy feelings inside me. "What channel is the game on?"

"Let me see the remote. I'll find it." He sits on the floor, back against the mattress, legs spanning the length of the rug, and scrolls through the channels so quickly it's dizzying. "This is a nice TV. Nicer than mine. I'm surprised she didn't store it with everything else."

"It's mine. It was a gift," I say without thinking.

"A gift?" He peers at me with that probing gaze, still clutching the remote. "From who?"

From Father Jesse. You know, the priest you think wants to fuck me. I am not having that discussion again. "From none of your business."

"Must be from a guy, then," he mutters. "Boyfriend? Secret

admirer? Daddy?" he ticks them off one after the other, pausing for a beat between each to see if I respond in some way. "Only a guy would give you a TV."

"There are differences between the gifts guys give and the ones women give?"

"Yeah. Don't change the subject. Where did the TV come from?"

Nosy bastard. He's not going to stop until I tell him. "It's from Father Jesse at St. Magdalene's, okay?"

Smith takes a bite of pizza, chewing carefully. "The priest gave you an expensive television? Did I get that right?"

"A parishioner brought to him, and he already had a TV. He didn't need another one."

"So he gave it—to you."

"It's really not that complicated. I volunteered to help the church create a new bulletin, and I'm sure the TV is a way to compensate me for my trouble. Surprised your boy Josh, who keeps track of me, didn't report it."

"*Mmhm*," he says. "Not too complicated at all." He drains the beer bottle and stretches to place it on the wood floor at the edge of the rug. "Josh is a grown man. Served two tours in combat—I doubt he'd appreciate you calling him a boy in that disrespectful tone. But he's on a more pressing assignment right now. I doubt you've seen him recently."

I hardly saw him before. "So who's tailing me?"

"Nobody was ever tailing you."

"Keeping an eye on me, then?"

"That would be me." He gets up and approaches the doorway.

Disappointment settles into my bones like a late January chill, but it comes disguised as anger. "*What?* You pretend to hang out so you can spy on me?"

"Calm your titties or that pizza will give you terrible heartburn. You want another slice or a beer while I'm up?"

God, I'm an idiot, or delusional. While I realize there is little difference between Sinclair setting up surveillance, and actually doing the surveilling himself, to me, there's a world of difference. "No. I want answers," I call after him, but he doesn't say a word in response until he returns and is sitting comfortably on the rug with a full plate.

"I told you when I agreed to help you get to the bottom of the King story, that it would help me keep tabs on you, too." He did say that. But I hoped his hanging around was about more—about wanting to be with me.

"I know it's gotten more complicated between us. And to be honest, most of the time I have no fucking clue what I'm doing. It's why mixing business and pleasure is never a good thing. I like you," he says, bringing a slice of pizza to his mouth. "My life would be easier all around if I didn't, but I do."

I'm not sure how to respond. *Get the fuck out* is my first inclination, but there's the matter of the restraining order, still. And then there's also the small fact that I put on my best panties and bra after my shower. That must mean I like him too, even if my life would be easier all around, if I didn't. "Can we talk about the restraining order?"

He nods solemnly, and the tenor of the room shifts. It's still serious, but the baggage has been packed away.

"I want you to think carefully about anyone you might have told about the visit to Sorlin. Even if you just mentioned it in passing."

"Other than you, Fiona is the only person."

"Fiona. Your friend from Boston?"

"Yes."

"Did you see anyone at the nursing home today who might have recognized you?"

That's such a tough question. How can I possibly be sure? "I didn't see anyone that I knew while I was there, and I was careful not to wear Judge Sorlin out, or to ask him too many questions that might upset him. He was in a good mood when I left. A dietary aide came into the room when I was there, but she didn't say a word to me. She just left him a couple graham crackers and some apple juice."

He looks at me with an alert gaze. "Do you remember her name?"

I shake my head. "She was a petite brunette and wore a light blue scrub top with teddy bears on it."

"Well someone saw you and reported it. It might have been her," he mutters mostly to himself. "Did you learn anything while you were there?"

"Not really. His dementia appears to be somewhat advanced. He had a brief moment of clarity when I arrived, but he wasn't lucid for long enough to tell me much about King beyond someone named Gigi who didn't want an abortion. I'm not even sure the two are related."

"What exactly did he say?"

"*Gigi doesn't want an abortion. Warren's in a hell of a pickle now. So much promise.* But in the next breath, he was asking if his wife was visiting today. She died ten years ago. Then he started calling me Noreen. That was his wife's name." Things deteriorated quickly after that, and I didn't want to push him too hard. Nana would always get agitated when visitors asked too many questions. It made the rest of the day rough, and it sometimes required sedating her so she could calm down enough to sleep. I wasn't going to do that to Judge Sorlin.

Smith shakes his head. "I hope someone puts a bullet in my head before I get to that stage."

"That's a terrible thing to say. He's a sweet, sweet man."

"I'm not talking about him. I'm talking about me." Smith gets up and makes himself comfortable in the center of my bed, his hands folded behind his head.

"What are you doing?"

"I'm tired of sitting on the floor," he says rearranging the pillows behind him and making himself right at home. "Why don't you come keep me company."

All that gorgeous muscle in my bed is so tempting, but he is a bad idea on steroids. "Don't get any ideas."

"Too late."

"It's not too late. Get off my bed."

"You think lying on your bed is what gives me ideas?" He snickers. "Or that I wouldn't fuck you on the floor, or against that door, or the dresser or—"

"Okay. You made your point."

"When's the last time you had sex?" he asks, in a voice that's not any different from the one he used to ask me if I wanted another slice of pizza. I turn and glare at his brazenness. "It's a simple question. It shouldn't require a calendar and a calculator —I hope."

"The alley," I huff. "If you want to call it that."

He whips a decorative cushion from the bed at me. "Before that. Was it more than a month ago?"

"Why do you care?"

"I'll take that as a yes. Six months? A year?" he asks, when I don't respond.

Longer. "Why is this germane to anything?"

"You know as well as I do that we're going to end up naked. Or at least you are. Maybe not tonight. But it's in the cards."

I do know. Most of the time, I even want it to happen. Although I expect him to be naked too. I pick at my pizza, pulling off a green pepper that's embedded in the melted cheese. But I'm a little afraid of him. There's something about him—his intensity—his demanding nature—I don't know for sure what it is, but it frightens me at times. Maybe I'm afraid of getting hurt. He's the kind of man that could, *and would*, break my heart. I have no doubt about it.

"Kate?"

I turn to meet his eyes.

"There are things worth sharing with me before it happens," he says with a gentle warmth, thawing the protective layer around my heart just a drop more. I hope he doesn't notice the thinning shell. "And we've got time right now—it's halftime and I'm not going anywhere until the game's over." The last part is laced with a bit of sarcasm that lightens the mood and puts us both back on safer footing.

"It's been more than a year," I mumble. Since before I left Boston.

"You on any kind of birth control?"

"No." I've only used condoms.

"Are you healthy?"

"Yes. Do you want to know what I ate for breakfast?"

"Not necessary. But you should be happy I'm asking these questions. And you should ask some of your own."

I just might do that. "When's the last time you had sex?" I ask from the rug at the foot of the bed.

"With my hand? That would be last night in the shower. Do you want to know what I was thinking about?"

I feel my neck flush. "With a woman?"

"The alley."

Now I'm curious. "Before that?"

"A few days before we had supper at Miss Macy's."

I swallow. "With a girlfriend?" *Please don't say yes.*

He maneuvers on the unstable mattress so that his head is at the foot of the bed, with his face close to mine. "No. If I had a girlfriend, I wouldn't have been in that alley. I'm not a cheater."

I curl my hands into tight balls, thumbs caressing the ridges and bumps of the outer knuckles. He opened the door, so I might as well ask. "Have you ever shared a woman—with friends?"

"At the same time?"

I nod, holding my breath while I wait for him to answer.

"No." He leans closer, his lips grazing mine. "Although once or twice women have shared me." I pull back, recoiling without even the pretense of subtlety.

"Don't ask a question you don't want the answer to, princess. You'll never hear me ask how many men have been in your bed before me." He tugs on my arm. "Come back here. Finish that line of questioning, or ask whatever else you're dying to know about me."

Smith is unlike anyone I've ever met. While he can be demanding and judgmental, he has an openness that is both seductive and scary at the same time. I have no doubt he's experimented with things that would make me uncomfortable. One more than any other. "You've never shared a woman—sexually? Not even with JD?"

"That would require our cocks to be in very close proximity to one another. Too close for either of our tastes." He pulls me up onto the mattress, until we're lying on our sides facing each other. "Is this something you're asking for?" He brushes my cheek with his fingertip. "Because you don't strike me as the type—"

"No." My voice is wobbly. "It's not at all what I want."

We lay there quietly for a minute or two. Me, swatting away the thoughts creeping in to ruin the evening. Him, searching my face for answers. "One day you'll tell me what this is all about," he says, smoothing back my hair with his hand. "Doesn't have to be tonight."

"No more questions?" I aim for the right amount of sarcasm to hide behind, but the words emerge shaky. I'm not fooling anyone.

"Plenty more. I'm just takin' a break to taste you." His lips are smooth and firm when his mouth crushes mine. There's no gentle exploration tonight. He takes and takes until I'm breathless under him. Until I can't remember ever being afraid.

My impatient fingers rake into his muscled back, tilling the terrain, until the lush tendrils of desire wind their way through the fertile ground, enveloping us, until there's no turning back.

It's then that his phone rings. A shrill alert dragging us from a shared weightless dream.

Smith throws his head back with a primal growl and pulls the damn thing from his pants pocket.

"Yeah?" He rolls off of me, taking all the warmth with him. "You are fucking kidding me." He says a few more things, none of which I grasp completely because I'm too busy bemoaning what is clearly not going to be happening tonight. When he ends the call, his lips brush my forehead in a chaste reminder that we're done here.

"There was an attempted break in at Sayle Pharmaceuticals—it's a Wilder property. I need to meet the police there. I'm sorry."

"It's okay." I say it, and of course he needs to go, but I'm not feeling okay. I miss him already.

"Don't worry about the restraining order," he reassures me. "We'll get you a lawyer to make it go away if we need to." I nod. "I want a raincheck for tonight," he says, tying his sneakers.

I respond with a sad excuse for a smile. A pathetic little tug of the lips, but he's already at the doorway so it doesn't really matter.

"Kate."

My gaze flickers to his eyes. "Hmm?"

"The break in is off the record." His voice is hard and unforgiving.

The break in is off the record. It's a warning shot. Not delivered with the violence of an AR-15, more like birdshot, leaving a smattering of ugly, painful pox that last for weeks.

A moment later the backdoor shuts firmly and he's gone, leaving me to tend to my wounds.

22

SMITH

I spoke with Kate briefly this morning and something seemed off with her. She was cool and detached. Not like herself.

It almost seemed like I did something to piss her off, but I haven't spoken with her since the other night when I brought pizza over to her place, and we almost ended up fucking on that ridiculous air mattress. There were no problems up until the time I left to deal with the disgruntled Sayle employee who thought he could break into his former lab and take his work. At least no problem aside from my hard, aching dick.

You could say I dodged one the other night. One being my own stupidity. I'll be smarter next time. Charleston has plenty of attractive women. I should not have sex with Kate McKenna. It's all true, but the story doesn't end here. It ends in some bed, somewhere, after we've both come a half-dozen times. I can pretend otherwise, but that's the reality. She's too far under my skin, taking up too much space in the spank bank, and I think about her too damn much.

Every guy knows the best way to get a woman out of his mind is to fuck her out. They don't all go away easy. Some linger, and it takes a repeat, or ten, to get rid of them, but it can be done. Kate's going to be a lingerer. I already know it.

That's neither here nor there because right now I'm in front of the library with my hands full of sweet tea, like the pussy I am. My first stop is the circulation desk. "Afternoon, Miss McCrae." I plop down a cup of iced tea in front of her. "I know you don't take your coffee with sugar, but I assume you take your tea sweet."

A bony hand flies to her chest. "Do people drink it another way?"

"Not our people," I say, halfway up the stairs to find Kate.

"Thank you for the beverage, Mr. Sinclair. Don't overstay your welcome."

The woman's got balls. When I get to Kate's office, she's saying goodbye to a client. The door's closed, so I can't hear the conversation, but Kate has her hand on the woman's arm. Whatever she's saying is kind and encouraging. I can tell from watching them. Aside from whatever beef I've had with her, she's a good person. I knew that from the moment I met her.

The problem is that even good people are sometimes motivated by outside sources. She's made it no secret, at least to me, how much she wants that Pulitzer for her mother. If I were smart, I'd turn right around, head down the stairs and out the door, and drink the damn tea I'm holding myself. But I'm not smart.

When the woman opens the door to leave, Kate sees me. But instead of saying hello, she turns her back and walks over to the table where she sits down in front of her laptop. I hope she doesn't expect me to leave that easily. By now she should know how much I love a challenge.

"Hey," I say, taking a seat without being invited. I put the iced tea in front of her. "It's hot out. Thought you might appreciate a cold drink."

"Thank you." Poor woman. She wants to be pissed at me, but I brought her some tea and now she's torn. "I'm really busy," she says. "I don't have time to chat." She is the worst liar.

"I'll only stay a minute. The restraining order has been dismissed."

"How did that happen?"

"My lawyer took care of it. It was apparently faulty. It needed to be filed by Sorlin's daughter and it wasn't."

"Who filed it?"

"His old firm." I slide the paperwork across the table. "Take a look at the name of the firm. Look familiar?"

"It's King's old firm."

"Yep. They could refile the request on behalf of his daughter, but the lawyer doesn't think they will as long as you stay away from Sorlin."

She nods. "I would be happy to go to court and contest the order. I've been doing a little research. I didn't do anything wrong."

"That's debatable. They could argue that just showing up and questioning him was wrong. But it doesn't matter, right or wrong, you were never going to be successful against them. Don't go back to see Sorlin."

"I'm sorry?" she asks with a pissy tone.

"Don't go back there. He didn't have anything for you, and next time, the order will stick. It'll follow you around forever."

She wants to tell me to go to hell, but she knows I'm right. The last thing an investigative journalist wants dogging her is an order to stay away from an old man with dementia. It will be brought up every time there's an issue. Doesn't matter if it's expired or not.

"I appreciate you handling it. How much do I owe you for the lawyer?"

"Nothing." She glances at me. "Lawyer's on retainer, and this took a couple phone calls. No big deal."

"Thank you."

"If you're interested in returning the favor, why don't you tell me why you're pissed."

"I'm not pissed. I'm busy."

"Bullshit. You were pissed when we spoke this morning. Couldn't wait to get off the phone."

"The other night, you left—"

"I had to leave. That's what my job entails. Trouble doesn't strike between nine and five. Well it does, but it also happens at other times. Inconvenient times." I reach for her hand, but she pulls it back into her lap. "Kate, what do you want me to say? If that had been someone calling with an important lead on the King story, you would have been out the door in a flash."

"It's not that you left," she says, staring at her hands. "It's what you said before you left."

What I said? Jesus. That could be anything. "I said a lot of shit that night. Help me out here."

"You said, 'the break in is off the record,' as though I would run to a tabloid as soon as the lock clicked behind you. It never crossed my mind." I hear the hurt in her voice.

I do remember saying it, and although I'm sorry it upset her, I would probably say it again. It's just the way it is. We each have a job to do, and there will be times when our jobs will be at odds.

When I'm through defending my behavior to myself, I try to see it from her perspective. It was a dick move.

"I own it," I admit, without making excuses. Sometimes with women, it's just less trouble to eat the humble pie, especially when you were wrong. "I straight up own it. It's going to take time to learn a new way of thinking—for both of us." I get up and go around the table, pulling a chair close to her. "I'm sorry I hurt you. Hurting you was the last thing on my mind that night." She doesn't pull her hand away when I reach for it this time.

"You going to be mad all day? Because if not, maybe we can grab a drink after work." She smiles. It starts small, but soon she's laughing, and I know I'm not in trouble anymore.

"I'll probably be done being mad by six o'clock. But then I have my class, and later Lucinda and I are getting a bite to eat."

I lean in to nuzzle her neck, sliding my hand up her skirt. "How about after dinner? Lucinda's old. I bet she doesn't stay out late."

She pushes me away. "I work here. This is a library. You need to behave." She doesn't want me to behave—or at least she's torn about it.

"I'll stop for now. Because the next time I have your panties off—let's just say we would be better off not to be in a library."

23

KATE

Getting through security at the front gate at Sweetgrass is akin to getting on base at Camp Lejeune where my brothers were stationed.

"Ma'am." A beefy guard nods at me, looking into the backseat of the car. "Any weapons with you?"

Oh God. "I have a gun in my purse," I confess with some apprehension.

"We'll safeguard it while you're on the property. You can have it back when you leave." I reach for my bag. "Please hand me the purse and I'll remove the weapon."

"Can you pop your trunk, Ma'am?" the second guard asks in a voice that indicates it's more of a command than a question.

Why am I here again?

Because I accepted Gabby's invitation, and because Smith didn't make excuses when I lectured him about how hurt I'd been about the *break in is off the record* remark.

I'm glad we talked it through, because no matter how I tried to justify it, I couldn't move past the hurt. And I refuse to let any more men into my life who I need to make excuses for. I already have plenty, thank you very much.

I can accept that we need to work on breaking old habits. Although in my mind, I've given him a deadline. If he can't make measurable progress by the end of the summer when my lease is up, there's no point in—remaining friends. And let's face it, we're nothing more than friends with benefits, and that's all we'll ever be.

We're too different—not just where we came from, but where we're going. Boston is my home and my ultimate destination, bed or no bed, and Smith doesn't like the cold climate. But for now, we're friends with a strong physical pull that might, or might not, get the chance to burn itself out before the leaves begin to change color. That's good enough for me.

When I'm free to enter Fort Knox, I park the car where the security guard instructed, and climb the front steps of the beautifully restored antebellum mansion. The house is magnificent, with stately columns, and generous pots of bright red geraniums and wave petunias lining the steps. Two iron urns flank the doorway, each holding a boxwood topiary draped in lights that I'm sure twinkle after dark.

With a growing apprehension, I ring the front doorbell. The lock clicks while I'm still admiring the foliage and the glossy black door opens. JD Wilder, himself, stands just inside, staring out like I arrived from a distant planet. After a few long seconds, he glances over my shoulder, perhaps looking for the spaceship. "Hello, I'm Kate—"

"I know who you are," he snarls. "How did you bypass security, Miss McKenna?"

"I left her name at the guard house," says a kind, familiar voice from behind him. "Like I did for each of the guests *I invited*."

Gabby hands off a drooling baby with a fist stuffed in her mouth to her husband, and pulls me inside. "Come in." She wraps me in a warm, friendly hug. "I'm so glad you made it!"

"This is for you and J—your husband," I say, when we separate, handing her a jelly jar of strawberry preserves I picked up at the local farmers' market. "And this is for the baby. It's a book. It was my favorite growing up." Anxiety has taken control of my brain, signaling for more adrenaline like it's planning a party. If I don't control myself, I'll soon be telling them about every book and toy I loved as a child.

JD stands several feet away, fuming. I can practically see the smoke pouring out of his ears. It's not helping my stress. I eye the door. It's still open, and there's nothing more I'd like right now than to run out and back to the safety of my little house without a sofa or a proper bed.

"Gracie and her daddy will love this book. They read together every night." It's difficult to believe this man, who is barely controlling his rage, reads to his daughter at night.

The baby starts to fuss and Gabby turns to her husband. "Why don't you take her upstairs and play with her? I'll join you after I show Kate to the kitchen."

He places a protective hand on Gracie's back, murmuring softly to her, and turns a simmering glare on his wife, before striding toward the stairs without a single word to either of us.

"I'm sorry about that. He beat me to the door." She squeezes my arm. "Don't worry. It's just a hiccup. JD will be fine."

She has a persuasive manner, but I don't believe for one second her husband is going to come around. I'm not even sure she believes it.

"If you need to be with the baby, I don't mind waiting here."

She glances in the direction of the stairs and clasps my hand. "Promise me you won't leave?"

I don't know if it's the nerves, but I start to laugh.

"You were thinking about it, weren't you?"

I nod sheepishly, and she laughs, too. "I won't go anywhere until you come back. I promise."

"I can't have you waiting here. But if you go down this hall to the end," she points toward the back of the house, "you'll run into the kitchen. Everyone there is a whole lot friendlier. And Delilah is making Devil's Margaritas." I must look as apprehensive as I feel. "You know what? They can wait a few minutes upstairs. Let's go to the kitchen and I'll introduce you to everyone."

I touch her arm. She's needed upstairs, not just to pacify the baby, but to pacify her husband. I'm not a child. I can brave the kitchen, especially if there is some booze there to calm me. "It's okay. You go up and smooth things over, and I'll find the kitchen. I can get along with anyone who knows how to make a decent margarita."

She eyes me carefully. "Do not leave, or I will chase you down. I won't be long."

I follow the sound of laughter to the kitchen. Smith's laugh booms over everything else. I stop right before the doorway to quell a small panic. What if he doesn't want me here with his friends? What if he asks me to leave? *Whatever it is, you'll survive it.* I practice a bright, cheery hello, smooth the flirty sundress I put on with him in mind, and step into the kitchen with my chin up.

"Kate," Smith says, freezing in place before my cheerful hello hits the air. "What are you doing here?" I suck in a lung-full of air. "Is something wrong?" he continues, tentatively. There's worry all over his face. I'm sure it never occurs to him that I was invited.

"Mrs. Wilder—Gabby—invited me," I squeak. "She dropped by the library and asked me to come. Said she wouldn't take no for an answer." The more I babble, the deeper his frown becomes, but I'm on such a roll that it will take a force of nature to stop me at this point.

"I'm Lally," a woman says draping a substantial arm around my shoulders, "and this is my kitchen, child. *Gabby invited me* is more of an explanation than he needs or deserves." She scowls at Smith. "Is this your house? *No?* Then it's none of your damn business." She squeezes my shoulder and releases me. "That's how we talk to men around here. Don't raise their expectations by answering stupid questions. Otherwise, before you know it, he'll be askin' about everything. *How many pairs of shoes you got in that closet?* And, *How long is your mama plannin' on stayin'?*" She shakes her head, with a chiding tsk-tsk. "I can see you're not a southern girl."

Lally is short and curvy with wide streaks of golden blonde covering what looks to be her natural dark hair. It's an odd hairstyle, but it works on her. I think she could make anything work.

She fills a glass, and nudges Smith out of the way, stepping between us to offer me an iced tea. "Take a drink. Go on," she encourages. "It's hot out, and you look parched." I can still feel the sear of Smith's eyes on me. Lally's not anywhere near tall enough to shield me from his glare, or from the security team that I expect to rush in at any time and drag me away.

I take a sip of the cool drink, and then another. "It's delicious. Thank you."

She turns to Smith. "I like this girl. She has good taste—in tea. Apparently not in men."

"Lally, this is between me and Kate," he says, still glowering at me.

"Then don't be bringin' it into my kitchen. Go tell Gabby I need her here. And don't be in a hurry to come back, because we're going to be talkin' about things that don't concern you."

"Like what?" he says with much more impertinence than is wise.

She rests both hands on her ample hips and raises her brow. "Like monthly visitors and sanitary products, and whether slips will ever make a comeback or if they're truly a thing of the past. Go have a drink with the boys. It'll settle your nerves."

"You're all damn crazy," he says, waving a hand in the air and stalking out.

"I'm Delilah." A buttermilk blonde with clear blue eyes, and a more pronounced southern accent than anyone I've met so far, approaches me. "I'm part of Gabby's let's-see-how-uncomfortable-we-can-make-the-guys plan, too. She means well."

"I'm Kate, but I guess you've figured that out." I take another sip of tea and place the glass on the counter. Coming here was just plain stupid. There's no other way to describe it. "I should probably go. I'm ruining Smith's birthday celebration." It's the last thing I want.

"You have to stay. Even with Lally, who accounts for half a dozen women, we're still outnumbered."

"I hope you're not referring to my waistline, Miss Delilah," Lally calls from near the sink.

"Of course not. I'm talkin' about your feistiness."

"Here," she says handing me a red-tinged margarita. "Taste it and let me know if it's missin' anything."

I look at the drink longingly. A little alcohol could go a long way right now, but I don't think getting drunk is a great idea. I'm clearly not among friends. I take a small drink from the unsalted half of the rim. "It's not missing a thing. What makes it red?"

"Wine. It turns it a pretty color and cuts some of the sweetness so you can drink more of them."

I take another sip. "How long have you and Smith been friendly?" she asks, while I try not to choke on the drink.

"We met when he tried to chase me out of town about a month ago."

Delilah's shoulders shake gently, but her lips are pressed tight, so she doesn't laugh out loud. "That's so romantic," she gushes, playfully. "A story to tell your grandchildren."

"Behave yourself," Lally calls from the stove. Her hearing is clearly as sharp as her wit.

"What fun would that be?" Delilah sips her drink. "*Mmm*. This is good. You know, Kate, I work for Smith, but it's more than that. He's like the big brother I never had." She pauses, dropping an ice cube into her glass. "Don't toy with him carelessly," she warns, "otherwise you'll have to deal with me."

With a ghost of a smile, Delilah raises her glass. "Sláinte," she says, in an Irish toast to my good health.

24

SMITH

By the time dinner is served on the piazza, I've had my fill of drinks with the boys. Although since Kate arrived, nothing more than *take it up with your wife,* and *I fully intend on it* has passed between JD and me.

Kate seems more at ease now than she did in the kitchen. Of course, anyone could relax with Delilah at their side fending off trouble. Kate's smiling at Chase, JD's youngest brother, like she's knocked back a couple drinks herself. Chase's interests are limited to hacking, bad music, and the gym. He isn't that amusing, although tonight he's uncharacteristically animated.

The guys who work for me have been paying Kate plenty of attention, too. Even the ones who know she's a target. *Bastards.*

They're all here because Gabby invited them. I didn't know JD's mother. She was murdered long before we met. But everyone agrees she had a heart of gold, and there was no *them* and *us* in her home. Everyone who worked for the Wilders was family. Gabby has taken up her example.

Gray hasn't said a single word to Kate, but he hasn't come to me bellyaching about her, either. That's a surprise. Might be because he's too busy eye-fucking Delilah, or maybe he's enjoying her eye-fucking him. It's quite a group assembled here.

Kate tucks some hair behind an ear. It's shiny and sleek tonight, without a single one of those waves my fingers itch to run through.

I need to talk to her and make things right. I *want* to talk to her. I *want* to make things right. My behavior in the kitchen left a lot to be desired. If she was mad the other day, I'm sure she's livid now, although the booze might have softened her. She won't make a scene. The worst that happens is she tells me to go fuck myself. I'm a big boy, and she won't be the first woman to say it.

I catch her eye with a discrete wink as I approach the small circle. "Hey."

She flashes me an apprehensive smile before turning her attention back to Chase. After about thirty seconds of listening to him pretend he likes women, I take hold of her elbow and drag her away from his inane flirting. "Come sit with me."

She gazes into my face warily.

"It's my birthday—I want to have you all to myself for a few minutes." That does little to ease her mind. She probably thinks I want to get her alone to dress her down.

"I'm sorry—I spoiled your evening," she says softly.

My stomach twists into a guilty knot. "You did not spoil my evening. Let's sit here." I stop at the wicker swing. It's at the edge of the party, where we can still be a part of it, but far enough away to talk privately.

"I mean it," she says. "I-I don't know what I was thinking coming here. I'm so sorry."

I squeeze her fingers. My parents raised their daughters to be unapologetic. Or at least not to apologize any more than their son. Kate apologizes for everything, like her very existence is a gross offense. Her family didn't do right by her. I don't know the details. Don't need to. There's no other explanation for a woman like her, smart, beautiful, with a good heart, to *always* step up and take responsibility for things that are not her doing.

"I'm happy you came," I tell her. It's the truth. Now that I've gotten past the initial shock, I am happy she's here. "And I'm the one who should be apologizing. My behavior in the kitchen—that was just plain bad." I gaze into her eyes. They're less emerald and more bottle green today, and the deep copper specks in the center are missing. "I was surprised to see you."

"Shocked, you mean."

I chuckle. "Pretty much. I wasn't sure I was ready to introduce you to this motley crew."

"Well, you weren't quite as *surprised* as JD."

"I'm sure." I shake my head. "Gabby probably should have told him beforehand. But she handles him better than anyone."

Kate smooths the wrinkles from her skirt, coaxing the fabric closer to her knees, so less leg is showing. I resist reaching over and hiking the material back up again.

"JD is a good guy," I tell her, "but often misguided. He has his own code he lives by. Gabby brings out his better angels. He was a miserable bastard without her."

"I'm glad I missed that."

It's quiet between us. Awkward, to be honest, like we're teenagers grappling with where to begin. It's not us—we've gotten comfortable with each other—it's the environment. The people, not the place. I'm not accustomed to feeling this way, and I hate it.

"I brought you a gift," she says finally, after a few more self-conscious minutes. "Is there a time set aside to open presents later, or is it okay to give it to you now?"

"Hell, no. This isn't a baby shower." I tug on her hair. *Mistake. Mistake. Mistake.* My brain blasts the warning, as a shiver runs through Kate. But it's too late. We both recognize it.

"I want my present now." It's an attempt to recover, but it

comes out sounding like the gift is her, and I'm demanding she spread her legs so I can lick her cunt.

"I'll—I'll get it."

I watch her walk away, hypnotized by the swell of her hips and their gentle sway. My gaze skims her legs, all the way down to *those* shoes—laced up her ankle, that made me hard the second I laid eyes on them. I intend on being the one who unlaces each one, slipping them off her feet after I fuck her.

I'm still thinking about the shoes when she returns with that big bag she lugs everywhere. "Open this one first." She hands me a rectangular box, wrapped in matte navy paper with shiny red stripes.

"There's more than one?"

"I guess it's time for presents," Gabby calls from the other side of the porch, before Kate can answer. "JD, get some champagne. I'll get glasses."

"She's going to be the death of me," I mutter, standing up.

"No, stay right there," Gabby says, pointing to the swing. "That's a good spot to do presents. We'll come to you."

JD pours everyone champagne or whiskey, depending on their preference. Good whiskey. Not the brand he reserves for when it's just me and him celebrating, but an excellent choice by anyone's standards. Good enough to know I'm not in the doghouse forever.

"Okay. We're ready," Gabby announces, sitting on the arm of her husband's chair.

I open Kate's gift that I've been holding, trying not to trash the paper completely. When I lift the lid from the box, I laugh at the trio of hot sauces before gazing at her. Not a sound is coming from her, but she's laughing too, eyes dancing, beaming like the sun. "Couldn't get Beau to make you a fresh batch of corn nuts?"

She's still glowing, and I'm sure everyone's waiting for me to let them in on the secret, but I'm not doing that. This belongs to us. "Where's my other present?" I ask without a drop of shame.

She pulls a cellophane bag, secured with a wide silver ribbon, from her tote. "It's Irish soda bread. You can eat it as is, or toast it for breakfast. It was my mother's recipe," she adds, with a gentle pride, her eyes shimmering with a tenderness I've never seen. "I think you'll like it."

I clasp her hand in mine, and lean in for a kiss, lingering too long on her lips—*in front of my friends*. I'm sure she's acutely aware of all the eyes, too. When I pull away, a flush stains her cheeks.

"Show's over," I tease, regarding the rapt audience. "You'll need a paying ticket to see the rest." Kate swats my arm, just as I catch Gabby's sweet smile. But I don't see JD anywhere on the porch. I'm sure he's disappeared inside, pissed off and pouting. I swallow a wad of disappointment.

His concerns about Kate are irrational, and I'm starting to lose patience with him. We've been friends for half our lives. There are brothers who don't share the kind of bond we have. Don't get me wrong, we've squabbled plenty, even raised our fists once or twice, but nothing has ever threatened the friendship. Not like this.

I glance at Kate, her graceful fingers folding the discarded paper, the bread she baked sitting in her lap. She swings her head to say something to Delilah, and her hair gets caught in the breeze, filling my nose with her sexy scent. I feel the pull in my groin.

JD's going to have to suck it up if he wants the friendship, because I have no intention of being the bigger man.

———

I don't know what kind of prodding it took, but JD shows up in time to make a heartfelt birthday toast when the cake is served, and shakes my hand when Kate and I say goodnight at the door. He even wishes her a very pleasant weekend, although that appeared to take more effort.

"I don't suppose you'll be up for a morning run?" he asks drily, glancing sideways at Kate.

"Not sure. But all that cake and booze—I should probably sweat some of it off. Can I text you later?"

"On second thought, why don't we skip tomorrow," he says, gazing at his wife. "It's going to be a *long* night here."

Oh, for fuck's sake. He's going to be all over Gabby's case about Kate. But before I can say anything in her defense, she tips her head, and sends him a smoldering look. A look he returns in spades. *Their plans for a long night don't involve Kate.* Whatever it is passes quietly between them.

"Good night, and thank you," I say, again, hustling Kate out the door. I don't let go of her hand when we get outside, or as we make our way to the driveway. We chit chat about where her car's parked, but that's all I remember. My head is somewhere else.

I can't stop thinking about those last thirty seconds with Gabby and JD. I want that—not what they have, that's their thing. I want my own thing. The kind where words aren't needed to convey volumes. Maybe it's the booze, or maybe I'm all hopped up on sugar, but I want it right now. And I want it with Kate. It's all I can think about.

When we get to the car, I pin her between my aching dick and the hood, my legs caging her like a predator. I have no intention of letting her go—not until I've satisfied us both. But that is not happening here. "Spend the weekend with me," I demand, lowering my mouth to hers, roughly licking my way inside.

"The weekend?" she gasps, when we come up for air.

"A night is just enough to get our feet wet. Not enough to do any real exploring. I want more." I sound like the greedy bastard that I am. But what the hell? It's my birthday, and this is the only present I really want.

She runs her fingers over my scruffy jaw, and it takes everything I have not to pop her on the Jeep, shove her panties aside, and take her right here. "It's inevitable, Kate. I already told you. We both know it's a bad idea, but I'm not sure there's anything I've ever wanted more."

"It sounds so romantic. How can I possibly resist?" She's doing that thing she does—a sassy comment to hide a shaky voice. Like she can fool me.

I take her hand and put a small kiss on each fingertip. "I'm not much for romance. But I promise I'll make it good for you, princess. So good."

"I don't need romance," she says, pulling me closer to her lips. *But you should have it,* I want to shout. *You should insist on it.* But I don't say any of it, because I'm a selfish sonofabitch, and all I can think about is her wet pussy sliding onto my fat cock.

25

SMITH

I leave Kate's car keys with Josh who's at the guard house. "The car is parked near the garage at the main house. Drive it to Kate McKenna's place at the end of your shift. I'll let you know in a minute where to leave the keys."

Kate watches us out the Jeep window. I don't want to leave her alone for too long creating a laundry list of reasons why she shouldn't spend the weekend with me. I'm not prepared for her to change her mind, so I don't waste any time making the call.

"Good evening, The Blackberry Inn."

"This is Smith Sinclair calling from Sweetgrass." I don't normally use my connections to the Wilders, but this isn't the kind of place you wander in off the street at midnight with a woman and expect a room. "I'd like to book a room for the weekend."

"This weekend?"

"Yes."

"We have a small suite available on the top floor, and a more modest, but well-appointed room a floor below."

"The suite, please. A young woman will be joining me,

without luggage. Can you arrange to have some toiletries sent to the room?"

"Of course. I'll have a basket of incidentals sent to the room within the hour. If it's missing anything, just call down to the desk and I'll take care of it."

After ending the call, I turn to Josh. "Leave the keys with the front desk at the Blackberry Inn under my name. And wipe the smirk off your face or you'll be looking for another job before the sun rises." *Eavesdropping bastard.*

That was the easy part. Now to deal with the woman who is wringing her hands in the passenger seat. I climb into the Jeep, beside a fidgeting Kate. "Josh is going to drive your car home and he'll leave the keys at the front desk."

"What front desk? There's no—"

"At the Blackberry Inn."

"Please explain." There's a twinge of *don't fuck with me* in her voice. That's a whole lot better than anxiety. At least I'm better at dealing with it.

"I made a reservation at the Blackberry Inn."

"For the weekend?"

I nod. "For the weekend." She looks out the window, and the uneasiness is palpable. I snatch her hand off her lap and bring it to my mouth. "It's a nice place. You'll like it."

"I've never stayed there, but I've walked through the lobby. It's beautiful." Her head snaps toward me. "I don't have anything with me. Not a toothbrush or a change of clothes. They'll know we're there for—sex. Like you picked me up at a bar, or I'm a hooker."

"Sex is their business. Everyone has sex in hotels. Do you really think the staff gives a damn about us? Besides, I did pick you up." I squeeze her hand to reassure her I'm teasing. It's ice cold, even on this warm evening. She's nervous. After that comment about the hotel staff, it's clear she hasn't spent a lot of time with men in hotels. But I already knew that—I'm not exactly sure how much time she's spent with men, period.

"They have toothbrushes," I add when it's too quiet again. "And you won't be needing clothes for anything I have planned." I can almost hear her heart hammering. Thankfully the trip downtown is quick.

When we get to the inn, I toss the valet my keys, and pull out a gym bag from the back of the Jeep. There's a change of clothes in the bag, and more importantly, condoms and lube. I check in while Kate uses the ladies' room.

When she comes back into the lobby, she's still wearing that timid smile, but I have a remedy for jitters. As soon as the elevator doors shut, I corner her in the small space and slide my hands into her hair, kissing her breathless, my body teasing hers, or maybe hers teasing mine. There's been nothing but foreplay since I met her. Too damn much foreplay. I'm ten seconds away from taking her against the wall in this tiny box.

The elevator pings, and we make it down the hall and into the room without my hands, once, leaving her body.

The suite is actually one expansive room with floor-to-ceiling windows overlooking the city. On one end there's an alcove with some furniture and a fireplace, on the other, a king-size bed with the covers turned down for the night. I toss the room key onto a small table near the bed and put my bag on the floor.

Kate examines the room from the sitting area, holding the back of a small sofa like she needs it for support. She seems lost again, but before I can deal with it, the bell rings. Her eyes dart suspiciously from the door to mine. "It's probably just the things I asked them to bring up," I assure her, opening the door.

"Good evening." The bellman wheels in a cart and takes a basket of toiletries into the bathroom. Then he sets out a bottle of Port and tea service with delicate cookies on a round table near the window. Kate and I don't say a word to each other while he's in the room. I half expect her to run out the door any second.

"Is there anything else you need?" the bellman asks.

"Kate?"

"No, thank you. This is lovely," she says, smiling. It's one of those fake smiles she paints on when she's anxious. I hand him some bills and he leaves quietly.

As soon as the door clicks, I sit on the edge of the bed. The sooner I give her something to do, the sooner she'll relax.

"Take off your clothes, Kate," I tell her, toeing off my shoes. "But leave on those sexy-as-fuck sandals."

She hugs her body tightly. "We've already played that game."

"Last time you played under duress. This time I want you to take them off willingly."

"And this time, you're going to take your clothes off?" she asks so softly, I can barely make out the words.

"Count on it."

She's motionless, feet glued to the floor, with her arms still wound around her body. "I'm waiting," I say, in a gruff impatient voice. It's meant to let her know that she doesn't need to worry about anything, that I'm in charge. But she doesn't understand that signal.

She lifts her chin. Her green eyes flaring in the dim light as she shimmies out of the little dress that's been swishing around her thighs all night. I dig my fingers into the mattress to keep me back. No smiley face underpants today. She's wearing a thong and a lace bra that are *very* grown-up. My eyes flit between the tiny scraps of purple fabric and her creamy skin. *"Kate."* I can't force myself to stay seated.

With a few long strides, I'm behind her, my hands on her upper arms. "Let me help you," I murmur above her ear, pushing her hair aside, to unclasp the delicate bra. I slip it off her shoulders and toss it on her dress, adding my shirt to the growing pile.

"Turn around. Let me see you." My voice is rough and low, emerging from the ache in my chest. She's beautiful, and I want her. Truth is, I've wanted her for a long time.

She swivels slowly. Her apprehension fills the space around us, making the air heavy.

I give myself a moment to enjoy her gorgeous tits, the erect pink nipples daring me to touch. The pull in my groin is relentless. My dick is weeping. I need to get better control, otherwise, this isn't going to be what I want for her—for either of us.

I maneuver us toward the window, her ass against my cock, with only my pants between us.

"The view is breathtaking." Her voice is little more than a squeak.

My hand splays flat on her stomach, cradling her against my aching cock. My free arm supports her breasts. "Not as breathtaking as you."

I love that she's tall. That I can lower my mouth and reach her neck easily. I'm buying time. Trying to get my dick to calm the fuck down. I can't ask her to suck me off, to take off the edge. At least I won't—not yet. She seems too inexperienced, and there's something that still bothers me—all that talk about sharing women with friends. Something about it didn't add up, and it's been on my mind ever since.

"Any trauma, Kate?" I ask as gently as I can.

"Trauma?"

"Yes. Has anyone ever hurt you? Forced you to do something—sexually—you didn't want to do?"

She shakes her head. "No."

"Not very convincing, Mary Katherine."

She rocks her hips all over my dick, and I swat the side of her ass. She jumps. "Stay still and let me focus." I draw a breath. "Trauma?"

"No trauma. How many ways would you like me to say it?"

Maybe not, but there's something. I know it.

Let's approach this from a different angle. "Anything off the table?"

"I'm sorry?"

"Is there anything that you absolutely don't like in bed, or don't want to do? Some people call those things hard limits."

"Oral sex." *You have got to be kidding.*

I let my hand wander over her belly with light strokes. "Giving or receiving?"

She lifts her shoulders with a slow, uncertain motion. "Receiving."

That's an easy fix. "Anything else?"

I feel her stiffen. "Anal—anal sex."

I pause for a few seconds, wondering if she's had a bad experience, or no experience. Not everyone is into it or has tried it. It's not that unusual. "What about anal play?" She shakes her head emphatically. "That's a lot of good stuff you've taken off the table. Is there anything else?"

"No." She says the word so softly I strain to hear it.

"Let me get this straight. You don't like to have your pussy licked, but you're okay with being tied to that bed and flogged or caned? And you don't mind me dripping hot wax on your breasts?"

Her head jerks, and she stares up at me with wide eyes. She's pale, and even with a throbbing dick, I'm beginning to have misgivings about this. In truth, if I met her at a bar, she's not someone I would ever take home. Not because she isn't attractive —she is—in every way that matters to me. But I prefer to play with seasoned women who understand the game. I'm not someone who likes to spend a lot of time convincing a reticent woman she should let me fuck her. But somehow—I got caught up in her, and—

"You—you do that? Beat women and pour hot wax on them?" she gasps.

I cringe as she says *beat women*. "I don't touch a woman without consent. And we don't have to do anything like that. Not tonight—not ever, if you don't want to. But sex is a whole lot more fun for everybody involved if we understand each other's preferences. You've never had this discussion before, have you?"

"No." Her answer wedges itself under my skin. I knew what she was going to say, but it still pisses me off.

"So you've only fucked mind readers?" It's not really a question, just me being an irascible asshole, and she doesn't say anything. "If you don't talk openly and honestly with a partner, you can end up being handled with all the finesse of someone stuffing a Thanksgiving turkey, or worse. Is that what you want?"

She laughs. It has a nervous, almost delirious edge. "I don't think I'll ever look at a turkey the same way again. Thank you very much."

Oh, no, Kate. You don't get to blow me off tonight by being a wiseass. That's not how this is going to work. "I want us to put *everything* on the table—I want you to give it all a try, just a small taste—even the things you think you don't like, because you might enjoy them with me."

She draws a long breath but doesn't release it.

"Breathe, Kate." I watch her take two shaky breaths, before continuing.

"I'll stop whenever you want. You just say the word and it's over." I kiss the top of her head. "Let's explore. Let me test your boundaries, just a little." I pause for a moment to allow what I'm asking to set in. "We'll go slow. Even if you feel afraid, because of something I say or do, or because of whatever games you play inside your head—you never have to be afraid with me. You have the power to stop it, at any time. That's the deal I'll make with you."

"I thought you didn't deal? That dealing was only for desperate people."

I take her hand and place it on my cock. "Feel the throb? That's what desperate feels like." I move her hand away because I've finally gotten some control, and I don't want it to evaporate into thin air. Or in this case, thick, chewy air. "It's a good deal. You should take it."

"Are you going to make me afraid tonight?" If I read the words, they would seem awful, but that's not how they sound when she asks the question. She's not frightened—anxious about the unknown, but not frightened. There's a difference.

"Not tonight." I watch her reflection in the window. Her mind is churning. This is new, and she's nervous, but she's going to take the deal, because she's curious, and although she's not ready to admit it, she wants to explore too. At least some part of her does. "We'll spend the weekend working up to it, if that's what you want."

She places her arms over mine and tips back her head against my shoulder. As much as I'd love to be inside her body, what I'd like most right now is to be inside her restless mind. It doesn't ever seem to quiet. I can fix that, too.

"Let's move closer to the window," I say, nudging her forward. "Put your hands flat on the glass. That's it. Press your breasts there too. Lightly." She shivers when her nipples make contact with the pane, and my dick throbs hard. "Cold, isn't it?" She nods. "But it feels good, doesn't it? Like the nerve endings all over your gorgeous little body are singing."

She nods, again. "Can anyone see us from outside?"

"Not enough light in here." I feel her relax against me. "But if you take the deal, before we leave here on Sunday, I'm going to fuck you against this window. Lights on, so that everyone can see you from the street. And you're not going to care. You're not even going to care if the pane is strong enough to hold, as I pound you against it. You're not going to think about any of it. All that will be inside that pretty little head is coming around my cock. That's all either of us is going to care about."

The pulse in her neck is thrumming, and I'm teetering at the edge of restraint.

"Okay," she whispers.

"Okay what, princess?"

"I'll take the deal."

Without another word, I lift her off the floor and carry her to the bed. *Trust. That's what the deal is really about. She gave you her trust. Don't abuse it.*

I sit her on the edge of the mattress, where I can have better access to everything, and slide my hand into her thong, tracing the tight little seam with my thumb, while gorging on her soft mouth. She tips her head back and moans, fisting the quilt like it will save her. "Open your legs for me, Kate. Let me make you feel good."

Her legs ease apart, but nowhere near enough to give me what I need. From my haunches, I tear the skimpy little fabric that's keeping me from her cunt. When my mouth is inches away from the sweetness, when her musky scent has taken over my brain, she whispers, "Can we start with something else? How about if I—taste you?"

She asks so timidly, so sweetly, and I want nothing more than to feed her my cock. Let it rest between her plump lips, while her tongue laps at the taut skin. But there's no fucking way I'm doing that. She's uncomfortable with my mouth on her pussy, but she's fine with hers on my cock? I'm sorry, but that is *not* okay.

"No. We made a deal," I say plainly, before my better angels intervene. "But we can stop, if that's what you want. We can get dressed, crawl into bed and go to sleep, or I can take you home, if you prefer."

I want her bad, but I'm almost at the point where I don't care whether we do this or not. I've been hard for so long that I need the release, but my hand will do, if necessary. It's been forever since I've been with a woman who is this timid, this uncertain, and I'm not interested in freaking her out any more than she is already. *This is why I don't play with rookies.* I tilt her chin, and peer into those frightened eyes. "Should we stop?"

She shakes her head vigorously—doesn't hesitate for an instant.

There's a tug inside me I don't understand. Something that goes beyond the physical release I'm chasing. "I need to hear the words, Kate."

She gazes at me with an innocence—an openness—a trust, that steals my breath. "I don't want to stop."

This time I move more slowly, beginning with her mouth, sliding my lips over her throat, murmuring into her skin, before sucking each hard nipple between my teeth until she writhes under me. I graze slowly, taking my time, my fingers following a patient path to her pussy.

When I get there, I spread her wide, my palms holding her open against the mattress. She presses her thighs into my hands, trying to clamp her legs together as I lick her. But she doesn't protest, and the little sounds emerging from her lips are the gasps and sighs of pleasure. The push and pull makes my cock swell, and the ache to plow into her is clawing. I'm having a lot of trouble fighting it back.

"You taste so sweet, princess, but you need more. I'm going to slide my fingers inside you. Remember how much you liked that in the alley?" She's so wet my fingers slip in without much resistance.

She's also squirmy as hell. "If you don't keep your legs spread, I'm going to tie them open. I need my hands." I find the pleated rosebud between her cheeks, teasing it with my tongue.

"No!" she gasps. But my tongue is already licking a path to her clit. I draw the sweet nub into my mouth, scraping the swollen flesh with my teeth. Her movements are jerky, and I feel her body tense as her slick walls choke my fingers. "Take it, Kate. Let go."

I coax her with my tongue, sucking on the hard little bead until she screams my name. Her hand flies to her mouth to muffle the pleasure and I want to push it away. I want to hear every sound she makes, but I'm a man possessed, and all I can do is slide the condom onto my weeping cock.

I let my mouth crash into hers in a brief attack, before I flip her over, and hoist her hips into the air, gripping them so tight I know there will be bruises. But I don't care. I plunge into her. There's no gentleness. No letting her get used to me. Nothing. I just sink into her hot pussy. It's only when I hear my balls slap against her tender skin, that I force myself to take a breath. "You okay?" I ask, slowing, but never stopping the assault.

"Yes," she groans, reaching behind to grasp my thighs. I lean over her and sink my teeth into the back of her neck. "Touch yourself, Kate. Play with your clit. Rub it real good, just the way you like." She hesitates, but I don't want to let go of her hips. I want them in my hands while I fuck her. "Now, Kate." I slap her ass. "Don't make me wait."

The smell of sex whirls around us, musky and dirty, and I fill my lungs with it until my chest is about to explode. Her quick fingers brush against my cock while she circles her clit. I want to watch her play with that dripping pussy. I want to watch her rub it raw. I grip her hips tighter. "You're such a good princess. I'm going to fuck you nice and hard until you come all over my cock."

Her breathing is labored, as she grinds against her hand.

"Kate. I don't have much control left. I need you to take it." Her hand works overtime. Her moans are strangled pleas. She's sandwiched between me and her hand, when her body tenses. She buries her face in the mattress as she bucks, finding her release around my cock.

I press my mouth to her shoulders, fucking through her orgasm with mine in reach. My spine prickles with the familiar tingle before my sight disappears, before there's nothing but a black hole melting into the fuzzy outer corners of my vision. I erupt inside her with a roar that bounces off every surface in the room.

26

KATE

Smith arranged for late check-out and we're laying on the sofa watching the basketball game. He's on his back and I'm nestled between his legs, on my back, too, wearing just a thin T-shirt he had in his gym bag. Eat, sleep, watch a little TV, and have sex, rinse and repeat. It's the best kind of lazy Sunday.

I scroll through my messages until I come to the one from Father Jesse, and as I read, guilt claws at my happiness, threatening to destroy a wonderful weekend. *I hope you're okay,* he wrote. *Missed you at Mass.*

He expected me at Mass. Until Friday night, I expected to be there too. Instead, I spent the weekend engaged in debauchery. *So much debauchery.* Where boundaries were tested, and the goalpost moved repeatedly, although not too far each time. I even ate a piece of sausage, which I still don't really care for, even when it's eaten from Smith's deft fingers. But the sex? The sex was—there really are no words. Even a woman who makes her living with words can't come up with the ones to do it justice.

"Do you know what surprises me?" Smith asks during a commercial.

"What?"

"Even though you were tentative about sex, you're comfortable naked."

Were tentative. It makes me smile and the guilt all about Father Jesse and missing Mass disappears. "That's what you're thinking about?"

He pinches my thigh and I squeal. "Among other things."

"I was on the dive team up until my sophomore year in college. Spent a lot of time in a bathing suit. It made me comfortable with my body. It's not perfect by any means, but it works the way I need it to and it's strong." It's something I like about myself—that I'm not always at war with my body, starving it, and punishing it with excessive exercise.

He flips me over, so I'm facing him. "Your body is perfect. And it's damned sexy that you aren't embarrassed to take off your clothes or walk from the bed to the bathroom naked. It's a huge turn on." His hands cup my ass gently.

"Is there anything that doesn't turn you on?"

He closes one eye, pretending to think hard. "I'm not big into golden showers." I give him an exaggerated eye roll. "Oh, and you are, miss don't-lick-my-pussy? Although I doubt you'll ever say that again."

"Humility is food for the soul. You should try it sometime." I whack his chest. It doesn't make a ripple, but that doesn't stop him from grabbing my wrists and pinning them against the small of my back.

"What was your favorite event?"

"The high dive."

"Really?" He says it with great reverence, and a hint of surprise. I smile proudly. It's the most common reaction from anyone who has ever seen the height of a high diving board up close and gauged its distance from the surface of the water.

"Takes a lot of courage to jump from that height into a dark pit."

"I'm a person of faith. I don't take unnecessary risks, but I'm not afraid to die."

He lets go of my wrists and gathers my hair in his hands, gently tugging it off my face. He has that alert gaze. The one he wears during careful studies, while he takes note of small tells, and collects bits of information to sort through at his leisure. I change the subject before we get into some intense conversation about faith and death that is heavier than anywhere I want to go right now. "You think I'm tentative about sex?"

One corner of his mouth curls, and his probing look softens. "You're passionate—and you've got fire in your blood. You have some hang-ups that get in the way at the beginning. Once you're past it, you're sexy as fuck." He kisses me, his lips smooth and tender against mine. "And highly responsive. I think you have all the makings of a dirty girl in you."

I don't know about a dirty girl, but I could easily become addicted to sex with this man. "*Hmm.*" I sigh contentedly, laying my head on his chest, while he runs his fingers through my hair, playing with the wavy strands.

"Tell me about it," he says softly.

"I don't understand what you're asking."

"Sure you do." I don't say anything. "Tell me why you're so anxious about things that feel good to you. Did you have a bad experience?"

A small panic worms its way into my chest. I know what's coming. He's going to nudge and nudge, and I'm going to tell him. And then—I don't know what happens.

"Does it have anything to do with what you asked me about sharing women with friends? Because my mind keeps going back to that."

He strokes my back with his fingertips. "Think about the last thirty-six hours, Kate. How much you trusted me. I don't think I took advantage of your trust, did I?"

I shake my head. "No." I take a breath. "I-I-I don't know where to begin."

He wraps his arms tighter. The warmth against my skin is welcome, but it's not enough to thaw the ice deep inside. "Start where you feel comfortable. For most people that's the beginning. But you start wherever you want." He kisses my head. "Take as long as you need. I've got you."

I've got you. I so want to believe it. And right now, I allow myself that indulgence—even though Father Tierney's words are tattooed on my brain in neon: *don't mistake lust for love*. I'm not a fool to think this is love, but I believe it's something more than simple lust. *I do.* And that belief nudges the well-protected pain from the dark corners of my soul, luring it out into the open where it hangs vulnerably.

"When I was a teenager," I start at the beginning, "I had a boyfriend who was older. We were together for about six months. I was totally inexperienced, and he wasn't. We—experimented. I was young and not ready for most of it. I don't mean kink or anything."

The shelter of Smith's body, and the gentle touch of his strong hands make it easy to keep talking. "But I traded—I was basically like a prostitute—trading sex, not for money, but for affection, maybe for some misguided idea of love. I'll never know for sure. But I wanted it so bad at the time, I did things that didn't feel good or seem right to me."

"How old were you?" His voice is low and hoarse.

"Fifteen," I say calmly, hoping he won't judge me harshly like the others.

"How old was he?" Smith stiffens under me, even before I say the word.

"Twenty."

His heart is hammering, and as much as I want to, I don't dare turn my head to look at his face. I'm not at all sure what I'll find there.

"Twenty," he repeats in a carefully modulated voice. "How did you meet?"

"A party. I went with friends. It wasn't his fault—not initially. I was tall and looked older. I let him believe I was older." *Although he never asked my age.*

"It was totally his fault—all of it," Smith barks. "What's his name?"

"Ryan. What difference does it make?"

"Ryan what?" I flinch at the demand.

"He said it was Cleary. But it wasn't."

"I want the rest, Kate. The part you're not telling me because it embarrasses you. The only person who should be ashamed is the man who touched a little girl." Smith's voice has a cutting edge—all pretense of control has slipped away.

His response makes me uneasy. I don't know what to make of it and I get defensive.

"I wasn't a little girl. I own some of the responsibility too." At least that's what everyone said when it happened—everyone but Fiona. My brother Tommy thought I owned all of it for sneaking out and lying, and for being a stupid whore. That's what he called me when he picked me up from the party with his girlfriend Tessa in the car. Tessa told her sisters, and by Monday everyone at school knew I had been found half undressed, in a room at the frat house with four boys. I squeeze my eyes tight, but it's not enough to stop the memories from flooding me.

"Kate," he prods, stroking my skin with his fingertips. "I need to hear the rest."

I run the pad of a finger over Smith's ribs, counting each one as the awful words tumble out. "One night, there was a party at the frat house and I drank some punch—usually I only had a beer, but Ryan urged me to try it that night, and I wanted to please him. After a couple glasses, I went upstairs with Ryan. That wasn't unusual. We always went up to his room during the parties. But this time, a few of his friends came in. That had never happened."

"I need a minute," Smith chokes out, lifting me off of him. He opens the balcony door but doesn't go outside. Instead, he rests his hand on the doorframe near his head, staring out over the city.

This is where it ends. Like it did the last time I cared about a man. The pain in my chest is excruciating. I should have never told him.

After a few minutes that seem to go on for hours, I get up to find my clothes. "Where you going?" he asks, from the balcony door.

"I-I think it's best if I leave."

He tilts his head to the side. "Best for who?"

Best for both of us, but mostly for me.

When I don't say anything, he strides over and leads me back to the sofa. "I am so pissed off right now—I want to hunt the bastard down and twist his neck until he can't breathe—not just him, all of them." He kneels beside me, an angry vein throbbing in his neck. "Did they rape you?"

His voice is calm, but his eyes are aflame with dangerous sparks flickering wildly. And I know before this discussion is over, I will be burned. But it's impossible to change course now. The embers have caught, and there's no way out.

I shake my head. "They kissed me and groped my breasts. Pulled off my shirt. Then the police came and broke up the party."

"Were they arrested?" I hear hope in his voice, but it's not how that night ended.

"No. The officers who responded called my brother Tommy—they wanted to avoid a scandal. My father had just been named a captain on the police force. It was a huge deal. Tommy was so mad." I'll never forget his face—or his words. "He called me a whore, and took me to St. Claire's—to the rectory—and woke up Father Tierney. He didn't know what else to do."

"He called you a whore?"

I hadn't meant to say that out loud. I'm not even sure I did. I glance at Smith. His eyes are black, and his snarl mean. I must have.

"Your brother managed those bastards by blaming you?"

"They didn't force me to do anything. They wanted oral sex and I would have given it to them."

"You were an intoxicated fifteen-year-old and those bastards were miserable excuses for grown men. Despite what your religion teaches, there are no rewards for martyrs. Stop blaming yourself."

He sits on the edge of the sofa beside me, his head in his hands. "I can't believe ... I can't—why didn't you tell me this before we had sex? I specifically asked you about trauma, Kate. You lied to me. Why did you let me talk to you the way I did, and push you—I knew you were inexperienced. I fucking knew something was amiss. But I didn't listen to my gut." He strikes the coffee table with his fist and it splits in two, dumping the decorative art books and my water on the floor.

I pick up the water, gripping the bottle in both shaking hands, gawking at the table in disbelief. It was almost the perfect weekend. How can it end like this? But it will, because I don't know how to fix it. My internal monologue goes on and on, moving faster and faster, but never getting anywhere.

I'm not sure how much time passes before he speaks. "I could have made it better—easier—on you. Cleaned my act up a little." He picks up a long shard of wood, twirling it between his fingers.

"You're going to get a splinter."

"A splinter? That's the least of my fucking worries."

"That's exactly why I didn't tell you."

He turns his head to look at me, his brow furrowed deeply.

"When I was in college, I had a boyfriend—my first boyfriend after... We were friends before things got more serious. I really liked him. We were working up to sex when I told him about what happened in the frat house." *He recoiled. Just like you did.* "It was a lot for him to handle—too much. He tried, but he could never get past the fact that if the police hadn't come, I would have given them all blow jobs and probably anything else they wanted."

Smith fills his cheeks with air and blows it out. The man who hasn't been able to keep his hands off me all weekend hasn't touched me since we sat down.

"Have a little faith in me. I'm not a stupid college boy."

"No. But you would have treated me like a girl with special needs. Like I was emotionally fragile and you needed to be careful so I wouldn't shatter. What kind of experience would that have made? I didn't want that. I wanted you to treat me like the other women you've been with. I like you—and I know it's premature, but I wanted us to have a chance."

He flicks his wrist and the long fragment of wood glides through the air like a paper airplane, landing just beyond the ruined table. "If I hadn't pushed, would you have ever told me?"

"I don't know." I shrug. I really don't. "I'd like to say yes, but I don't know. I didn't want the past to soil the future."

He doesn't say anything for a few moments, but his thick dark eyelashes flutter as the realization sets in.

"I've been in some hellish places." He leans back against the sofa, pulling me with him, until my head is resting against his shoulder. The emotion wells up inside my throat. I wasn't sure he'd ever touch me again. "I mean, places that make hell look like a fucking walk in the park. I can get through anything—as long as I know what I'm dealing with. But keeping this kind of thing from me, Kate, isn't going to work. You want me to trust you, but you need to trust me, too."

I tip my head up. "I—"

"I understand why you did it. I know all about not dirtying life with ugly details from the battlefield."

He kisses me gently like I'm made of candy glass. When his

kiss doesn't turn rough and demanding, I can't help but wonder if it ever will again, or if this truly is the beginning of the end.

"Don't pity me, and don't treat me like I'm broken. Anything but that."

He trails his nose along the edge of my jaw. "Broken? I'm just marshalling my energy. We only have this room until five and I believe I promised you a fuck against that window, so hard you wouldn't remember your name."

There's an edge of bravado to his voice that's never been there before. It's the decent, human part of him that's unsure about how to treat me. It makes me want him all the more. Not in a trade for affection—I can get that from him without the sex. I want all this man has to offer. Everything.

I throw my arms around his neck. "Thank you," I murmur into his warm skin, as he pulls me tight against him. "Thank you."

"Let's see if you're still thanking me tomorrow when it hurts to sit. Go stand in front of that window. Give me this," he says, pulling off my shirt. "I want your feet apart and those ripe rosy nipples grazing the glass while you wait for me quietly, like a good little princess."

———

The pounding against the window requires a nap and a long shower that involves Smith shampooing my hair. Having his strong fingers massaging my scalp was almost as good as the sex. When we're done, he gets out of the shower and tosses me a warm towel.

"What's this from?" I ask, taking a break from drying my legs to run a finger along a scar on the right side of his abdomen. It's larger, and although it's healed, it's fresher than the others that are scattered over his body. I've wondered about it since I first saw him with his shirt off.

"Should we order room service before we leave, or do you want to stop for food on the way to your place?" Nice pivot, Sinclair. But not today.

"Up to you. I can wait." I reach out and touch the healed wound. He stiffens under my fingers. "What is this?"

"A scar," he says in an *I'm not answering that question* voice that he hasn't used with me since we met.

"I can see that. It doesn't look as old as some of the others. What happened?" He doesn't say a word. "I realize you can't give me details, but you can tell me something about what happened."

He finishes drying himself with his back turned toward me. "Not your business."

I'm sorry? He can't possibly think— "You think I'm going to write a story about how you got your scar?"

"No. That's not what I think. But how I got the scar doesn't involve you." He tosses the towel over the tub ledge and stalks out of the bathroom. *Oh no, you don't.*

I follow him into the living area, where he's pulling on his pants.

"I just poured out my soul. You expected it because you hadn't betrayed my trust. I'm quite certain I haven't betrayed yours, either. And now I expect you to tell me about the scar. Not the classified part, but everything else, because from the way you're acting, it's a big deal."

There's not one peep from him while he buttons his shirt, like it's delicate neurosurgery that requires his full attention. "Get dressed," he says finally. "I'm going down to the front desk to explain the broken table. Meet me in the lobby when you're ready."

Like hell. "If you leave this room without talking to me about the injury, you don't need to bother waiting downstairs. I'll find my own way home." He stops short, just inside the door. "While I understand that fair does not always mean equal, I believe relationships, of all sorts, thrive on give and take. I won't have another man in my life whose behavior I have to justify to myself to keep my heart from breaking. You go, we're done."

He hasn't faced me, but he's still here.

"It happened three years ago. My niece needed a liver transplant. Her mother was a good match, but had she donated, she would have been too weak to take care of a sick child who needed her—but my sister would have pushed herself to do it anyway." Smith takes a breath, and blows it out with a long sigh.

"I was also a good match," he continues, as though this is the last discussion on earth he wants to be having. "I donated part of my right lobe. A healthy liver regenerates within a short time. It wasn't a big deal." He takes a step closer to the door while I do the math in my head.

"That's why you left the military."

"I didn't have to leave. They would have found something for me, but I was out of field operations forever—at least out of the kind of operations I'd been trained to do."

My body is swamped with a dizzying array of emotion. I'm overwhelmed that he would give that precious gift. Overwhelmed that a little girl is alive because of his selflessness. And overwhelmed by the realization that she will carry that burden one day. It all hits very close to home. "You gave up a career you loved to give your niece life," I say, the tears trickling down my cheeks.

Smith spins toward me. "It's not at all like that, Kate," he spits out. "Don't make me out to be some kind of fucking hero. I didn't storm the beaches at Normandy. I wanted out of the Army. It was a convenient excuse. Now if you're done probing my subconscious, I'll meet you downstairs."

I'm left in my towel, tears still trickling as the door clicks behind him. There's clearly more to this story, but what he shared will do for now. The fact that he told me about it at all gives me hope for us.

27

KATE

*I*t's been two weeks since Smith's birthday, and we've spent all our free time together, most of it naked. But tonight, we have a date before naked, and I need to finish getting ready or I'll be late.

Just as I finish brushing a final coat of mascara onto my lashes, there's a knock at the front door. *Hmm.* I'm supposed to meet Smith at the bar, but maybe his meeting finished early and he decided to swing by to get me.

I peek through the window. It's Father Jesse. My conscience twinges as soon as I see his face. After I missed church *again* last Sunday, I emailed him some samples of the bulletin I had planned on taking with me so he could make a final decision, but I haven't heard back.

I open the door, glancing at what appears to be some kind of *pet carrier*? "Hello," I say, trying not to stare at the thing in his hand.

"I'm sorry to drop in like this. I realized halfway here I should have called."

"Please don't apologize. It's fine. Come in," I assure him,

trying to wrack my brain about whether there's anything lying around that a priest shouldn't see.

"I brought you a gift. It's another one of those regifts that I hope you'll accept." He holds up the carrier. "Someone left this little guy at St. Maggie's last night. Hoping that we would take care of him, I suppose. But I can't keep a pet, and Virginia is terribly allergic. I don't want to have to call animal control." I peer into his sober face. I don't want that either. "Although frankly," he continues, "as soon as I laid eyes on this sweet cat, I thought of you, and how as a child you had longed for a pet."

"A cat? For me?" I try to sound less surprised than I feel. Actually, I'm not sure how I feel.

"He came without instructions. Just with some dry food. Like Magdalene herself, so much about this kitty is unknown."

While Father Jesse compares the cat's history to Mary Magdalene's, I rack my brain trying to remember what my lease says about pets. *Pets under twenty pounds are permitted. Yes, that's right.*

"Why don't we put the carrier on the counter? It looks heavy." I peek at the cat through the small grate at one end. He's cowering in the back of the carrier. *Poor baby. You don't need to be afraid. I won't hurt you.* "Does he have a name?"

"I'm sure he does, but I don't know it. Maybe you can come up with something fitting."

"He's so sweet. But he's shivering. I bet he's scared to death. Do you know for sure that he's a he?"

"I had him out for a bit last night. I haven't had much experience with cats, but I know all about the male species."

I smile at the roundabout way he describes the cat's sex. Smith would have gone straight at it and made some sarcastic dick remark. I take another peek at the Tabby with his shiny orange coat that makes him seem like he's meant for me. He looks back at me with a vulnerability that steals my heart without any effort at all.

"Cat's aren't as much work as dogs," Father Jesse explains. "At least that's what I've always heard. And this one isn't a kitten."

I take another peek into the carrier. "Sold," I say cheerfully. "You're right. I've always wanted a pet and this little guy needs someone to love him."

Father Jesse glances around the kitchen. "How's the TV working out?"

"I love it. I've been watching more of it than I should."

"Good." He gives me a lopsided smile. "I hope you love the cat even more. I should go. I have to stop by the hospital and visit a parishioner who was admitted this morning. Will I see you on Sunday?"

"Yes." I lower my eyes, staring at my shoes like a child about to be chided for misbehaving. "I'm sorry about last Sunday." *And the Sunday before that.*

"I'm sure it was important," he says, and my conscience pings while I think about my nipples pressed against the cold glass and Smith's—

"Did you have a chance to look at the sample bulletins I emailed?"

"Kate, I'm not very good at email. I couldn't open the fancy attachment. What is it called?"

"A zip file."

"I realize it's a shameful waste of resources, but could you please bring paper copies on Sunday when you come to Mass? I'm a technological dunce, I'm afraid."

"Of course."

He starts down the stairs, turning to me before he reaches the bottom. "Someone left the cat in my care so that I would find a new home for him. I feel it in my bones. You'll make sure to lavish him with love and attention, won't you?"

"I'll take good care of him. I promise." He nods, and I watch him get into his car before shutting the door.

I traipse back into the kitchen, and peek inside the carrier.

"Okay, kitty-cat," I murmur. "There's something you should know. I've never taken care of a cat, or any pet for that matter. You'll go easy on me, won't you?"

The poor thing is still cowering in the corner, even as I speak gently. I'm not sure whether to open the crate or let him be. But I better figure it out soon. I'm sure there's a ton of information online. I grab my laptop and pull up what seems like a reputable post about bringing home a new cat. Then I call Smith.

"Running late?" he asks above the noisy banter in the background.

"I need to cancel tonight."

"This better be good, because I'm already at the bar," he says coolly.

"I'm the proud owner of a cat," I announce, the smile on my face reflecting a heart bursting with excitement.

"A cat? The kind that meow and claw up everything they can get their little paws on?"

"Yes."

"When did that happen?"

"About thirty minutes ago. I'll admit the timing isn't perfect, but he needs me."

He grunts. "Cats don't need babysitters. They're independent little assholes that are gleeful when you leave so they can destroy your house while you're out."

"Will you stop? I realize he can be left alone, but not tonight. The poor little thing is so nervous he's shaking." *Don't worry kitty, I'm not leaving you alone.*

"Understood," he says, without any sullenness. "Why don't I come over and we can figure it out?"

As difficult as he can be, in some ways Smith is easy and flexible. "I would love that. But would you mind stopping by the pet store first? I need some supplies and I don't want to take him out. Or if you'd rather, I can go and you can stay with him."

"Have you ever had a cat?"

"No. No pets. You?"

"Enough to make Old MacDonald jealous. Where's the cat now?"

"Right here. In a carrier on the kitchen counter."

"First, put the carrier on the floor. If he starts to go crazy, he can knock it off the counter and get hurt. Is there anything laying around in the second bedroom?"

"No. The walk-in closet is packed with storage, but the room itself is empty."

"Isn't there a rug?"

"Yes. An area rug."

"Roll it up and take it out of there. Or leave it in a corner and I'll take it out when I get there. Remove any curtains and pull the shades or window blinds all the way up. Don't let the strings dangle. Put the carrier inside the room with the latch closed. That way he can feel safe while he gets used to the smells in the room. I'll be at your place in less than an hour."

"Are you going to stop by the pet store or should I plan on going?"

"I'll stop. The only pussy I'm babysitting tonight is yours."

Smith shows up fifty minutes later with a cardboard box filled with supplies and a tall carpeted tree limb.

"A scratching post?"

"You're going to be happy you have it. Every guy needs an outlet."

I laugh and wrap my arms around him. I can't get enough of his playful side. "Thank you. I don't know the first thing about cats."

"Where is he?"

"In the room, like you told me. I've been sitting with him, so he won't be alone."

"If you wanted something that gave a shit, you should have gotten a dog." He hands me two shallow bowls. "Wash these, and rinse them good," he instructs. "Fill one with fresh water."

When I get to the bedroom the litter tray is set up on one side and the scratching post on another. Smith is talking to the cat in a gentle voice. "I hope you're a mouser, and not just some freeloader taking up space. And the redhead's mine. Don't get any ideas."

I grin foolishly as I eavesdrop for another minute. The man can be tough and bristly at times, but it's all on the outside. Inside, he's good to the core.

"Here's the water. Where should I put it?"

"Give it to me." He places it on the floor a few feet from the carrier next to a bowl with wet food. "You can move the litter tray and the post anywhere you want after a week or so, but just a few feet at a time, so he gets used to it. Eventually they can be closer to the edge of the room." He opens the carrier door, and motions for me to follow him out of the room.

"Why are you closing the door? We won't be able to see him. What if he's terrified with it closed?"

"He'll be fine. When he's hungry, the smell of the food will draw him out, and he'll start to get used to the space."

"Too bad I don't have a baby gate. Then we could watch him while he adjusts. I don't like not being able to see him."

"He's a cat. He climbs."

Of course, I know this. "Right." Smith must think I'm an idiot—and with good reason.

"What made you decide to get a cat out of the blue?"

"I didn't exactly decide," I say, while Smith washes his hands in the kitchen sink. "It was—a gift."

He glares at me over his shoulder. "A gift? Don't tell me from the priest."

28

KATE

I'm not having this discussion with him. He's already made his feelings about Father Jesse abundantly clear.

"What should we do for dinner?" I ask. "I can make pasta, scrambled eggs, or cereal. That's all I have in the house. I normally grocery shop on Sunday evenings, but I was busy having my boundaries tested last weekend." I smile at him while he dries his hands on one of my yellow dish towels. One day soon, I'm going to have a talk with him about not washing his hands in the kitchen sink, and that yellow dish towels are strictly for drying dishes. The blue ones are for hands.

"The priest brought you a cat?" *Oh, God. He never lets a damn thing slide.*

"Yes," I say with little patience for what he's insinuating. "Have you decided about dinner?"

"Chinese from the place on King that delivers. You don't think it's odd that a priest gives you presents?"

"No. I'll order. What do you like?"

"Anything with meat. For the record, I think it's odd. And if you stopped people in the City Market and asked them about it, they would agree with me. And it wouldn't matter if they were from Des Moines, LA, Boston, or Charleston. They would all be weirded out by a priest bringing a woman gifts like he was fucking Santa Claus." He snatches the phone from my hand.

"What are you doing? I'm in the middle of ordering food."

"Using a lifeline. I'm calling a friend."

He fiddles with the phone.

"It's locked. Now give it back and call your own friends." I hold out my hand.

"Was locked."

"How did you do that?" I demand while the phone is ringing on speaker. "Who are you calling?"

"Hey! I was just thinking about you," Fiona says when she answers. I try to grab the phone, but he holds it out of my reach.

"Really?" Smith drawls. "What were you thinkin', darlin'?" I want to laugh, but I won't give him the satisfaction.

Fiona is quiet for a few seconds. "This is Smith Sinclair, Kate's friend, and don't pretend you don't know who I am. I'm sure you already know how big my watch is."

She snickers, holding back a full laugh. "Is Kate there?"

"Hi, Fi. Do not listen to anything he says."

"We're calling for an unbiased opinion. There's a priest who's been bringing Kate presents. First, he gave her an expensive TV, and then today, he brought her a cat."

"What kind of cat?"

"An orange tabby."

"I want a cat."

Smith throws his head back. "Focus here, Fiona. Don't you think it's strange that a priest brings Kate presents?"

"Not really."

"Not really?" He shakes his head.

"Kate is comfortable with priests and that makes them comfortable with her. She isn't like most people." *Thanks, Fi. Why don't you tell him everything you know about me*? "Her childhood home abuts St. Claire's. She was always over at the rectory. Father Tierney used to babysit her."

"Babysit her?" Smith pauses, his forehead crinkling like he's trying to understand what the hell she's saying. "I don't know anything about that. And I'm not sure I want to know about it," he mutters. "But this priest," he continues, sparing me a scowl, "looks at Kate like he wants to eat her."

"Bullshit," I say loudly.

"I've seen it with my own two eyes."

"Is it true, Kate?" Fiona asks.

"*No.* The TV was something a parishioner gave him that he didn't need. I already told you the story, and when we had dinner *to discuss the bulletin I'm helping him with,*" I return Smith's scowl, "I mentioned that I've always wanted a pet. So when a cat was abandoned at the church, he immediately thought of me." I glare at Smith. "What is so hard about that to understand?"

He ignores me. "This isn't weird to either of you?"

"I don't care how big your watch is, you sound like a jealous boyfriend. It's not a good look, Smith," Fiona says, calmly but firmly.

"You're just agreeing with her because she's your friend. I bet if I asked your husband, he'd be thinking exactly what I'm thinking."

"Two fools do not a genius make. Unless you want to tell me more about your watch, I need to feed my children. Kate, call me tomorrow."

He disconnects the call and tosses my phone on the counter. "What do you want to do about dinner?"

"I thought we were having Chinese. How did you get into my locked phone? Let me guess, special commando training?"

"*No.*" He draws out the word, impatient with me. "It's not part of special operative training. If you can't get into a locked phone, you're not getting anywhere near the training program."

"It's a neat trick." *Hopefully this is the first time you've unlocked my phone.* "Do you want a beer?"

"Please."

Smith disappears while my head is in the fridge. I find him in the bedroom doorway, the door ajar, watching the cat eat. For the first time, I get a good look at the tabby. He's actually bigger than he looked in the carrier—a bit pudgy, actually. I squeeze Smith's arm. "Poor thing must have been starving." *Don't worry sweet kitty. We have plenty of food.*

Smith holds a finger to his mouth and shuts the door quietly.

"The cat should see a vet," he says when we're back in the kitchen.

"I'll set something up for a couple weeks from now. Maybe by then he'll be more accustomed to me and won't be so scared when I take him out in the car."

"I don't think you should wait. *She* looks pregnant."

"Pregnant?" I should have known from the way he talked about the male species that Father Jesse wouldn't be able to tell the difference between a male and female. "I thought he was a boy?"

"Did you see a dick anywhere?"

I grin until my cheeks hurt. "Only the big one in the kitchen, but I think he's hiding a smaller one under his clothes."

Smith laughs and pulls me into his chest. "I don't like that priest."

"Duly noted. But I do. Now let me finish ordering dinner and then you can help me find a vet."

"You order, and I'll call the vet—I know a good one who makes house calls."

"I'm not sure I can afford a vet who makes house calls."

"Just order dinner. I'm starving."

———

We finish dinner, and Dr. Long, the vet, comes by at about nine with a portable ultrasound machine that the cat wasn't crazy about. "What's the kitty's name?" she asks, setting up a small table.

"I was going to call her Fenway when I thought she was a he. Not sure now."

"Fenway's a nice name. As long as you love her and say her name with affection, she won't care what you call her." She sits on the floor next to the carrier and opens a bag of fishy smelling treats, so pungent they could attract cats from all over the city. "I'm going to give her a few minutes and see if she comes out on her own."

After a short time, Fenway slowly makes her way into the room, tracking the fishy smell to Dr. Long.

"She's pregnant, alright. There's the pinkening," the vet says pointing to the cat's underside. "Good call, Smith. She seems healthy and well-cared for. I bet your family misses you, Fenny," the vet coos.

After a few minutes of treats and gentle petting, the cat lets Dr. Long examine her.

"I can feel the microchip in her neck, but it doesn't appear to be registered when I scan it. That's not uncommon. People bring home kittens and puppies that are chipped, but they don't pay the twenty dollars to activate it."

"I don't know about her family. She was left at St. Magdalene's church."

"Is that so, Fenny?" the vet says, feeding her a treat. "Sometimes the prospect of kittens is too much for pet owners. I can't say enough about spaying and neutering. At least they didn't drop her off in the woods for a predator to find." I shudder at the thought.

"Do you know when the kittens will be born?" I ask, watching how quickly the cat has warmed up to Dr. Long. I'm thrilled she's not so scared anymore. Maybe it won't take her too long to warm up to me, either.

"About a month. She's a young mama."

"Is there anything special I need to know to prepare for the kittens?"

"I'll leave you with some reading material. She'll mostly take care of business herself. But I wouldn't let her outside, even if she begs at the door."

"Can she stay alone while I'm at work?"

"Yes, of course. Although if you can come home during the day for a short visit, that might be a good thing until she has her kittens." I can definitely rework my schedule to come home at least once during the day.

She gives me some papers and tells me to call the office on Monday to set up an appointment for two weeks. "Unless you want me to do another house call?" she asks, glancing at Smith. "I don't mind."

"I can take her into the office. By then I hope she's more comfortable with me. What do I owe you for today's visit?"

She gathers her equipment. "Nothing for today."

"Are you sure? That doesn't seem right."

"Take good care of Fenny. That's all I ask. And don't worry. Cats are much better prepared for babies than humans are."

Smith sees Dr. Long out and comes back into the bedroom. Fenny lets me pet her before she crawls back into the safety of her carrier. I think she's warming up to me.

"I don't understand why she didn't want to be paid. Did you work something out with her when you called?"

"I tried. She won't take money from me."

"Someone you used to play with?" *That's ugly, Kate.*

"Claws away, princess. Never played with her. She had some trouble with an ex-husband that we helped her with. That's all I'm going to say on the subject."

Now I feel like a total ass. Jealous girlfriends aren't any better of a look than jealous boyfriends.

"Let's leave Fenway in peace," Smith says. "We can check on her in a little while." He tugs on my hair as I shut the door quietly. "I wouldn't like to see it all the time, but a little jealousy is hot on you."

I smile shyly, the flush of embarrassment coloring my warm cheeks. "Just sayin'," he adds, with the smug, self-satisfied preen of a peacock that makes my pussy tingle.

"Do you want to watch a movie and have a sleepover? Maybe you'll show me your watch, if you're not embarrassed by the tiny thing," I tease over my shoulder, on the way to the bedroom.

He lunges at me, tossing me over his shoulder like I weigh nothing. "I'll show you my watch, princess. And then you're going to worship it from your knees."

His words and *that* voice he uses make me want to rip off his clothes and rub my body against his like a feline desperate for attention. But if history is any indication, I'm going to get all the attention I can handle.

"Now take off your clothes. And be quick about it," he commands, slapping my ass while dumping me squealing onto the air mattress.

29

SMITH

We slept on the floor at Kate's for the last time two nights ago. She's going to be pissed about the bed and the sofa, but too bad. I haven't been there every night, but we've still managed to wreck six air mattresses in the last three weeks. *Six.* Including two that were supposed to be indestructible. Although that kind of advertising is nothing more than a challenge, anyway.

The delivery guys texted me an hour ago to say they were thirty minutes away, so I expect a call from Kate any time now. *Bingo.* My dashboard lights up with her name. Bring it on, *Mary Katherine.*

"What possessed you to buy me a bed and a sofa?" She starts, before I even say hello.

"I don't want to be out-gifted by a priest."

"Please tell me that's a joke."

"Mostly. I'm too old to be sleeping on the floor. So are you. And I like a comfortable place to take a nap and watch the game." Plus, I'm tired of indulging your *I'm just here as a temporary thing* bullshit.

"Wait a second," she says, before the banging. "Dammit!" she cries.

"What the hell happened?"

"I'm making Fenny some fish broth to add to her food, and it boiled over. When I moved the pan off the stove, I burned my finger. Nothing serious."

"You sure?"

"Yeah. It's fine. Startled me, that's all."

"The cat's getting homemade fish broth?"

"She's pregnant. She deserves a few treats, and Dr. Long said the extra nutrition and fluids are good for her."

Kate is ridiculous about the cat, and I give her a ton of shit about it, but the truth is I love that side of her. She is going to flip out when those kittens are born. I'm kind of looking forward to it, myself. The question is, what are we going to do with all those kittens when they're weaned?

"That cat gets treated better than I do. Just make sure she stays off my couch."

She clicks her tongue. "Poor baby. Speaking of the couch. Did it occur to you to ask my preferences?"

"I'm working on finding out every one of your preferences, princess. It's a job for a special operative, because you're not very forthcoming. But I'm working on that, too."

"That's not what I meant."

"The bed is the bed. I picked out a decent mattress. As far as the sofa—I don't know a paisley print from a blooming hydrangea, so I chose something safe. Besides, leather is easy to wipe down. I plan on making that sofa real dirty."

"I'm not going to be in Charleston much longer. Even with both of us chasing down clues, the information has pretty much dried up. My lease expires in August, and by then the Boston Police Commissioner's job will be set. It's wasteful to buy furniture." I hear the regret in her voice as it trails off. Or maybe that's just what I want to hear.

"I'm getting tired of that excuse. Almost as tired as I am of sleeping on the floor." I'm short with her. The truth is, I don't want to hear it. Every time she says she's leaving soon—every fucking time—my stomach balls into a tight fist. I'm not ready for her to go. Although, it's still a month away. Maybe I'll be ready by the time the summer ends. Maybe more than ready. *Right.* Even I'm starting to have trouble swallowing the bullshit.

"Do you want to come over tonight?" she asks. "I'll make that crab dip you like."

"Let's go out for drinks and then grab some supper."

"I don't know about leaving Fenny alone. She's close."

"She's not that close. Besides, she's a cat, not a pregnant teenager. She'll be fine alone for a few hours. We haven't been out since you got her." *Not that I'm complaining, because I've enjoyed every second that we've spent holed up with you naked and needy, begging for my cock.* "You're due for a night out."

"Alright," she says hesitantly. "But let's not go too far."

"I'll come by about seven—make that six-thirty—in case we want to take that mattress for a spin before we head out."

"You're impossible." She sighs. "Thank you for the bed and the sofa. You're right about sleeping on the floor." She pauses for a second. "I know what you're going to say, but I'd feel better if I paid for the furniture. At least for some portion of it."

"I don't want your money." I hear her getting ready to fuss on the other end of the call. "But if you're dead set on paying me back—you can work it off. But I warn you. I'm demanding and difficult to please."

She's smiling. I know she is, while she's coming up with some smart-ass thing to put me in my place. But instead, she surprises me, like she often does. "I'd like the opportunity to work off my debt, sir. *Anything* you'd like. I'm told I follow instructions well."

Her voice is low and sultry, and my dick is pushing against my zipper. *Fuck six-thirty.* "I'm on my way over now. When I get there, I want you naked on that bed, with your gorgeous ass in the air."

It's late by the time we get back to Kate's for the night. The bed was well broken in before we left, which I'm not griping about. But then it took forever before I was able to drag her away from the cat.

Kate insisted on feeding it a dollop of whipped cream, *freshly whipped cream*, from her finger before we left. When I begged for a taste, she shut me down. That, of course, led to christening the sofa. By the time we made it out the door, the sun was dipping into the horizon.

I see it the minute we pull up in front of the house. My gut twists into a knot. *I hope to hell I'm wrong.* Kate doesn't notice because she's too busy telling me about an email she got from a former colleague at the Sun. Apparently, Warren King might not actually be sick. Big surprise.

It's dark, and I can't be certain, so I ask her to stay in the car. I don't want to alarm her, and I sure as hell don't want her to see—
"Wait here for a minute. I need to check something."

"What? Why can't I come with you?"

"Please don't argue. Just wait in the car until I get back."

As I make my way closer to the stairs, I see Fenny sprawled on the sidewalk, not moving. *You have got to be fucking kidding me.* My first instinct is to pull off my shirt and cover the cat so that Kate doesn't see it like this, but I pause to make sure it's dead, and then it's too late.

"What is it?" Kate says, opening the Jeep door.

"Stay back. Get back in the Jeep, Kate. I'm not dicking around." I try to block her view of Fenway, but the piercing scream and the mournful wail that follows tells me I'm unsuccessful. My heart breaks for her as she fights me, kicking and scratching as I carry her back to the Jeep.

I've seen death up close. Some of it grisly. I've comforted soldiers under my command, and friends who have witnessed the horrors of war. In their grief, they don't want promises that can't be kept. They need someone to stand strong beside them. I've also lost pets, and it can be every bit as heartbreaking. It never occurs to me to tell Kate *it's going to be okay* as I force her into the Jeep. "I've got you," is what I promise. "I've got you."

Once she's situated, I grab a towel from the back of the car and place it over Fenny so that she doesn't have to see the damage. Someone sliced her down the middle. That's what it looks like, anyway. *Jesus Christ! How am I ever going to explain this to Kate?*

The cat got out of a closed house. It's not Houdini—someone let it out. There were no open windows when we left. I checked myself. *This was King's people. I know it was.*

I move Fenny a bit so I can take a better look at the wound. This is bad. A fucking nightmare kind of bad.

Kate is sobbing when I get back to the Jeep. I hold her while she cries in my arms. When I find the sonofabitch who did this, I will show them no mercy.

I don't want to leave her out here alone, but I'm not letting her go inside until I know it's safe. "Someone might have broken into the house and let Fenny out. I want to take a look around before you go in."

"No." She grabs my arm, clenching tight. "Let's call the police. I don't want you to get hurt."

"No one's going to hurt me. I want you to lay on the horn if anyone approaches the vehicle—actually, lay on it if you see another human being on the street. I don't care whether you recognize them. Lay on the horn until I get here. Do you understand?"

She nods. "Please call the police."

Kate has more faith in the police than I do. "I'll call them if you promise not to get out of the car until I get back."

She nods.

"Give me your keys." Her hands are shaky. I kiss her right above her ear. "I'll be right back. Doors locked. Stay in the car."

I call my office and have them contact the police while I search the perimeter. There's a blood-stained towel behind the bushes in the front yard, not far from where the cat was lying, and a screen in the back of the house is on the ground. It's been cut.

I dread what else I'm going to find inside, but it's not too bad. Some drawers are open and appear to be ransacked, and her laptop is gone from the dresser, but the backup and the television are still here. This was not a robbery. More reason to believe that the King camp is behind this.

When I get back outside, Kate's kneeling on the sidewalk with Fenny in her lap, stroking her bloody fur and sobbing. "Kate. Come here. Let me take Fenny." I wrap the cat in the towel and place her on the grass. "I told you to stay in the car." It's a stupid, unhelpful thing to say, but Kate doesn't even notice.

"I didn't take good care of her. She was counting on me. I let her down. And her babies. I let everyone down."

I wrap my arm around her shoulders. The guilt this woman is going to carry about this is already gnawing at me. She wanted to stay home. I was the one who pushed to go out. "There's not a single person—not a single thing that you've ever let down in your life. Let's go inside and clean up. Then I want you to pack a bag. I'll take care of Fenway."

"Pack a bag? Where are we going?"

Good question. I can't take her back to my house at Sweetgrass, because—I can't. When a grown man can't bring women back to his house, it's time to find somewhere else to live. But that's for another day.

I glance at the time. By the time the police get here, take a statement and a look around, things will be winding down at Wildflower, and it's closed tomorrow. It'll buy me some time. "Someone cut the screen and broke into the house. It's not safe to stay here tonight. I think your laptop was taken, but not the backup. I need you to look around and see if they took anything else."

We go inside through the front door, and I follow her as she wanders around the house. When she gets to Fenny's carrier, she picks up a small toy mouse. "She loved this. We should bury it with her." I lead her away from the room with Fenny's things as quickly as possible.

"I don't see the laptop," she mumbles. Her voice is hollow, and I want to take on her pain and carry it for her. "But it's all backed up and saved to the cloud. Some jewelry is missing. Costume jewelry. It's not important. Not like Fenny." She holds up her hand and touches the Claddagh ring on her finger that belonged to her mother. "Should we call the police?"

"Already done." I open her bottom drawer where she keeps a small gun safe. It's empty. "What about your gun?"

"I didn't take it out of my bag before we went to the restaurant."

"We're going to the range tomorrow. I want to see if you can actually shoot that thing."

"I already told you I can."

More than once. But I want to see it with my own two eyes. Whatever sick motherfucker killed the cat was inside this house. "When's the last time you shot it?"

"Boston."

"Then you need practice."

"Her belly looked like it had been cut. Fenway. Could a car have done that?"

I shrug.

"If a predator—I would have expected her to be—did she get caught on the screen?" Tears are falling again.

She doesn't need to hear the truth tonight. "I don't know." I swipe a tear from her face with my finger. *But I'm going to find out. That's a goddamn promise.*

30

KATE

I open my eyes and look around the room. It takes me several seconds to remember I'm at Smith's apartment at Wildflower. I fell asleep in his arms sometime late last night, but he's not here now.

Once I'm fully awake, it all comes flooding back. Fenny's dead. Someone broke into the house while I was enjoying dinner, laughing, flirting, and basking in Smith's light. They let her out. She must have been terrified. I pull up the covers.

Leaving her alone was a mistake. If I had been there, she would still be alive. Her kittens would still be alive. I'm cried out from last night. Now, I'm just numb. And I'm cursed. Everything I love dies.

I reach for my phone. It's almost noon. I want to talk to Fi, but she's either at church or on her way to one of the Nanas' for Sunday dinner. Maybe I should call my father? No. It would only worry him—*and he'll find a way to blame you*. I already blame myself. I don't need him to pile on. But I do need to get up and find Smith. I want to make sure that Fenny is buried. But first, I need to pee.

I take care of business and use the toothbrush he gave me last night. I start to finger comb my rat's nest, but right now, I don't care about my hair.

My clothes are not where I left them last night. Maybe he hung them in the closet. I open the closet door, but I don't find any clothes there. Not a single stitch.

What I do find is a large room, even larger than the bedroom, with the same high ceilings and wood floor. There are hooks on the ceiling in the corners of the room, and an array of items hanging on the wall. One is definitely a flogger, but I don't recognize the rest. The room is otherwise empty except for a chest, a couple chairs, and two large items I don't recognize, although one resembles a hammock, and the other—

"Good morning," Smith says hesitantly from the doorway. "I brought you coffee."

I don't take the coffee. "What's all this?" I ask, cupping my elbows. I know what these things are used for, but I'm not sure what to call them.

"Toys."

Toys. Of course. I might not know much about kink, but it's pretty obvious. What else would they be? "Are—are they yours?"

"They're on loan."

On loan? Where exactly does one borrow this sort of thing? "From whom?"

"A friend." He's terse, like he's already getting impatient with the questions. Well, I have a lot more.

"What's that?" I ask pointing to the hammock contraption.

"Just a swing."

"Just a swing. Really? The kind you would put your nieces in?"

I glance at him. His face is hard. "That's a low blow, Kate. I get that this might be unfamiliar to you. And surprising. That's all well and good, but leave those little girls out of it."

I feel a bit of remorse. I shouldn't have mentioned his nieces, but I'm not ready to apologize. "What about this thing?"

"It's a saddle."

"A saddle?"

"Yeah."

"What do you do with it?"

He cracks his knuckles. It's not to intimidate me. He's uncomfortable. "It's a saddle. Pretty self-explanatory."

"Really? Because I don't understand it. But clearly, I'm stupid."

"You want to know what it's used for?" He slaps the seat of the leather saddle. "You really want to know? Because you're pale and you look pretty damn horrified. You should have never come in here."

I curl my lips over my teeth, and press my mouth together, weighing my words carefully. "Pale is my natural coloring, and I wasn't snooping. I was looking for my clothes. I thought it was a closet. And don't change the subject. What is this used for?"

"There are phallus shaped accessories you attach here." He points to an area in the center of the saddle. "You pick the one that suits you. And here is where you connect an attachment that stimulates the clit." He's dispassionate and clinical. If I didn't know better, I would say there was no pleasure for him in these toys. *But that would be stupid.*

"What do you do?"

"Watch."

We're back to one-word responses. Soon it'll be grunts. This is what he does when he doesn't want to talk about it. Well, Sinclair, I wish I hadn't walked in here too. But now that I have, you are going to talk. "Watch? With your cock in hand?"

He lifts his chin. "Sometimes. But other times, I stand behind the saddle and slide my dick into her ass." I swallow hard. "Bite her neck. Play with her tits. I might even grab that riding crop off the wall," he says, pointing to the item near the flogger. "It doesn't matter where I'm standing, I can see her pleasure reflected in the mirrors on the wall."

That was a big fuck you to me. And it takes me a long moment to regain my equilibrium.

"So this—this is what—you're into? That wasn't some off-handed remark at the Blackberry Inn about floggers and hot wax. What we've been doing has just been a warm-up for what you really like."

"Kate."

I put up my hand to stop him. "Have you been using these with another woman—with other women since we've been—having sex?"

"I haven't been with anyone else besides you."

"When was the last time you *played* with someone?" I'm defensive and confused, and I don't give a shit.

"I think that would be yesterday early evening."

"Don't be a smartass. When is the last time you were with a woman that wasn't me?"

"I already told you, a few nights before your birthday."

"Here."

He nods.

"That was weeks ago," I mutter, under my breath. "Why do you still have this on loan?"

Smith scratches his head but doesn't say anything for a moment. "I'm not exactly sure." He shrugs.

I walk over to the swing, and finger the mesh, imagining a faceless, naked woman reclining in the thing. I give it a push. It twirls, almost innocently. But there's nothing innocent about it. "You wanted me to know."

"No." He shakes his head.

"Yes, you did. Otherwise you would have returned it to your *friend*."

"It's not like we ever come here. If it hadn't been—"

"Stop lying. Stop."

"I'm not sure." He closes his eyes, squeezing the back of his neck a few times. "If you gave me truth serum—I would probably tell you I keep it here to remind me that this is an important part of my life. Something I shouldn't forget about—just because—I like you."

I glance at him before going over to the saddle and staring mindlessly at the groove where the phallus attaches. I don't think about the devices hanging on the wall, or what might be in the chest of drawers. All I can think about is that what we do is not enough. That I'm not enough. Of course, I'm not enough for someone like him. *God, I'm an idiot.*

"Talk to me, Kate," he murmurs in that voice he uses to coax me into telling him secrets.

My fingers find my hair, and I begin to play with it, because this is too much. "I thought we were having pretty great sex. That it was something special. I thought you were enjoying sex with me. But I guess I was the only one enjoying it."

He comes over and puts his arm around me and drags me toward him. "I have enjoyed every second of you. Don't you dare start conjuring up shit in that overactive little mind of yours."

"But what we have isn't enough?"

"It's enough. More than enough."

I pull away and search his face. It's earnest, but— "You're lying. The proof is right here in this room."

He doesn't look at me as he nods. The movement is so small it's barely perceptible. "It's enough—for now. But kink has been part of my life for a long time. A long time." He gazes at me. "I like it. A lot. What we have is enough, but I'm not sure for how long it will be enough. I'd be lying to say otherwise."

Everything is a little fuzzy, and if I hadn't thrown up twice last night, I'd be puking on my bare feet right now. *Fenny. Oh, God. One thing at a time, Kate. Stay present.*

"Tell me about the women you play with. The ones who like this."

"No. I won't do that. I can talk to you about the kinds of sex I've had, but my relationships, including the one I have with you, are private. All you need to know is that this," he waves his hand between the swing and the saddle, "was all consensual. And that I respected my partners while we played, and after."

I glance at the few items hanging on the wall that look like they are on loan from The Tower of London. "Consensual."

"I guess you could say, at times, it was consensual, non-consensual play."

What the hell does that even mean? "You need this in your life?" *Because this is so far out of my experience that I'm having trouble. And I don't know if I can ever fully accept it.*

"Need it? No. We both know I get off without it. But it would leave a large void if it was gone forever."

"And the vanilla sex we've been having will never fill that void?" *No, Kate, it won't. How many different ways does he need to say it?*

"I wouldn't say that it's all been vanilla. More like butter pecan, rich with some crunch." I ignore the tug at the corner of his mouth and the dimple winking at me.

"And what's this?"

"Midnight cookies and cream," he says matter-of-factly. "We're making progress, but we're a long way away from this."

Progress? "You've been grooming me? For this." Oh. My. God. He's a predator.

"Whoa." He raises both his hands. "That's a loaded word. It implies manipulation. I told you straight up I was all about exploring and pushing boundaries. You were well aware."

"Are you a dominant? A sadist?" I'm not even sure of the correct language to use.

"Those are complicated words. I consider myself a top. Although I'm occasionally, and I do mean occasionally, willing to let someone else take charge."

"What does that even mean? I don't speak kink. Speak in terms I can understand." I'm trying to stay calm, but my insides are shaking.

"I prefer to be in control. In all aspects of life, including during sex. It's not some deep-rooted psychological need. I didn't experience abandonment or any other childhood trauma. I just like it. It's how I'm built." He squeezes my shoulders and presses a tender kiss to my head. The clean smell of the sandalwood soap on his skin relaxes me—unlike everything else in this room, it's familiar.

I take a deep breath and hold it for a few seconds before I let it go. "I don't know, Smith. This isn't what I signed up for."

"I know." He pulls me closer. "But you've been enjoying it. Even the things you thought you didn't like."

It's true. "But what we've been doing isn't this. And just like you can't imagine a life without this, I can't imagine a life with it."

He hooks his finger under my chin, until I'm looking into those serious whiskey-colored eyes. "That's not entirely true. I've thought about a life without kink. But you've never really thought about a life with it."

"But—"

"You're still upset about Fenway. You're letting your emotions cloud your thinking."

I jerk away from his grasp. "Don't you dare. Don't you dare tell me that I'm over-emotional and can't think straight. Have some respect for me. I just walked in on this. I've been falling in—developing feelings—having sex with a man who has a whole secret life that I didn't know a thing about."

"What I do is no one's damn business." Now who's defensive? "But it's not a secret, Kate. At least I didn't want it to be from you. But I didn't think you were ready—and I didn't want to chase you away."

"You decided I wasn't ready? Well here's a little nugget you can slip into your back pocket: I'm always ready for the truth."

We stand there, still, for what feels like months. The longer we stand there, the stronger the realization becomes that we aren't meant to be together. We're too different.

"The truth is," he says, "this is fun—it can take even great sex to a whole other level. But I wanted to introduce you to it slowly. I hoped it was something we could share together."

The sorrow in his face mirrors the one I feel in my heart. I'm confused and defensive, but I'm not ready to give up on us. Not without more information. *Well then, grow up, Kate. Figure it out.*

"I'm not a submissive," I say haughtily.

There's a glimmer in his eyes. "Good. Like I told you earlier, I'm not a dominant."

"Does this mean we can never have normal sex?"

His hand moves to my hair, tentatively reaching for a curl. "It's all normal, Kate."

"You know what I mean."

He reaches for me, and I don't pull away. "We can have it all. I want to have lots of vanilla sex. I want to wake you up in the middle of the night and slide into your pussy while your body is warm and sleepy and my dick is hard from dreaming about you. But I also want to try all the kink with you. Kink so filthy it makes you pink when you think about it in the light of day. I want all of it. With you."

I see the vulnerability in his face. I hear it in his voice. I know it cost him to lay out his feelings.

"I don't know … what if … I don't want any of this." I shrug. "But while I'm deciding, there can be no other women—no matter how bad the urge gets."

"This is not an addiction, and I am not an addict. And there have been no other women—the day you laid your head on that pillow at the Blackberry Inn, this—us—was exclusive. I made the decision that day."

"What about asking what I wanted?"

He pulls me away, just enough to look at my face. "You wanted something else?"

I shake my head. "No. But I want you to ask—I don't want you just to assume."

"Fair enough. But about those *other women* you keep bringing up. It's never going to work between us if you can't trust me. My line of work takes me to all sorts of places with all sorts of people at all times of the day and night. I can't share everything about what I do. As a matter of fact, I can't share most of it. But I'm not a cheater."

"Trust is a two-way street."

He nods. "I'm getting better at it." *He is.* There are still occasional lapses of trust, mainly involving the Wilders, but overall, things are better in that regard.

"You can give this up, until we figure it out? What if it doesn't happen right away? What if it never happens?"

He places his hands on my upper arms, his fingers digging into the pliant flesh. "Look at me," he says, in a sober voice. "This is not an open relationship, and I repeat, I am not a cheater. When we're done with each other, we'll talk about it. It might not be pleasant, but it will end with a discussion, not with another woman in my bed. You have my word on that."

When we're done. My stomach contorts into a painful knot that makes it difficult to take full breaths. My mind sprints from one awful scenario to another, but each with the same tragic ending. *I wanted it to work,* but *this is an important part of my life. I can't give it up forever.* No! I will not play the victim in this story. I will fight for this. *For us.*

"I want to try the saddle," I say in a clear, determined voice.

His brows are knitted together. "I'm sorry?"

I square my shoulders and approach the damn thing like Joan of Arc riding into battle. "I want to try the saddle."

"Now?"

I look him straight in the eye and nod.

"*No.* Absofuckinglutely not."

"Why not?"

"Because you're not fifteen, and I'm not an asshole in a frat house."

I gasp. "I can't believe you just said that. You think I'm forcing myself to tolerate this so that you'll love me?" As I say the words out loud, I realize there might be a grain of truth to them.

He just stands there, the knob in his throat bobbing before he speaks. "That's not what I meant. Don't put words into my mouth. I think you're willing to try things you're not ready for because you think it will make me happy. You're always too willing to disregard your feelings when it comes to people close to you. You don't strap on a pair of skis for the first time and take a run down the expert trail. That's a sure way to guarantee you'll never put on those skis again. You're not ready for this."

"Why is it that you always get to decide what I'm ready for? I'm an adult. I want to see if this is something I can ever be into, or if we should go our separate ways now."

"I want you to like this." He gestures toward the *toys*. "Maybe not these particular things, but I want you to love kink as much as I do—as much as I know I can with you. This isn't fiction where a virgin is taken to a dungeon and ends up a pain slut before the night is through. That's not how it works in real life. If we play too much, too soon, you could be turned off and shut the door on it forever. There's no reason to take that risk."

"This is what I want." I sound much more confident than I'm feeling. The pain slut comment rattled me a bit. "You can join me, or you can watch, or you can leave and think about me mounting that thing." I reach for his hand. "Or you can help me learn. I'm going to do this with or without you." I give him a minute to settle in. "Where are the attachments?"

He shakes his head and turns toward the door.

"You're a coward," I shout after him. "Nothing more than a bunch of big talk. You don't want to do this with me. You just want this to become the excuse when you've had enough of me, and want to walk away, guilt free."

31

KATE

He stops in his tracks, pivots, and stalks toward me. "You have no idea what you're asking for."

"Then show me."

I see the turmoil in his eyes. The flicker of uncertainty across his strong features. I'm sure there are reels in his head playing on a non-stop loop. A drunk fifteen-year-old girl surrounded by young men in a frat house, pawing lewdly. He doesn't want to add to her pain.

"I want to understand this."

"I know." He throws up his hands. "But what you're suggesting—isn't the way to understand it."

"I want to know if this can be a part of my life. If I'm in it for the long haul. I need to know before I get any deeper."

His tongue emerges, the tip nestled in the bow of his lip. He's considering it.

I wait impatiently for him to decide. "Fine," he says, his palm scrubbing a stubbled jaw. "I'll play, if that's what you need."

I don't believe him. He's going to give me some watered-down version of what he likes. It will serve as a reminder to him that we're different, and in the end, neither of us will know if we can reconcile those differences.

"Don't you dare." I pound my fist against his chest over and over. "Don't you dare. I am not a fragile glass figurine, and this is not a Tennessee Williams play. I want to be treated just like all those other women you claim to respect so much. I want the same things you give them, during and after."

He drags in a breath and blows it out with a long hiss. "Fine." This time the word pulses with life and fire. "If that's what you want. But you are not in charge today, princess." His body language shifts as he speaks. His eyes turn cold—his voice hard. He steps closer, mere inches away from me.

"Take off that T-shirt and get on your knees. Get comfortable there because you're going to take out my cock and suck it like your life depends on it. Do you know why, Kate?" He grabs a fistful of my hair. "Because despite all your foolish bravado, you're going to want me patient with you today. You're going to want me to have some measure of control. So you're going to use that sassy little mouth to settle me, and you're going to do it real good, just like I showed you."

He tugs harder on my hair until my scalp tingles. "Then I'm going to fuck you until you can't remember if your name is Mary Katherine, or Katherine Mary, or Jenny from the block."

Is this what I want? Should I be afraid? I push the thoughts away, every last one, and force myself into the moment.

When he lets go of my hair, I pull off the thin T-shirt and drop to my knees. It's not an elegant landing, but I'm where I need to be to unbutton his jeans. His cock pushes its way out before the zipper is fully down, and I cradle it in a shaky hand.

I gaze up at him and see a myriad of emotions in his face. He's still unsure. He could end this at any moment. I feel it. "Don't you treat me like I'm broken, Smith Sinclair." Then I lower my mouth and lick his shaft from root to tip, my tongue flicking the ridge of the flared crown. I use my teeth to gently scrape the dusky head before drawing it into my mouth.

"*Kate*," he groans, sliding his hands into my hair, cupping my head with gentle fingertips so that I'm still setting the pace. I want to know if his head is tipped back and his jaw is slack, or if he's watching me tease him with my lips. I let his swollen cock slide over my flat tongue, and that's when he takes control. He doesn't wrest it from me. I hand it to him, willingly.

In seconds, my eyes are watering and my gag reflex is working overtime. "Swallow," he instructs with a raspy voice, each time he shoves deeper into my throat. "Breathe through your nose."

I'm grateful for the reminders.

His breathing is labored. My fingers feel the tightening in his groin, and the jerky movements of his hips right before he pulls out of my mouth, spraying his seed on my breasts and belly, bits bouncing off my skin and splashing onto my hair and face. I gasp, gulping mouthfuls of air, like I've been holding my breath underwater for an extensive period of time. It's shocking and exhilarating, and I want more.

He yanks me off my knees, kissing me roughly. "You just need to say stop," he murmurs, backing me up against the saddle, where he owns my mouth until I'm submerged again.

After a few minutes, he sweeps the T-shirt I'd been wearing from the floor, and wipes his mark off my skin. But it's not gone. It's smeared deep into my pores, where I'll smell him every time I sweat.

"Turn around and bend over that saddle you're so interested in riding."

I do as instructed. Draping my body over the worn leather saddle, my chin resting on the very edge. He stands over me, quietly. "Can I choose the phallus?" I ask softly, when the silence becomes too loud.

Smith slaps my bare ass in response, and I yelp at the sting. "I already told you we are not playing with that saddle. Today, you're just going to be anchored to it." He slaps my ass again, and the sting begins and ends in my cunt. "Don't move, and don't say a single word until I give you permission to speak."

He comes back holding a long bar with cuffs attached to it, and a glass plug with spheres attached to one another in increasing size as they approach the base. I recognize it immediately because we've been playing with butt plugs. Smaller than this though, and made of pliable material.

Smith holds up the bar. "This is a spreader bar. I'm going to attach the cuffs to your ankles and then to the bar. The bar is going to keep your legs open nice and wide for me, Kate. You tend to squeeze your legs together before you come. It deflects some of the intensity you're feeling. With this, you're not going to be able to do that. I'm going to lick your sweet cunt until I've had my fill, and you will take every orgasm, all the pleasure, I give you. Do you understand?"

"Yes." My mouth is so dry, I can barely form the word.

"Do you know what this is?"

I nod. "A butt plug."

"That's right. It's made of glass. Do you remember how cold glass is against your skin until it's warmed?"

When I don't respond, he slips the long plug between my legs, dragging it over my clit. I shudder and gasp at the cold. "We're going to warm it just like this." He holds it against my entrance and pushes it inside. I groan as it fills me.

He pulls it out, coated and slick, and holds it in front of my face, licking the glass like it's a popsicle to be savored on a blistering day. "Do you want a taste? Take a small taste." I slide my pointed tongue over the smallest sphere, acutely aware of where it has been and where it will soon be.

"You're delicious," he murmurs, taking another long taste.

He discards the plug, and standing behind me, he gently pulls back my hair. "I'm going to tie your hands to the base of the saddle so you don't fall over when the spreader bar is in place."

He ties my wrists with binding, slipping his fingers between the fabric and my skin. "This won't cut into your wrists, but it will save you from a nasty fall if you let go of the base. I don't want you to get hurt." I'm grateful for the care he takes, but I can't help but wonder if this is an extra precaution for me, or just the norm.

He crouches, biting my ass, while he attaches the cuffs. I jump every time his teeth sink into the fleshy cheeks.

"Spread those legs for me, Kate. Nice and wide." The lever clicks and I grip the long thin base of the saddle tighter.

"Stop. That's all you need to say to end this immediately." He brushes his fingers down my back. "Say it, so I know you can."

"Stop."

"Say it again."

"Stop."

"If you don't stop me, I'm going to push hard, and I'm not going to stop until you're a muddled mess." He kisses the back of my head after he says it. I feel the reticence on his lips.

Smith licks me back to front, again and again. He sets his own pace. I shudder at each long stroke, overwhelmed by the feeling of being restrained while he tongues me with abandon. When his fingers join the party, I am filled with the urge to squirm. But my movements are restricted, and I am at his mercy while his fingers fuck me, twisting in and out with a rhythm that he controls. It's too much. *Too much.*

"Regulate your breathing, Kate." I concentrate, taking a couple carefully controlled breaths. "That's it."

His fingers have slowed, and his mouth has moved away from my pussy. *I need it back.* But I can't grab his head and pull it toward me. "Smith, I need more. I was almost there," I plead.

"*Shhh.* You can have more. Right now." I flinch when the cold lube makes contact with my ass, sliding between my cheeks. "This is a special plug," he says. "It will feel a lot like the others we've played with going in, but these little balls are going to blow your mind coming out. Push out," he instructs, sliding the glass inside me. "Breathe."

I am dripping. I don't know if it's all the lube he applied or if it's my arousal. My pussy is clenching. I want him inside me. His fingers. His cock. I don't care.

His nose brushes my clit. He grunts his approval, and then he eats me. His lips, his teeth, his tongue, they're all at the table, while he sucks on my clit, occasionally rocking the plug. "Go ahead, Kate. Come all over my mouth." His tone is lewd, almost taunting.

I feel his fingers slide into my pussy. *Two? Three?* I don't know. But my walls clench, hugging tight. My hips buck, but the movements are small, controlled by the restraints. It's maddening. I feel my body tighten as I soar. Up, up, up. *Yes!* All of the pent-up energy—the frustration of not being able to move, bubbles up and pours out, filling the room in a long loud scream.

Smith slides up behind me. He presses a kiss to my cheek. He's trembling, fighting for his own control. "I'm going to fuck you, princess. It's going to be so tight with that big plug in your ass."

I whimper, as his teeth sink into my flesh, biting along my shoulders and back, like he's tasting my skin.

"*Ahhh!*" The sensation adds to the sensory overload.

"Do you like being restrained?" he murmurs in my ear. His voice is thick, bathed in a delicious lasciviousness. I feel him at my entrance before I can answer, rubbing the flared crown against the tender flesh.

I open my eyes and gaze into the mirror to watch this beautiful man enter my body. The smell of sex wafts around us like frankincense in a holy ritual.

His jaw is slack. His eyes shutter as he ruts deep. My mouth falls opens in a gasp, and I struggle to keep my lids up. He moves with a graceful command, emitting the low growl of a predator who has captured his prey. His lashes flutter, exposing dark slits that catch me watching in the mirror.

His mouth eases at one corner, the glint of hedonism lighting his dark eyes. He bends over my body, wrapping my hair around his fist. "You're such a dirty little princess. Look at your pretty face with traces of my cum still on it."

I squeeze my eyes tight, losing myself in the punishing rhythm of his powerful thrusts, enjoying his fingers digging into my hips. I'm a blissful mess, bursting with need. "Please," I beg.

"Please what, princess?"

I don't know. I don't know what I need.

"Please, fuck you harder?" He picks up speed and delves inside the tight channel with a vigor that pulls silent screams from my well-used body. "Please, your tits need some attention?" He palms my breasts, pinning me more securely between the saddle and his hips, impaled on his long thick cock. My nipples are so sensitive, every squeeze, every roll, sends a zing of pleasure to my core. I moan loudly, my desperation filling the air, as I grip the base of the saddle tighter. "Please, let you come?"

He lowers his head, murmuring in my ear. "Because that's not happening yet." His hot breath curling into the shell lights a nerve, and the fire runs wild, reigniting itself when it reaches the tips of my toes.

He has one hand on my hip, anchoring me, and the other on my clit. His fingers circling, my legs trembling, and just as I am certain I'll die if I don't find my release soon, he pinches my swollen clit, and pulls out the plug one bead at a time as I fall apart. I tremble and grunt, writhing under him as each ball finds its way out. His thick cock works furiously inside my throbbing pussy, and I scream his name and shudder with the final wrench of the glass.

He pulls my hair back in a rough tug. "Watch me come inside you, Kate." His eyes are heavy. The sweat is dripping from his skin. My hair is twisted around his hand. With two violent thrusts he roars his release. His features ease, occasionally contorting until he stills.

Still breathing hard, he gazes at me in the glass. I'm not sure what I see in his face. In his eyes. I'm too afraid to think about it. Too afraid it will break my heart if I'm mistaken, or if it's not real. I only know that I want to look at it forever.

He leans over and places a gentle kiss at the base of my neck, before pulling out. "Are you okay?" I gasp at the emptiness, mourning the connection, and simply nod because I can't speak.

Smith ties the condom—which I'm glad he remembered, because I certainly didn't. Then frees my wrists, rubbing them vigorously between his hands. "Just hold on, babe, while I get the spreader off. You might be a little unsteady, so just hold on."

When I'm free, he carries me into the shower and turns on the water, using his body to shield me from the spray until it warms.

"Let me take care of you," he murmurs, taking the soap out of my hands. He slides his soapy fingers all over my body, up into every crease and down every slit. Then he soaps himself while the water rinses the suds from my skin. He shampoos my hair, and gently combs out the tangles like a pro. It occurs to me that he's done this before. But I don't let the thought spoil my happiness.

"Drink a little juice," he says, sitting me on the edge of his bed. "That's it. Now lie down. I'm going to hold you, like this, while you nap."

"Smith." I squeeze his arms, wrapped protectively around me.

"We'll talk about it later." He kisses my head and pulls me higher onto his chest. "You're a warrior, Kate. Don't ever lose that spark. Sleep, Princess Badass."

"I—I—" The words fade with me into the warm darkness, Smith's heartbeat a reassuring pulse against my cheek. I feel more like a sleepy princess than a badass.

32

KATE

When I wake, Smith is on the phone. I hear his muffled voice from the other room. I wonder if he knows more about the break in—about what happened to Fenny. My heart still hurts.

I dreamt about her while napping. The kittens were born, and Fenny was sunning herself in the morning light that pours into the bedroom while her babies played nearby. But it was just a dream, because in the end, there were no fluffy kittens and no peace for her. How could it have happened? The one evening I go out, someone robs the place. I'm not numb anymore. I'm mad as hell.

The police were sympathetic but acknowledged that it was unlikely we'd find the culprit. But Smith feels differently. I remember exactly what he said. *Oh, we're going to find them. And they better pray the police find them first.*

After I brush my teeth, I get dressed, but not before peeking into the room where we *played*. I say the word out loud, let it tumble off my tongue. It rolls off in a confident, fluid motion that almost surprises me.

I wander inside the quiet room, much like I did earlier. But this time I don't hug myself, confused by what I find. This time I touch the saddle with great courage, in the very spot where I lay splayed and open to him. There is a great sense of relief.

"You ready for round two?" I turn toward the deep silky baritone in the doorway. His mouth is lifted at the corners. Not in a smile, but in something that could easily become one.

"I could probably use a small break." My voice is small, as though I'm suddenly shy.

He enters the room, eating up the space between us in a few long strides. "You okay?" he asks with an alert gaze. "That might have been more ambitious than it needed to be."

"I'm good. Totally good," I say through a forced smile.

"Did you enjoy it?" Smith searches my face, touching a fingertip to my lips. "Don't tell me what you think I want to hear. Tell me the truth. Dig deep for the honesty."

I blink several times, trying to unearth the right words. "More than I thought." I smile, shy again. "A lot more." The lines on his face smooth.

"It's new to you. New to me with you. It gets better."

"None of this is entirely unfamiliar—well except the saddle."

His brow scrunches, forming strings of puzzled lines. "Oh yeah, you read porn. I almost forgot."

"Romance." I punch him in the arm.

"But?"

"But I never expected it to be a part of my life. Honestly, I wasn't even sure how much of it actually existed outside of fiction. How about you?"

"I knew it existed outside of fiction." He smirks, the dimple appears, and my knees wobble.

"That's not what I meant."

His head tilts. "It was—pretty amazing."

I think so too. The tension slides off my shoulders in big sheets, evaporating into nothing.

"Even though I'm a newbie?" *Leave it alone, Kate.*

"Something to be said for teaching a newbie." His eyes are bright, and soft. "Thank you for doing something so far out of your comfort zone. You're not the only one developing feelings."

His words are more difficult to accept than the punishing rhythm as he pinned me against the saddle, chasing his release.

"Thank you for trusting me," he says. The words are heartfelt and it's impossible to miss the gratitude in his voice.

"It's not that hard to trust you." What's hard is not to let myself get too comfortable in the cocoon we created. Not to feel too safe there.

He tucks a wilted curl behind my ear. "We need to talk, Kate." His face is somber, and my mind flies somewhere terrible, second guessing everything he just told me. *Maybe it wasn't enough.*

"Fenway wasn't a hit by a car and placed on the sidewalk by a good Samaritan."

After holding her last night, I didn't think so. But please, please don't tell me a predator gutted her. I don't know why, but this seems like the worst kind of death. "Do you think she cut herself on the screen jumping out the window?"

He shook his head. "No. There was no blood on the screen or anywhere near it, but there was a puddle of dried blood on the mattress under the comforter. We didn't notice it last night because it had soaked into the sheets, and was covered, but by this morning—my guys found it when they went to check the place. We think someone killed her there and carried her outside."

"In my bed? Who would? Why? The cat didn't hurt anyone. Who would do something so awful?"

"I don't know."

"Oh my God." I sink to the ground. "It's my fault."

"Kate, it's not your fault. It. Is. Not. Your. Fault."

"But if I'd been home. If I had kept a better eye on her."

"We can 'what if' this to death, but it's not going to help us find the bastard who did it. It's not your fault, but I am worried about you."

You don't need to worry about me because I'm a survivor. It'll take time, but I know how to do this. "I'll be okay. I just need some time to come to grips with what happened. Think about how frightened she must have been. I want to help you find who did this."

"It's not about your mental health. I'm worried that this was a signal meant for you. Are you working any angle of the King story I don't know about?"

"No."

"What about the societies?"

"No. After the restraining order—I've been so busy with Fenny, and work, and the bulletin for St. Maggie's, ..." *and you*, "... that I've let it fall by the wayside." I'm embarrassed to admit it. After all, isn't that why I'm in Charleston?

"Are you sure you haven't spoken to anyone?"

"Other than Lucinda, no. I'm sure."

He has that faraway look he gets sometimes. He listens and soaks up everything in the environment, but it's like his brain is running on dozens of different circuits, all feeding him information that he's cross-checking.

"I want you to stay with me. Make a list of things you need for a week or two, and we'll go by your house to get them."

A week or two? "No, Smith. I want to go back to my place. I want to bury Fenway."

"She's been buried. My guys did it when they secured your house. They put the mouse toy she liked with her like you wanted," he adds gently.

"Thank you."

"You can go back today, but then you're coming with me for the foreseeable future."

"I—"

"This is non-negotiable. Whoever killed Fenway is a monster. They are either sick or doing a sick person's bidding. Either way, it's unsafe for you right now."

33

SMITH

I left Kate at her house with Ty and Josh. Ty is one of my best men. The best of the best. Josh is new to a civilian-protection detail, but he's had plenty of experience dealing with an enemy. He likes Kate, which isn't crucial to the job, but it will make it more pleasant for her.

When I arrive at Sweetgrass, Zack's nurse is leaving and lets me inside. I'm grateful it's Sunday and I don't have to stop to chit-chat with Lally in the kitchen or with Patrick, JD's assistant. I go directly to JD's study where I know he's waiting.

I knock on the door, but don't wait for an invitation to enter. There was a time when I would have said that nothing would ever come between us. But that was before Kate. The relationship is bruised right now, and I'm about to put it on life support. "I'm sorry to barge in on a Sunday evening, but I need a favor, and wanted to make the ask in person."

"You're always welcome here. What's up?"

I sit at the edge of his desk. "Someone cut open the screen to a window at Kate's. They killed the pregnant cat in her bed. We found it last night when we came home, clean slice through the belly. Looked like it was done by a hunter, or someone who has gutted an animal before."

"*Jesus.* Do you have any idea who might have done it?"

"No. They made it look like a burglary, but all they took was some worthless jewelry and her laptop—not the backup, which was sitting next to it. They left the expensive television sitting there in the open. It was staged. Poorly staged. I suspect it has something to do with King. A warning of some sort."

He nods. "They took her laptop. Is she close to something?"

"No. That's the thing. Although sometimes you can be standing in a pile of horseshit and not know it. If they were afraid of what was on the computer—they would have taken the backup too. It's a warning. I'm positive."

"What's your favor?"

"I want to move Kate into my place, here."

"I'm sorry?" He grips the edge of the desk with both hands, his thumbs hooked under the lip. "You want to bring trouble to my doorstep?"

I lean across his desk to make my point. "There's no safer place in Charleston than Sweetgrass. I've made sure of that. I just need her here long enough so that I can put together some airtight security at her place. I'm already working on it, but it can't happen overnight."

"Fuck no, she can't stay here. And don't you think you're blowing this just a tad out of proportion?"

"No," says a voice from the doorway, with one hand propped on her hip. I turn to face her, my blood at a full boil at JD's callousness. "I don't think he is blowing it a *tad* out of proportion. But it's a damn funny accusation coming from your mouth." Gabby stomps into the room, standing in front of JD's desk, with her chin lifted for a fight.

"She cannot stay here," he barks, standing and glowering. "You have a daughter. Have you forgotten?"

"You mean the one I pushed from my womb and fed from my breasts?"

The gravity of the situation hits me, and I feel awful they're arguing over something I stirred up. But I'm not going to stop it. I need Kate here, where the security is essentially impenetrable.

"I forbid it." JD raps his knuckles on the desk for emphasis.

"You forbid it? Is this not my home, too?"

"This is our home. Where Gracie should be safe, and Zack, and you," he adds, his eyes darting to me. "I am so pissed off you would put my family at risk for some woman. I'm not sure I can ever get past this, Smith."

Gabby walks around the desk and rubs JD's arm. "Is this who we are? Is this who you are? Because it's not who I am."

"We have a daughter to consider."

"This is not who I want my daughter to be. It's easy to throw money at problems, or hand generous checks to people in need. This is the hard stuff. Sacrifice that demonstrates real charity and genuine compassion. The rest is window dressing."

JD pounds his hand on the desk. His eyes are black with a fury that I haven't seen since Grace was born. "Goddamn you, Smith." His eyes flit from his wife to me. "Fine. You want her to stay here. You put your plan for the new business on hold indefinitely, because she's your responsibility while you're putting my family in harm's way. And you," he spits at Gabby, "you forget about going to Georgie's Place while she's here. You're under lockdown along with the baby." He glares at me. "Put the whole damn place under lockdown."

"JD," Gabby says. "You—"

"Do not say another word," he warns her. "If you want that woman to stay here, that's the way it has to be."

"JD," she pleads, squeezing his arm.

"No, Gabrielle. I almost lost you twice. I won't tempt fate a third time." He stalks out without another word to either of us.

"Is he right, Smith?" she asks. "Are we inviting trouble here, or is it just his usual paranoia?"

"I don't know. I can't say for certain." My conscience is biting. Not just because of the fight. Not just because I put our friendship at risk, but because I have no way of knowing for certain what kind of trouble will follow Kate to Sweetgrass. And I have no way of knowing whether the security here will hold up. It's never been really tested.

We have a saying in the army, *no battle plan, no matter how well-designed, ever survives first contact with the enemy.* It was my father's response every time someone asked if the plan was foolproof.

"Look, this was a mistake. I should have never put either of you in this position. I'm perfectly capable of protecting Kate, anywhere. We'll do something else."

"No," she says firmly. "Bring her here. There's no safer place for someone who needs protection than Sweetgrass. We all know it."

34

KATE

*J*osh pulls up to the guard house at Sweetgrass, and we're waved through. Getting onto the property is nothing like the night of Smith's party. He takes the familiar tree-lined drive, but we don't turn left toward the main house. Instead, we cross a small pond and continue past a stable, and a couple of barns on the right. I can't see it from the road, but the ocean is somewhere to the left. The property is enormous.

We pull into a cul-de-sac with three houses. All are more modest than the main house, but still lovely, with lush plantings and colorful flowers cascading from painted window boxes. Ty gets out and opens the door for me.

"We'll get your bags," he says. "Smith's inside waiting for you."

I don't bother to ask any questions, because I'm sure I'll get the same answer they've each given me at least a dozen times today. *You'll need to talk to Smith.*

When we get to the porch, Josh knocks on the door.

"It's open," Smith calls from inside. He meets us in the entryway, and gives me a quick, reassuring smile. "Just leave the bags," he instructs Ty and Josh. "I'll take them upstairs. Thanks, guys."

"We'll be in the office," Ty says, before they turn to leave.

"Appreciate it," Smith says, rubbing the back of his neck. "Wait a second." He turns to me. "Josh and Ty are your security team. There will be others, too, but they're the core of the team. The security office is located in the house next-door. That's where your team will be while you're on the property. It's also where my office is located."

He pauses, crossing his arms across his chest, his biceps straining the T-shirt fabric. "They're in charge. You need to listen to them. To *everything* they say. They will protect you, with their lives, if necessary."

A small panic begins to rise. "I-I don't want that." I cup my elbows, squeezing tight. "I don't want anyone to risk their life for me."

"It's what we do. But it won't likely come to that—and the risk is lower if you do as we say. It's the best way to keep everyone safe. I need your promise."

I glance at the two beefy guys. Both are well over six feet tall with muscle to spare. Josh has such a baby face the thought of anything happening to him because of me ..."I promise. Do you have children?" I ask them.

"Not yet," Josh says, not blinking an eye.

"A boy and a girl," Ty responds.

I peer into both of their serious faces. "Not one more person dies. Not one more animal dies because of me. Don't do anything stupid on my account. Please. I couldn't live with it."

Smith squeezes my shoulder. "I'll talk to you guys later."

"I appreciate all this," I tell Smith after they leave. "I know you're trying to help, but it isn't going to work for me."

"What are you talking about?"

"No one—not one more person puts themselves at risk for me. I mean it."

"Alright. Let's get you settled and then I'll show you around."

I glare at him. I know a blow off when I hear one. "Don't think this discussion is over."

He grabs my bags, muttering under his breath.

The house isn't huge, but no expense was spared. The kitchen has professional-style stainless steel appliances and granite counters. It's nicer than anything I've ever worked in. It's also vastly different than the apartment. It's hard to believe they belong to the same man.

Unlike his place at Wildflower, it's warm here, with dog-eared books on a small table near a recliner, and photos of smiley little girls on the mantle. But it's the stick-figure drawings attached with magnets to the refrigerator that make my heart swell, and for a few minutes, I forget my life might be in danger.

I follow Smith up the stairs to a bedroom that is decidedly masculine. There is a wall of windows with an impressive ocean view. "Is this your room?"

"Our room." He puts down the bags. "I brought in a dresser from one of the other rooms and made space for you in the closet. There are two more bedrooms in the house, but it seems ridiculous to pretend you'll be sleeping elsewhere. I'd drag you into my bed every night anyway."

I smile at him. "The Neanderthals really had nothing on you." I'm rewarded with a dimpled smirk, arrogant as the day is long.

"The bathroom's through here." He points to French doors, which I suspect lead to a luxurious bath. "There are towels in the closet and extra toiletries. Take whatever you need. If we run out of something, or if there's something you want that I don't have, add it to the list on the corkboard in the kitchen. Same with food."

"It looks like you thought of everything, and I brought stuff with me. But if I need anything, or if you need anything, I can pick it up on my way home from work tomorrow."

He rubs his hand over his jaw, studying me. The hand scrubbing the jaw, or squeezing the back of the neck is never good news with him. "We need to talk."

This is going to be particularly bad. I already sense it. "Let's go downstairs," he says, leaving the room. I follow him to the kitchen. "Do you want a beer?"

"No."

"Some water?"

"No. I'm fine."

"*Fine.* You keep saying that, but I don't believe it."

"I'll actually be fine after you tell me whatever it is you're avoiding telling me. Not that I don't enjoy watching you play hostess."

He sniffs, and his mouth twists into a snarl. *It must be worse than I imagined.* "Sweetgrass is on lockdown."

"What does that mean?"

"It means that there are limitations on who comes onto the property and who leaves." He has the impatient tone he gets when the conversation is unpleasant.

"I'm not sure what you're getting at."

"You can't go to work while you're here."

What? "I have to go to work. I have appointments, a class, people who are depending on me." He drums his fingers on the counter while I speak.

"It's not happening. I'm sorry."

"Take me home," I demand, with all the dignity of a five-year-old.

He sits on a stool and pulls me between his legs. His hands clutch both of mine. "You are not safe at home. You need to stay here until I can make it safe. I'm working as quickly as I can to make it happen."

"I'm a prisoner until then?"

"Not just you," he responds soberly. "Gabby can't leave here to go to Georgie's Place or to go anywhere. There will be restrictions on Lally, and on many of the other people who work and live here. And no one else is complaining." The last part stings, but I deserved it.

"*No.* I don't want that. I don't want everyone to be inconvenienced because of me."

"They're happy to do it, Kate. We don't know what's going on, but you're safer here than anywhere. Everyone is aware of it." This is a lot to swallow. Maybe too much.

"Please work fast on getting my place secure. I know you're busy, and it's a lot to ask, but I can't have everyone inconvenienced. It's not fair to them. I barely know these people."

"They're my friends. You're important to me, and they know it. I would do the same for them—without hesitation."

I nod. "There is one thing I do need to do—somewhere I need to go—it's safe. Totally safe."

"No place is totally safe. But where do you need to go?"

"St. Maggie's." His expression tightens, but I don't let it dissuade me. "I need to talk to Father Jesse. I want to tell him in person about Fenway. He trusted me to take care of her. I promised I would. It's weighing heavily on me. I'll go straight there and come right back, and I won't ask to leave again. Please let me do that one thing."

He considers the request carefully, before grasping my hips, and pulling me closer. "You can't go by yourself. Regardless of how safe you think it is on the island, you have to get there and back. I'll be out of town for most of the day tomorrow at a meeting. My guys will be working on the extra security. I can't afford to be paying a visit to the clergy."

"You don't need to go. They can search me at the guard house when I come back. Please, just this one thing."

The tip of his tongue is resting on the bow of his lip. The skin beneath his eyes is smeared with black from not sleeping. *Because he's been worried about me.* Regret twists like a knife in my conscience. I can make this easier for him. I cradle his cheek in my hand. "I don't need to go. It's okay."

He presses his warm cheek into my palm. "Ty and Josh will take you. No stops between here and the island, or on the way back. You will listen to everything they say. You will not argue with them, and if they give you instructions, you will obey immediately."

I nod. "Yes."

"You cannot let the priest know you're coming, and you cannot tell anyone that you're going. That includes Lucinda and Fiona. We don't know if anyone's listening. If they are, it could put everyone in danger."

"Do you believe I'm at that much risk?"

"I'm not sure, Kate." He reaches for an errant curl, twirling it around his finger. "But I'm not taking any chances with you, or with anyone else I care about. Why don't you shower, and I'll make sandwiches for us? We should go to bed early." I expect him to make some suggestive or lewd remark about going to bed early, but he doesn't. "I want to take you to the range first thing in the morning and see what you can do with that gun of yours."

35

KATE

I have a new laptop, a new phone, because apparently my old phone isn't secure enough for Smith's tastes, and I'm being chauffeured around like royalty, or perhaps like a prisoner. It depends on one's perspective.

The hardest part, aside from the fact that Fenny is dead and everyone at Sweetgrass is under lockdown, is I can't talk to Fiona about any of it. She leaves for their Cape house tomorrow with Brett and the boys, and she doesn't need to know about my predicament before she goes, otherwise, she'll spend the entire month worrying. It's the one time during the year where they are free from family obligations and the Nanas' prying. I don't want to spoil it for her.

Josh and Ty are quiet in the front seat. When they picked me up, they brought me a thermos of coffee and two muffins, courtesy of Lally. But I can see they're not crazy about this trip. The worst part is that Father Jesse might not be here. He's normally available on Mondays, but he could have been called away because someone has taken ill.

Josh pulls into the parking lot closest to the rectory, and a tall man with salt and pepper hair is raking the beds.

"Who's that?" Ty asks.

"The gardener who works here. His name is Silas, but I've never met him. He has a house on the property down that lane." I point to the dirt road, contemplating whether I should tell them about Silas's prison record, but decide that it was a long time ago, and it was told to me in confidence.

Thankfully, they agree to wait outside. "What should I tell Father Jesse, or the church secretary, if they ask about you?"

"Tell them we're providing security. That Smith Sinclair feels your connection to the Wilders requires you to have a security detail."

"I can't lie to a priest."

"It's not a lie. You're protecting them. Everyone who knows the details is at some risk."

I'm not sure if that's exactly true, but I don't want to risk anyone's safety. Josh and Ty know this, and I expect this is a bit of manipulation on their part, but I can't take the chance. "I won't say a word."

I walk toward the rectory, admiring the giant stone turret against the bright blue sky. As I climb the steps, I catch Silas watching me. As soon as he's caught, he averts his eyes and goes back to the garden. A chill runs through me. There's something about the way he looked at me. *It's your imagination, Kate. You're holding his history against him. It's not fair. He paid his dues.* "Hello," I call to him, but he keeps weeding as though he didn't hear me.

When I get inside, Virginia is on the phone. She waves and motions for me to sit. A few moments later, Father Jesse sticks his head out of the office.

"Kate," he says softly with a smile. "Come into my office where we can talk freely." I go meekly, my heart heavy with the news I'm about to deliver.

"Did you get a new car?" he asks after he shuts the office door.

"No. I—Smith Sinclair has some concerns—because of the

Wilders—and he's insisting that I have a security detail assigned to me." I hate myself for the lie.

I'm so nervous, sitting still is a problem. "I brought the mock-ups for the newsletter, but first there's something I need to tell you," I blurt.

He stands and comes over to where I'm sitting, and places a hand on my shoulder.

"You look a little pale. Let's go into the reconciliation room. It's the perfect place for telling me things, and we won't be interrupted. You'll be happier talking there."

The last place I want to go is to the reconciliation room, but I follow him, leaving the mock-ups on the desk. When we get to the room, he flips the sign that says welcome, to the side that reads *God is in Session, Do Not Disturb*. The corny sign suits him.

It's a lovely space, overlooking the garden where Silas had been working. But I don't see him now.

We sit in two upholstered chairs near the window. There's a box of tissues on a low pedestal table between us, and he brings me a cup of water.

"What has you looking so forlorn?" he asks gently.

"Fenway is dead. All her kittens are dead."

He reaches for my hand. "Oh, Kate. I'm so sorry. You must be crushed. Tell me what happened."

"Someone broke into the house and killed her during a robbery. It was awful." I realize as soon as I say it, that I divulged too much. He's a priest. This is a reconciliation room. He won't say anything.

"That is awful. Were you at work when it happened?"

"No. I was out with a friend."

He lets go of my hands and sits back in his chair. "I see." The words seem laden with accusation, but I suspect it's my conscience biting me.

"We were gone for a few hours. I don't normally leave her alone unless I'm at work or running an errand."

"You were with Mr. Sinclair?"

"Yes." I clasp my hands in my lap.

"You've been spending a lot of time with him, yes?"

I nod.

"He's the reason we haven't seen you at Mass?"

I shrug. "Yes."

"Kate," he takes both my hands, again, holding them in his. "You look miserable, like the weight of the world is on your shoulders. Although, I think it's your conscience that's heavy. Would you like me to hear your confession?"

No. I don't know. "I'm not sure."

"God wants to absolve you of your sins. Let Him carry your burden."

I suppose it makes me spineless, but I don't say no. I don't know how to. "Okay."

He gets up and brings over a kneeler. "We can sit, or you can kneel there, whatever you prefer."

I'm accustomed to kneeling during confession, and maybe this would seem less awkward if I got to my knees. "I'll kneel."

"Whenever you're ready," he says, pulling a chair closer to the kneeler.

I lower my head and close my eyes, while making the sign of the cross. "In the name of the Father, the Son, and of the Holy Spirit. Bless me Father, for I have sinned. It's been eighteen months since my last confession, and these are my sins."

I confess to lying, swearing, and using God's name in vain. I confess to vanity and willfulness, and the list goes on and on, because I am a sinner. And while I don't fully embrace the sacrament of reconciliation, here in a church, on my knees before a priest and God, I choose to believe that my sins will be forgiven.

"Do you want to tell me about your relationship with Mr. Sinclair?" he asks when I quiet.

No. I don't. But I will, because if I don't, I'll be committing another sin while on my knees in the confessional. "I have had sexual relations outside of marriage. And used birth control." *Another sin.*

"Were you forced or coerced in any way to have sexual relations, or did you give your body willingly?"

I know confessing can be like this, especially during the modern reconciliation, but I'm not accustomed to having such frank discussions about my sexuality with a priest. Usually we both skirt around the issue with some embarrassment and dispose of it as quickly as possible.

"Kate?"

"I gave myself willingly."

He is quiet for a moment while I fidget. "Are you sorry?"

I attempt a deep breath, but the guilt and shame are heavy in my chest, clogging the airways and the most I can muster is a shallow breath. "No."

"Will you continue to have relations with him?"

I squeeze my eyes together. "Yes."

"Is this something you enjoyed?"

I don't understand the question. It's a sin, whether I enjoyed it or not. I want to get this over with. "Yes." I feel so exposed.

My head is bowed, but my eyes are open. I see a flash of anger in Father Jesse's eyes. Maybe I'm wrong. It's hard to tell from this angle.

"Let's sit, Kate."

It's quiet until we're both seated at the window, again. "I can't absolve you of your sins unless you have a pure heart."

I know this.

"I don't know how to put it delicately, so I'm just going to share with you my perspective as a priest, a shepherd, with many years of experience bringing lost lambs back into the flock." He pauses for a moment. "Sinclair is a bad influence on you. He's the devil tempting you into sins of the flesh. Bad things happen when you don't resist him. It's not a punishment, but rather a sign from God who loves you. Your conscience will not be light again until you shun the devil's advances."

The devil? No. I don't accept that. "He's a good man," I say peevishly, in defense of Smith. "And he's my friend. I have feelings for him. Strong feelings—not just physical—I care about him. I might love him. I'm not certain."

Father Jesse moves to the edge of his seat, closer to me. "Lust and love are two emotions often mistaken for one another." He says it matter-of-factly. I feel like I'm fifteen sitting in Father Tierney's office on that awful night in the frat house. He said something very similar to me.

"God doesn't always make it easy for us, but He is always there to light the way. I will absolve you of all your sins, but for the sin of fornication. I will be here when you begin to see things more clearly, when you choose a righteous God, because I know you will. Until then, I will pray that the Holy Spirit imbues you with wisdom."

I nod. I know the devil reference was to make a point. But I'm hurt and angry at him for the comparison.

"I'm not going to give you penance—not a traditional penance, anyway." I glance at him. "I want you to think about Sinclair, about who he is, and how he fits into your Catholic faith. In a week, you'll come back, and we'll discuss your thoughts. Deal?"

"Yes." I give him a small contrite smile. But my anger hasn't dissipated.

"Why don't we go back to my office and take a look at the bulletins you created?"

Yes, please. When we step out of the room, I'm finally able to take a deep breath.

When I get back to Smith's place, I change into shorts, and after a restless forty-five minutes where I can't stop thinking about what Father Jesse said about Smith, I decide to go for a walk. Maybe I can find the pond with the little bridge. I leave a note in case Smith stops in. Although he's in DC on business today, and I doubt he'll be back before me. I also text Josh before leaving the house.

Kate: I'm going to take a walk around the property. Is that a problem?

Josh: Not as long as you have your phone with you and you don't set one foot off Sweetgrass.

Kate: Yes to both. Smith said not to go anywhere without my gun. It's at the security office.

Josh: You can't have it on the premises. The property is closely monitored. You don't need it.

When we were at the range this morning, Smith told me I needed to carry my gun with me everywhere. I suppose he meant everywhere that wasn't Sweetgrass.

Being at the range with Smith was quite an experience. He's an excellent shot. Scary good. I've never seen anything like it, and I've clocked endless hours at the range. Me, on the other hand? I was rusty, and of course since I was trying to impress, I was off my mark a lot. But Smith was patient, and by the time we left, I was more confident, and hitting the target more often than not. He promised to take me back this week.

I walk past the stable, still thinking about the way Father Jesse talked about Smith. I realize Christians aren't very Christian when it comes to stomping out evil, and Catholics are no exception, but to call Smith the devil—even to make a point—that was wrong. Wrong in so many ways. I will do my penance and consider how Smith fits into my life, Catholic or otherwise. But I won't be choosing the strict teachings of my faith over him. That I already know.

Just when I'm sure I've lost my way, I stumble onto the pond in the center of the property. As I cross the bridge, I notice Gabby with the baby. They don't see me. Gabby is blowing bubbles, and Gracie is sitting in the stroller waving her hands and kicking her feet, trying to snatch bubbles from the air. I watch them for a few moments—deciding whether to spoil their fun, but more than anything, I am transfixed by the beauty of the pair. The natural simplicity of the bond between mother and daughter. In the ultimate act of indulgence, I allow myself to do something I haven't done in a long, long time.

I imagine a woman with wavy, burnt-red hair and alabaster skin, playing with her little red-haired daughter on a blanket in the park down the street from where I grew up. The woman's three older sons are off climbing on the playground equipment, so it's just the two of them. The mother tells the baby how much she loves her, cooing softly, while blowing raspberries on her belly. The little girl squeals in delight. It's fanciful, and exists only in my imagination because there are no photographs, no evidence of it ever happening. But every time I walked by that park on my way to elementary school, I imagined my mother, on one of the few good days she had, taking us to the neighborhood park.

I take out my phone and snap some pictures of Gabby and Gracie. I'll frame one and give it to Gabby as a thank you for allowing me to stay at Sweetgrass, despite all the trouble. I scroll through the photos and save the best one to the cloud. I can edit it from my laptop and pick up a nice frame when I'm no longer confined to the premises.

Gabby will love it, and one day, maybe Gracie will, too. Although I hope she never needs photos to remember her mother.

I fell asleep in the recliner with the TV on while I waited for Smith to come home from DC. I don't wake when he comes in, but the foraging in the kitchen rouses me.

He's leaning against the counter eating cold macaroni and cheese from a casserole Lally sent over with some chicken.

"I can heat that up for you."

"I don't need it heated up. I need you to come here." He wraps me in a warm embrace. "I would say I'm sorry I woke you, but that would be a lie." He licks his way into my mouth, placing the food on the counter behind him.

"Eat," I say after a few long minutes of kissing that I know is going to end in sex.

"I thought that's what I was doing."

I roll my eyes as he grabs the dish. "How did it go today with Josh and Ty?"

"Better than I expected. Ty is a little scary, but I guess it's because I'm used to seeing Josh lurking." I want to ask him if he found anything more about the break in, but he looks exhausted and it can wait until the morning.

He rinses the dishes and places them in the dishwasher. He has the neat and orderly habits of a soldier living in close quarters. When my brothers first came home on leave, they would be neat and tidy too, but after a few days they were back to their old selves.

"How was your day?" I ask, while he puts the leftover chicken in the fridge.

"Better than expected too. I caught up with a couple guys at the Pentagon from my old unit, and we had a beer before I came back. Rebel rousers." He grins.

"Takes one to know one. I bet you got into your share of trouble in the desert and left a trail of broken hearts in the sand."

"I didn't leave a single broken heart there."

"I don't believe you."

"Believe it. I never once touched a woman while I was deployed—let me take that back. In the desert, never. On leave in the Mediterranean, might have been one or two." He winks at me. "But never in the desert. Too risky."

"You afraid some girl's father was going to chase you down with a shotgun?"

"I wasn't afraid for myself. But women who are even suspected of having sex outside of marriage are stoned to death. No way to protect them. Even sex with me isn't worth dying for." He pinches my ass, and I yelp and swat his hand.

The devil. There couldn't be anything further from the truth. I'm angry at Father Jesse all over again.

"We didn't get much of anywhere on the break in today. Cops still have nothing. Your neighborhood is residential and doesn't have cameras that we can get into."

"You have that capability?" It's a dumb question, but it's too late to take back.

"What do you think I run around here, some lame back-ass operation? I have a couple guys who are good. But Chase Wilder is a pro."

"Chase? Really?"

"Yep. Little nerd's got game."

"It's funny, people aren't always as they appear. Delilah looked familiar. But it was this morning at the range, with her hair pulled back, when I finally put it together. I remember the trial and all the news coverage when she was outed. Her hair had been dark. It's funny how such a small thing can throw you off the trail."

"I don't want to talk about Delilah. I want to talk about why you're not naked in my bed, waiting for me, with a green-jeweled plug in your ass. The one that matches your eyes." He tosses me over one shoulder and slaps my backside on the way to his bed. "We're about to fix that."

36

SMITH

It's been nearly a week since the break in, and we're not any closer to knowing why it happened. All the leads are cold. Nothing points back to King or to any of his cronies. Not a single thing. Although that doesn't surprise me.

The robbery itself was amateur hour, but that's what they wanted us to believe. The people surrounding King are pros. They don't give a shit about him. It's all about protecting his judicial seat. We'll eventually figure it out, but it's taking more time and resources than it should.

I've been dragging my feet on beefing up security at Kate's. I had the mattress replaced and the apartment thoroughly cleaned after we swept it for evidence. But I've got to get my ass into gear. She agreed to take the week off, but that's it, and Gabby is beyond restless. I can see it in her eyes. She stopped by to talk to me yesterday, wanted to know if we'd made any progress.

JD and I haven't exchanged a single civil word since Sunday evening. He's blown off our morning runs and avoided me at every turn. In truth, I haven't gone out of my way to see him, either. He's right. I'm putting his family at risk. It's a tiny risk, but it's not nothing. This pains me. I love Gabby and Grace, and my job has been to protect them, above all else. Up until now, I've never let anything get in the way of that.

What JD's wrong about is that I did it for *some* woman.

Kate's not just some woman. And the last few days while we've been playing house, it's occurred to me that I would miss her if she wasn't here. Not just in my bed—although I would sure as hell miss her there, but I would miss the smell of her shampoo on the sheets. I would miss someone giving a damn about how my day had gone. I would miss her green eyes and her sassy smile and her clever retorts. And the way my heart stills and softens when she's in my arms.

I'm pretty much fucked. At least I know it.

I glance out the window to JD pulling up. From the looks of him getting out of the vehicle, I doubt he's here to apologize. It takes less than ten seconds from the moment the car door slams until he's breathing fire in my office.

"What the fuck is this?" He shoves a newspaper in front of me.

It's a photo of Gabby and Grace near the fishpond.

I stare at the image. But I can't fully comprehend what I'm seeing. It's as though my brain isn't firing on all cylinders. I'm not sure it's firing at all.

"That reporter took a picture of *my daughter* and sent it to the paper." He is spewing venom, out of his mind with rage, and I can't blame him. "From the moment she was born, I promised Grace, and myself, that I would not let her be dangled in public. That she would be a normal kid. That she would be safe."

He picks up the paper and slams it on the desk, like he's catching a fly. "The AP picked it up, and it's all over the internet. All over town. All over the fucking country—maybe the world. How much do you think the photograph of *my daughter* earned her?"

I still can't form a single fucking word. My chest is collapsing. It's as though a crane dropped a steel pallet on it.

"I want her gone. Now." He's going to want to exact retribution. I can't blame him for that, either. Right now, I want to hurt her, too.

"I'll escort her off the property myself if necessary." His voice is menacing. "I want her out of Charleston before the sun sets on the Sabbath. If you aren't man enough to do it, I'll find someone else to protect my family."

"I'll fix this."

"There's no fixing this. It's out there. Forever. We can only mitigate the damage."

"I'm sorry. I am so fucking sorry."

"You brought the enemy inside. Cozied up to her, and let her weasel her way into your bed until all you could think about was her pussy. You turned your back on the people who care about you. For what? For a stupid bitch that we knew all along couldn't be trusted."

After spewing venom all over the office, he turns to leave.

"JD—"

"Save it. If you give a shit about what happens to my daughter, help me pick up the pieces. Start next door."

The outside door slams behind him. No one from the other room, aside from Delilah, lifts their head. They all heard it, though. Every word. Some leader I turned out to be.

Delilah peeks into the office. "Do you want me to go next door and take care of it?"

"No," I bark. "Leave me alone for a few minutes."

I pick up the paper, and then pull the image up on my computer. Gracie's smiling little face. Her innocent little face. It's everywhere. How could Kate betray me like this? How?

I grab the newspaper, and stick my head into the conference room, waving the evidence of my stupidity in the air. "Get on this. Call Chase Wilder for help. We won't be able to shut it all down, but we can get the photo off the mainstream outlets." That just leaves the dark corners of the web. *Fuck.*

I stalk next door, the rage and the pain of betrayal, *yes, fucking pain,* all-consuming. Kate's in the shower. I take the steps two at a time, and drag her from under the warm spray. "Get dressed, get your things together, and get out. You have thirty minutes, so don't stand there with your damn mouth open wasting time."

"What? Wait!" She reaches into the shower and turns off the water, then wraps a towel around herself. She can stand there naked for all I care. She's never looked less appealing.

I shove the paper at her. "Did you take this photo?"

Her eyes widen in surprise. "Yes," she says softly. "I took it on Monday afternoon."

"How could you do this? How? And why? If you needed money, I would have given you money. You didn't need to exploit my friends like this. People, who despite the risk, opened their home to you."

"I didn't sell the photo. It—"

"You gave it away? For a damn Pulitzer?" I slap the paper against my thigh. "I don't know what's worse."

"No! I took the photo—"

"I don't want to hear your bullshit. You betrayed them. You betrayed me. In a way I can never forgive."

"I—"

"No. I don't want to hear another damn lie from your mouth. Get your things and Josh will take you home. Plan on leaving Charleston within the next two days."

"I have responsibilities here. I can't just walk away. You have the right to kick me out of your home, but you have no right to make me leave Charleston. I did nothing wrong. If you bothered to look into your heart for just a single minute, to see me as something other than the enemy, you would see that I love you. That I would never betray you—or the Wilders, for that matter."

"You took the photo. You haven't left this place with your phone since. The only way it could have gotten out is if you sent it to someone. You are the enemy. The one I let in."

I slam the door on my way out. *Pussy makes a man stupid.* It never has before, but it certainly made me a moron this time. *Jesus Christ.*

"Go next door," I instruct Josh, "and make sure she doesn't get into any more trouble while she packs. Then take her home, and you and Ty take turns with the surveillance. We're stepping back her security."

"One man on her at a time?" he asks, skeptically. Josh likes her, and I can see he doesn't agree with my decision to step back security.

I glare at him. "One at a time. I won't waste any more resources than that on her. If you have a problem with—"

"No problems," he responds coolly.

I'm tempted to pull everything, but—I crack my knuckles—but I can't. I don't have the balls to do it.

"The alarm is set up—teach her how to use it. Remind her to carry her weapon. But that's it. She'll be leaving Charleston in a couple days. Then she ceases to be my problem."

"Should we take the tracker off her phone and car?"

I blow out a breath. "No. I want to know where she is. Go." I glance at Gracie's face on my screen. "Delilah," I shout, as Josh is leaving.

"You need to calm down," she says quietly, so no one else can hear. "You're no good like this."

She's right, but I can't, so I ignore her and her damn warning. "Who was manning the surveillance on the property Monday? What were they so fucking busy doing that they didn't see Kate taking photos of Gabby and the baby?"

"LT."

"We had only one person on it?"

"Between the new venture, what we were already doing, and the extra security on McKenna—you were gone all day Monday. We were stretched pretty thin."

"Don't make excuses."

"I don't make excuses." Delilah's not like Josh. She doesn't back down from a fight with me—or with anyone—unless it's part of a strategy. I rock back in my chair, hands behind my head.

"I want to see LT as soon as he arrives, and have someone pull the tapes from Monday afternoon." She's studying me, arms perfectly still at her side. "Why are you still standing here?"

"Let me investigate this. You're too close to it. And there's no reason you should have to beat yourself up any more than necessary."

"Oh, that's where you're wrong. I need to beat myself up until I pass out, so that I remember never to do something so fucking stupid again."

37

KATE

The days since I left Sweetgrass have passed in a blur. Lack of sleep, too much wine, and not enough food make for a potent cocktail that has wreaked havoc with my system. The worst part is that there's no one to talk to.

Fiona knows something is up, but we don't talk on the phone much while she's at the Cape. Family time first—it's a deal she has with Brett. Fi minimizes her phone time, and he doesn't play golf. She'll be back at the end of next week, and I'll talk her ear off then.

My phone dings with an alert. I reach for it and turn it over. *Oh God.* The Boston Commissioner's job went to Moniz. The blows just keep coming.

I pull up one article after another. Most are measured, but there are a few that tear into my father. One in particular, that cites the information that leaked from the police department to the Sentinel. My chest hurts, but I'm cried out.

I didn't steal that information any more than I sent the photo to the paper. If Smith sees the article, it will just remind him that I've done it before. I don't know exactly what happened at the Sentinel. My guess is someone in the department who supported

Moniz fed it to a reporter. That certainly wasn't me. The issue with the photo is clearer. Someone hacked into my phone. There are no other possibilities.

A techie friend from the Sun tried to sort it out for me, but she could only get so far. It's too expensive for me to pay a forensic analyst to look into it. I don't have that kind of money.

Why? That's the question I keep asking myself. Why would anyone bother? I keep coming back to the same answer—Grace Wilder's photo was valuable because she's been so carefully protected. My phone must have been the weak link.

I can't think about it anymore. I need to call my father.

While the phone rings, all I can think about is how much I dread this conversation. He wanted the commissioner's job bad.

"Yeah," he answers gruffly.

"I just read about the job, Dad. I'm so sorry."

"After everything I've given those bastards. They screw me like this." He sounds like he's been drinking. It's not even eight in the morning.

"When did you find out?"

"They called me in on Wednesday," he growls. *Three days ago.*

"Is Joyce with you?"

"Nah. Bitch left yesterday. Said she won't put up with the drinking. I told her to get the hell out then." *Oh God.* The last time he missed a promotion, he went on a bender that lasted two weeks. It was years ago. If it hadn't been for his buddies staging an intervention and covering for him, he'd have lost his badge.

"Is Tommy staying at the house?"

"Nah. He hooked up with some broad."

"How about if I come home for a visit? I'll make you a meatloaf, and fill the freezer with things you can microwave. Maybe we can catch a Sox game. I'll see if I can get tickets."

He starts to whimper. "That job shoulda been mine."

"I know. It's not fair." I need to tell him to stop drinking. But I have to tread lightly or he'll push me away too. "I bet you haven't had breakfast. You might feel better if you eat something. And—how about if, just for today, you don't have any more to drink."

"Don't tell me how to live my life, little girl," he shouts. "I'm your father."

I finally hang up after another half hour of him grousing and sobbing, with a promise to visit in a week. I just took time off when I was on lockdown at Sweetgrass. I don't want to lose my job, but I need to make sure he's okay. If he loses his job, it will be a lot worse than me losing mine.

But I'm not going anywhere yet. Sinclair doesn't get to kick me out of the city like he owns it. First, I need to figure out where I'm going and what I'm doing. I need to talk it through with Fi.

I call my brother Tommy to send him to check on my dad. When he doesn't answer, I text.

Kate: Hey. Just talked to Dad. He's been drinking. Sounds like for days. Can you check on him?

Tommy: Sure. I never have anything better to do than clean up your messes.

Kate: This is not my fault.

Tommy: It's all your fault. Still can't figure out how you live with yourself.

Kate: Just check on him. Please.

I toss the phone on the bed next to me. I can't go back to Boston—not to live.

"Hello." I give Lucinda a peck on the cheek. "This place is gorgeous," I murmur, taking the seat across from her. We're having dinner before I leave for Boston tomorrow. Stacey, whose job I took at the library, is filling in for me while I'm gone.

"I wanted to take you somewhere special on your last night. I'm going to miss you."

"It'll only be for a couple weeks. Then I'll be back with a million questions for you about Charleston."

"You haven't given up, huh?"

"On the societies?" She nods. "I've pretty much given up."

"You done with Warren King, too?" she asks.

I shrug. "I have a feeling the final chapter of that story hasn't been written."

"You don't believe he's sick?" she asks, choosing a flaky roll from the napkin-lined basket between us.

"I have my doubts. What about you?"

"Sick? *Pft*." She rolls her eyes. "Not unless he's got the clap. It's a concocted story."

I smile. She tells it like it is, always. "You really don't like him?"

"Always found him to be a weasel." She leans across the table. "And nowhere near as good in bed as he claims to be," she says in a hushed voice. "Close your mouth, Kate. Women have been having sex with men they're not married to for centuries."

"Did you date him?"

"No! He was a bad mistake on a night I enjoyed one too many cocktails. I'm like Mae West. I never do the same mistake twice. Always look for new ones."

I press my lips together, trying to suppress the laughter that's bubbling in my chest from spilling all over the room.

"Tell me about your friend, Sinclair," she says, with a wry smile. "He a mistake?"

"It's complicated. I'm sure he sees me as a mistake. That picture of Gracie Wilder that ended up *everywhere*, I took it. I told you that. I'm not sure he'll ever forgive me."

"The Wilders should have sent a picture of that little girl to the press themselves after she was born. What did they expect? Sooner or later, someone was going to get a photograph of that child."

"I don't think it matters."

"You are a convenient scapegoat. Do you know why that is, Kate?"

I swallow some water. "No." Fortunately the waiter brings menus before she can explain.

"Because you allow it," she says as soon as his back is turned. I should have known better. She's not someone who is easily distracted by shiny objects. "You get all feisty about the women you work with," she continues, "but when it comes to sticking up for yourself, you let people pile on."

"Like Sinclair?"

"I'm reserving judgment on him at this time."

We order and settle in with our pre-dinner cocktails. Lucinda knows everyone in the place, and everyone knows her. I meet more people before dessert is served than I've met the entire time I've been in Charleston.

"I'm glad you've let the societies be. I know it's hard to believe, but there really isn't much there. Did they do some bad things? *Yes*. Mainly to keep the old ways, and the power in the hands of the same families. The result was travesty and tragedy for many people." She's uncharacteristically sad.

"How so?" I ask gently.

"Marriages were arranged. Not to a specific person—at least not in my time. We were mostly free to marry our choice from the stallions in the stable—monied young men with good breeding and family connections from the same society as our family." She's wistful. "The societies filtered out anyone who didn't have the proper lineage. The powers vested there, came between true love on many occasions. That might be the worst thing the societies have ever done."

Is she telling me her heart was broken as a result of the arcane rules? *I think she might be.* "You never married?"

She shakes her head. "Never."

"Have you ever been in love?"

"The man who stole my heart was a young public defender

who came to town right after I finished college. He was from New York, with a last name my father refused to pronounce correctly. We spent hours in each other's arms and talked about getting married—until the day my father, with all his society connections, ruined his career and chased him out of town."

"That's awful. There was nothing either of you could do?"

"It was awful, but not uncommon. The worst part was that when he begged me to go with him, I didn't. I didn't fight hard enough for him. For our relationship. I put my fate in someone else's hands. I kept hoping something would change my father's mind—that my profound unhappiness would persuade him to have a change of heart. But it never did."

"Did you ever talk to him again?"

She shakes her head. "It was a long time ago. There were no cell phones or internet. Communicating with someone so far away as New York seemed at the time, wasn't easy. Not if it had to be kept a secret."

Even after decades, she seems filled with regret. "I'm so sorry you never saw him again, Lucinda."

"Oh, I saw him." She gazes at me over her coffee cup. "I never forgot him. Built a shrine to him in my mind. There was never anyone as handsome, as smart, as kind, or as good in bed." She sighs. "After six years of trying to forget, I hired a private investigator to find him. He was a rising star in the New York legal circles, married to a pretty girl."

She glances at me. "Life waits for no one, Kate. Not even leggy redheads. But I couldn't stop thinking about him, so I went to New York, packed my prettiest dresses. Sat in the back of the courtroom while he tried a big case. I watched his every move, admired the way his crisp white shirts fit around his neck, the way his suits tapered at the waist, the sharpness of his tone when he cross-examined a witness. By the end of the week there wasn't anything about his courtroom mannerisms that I didn't know."

This is a heartbreaking story—and I haven't heard all of it. "But you never talked to him?"

She shakes her head. "He was married. He wasn't the kind of man who would ever step out on his wife, and I wasn't the kind of woman who would ask him to do it."

She smiles at me. "Don't look so forlorn, Kate. My life was full of fun and rebel-rousing. I've got no complaints. I've lived just the way I wanted." Even as she says the words, I don't believe them. Not after her story. "What would you do if you weren't a journalist chasing stories?"

"I would write books. In a pretty room that overlooked a garden, or maybe the ocean." I smile at the whimsy. "Someday."

"What would you write about?"

"I don't know. Maybe I would write a bittersweet love story about lovers who weren't destined to be together."

"Put some juicy sex in it, and I'd read it." We both laugh, and she orders a *small* after-dinner drink for us before insisting on picking up the check.

I wait with her outside the restaurant for the valet to bring her car. "If you leave me a key, I'll check on your place while you're in Boston," she says.

I've never told her about what happened to Fenny—other than that she's dead. "I would love for you to have a key. But there is something you should know." I give her as few of the grisly details as possible, just enough so she doesn't go there alone, and make a promise to drop off the key in the morning.

38

SMITH

Kate's leaving Charleston. It took longer than planned, but she told Josh this morning she was headed out of town first thing tomorrow. "Pull all surveillance as of six a.m. Write it up, and then take a couple days off," I told him when he called to give me the news. "You've earned it."

The rest of the day sucked. Up until now, I've been able to distract myself by throwing everything I had into the new business. Day and night, until I couldn't keep my eyes open. But today, nothing could get her out of my head.

I managed to piss off or scare the shit out of every person I encountered today. I drag my miserable ass into bed at ten so that I don't drown my sorrows, or worse, call Kate to say goodbye, or even worse, stop by to tell her in person.

As it turns out, I'm highly susceptible to pussy whipping. Surprised they ever let me near the elite ranks of the military. No failsafe way to rule out that trait, I suppose.

I climb out of bed and tear the sheets off the mattress, literally, then chuck them outside along with the pillows and quilt.

They smell like her. It doesn't matter how many times they're laundered, her scent dug itself deep into the threads and it won't let go.

I lay on the exposed mattress, my sweatshirt balled up for a pillow. But I still can't sleep. Her scent is still everywhere. *I need to get to hell out of here.*

After throwing on some clothes, I pop into the security office next door. "I'll be at Tallullah's if anything comes up."

"I'm just finishing this damn paperwork, and I would love a drink," Delilah says, grabbing her purse.

"Not looking for company," I snarl over my shoulder, on the way out. "See you in the morning."

There was a time when I could have strolled over to JD's with a bottle, or just showed up empty-handed and drank his booze. We'd shoot the shit until life's problems were in the rearview mirror, so far back we could barely see them. But we're still not talking any more than necessary, and it's unclear whether we can salvage a business relationship, let alone the friendship.

---

*T*allulah's is noisy and crowded, but there's a seat at the bar where I can be left alone.

Before I can get to it, some bastard lands the stool I have my eye on. I'm prepared to wage war for it, but the little cocksucker takes a second look at me and decides he wants to live to eat his mama's cookin' again. He steers his girlfriend to a table, and I sit my ass down.

"What's good?" Beau asks, setting a napkin on the bar in front of me.

"Not a fucking thing. Hook me up with a draft, and whatever you do, don't let me have any whiskey. I won't stop once I start."

He brings me over a beer. "This one's on me."

I'm on my third beer when a blonde sidles up next to me and sits down. "I thought you might have a change of heart about some company," Delilah says, rubbing her hands together as if to warm them. "And I haven't had a cocktail in forever."

"They stop selling drinks at the other bars in Charleston? All the liquor stores closed?"

"Got any apple cider, Beau?" she asks in that sweet voice of hers.

"Yes, ma'am. Any preference on whiskey you'd like with it tonight?"

"Surprise me."

Delilah is attractive by any standards, and she can turn on the southern charm like it's nobody's business. But make no mistake, she'll bat her eyelashes and smile at you while she's cutting out your kidneys. Even so, she has that nurturing gene a lot of women possess, and tonight she's determined to make me feel better, if it kills us both.

"Don't you have anything better to do than babysit me? I'll bet Gray Wilder could be convinced, without too much trouble, to use his dick instead of his eyes to fuck you." God love her, she doesn't blink.

"You can put it on his tab," she tells Beau when he brings her drink. *His* tab, meaning mine. She takes a sip and moans. "I needed this."

I finish my beer, ignoring her as best as I can.

"You're going to have to do a lot better than that Gray Wilder comment to get me to leave. It's not that you're not somewhere in the running to be the biggest asshole in the world, but you lack something. That *je ne sais quoi*." She smirks at me. "I've met real champions. You're not even the biggest asshole I've encountered today."

I start to laugh—not because she's funny, although she is, but because my emotions have topped off and need somewhere to go.

"I have the information you wanted on that guy with the alias, Ryan Cleary. His name is Ryan Donovan. Cleary is his mother's maiden name. He lives outside of Boston." She turns her head to look at me. "I figure it has something to do with Kate."

It's not her business, and I don't want to involve her, so I don't answer. "Leave it on my desk. I don't want a paper trail."

"No paper trail sounds right up my alley. Need help?"

"Nope."

It's after midnight and I'm still boozing, but Tallulah's has mostly cleared out. Delilah's in the bathroom when it happens. Some stupid bastard plays that stupid fucking song by Lady Antebellum. The one Kate likes. The one she sings when she thinks no one is listening. The one she got off on in the bathtub —*thinking about me.*

I'm sure it was one of the drunk college girls singing the lyrics in the corner who played it. But it doesn't matter. It hurts like a sonofabitch.

I drain my beer while the force invades, raining pain that blinds me. I'm out of my mind, desperate to fight back. My life, or at least my sanity depends on it.

I grab the baseball bat that Beau keeps behind the bar. Then toss a credit card near my empty glass—"Put whatever the cost is on it. Repair it, buy a new one, whatever you need," I tell him, following the music to the back of the room. When I get there, I lift the bat and take a swing, and then another and another, beating the shit out of the jukebox—until it stops playing the damn song—until Delilah wrenches me away.

"What is wrong with you?" she cries, yanking my arm.

I've been in real battles, with live munition and formidable opponents. My system doesn't overreact. The altercation with the music box was satisfying, but not enough to get the adrenaline flowing. My pulse barely registered it. "Didn't like that song."

"That's all you have you have to say for yourself?"

I shrug. "Pretty much."

"Have you ever considered that maybe she didn't send the

photo to the newspaper? Gabby doesn't believe she did. Neither does Josh."

"Gabby chooses to see the good in everything. Josh is green. But yeah. I've considered it." I've looked at every possible alternative—desperate to find a different answer. "I haven't seen anything that leads me to any other conclusion."

"Maybe you need to keep trying, because it's a bad idea to be wiping out innocent jukeboxes all over Charleston. They're practically extinct as it is." She lets go of my arm.

"I've heard what Gabby and Josh think. What do you think?"

She pauses for a few seconds. "Sometimes geese quack like ducks."

I have no patience to decipher low country talk right now. "What the hell does that mean?"

"The odds are it was her, but everything isn't always as it appears. Especially when bad men have power and money to throw around. They can turn ground beef into Salisbury steak, nap it with a tasty brown gravy and everyone gobbles it up like it's the best thing they ever ate."

Delilah knows that lesson better than most people. I run my palm over a scruffy jaw. "Call Chase Wilder in the morning. I know you've already talked to him about getting the photos taken down, but ask him to trace the digital prints. Unless the person who leaked the photo was exceptional, they left prints. Although I couldn't find any."

"Already talked to Chase. He's been conducting a forensic analysis for a few days."

"On his own?"

"Apparently, JD already asked him to find out who leaked the original image. Did I mention Chase doesn't think it was Kate?"

"Has he found evidence to support that it wasn't her, or is that his tiny dick talking?"

"No evidence yet."

39

KATE

After I left Lucinda, I spent hours thinking about her tragic love story. What would have happened if she fought for her public defender? Her true love. How might it have changed the course of her life? Maybe it wouldn't have mattered, but she would always know she tried. Not having done anything must make the regrets harder to bear.

Somewhere around two in the morning, I decided I wasn't giving up on Smith. There's too much about him that I love. I don't want to be a seventy-year old woman full of remorse. It doesn't matter how full my life becomes. I'll always be left wondering if it would have been fuller with him.

I'm at the library before it opens. Lucinda is always here early. We talked for a long time at dinner, but I want to give her the key, and hug her once more before the toddlers come in for story time.

I tap on the glass door to get her attention. "Good morning," she says, opening the door for me.

"Good morning. I only have a few minutes."

"I don't like that you're not making any stops between here and Boston."

"I'll take breaks, and I'm thinking I might stop in DC to say hello to some of my old colleagues. Here's the spare key and the alarm code. I have nothing to hide, but please don't go into the house alone. It's not safe."

"I'm sorry to hear it. A young woman like you should be hiding a few things in her drawers." She winks, clutching a long strand of pearls. She really is too much. "I know we already talked about this, but remind me. When can I expect you back?"

"Two weeks. Could be a little longer."

She pulls me into a hug. For such a powerhouse, there's nothing to her. I feel her ribs through her light cardigan. "Don't worry about anything here. You take care of your father and set him straight. Do not give in to any sob stories, or I'll have to make my way to Boston and that will just be unpleasant for everyone involved. We each create our own destiny and we live with the consequences."

I squeeze my eyes tight. She's right. And if I hadn't already decided to come back for Smith, her words would have spurred me there.

She pats my back before releasing me. "I'll keep an eye on Sinclair while you're away, make sure there are no floozies getting too close to him. But I suspect there's nothing to worry about in that regard. Although he wouldn't be the first man to act stupid."

I'm prepared for stupid. We're finished in his eyes, and it wouldn't surprise me if he got right back up on the saddle—so to speak. I have no illusions. My plan is to be the last woman he has sex with. The rest is out of my control. When I get back, I'll see to any *floozies* myself. "How did you know?"

"That you weren't done with him?"

I nod.

"I recognize the look. And you don't strike me as the type of woman who needs to touch the fire to know it's hot."

After we say goodbye, I walk the two blocks to the coffee shop where I'm meeting Gabby. It's strange not to have Josh or Ty lurking. But it also feels like a new beginning.

I see Gabby as soon as I walk inside the shop. I didn't expect Delilah to be with her, but try to rein in my surprise.

"I asked Delilah to come along," she says after our hello. "It was a last-minute decision, otherwise I would have emailed you." Gabby clasps her hands together, her index fingers sticking straight up, pressing against one another. "I have a long history of trusting people I shouldn't trust. I don't always agree with Delilah, but I value her opinion."

She's not pulling any punches. It stings, but I suppose it's fair.

"It's nice to see you both," I say, sliding into a seat across from them.

"We ordered coffee for the table," Gabby says, pouring me a cup. Her manners are so ingrained, she can be gracious even after making it clear she doesn't trust me. I pull the wrapped package from my bag but leave it on my lap. I'm having second thoughts about the gift. Not because Delilah is here wearing a charming don't-fuck-with-me look, but because it seems ill-advised now.

"I asked you to meet me because I want to apologize in person. I took the photograph that appeared in the paper. I actually took a few photos that day. I'm very sorry."

Gabby doesn't seem surprised, and I can't read Delilah. "Why, Kate?" Her brow is furrowed. "That's what for the life of me, I can't understand."

"In hindsight it seems so foolish. I'm not sure I can distill it into words. It was never really about words. It was all about a feeling." I swallow the lump in my throat. "I was out for a walk, when I saw you blowing bubbles with Gracie near the pond. You were both so happy."

I'm struggling with tears now, but I'm determined not to cry. I don't want to seem even more pathetic than I am. "Something about watching you with your daughter called to me. I cherish the photographs I have of my mother and me. I wanted to capture that moment. I wanted you to have it. I wanted Gracie to be able to look at the photo when she got older—and see the beauty of the moment."

My heart is filled with regret and sorrow, but my motivation had been pure. "At the time, it seemed like a nice way to thank you for all your trouble. I never meant for it to fall into anyone else's hands." I hand her the wrapped package. "This is for you—I totally understand if you don't want it—it's not the same photo that was published."

"If you didn't do it," Gabby asks softy, "then who did?"

I wish I knew. I've made dozens and dozens of calls, but no one has been able to give me an answer. "I have no idea."

Gabby nods, then unwraps the package. Her fingers gloss over the glass lightly, and she smiles, gazing at the photo. "Apology accepted," she says softly.

I release a small breath, but the relief lasts for mere seconds. "Why should we believe you?" Delilah asks, pointedly. Clearly, she isn't accepting apologies.

I return her hard stare. "Because it's the truth. Because even if I hated all of you, which I don't, I would never do anything to betray Smith."

"I'm not easily swayed by misty eyes," Delilah says, her own blue eyes as cutting as her words.

Gabby places her hand on Delilah's wrist. "Hush."

I glare back at Delilah, unwavering. It sounds easier than it is. "What could I have possibly gained by sending that photograph to the paper, anonymously? It doesn't make sense."

"It never did." Gabby's voice is resolute, and although she's not the final arbiter, I'm grateful for her generous spirit.

"I think you were currying favor with an editor or publisher," Delilah says callously. "You wanted something from them, and what better way to ingratiate yourself than to send a photograph of the never-seen-in-print, Grace Wilder, the former president's only grandchild? That's what I think."

I think you're a mean-spirited bitch. That's what I want to say. But I know this is about more than a photo. This is about her loyalty to Smith, and I can't hate her for it. "You're entitled to your opinion," I answer curtly, before turning to Gabby. "I'm leaving for Boston, and I need to get on the road."

"Smith has been away on a project," she says. "Does he know you're leaving?"

I shake my head. "No—we haven't spoken since the day the photo was published."

"This is goodbye?" Gabby tilts her head. "I hope not, Kate."

"I hope not, too. I hope you'll forgive me and that we can be friends at some point. But either way, I have family matters to take care of in Boston, and then I intend to come back for Smith —for our relationship." I hold my head high—*screw Delilah*. "I'm not giving him up without a fight. I don't know how to make amends for something I didn't do, but I'll have a lot of time in the car to think about it." I place my folded napkin on the table beside the coffee mug. "And I'll expect an apology from him, too. He flew off the handle without bothering to hear my side of the story."

"When will you be back?" Delilah asks, her tone less severe.

"Two weeks, give or take a few days. Please don't talk to Smith about this. I want us to be able to work it out ourselves." Neither woman agrees to keep quiet, but I'm through groveling and begging for today.

"When you get back and you're settled, will you still consider volunteering at Georgie's Place?"

"Are you sure you still want me?"

"I never believed you sent the photos to the paper. It never made sense to me."

"Not that it matters," Delilah chimes in, "but I'm coming around to that way of thinking, too."

The olive branch she holds out is from a young tree, but the sapling has potential to sprout roots if tended carefully. I don't allow my pride to squander the opportunity. "It matters to me."

"Are you driving straight through?"

"Not sure. I might stop in DC on the way."

After a round of goodbyes, and a dire warning from Delilah about the dangers lurking in rest stops along the highway, I leave historic Charleston.

40

KATE

On my way out of the city, I pass the sign to Albert's Island. I haven't been back to St. Maggie's since Father Jesse heard my confession. Since he called Smith a devil. It still makes me furious.

I dutifully completed my *Penance* assignment, and owe the priest my conclusions: I don't believe Catholicism requires me to choose between a man I love and a faith I love, but if it comes down to a choice between Smith Sinclair or the church, he wins. It's not even close.

At the traffic light, I bang a 'uey, as New Englander's say, and take the left onto the island road. It will add to my late start, but I'm going to pay Father Jesse a visit and get everything off my chest before I leave, because when I return to Charleston, I'll be focusing on new beginnings.

While I wait for Virginia to open the rectory door, I sense eyes watching me. I glance over my shoulder, but don't see anyone.

Virginia greets me with a warm smile. "Hello, Kate. What a nice surprise. Come in."

"How are you?" I ask, following her into the reception area. It's been almost three weeks since I last saw her.

"Good. We're all good. Father Jesse isn't here. Can I help you with something?"

"When do you expect him?"

"Not for several days."

"Oh—I didn't realize he was away." Well, this puts a crimp in my plan to tell him off.

"It's the only two weeks he takes for himself all year—readying his soul for the Feast of St. Magdalene. It's just a week away. Father Martin, from St. Ray's downtown has been filling in while he's been gone. But he's only here for Sunday Mass. If you need something—"

"I don't need anything." I don't want to get into the reason for my visit with Virginia. "I came to say goodbye."

She pales, propping herself against the back of an upholstered chair. "Where are you going?"

"To Boston. I'll be gone for a couple weeks myself. I'll talk to him when I get back." *As soon as I get back.*

"You can't go," she pleads. "Father Jesse—you can't go without saying goodbye to him. He'll never forgive me if I let you go."

She seems genuinely afraid of his reaction. "I'll only be gone for two weeks," I assure her. "Then I'll be back."

"Let me make you a cup of tea before you go."

She's frazzled and behaving oddly. More oddly than usual. "No, thank you. I can't stay."

"Let me try to reach him," she says, waving her hands around. "I'm not sure if I'll be able to. Please. Just wait while I call."

Another five minutes isn't going to kill me. I don't know what's going on with her, but I don't want to make it worse. "Sure."

She places the call, getting more and more agitated with each ring. "He didn't answer," she mutters, staring out the window. "The reception is poor there, and the calls don't always go through."

"Are you okay? You don't look well."

Her eyes dart to mine. She seems more alert now. "I don't feel well," she says, placing a hand on her chest. "I hope it's just a bad case of indigestion. Would you help me upstairs before you go? Father Jesse keeps antacid in the kitchen."

She's still clutching her chest, and I'm a little nervous to leave her like this. "I can run up and get it if you tell me where it is."

"It's easier if I show you."

I follow her upstairs and into the kitchen. "It's in that cupboard. Down there." She points to a lazy Susan in the corner.

I crouch down and open the cupboard, turning the top tray. "I don't see—"

41

KATE

My limbs are so heavy I can't move them, and my head is pounding. *Where am I?* Somewhere dark and musty.

There are voices in the distance. Father Jesse and Virginia—I think. St. Maggie's. I must be at St. Maggie's.

"I didn't know what else to do," the woman says. "I wanted to give her tea with Petey's sleeping medicine. But she wouldn't take it. I wanted to make you proud."

"You did, little slave. You made your Master very proud. I'm going to reward you later. But first, we need to make sure she wakes up."

Master? Little slave? It can't be Father Jesse and Virginia. I must be mistaken. The throbbing in my head makes it hard to think. Maybe I'm dreaming.

The heavy footsteps come closer. Maybe whoever they belong to will bring me some Tylenol for my headache. And some water. My mouth is so dry.

"Magdalene." Someone nudges my arm, brushing cool fingers across my forehead. "Magdalene, wake up." I try to open my eyes but the lids are so heavy, they don't budge. "Father

Jesse. Help me." I feel my lips move, but he doesn't seem to hear me.

"She's stirring a bit," he says, "but she's not ready to wake up. Let's give her a little more time. Why don't I give you your reward while we wait? Would you like that?"

"Yes, Master."

"Prepare yourself, then bring me your collar."

"In front of Kate?" *Kate. Yes. I'm Kate.*

"Magdalene," the man admonishes harshly. "She's Magdalene." *Who is Magdalene?* "And yes, here. We shouldn't leave her unattended. Don't look so worried, my little slave. How about if we play kitty? Would you like to be my spoiled little kitten who gets a special treat?"

"Oh yes, Master. I love to be your kitten." *It's Virginia. I know it is, but she's using a little girl voice. I don't understand. Why is she calling the man who sounds like Father Jesse, Master?*

"May I, Master?"

"You may undress your Master." *I'm struggling for breath. I want to wake up. Maybe I'm dead. I don't think my head would hurt so much if I was dead—unless—this is hell.*

"Master, if I may ask. What is my treat?"

"You will be allowed to fully worship your Master's body. And if you please me, you will be permitted to masturbate to orgasm."

"With a new toy? Can I use one of the new toys from the chest?"

"*May* I use a new toy? No, you may not. If you had convinced Magdalene to have the tea and put her into a gentle sleep, you would have earned a nice new toy and a warm bubble bath after we were through playing."

"I'm sorry, Master. I'll try to do better."

"Hold still," the man says. She gasps and groans painfully. *Is he hurting her? I listen as carefully as I can, but my head aches, and it's hard to focus. I don't think I can help the woman, anyway. I can't move.*

"Such a long pretty tail for my pretty kitten. I chose a nice big plug for you to squeeze. Don't you dare push it out, or you'll ruin our special evening. You don't want that, do you?"

"No, Master," she whimpers. *Is she hurt? Virginia! Are you okay? I scream, but there's only silence where the words should be.*

"Let me brush you before we begin. Head on my lap, but keep that ass high in the air, like an appreciative little pet. I want to be able to admire your pretty tail."

"Yes, Master." *She sounds happy now. I don't understand.*

"No new toys today, but I'll allow you to rub your cunt against the toe-box of my dress shoes. The ones I save for Sunday Mass. You know how much you enjoy that. But only if you please me, otherwise, you'll have to use your fingers to satisfy your dirty cunt, and that won't be nearly as much fun for you."

"Thank you, Master."

"Have you sedated Petey for the night?" *Sedated Petey? No! Petey, Petey, Petey! I struggle, but I can't move.*

"Yes, Master."

"Good. Now take your reward. Worship your Master with that hungry little mouth, Gigi."

"Magdalene. Magdalene. You need to wake up, now. It's time."

My eyelashes flutter for what seems like forever before they finally open. Everything is fuzzy at first, and my eyes are gritty as though someone poured sand in them. "I'm Kate," I croak. My throat is so parched it's painful to speak, but it doesn't hurt as much as my head.

"Kate was your sinner's name. Now, you're Magdalene."

I turn my head to the side. My neck is stiff, and it moves slowly. Virginia is on her knees, naked, beside Father Jesse. She's wearing a pink collar and furry ears. *Ears?* I try to make sense of it. But I can't. It's just a nightmare. I'm sure of it.

"I—I don't understand." My lips are cracked, and my mouth is split at the corners. It stings when I move my lips.

"You will understand. Soon enough. Rest tonight. Tomorrow, Gigi will bathe you and dress you in something clean. We need to keep you pure until your birthday. She'll wash you inside and out, because Jesus doesn't like dirty whores."

Gigi. Gigi. Who is Gigi? A thick fog envelops me, and my eyelids shutter, dragging me back into the darkness.

"Go to sleep, Magdalene." I don't respond, because I can't.

"Lie beside her bed, Kitten. She likely has a concussion, and we want her well by her birthday. Wake her hourly. Make sure she has a few sips of water each time. You sleep in between."

"What about Petey?"

"He'll be fine. Go home at six o'clock and see him off to camp. I'll take over until you return. When you get back, draw Magdalene a bath. Bathe her as you would me, then prepare her some lightly buttered toast with a poached egg. Sprinkle some salt on it, and make her a cup of tea."

"Yes, Master. I'll be back as soon as Petey's on the bus."

"Don't dawdle. I have Mass at nine."

———

When I wake, the room is dark. I need to pee. My head is pounding. *Where am I?*

"How do you feel?"

"Father Jesse?" I ask tentatively, turning toward the figure by the bed clutching a bible in his hand.

"Not Jesse. I'm Jesus, Magdalene. You are a sinner, and I am here to absolve you. We will pray together for your soul and purify your body until it is a worthy vessel for me."

"My head hurts—I—don't understand what you mean. Is this a dream? Are you Father Jesse?"

"Jesus," he answers impatiently. "I'm Jesus. I'm sorry about your head, but Gigi didn't know what else to do. You were leaving until after your birthday feast. We couldn't have that."

The rectory. I remember, now. Virginia wasn't feeling well. My eyes dart to the rounded stone walls at the edge of the room. *The turret*. I lift my head to sit up. I can't. My arms and legs are heavy. I inch them slowly until the rattle startles me. *I'm chained*. I remember it from last night when Virginia helped me to the bathroom.

"Calm yourself," the man says. "You are restrained. It will be easier for you if you place your fate in my Father's hands, as I have."

He thinks he's Jesus. *He's crazy*. I'm going to die here, like this, at the hands of a delusional priest. I try to control the rising panic. Prayer would be where I would normally turn at a time like this—I glance at the priest. But that source of comfort has been ripped from me.

"There have been others, but none like you," he continues in an eerie, detached voice. *Others?* "You were sent from my Father. But I don't know if I'm meant to keep you as a bride, until my work on earth is done, or if you are to be a sacrifice like the others. We'll pray for a sign from Him."

Terror digs in its sharp talons, as my brain fully registers the priest's words. My empty stomach seizes. I lift my head inches off the pillow, turning my neck when I begin to wretch. Sour liquid dribbles out of the corner of my mouth onto my chin, puddling on the cushion.

When I'm too weak to hold it up any longer, I lower my head beside the vomit, barely noticing the urine leaking from my bladder.

This is how I'm going to die.

42

SMITH

*A*nother fucking interruption. I'm never going to get a damn thing done today. "Yeah?"

"There's a woman at the gate in a brand new Cadillac, bigger than she is," Ty says. "Her name is Lucinda McCrae. She needs a word with you."

Jesus Christ. "Let me talk to her." I hear the back and forth, before Ty is on the phone again.

"She's says she wants to see the whites of your eyes while she's talkin' to you."

"Oh, for fuck's sake. Bring her to my office. Do not let her drive on the property." I'm sure this has something to do with Kate. Nosy old woman.

Before I turn around, Lucinda McCrae is standing in my office doorway. "Good morning, Miss McCrae, what can I do for you?"

"May I come in?"

Only if you have to. "Of course." I stand and usher her inside to a chair near my desk.

"I don't know what kind of people you have working for you, but you might want to shut the door, so they don't hear everything I have to say." I do as I'm told so I can get her the hell out as fast as possible.

"How can I help you?"

"Where is Kate McKenna?" she asks pointedly.

"No idea." I shrug. "Haven't spoken to her in weeks. I would guess Boston."

"Wrong. She's not in Boston. Try again."

"Miss McCrae, with all due respect, I don't see why Kate's whereabouts concerns either of us, especially me."

"I received a frantic phone call at the library this morning from a woman named Fiona Nash. She hasn't spoken to Kate for nearly a week. The last time they spoke, Mrs. Nash got the impression that something was bothering her. Perhaps something concerning *you*." She glares at me, waiting for an answer.

"You'll have to ask Kate." I'm dismissive, but I've already had enough of Lucinda McCrae, and she's only been here two minutes.

"I would. But no one has seen or heard from Kate since she left Charleston five days ago. Unless you have."

My heart drops into my stomach. There were at least a dozen messages from Fiona that I deleted without listening to.

"Ms. McCrae, I appreciate you coming by. I'll look into it."

"No, Mr. Sinclair, you will not dismiss me like I'm a doddering old woman. I need assurances that you will contact Mrs. Nash and that you will search for Kate until you find her. I will not leave your office without those assurances."

"You have my word. I'll keep you abreast of any news." *Now get to hell out so I can find her.* She's still sitting.

"Do you have a key to her house?"

"No."

"You are planning on going there?"

"Maybe. But if we do, we can get in without a key."

"Charming, I'm sure. But here," she says, placing a single key on my desk. "Take the one Kate left me. I want it back when you're through. And don't make a copy," she adds sternly, standing to leave.

"You have a key to Kate's place?"

"She left it with me on her way out of town in case there was an emergency. Made me promise I wouldn't go there alone."

"Have you?"

She stands taller, nose in the air. "On my way here. Mrs. Nash was so distraught. She's coming to Charleston, but won't be here until this evening." *Just what I need.* "Nothing seemed amiss. I looked in the closets, and her shoes were lined up in a row, and her clothes were still hung on hangers neatly. Nothing was disturbed."

"What do you mean her shoes were lined up in a row? She moved out, didn't she?"

"Her lease is up in August. She was planning on looking for a new place when she got back."

Wait. "She's coming back?" I'd like to say her returning to Charleston pisses me off, and while it does rile the emotion inside, I don't think it's anger.

"Yes. Stacey is filling in at the library. But only until Kate gets back. She wants to stay at home with the baby."

Right now, I really don't give a shit about Stacey and her parenting choices. "Miss McRae, I need you to go so I can get to work. Ty will see you back to your car."

She wags a boney finger at me. "I want to be kept in the loop. I'll be at the library until six. She was coming back to Charleston —because—it was a matter of the heart. You find her," Lucinda says, on her way out the door.

"Josh!"

"Yeah?"

"Did you take the tracking devices off of Kate McKenna's phone and car before she left Charleston?"

"No," he says sheepishly, and I want to plunk a big wet one on him.

"I need the coordinates on her location. As fast as you can get them to me."

I call Fiona, before he's even out of my office.

"You son of a bitch!" she shrieks into the phone. "Where is she?"

"Calm down, Fiona."

"Don't you tell me to calm down. I've left you a dozen messages in the last few days. Where is she?" I've never met Fiona, but nothing Kate ever said about her would make me think she's a drama queen.

"I don't know." *No one has seen or heard from Kate in days.* My heart thumps hard, as the realization sinks in. "Lucinda McCrae was just here. As far as I know, Kate was last seen on her way to Boston. Have you spoken with her family?"

"I paid her father a visit—the bastard was drunk as a skunk. He couldn't be bothered. I tracked her brother Tommy down, too." Fiona's breathing so heavy, she's panting.

"What did he say?"

"He said, 'She's probably shacked up with some guy. She'll show up eventually.' He's an asshole."

Who talks about their kid sister like that? I'd like to beat his face into the ground.

"I filed a missing person's report yesterday morning. They wouldn't let me do it before then. I've called twice to check about it, but I keep getting the runaround. I have a flight out late this afternoon. It's the soonest I could make arrangements for the kids. I'll be in Charleston by nine."

"Where did you file the report?"

"Charleston police."

That's a problem. I haven't heard a single word from them, and Lucinda didn't mention it, either. You'd think the first place they'd go, after her house, is to the library where she worked. The next thing would be to pay me a visit. They're not looking for her. It might not mean anything more than incompetence, but it could also mean someone on the inside doesn't want her found.

"Stay put for now in case she shows up in Boston. I have it covered on this end."

"Kate would have told me if she was coming to Boston. I would have talked to her—kept her company while she was stuck in traffic on the turnpike. Something happened."

That's becoming crystal clear. "We still have a tracking system on her phone and car. It will tell us where she is." *Or at least give us the location of the vehicle. I keep that last part to myself.*

"Smith—there are few people on this earth I love more than Kate. Few people who are handed the short stick every damn time, and who always take it without complaining. So many people have let her down. Not this time. We need to find her."

My feelings about Kate are so tangled up with my job, my relationship with JD, and my general mistrust of reporters. I'm not sure a relationship with her could ever work. But I am sure I won't stop looking until I find her. *I'm damn sure of that.*

"Stay in Boston. There is nothing you can do here. As soon as I find her—the very minute—I'll send a plane so you can be with her wherever she is. Until then, take care of your kids—Kate would want that."

Josh jogs into my office, green around the gills. "Fiona, I need to go."

"All we have is an occasional weak signal from her car—too weak and sporadic to gather coordinates," he says gravely. "Nothing on her phone."

Weak signals mean the car is well-hidden or submerged. Well-hidden in the way a professional could do. In the way King's people could do. I don't let myself think about submerged. "Any chance the tracking devices are the ones that store records we can access?" *Say yes. Please, say yes.*

He shakes his head. "She wasn't much of a threat when we started keeping tabs on her. We used the basic equipment. When we upped the security—I was going to swap it out before she went back to work, after the lockdown was lifted. But then—we cut back her security."

"Find Chase Wilder and have him call me immediately. Then meet me at Kate McKenna's place." He starts to leave, still looking ashen. He might be a seasoned veteran, but Kate was his first civilian gig. It's different.

"Josh." He turns. "*We* didn't cut back her security. *I did*. I gave the order." That knowledge snakes its way into my conscience, with a sharp venomous bite. "This is on me."

43

SMITH

I climb into the Jeep, hoping the change of scenery will help clear my head so I can think logically. If I had only listened to Fiona's first message, instead of acting like a bratty teenager, Kate wouldn't still be missing. *And if you hadn't cut back her security, she wouldn't have gone missing at all.*

My chest is tight. I don't have a single good feeling about this.

If a hostage is taken alive, the first twenty-four hours after an abduction are vitally important. But it's more complicated than that. I've rescued hostages who have been held for more than five years. It all comes down to *why* they were taken. If King's people have Kate, they're not looking for a trade. They're looking to shut her up.

My phone rings, interrupting one macabre scenario after another. I have to stop thinking like that, or I can't run the investigation—and there is no fucking way I'm handing it over to someone else.

"Chase," I bark into the phone. "I need your help. Kate McKenna is missing. We have her car and phone tagged, but the signal is weak and infrequent."

"I heard. Where are you now?"

"On my way to her place to see what I can find."

"How long has she been missing?"

"Five days."

"*Fuck.* I'll meet you there."

"No. We don't know what we're going to find when we get there. It's not safe."

"I can help with this," he says pointedly. "You're tracking her electronically, and I'm better at that than anyone on your payroll." Truth.

"I need you tracking her phone and car more than I need you at her house."

"I can walk and chew gum at the same time."

This is just another bad decision in a line of bad decisions. *Go big or go home.* "Do you know where she lives?"

"Give me the address."

"If you get there before I do, *do not*, I repeat *do not,* get out of your car." I give him the address, and call Delilah.

"Go to St. Maggie's on Albert's Island, and talk to Father Jesse Creighton and the church secretary, and anyone else you can find over there," I instruct. "Ask them about Kate. Make up some bullshit so you don't alert anyone that there might be a problem." I considered going myself, but I can't stand that fucking priest. I'm too biased to get a good read on him.

"Is he a suspect?"

"She's been gone five days. Today makes six. Everyone's a suspect." *Six fucking days*. I want to throw a huge tantrum, kick shit over, break things with my fists, but it'll have to wait until I find her.

"Gabby and I had breakfast with her the day she left."

What? "You're just telling me this now? What the fuck, Delilah?"

"It wasn't an issue until now. She didn't leak that photo."

"How do you know?"

"Because before working for you, I had a nice little career as a

CIA agent, remember? I sat less than three feet away from her. I pushed her, watched every reaction. Her eyes. Her body language. Her expressions. She isn't savvy enough to fool me. I'm telling you she didn't do it."

I don't say a word because what's on the tip of my tongue is so damn ugly, my relationship with Delilah will never recover from it. This is just another damn betrayal from someone I trusted. *Gabby, too.*

"She told us she was going to take care of some family issues, and then she was coming back for you. She wanted you guys to work it out on your own terms and asked us not to say anything. She loves you, Smith."

My mind is going in a dozen different directions. I don't let the *she was coming back for you* part in. There's nothing there that can help us find her, but plenty to trip me up. Delilah is nobody's fool. I'm not sure how Kate's innocence fits into the equation. Does it point more to King, or somewhere else? We need a tighter timeline.

I clear the lump from my throat. "This is what we're going to do. You're going over to the church like we talked about. Take Ty. Find out everything you can. Call Gabby and Lucinda McCrae—send someone to the library to pick her up. If you know of anyone else Kate might have spoken, or met with that would have anything to add, round them up. I want everyone in the conference room by one o'clock."

There's silence on the other end of the phone.

"Is there something about what I just said that you don't understand?"

"Do you want me to take the lead on this? You're awfully close to it."

"No," I bark. "And don't question my ability to manage this again."

"I'm sorry, but I can't do that." There's passion in her voice, and even though I'm pissed, I count on her to call me out when necessary. She's one of the few people willing to do it. "You're assembling a group together in a room without first debriefing them individually. That's a bad idea."

"I'm well aware." I grip the steering wheel tighter. "But she's been gone for almost a week. We ran out of time to do it by the book days ago. This is the best way to create a timeline of her last forty-eight hours in Charleston and pull resources together quickly. We're out of time, Delilah." As I say it, my heart pumps hard.

There's a long silence on the other end. "I'll get everyone there. If the priest or the church secretary have anything to add, should I bring them to the meeting?"

Kate trusts that priest. But I don't. There's something about that guy that rubs me the wrong way. I'm going with my gut on this. "Hold off for now. I don't want them to know too much. But I want your impression of the priest after you meet him."

"What about the homeless women she works with?"

"I've thought about that." If we have to start hunting them down—we're screwed. "It could be important, but we don't have the manpower to go there right now. It'll be like looking for a needle in the haystack. No one keeps accurate records of their comings and goings, for privacy reasons."

"I'm at Kate's. Call me right away if anything turns up at the church."

"Are we okay?" she asks softly. I can almost see the worry lines creasing around her eyes. It wasn't a betrayal. It was women sticking together, thick as thieves, the way they always do. I'm grateful Kate found that with them.

"Yeah. We're okay."

44

KATE

I don't know how much time has passed. But I'm pretty sure they're drugging me, so I eat and drink as little as possible. I don't have an appetite, anyway.

My situation feels hopeless, growing bleaker with every passing hour. I haven't fully accepted my fate, but it's settling in.

I'm chained securely, and I hear the lock click on the door as they come and go. There's no escape. *And no rescue.* No one knows I'm missing, so I never imagine anyone coming for me. Maybe it's less painful this way.

If only I had told Fiona I was going to Boston. But I wanted to surprise her—that's not entirely true. I didn't want to hear her beg me not to come or have her tell me my father would wear me down until I agreed to move back and take care of him—until the next time he didn't need me.

While I lay here waiting for the rape and death sure to come, I comfort myself by practicing gratitude—focusing on all the good I've enjoyed in my life. I'm not a Pollyanna and certainly not a saint. It's just that I have nowhere else to turn at this moment.

Most Catholics prepare for death with prayer, but there is not a shred of comfort for me in my faith. Only betrayal.

Instead, I think of Fiona and her boys, of all the happiness they've brought to my life. While I tick through the seasons, Fi is the one person who shows up consistently in my good memories.

Each spring, we picked lilacs together in the backyard and brought them inside to perfume my room, and we always shared the leftover cupcakes from Rita's that some kind soul brought to school on my birthday. Someone was always absent, leaving at least one for us to share on the walk home.

I think of my mother often, too, wondering if she would have made the same decisions, if she knew what my life would hold. At times, when I'm especially groggy, she speaks to me. *You need to stay strong,* she pleads. *Prepare yourself for a fight. It's not your time yet, angel. I love you.* There are times in the darkness when I'm certain she's by the bed.

But what I think about most is Smith. When I need comfort desperately, I find it in the memories we made together. I shut my eyes and feel the shelter of his protective arms. When the pain becomes too great, I imagine him smoothing my hair, murmuring, "I've got you," like he did the day I told him about the frat house, and the night Fenny died.

But my time has not all been spent wallowing in memories. While there is little chance for escape, I have formed a skeleton of a plan. It's not likely to save me, but at least it will be a death of my own choosing. When they discover my body, they'll know I made an effort.

Virginia is exhausted and stretched thin. I've been here longer than planned and she bears the brunt of responsibility. She's emotionally fragile, and the added anxiety has left her psyche even more vulnerable. Each time Father Jesse mentions keeping me as his bride, she tears up. I think she's worried I'm her replacement.

I've started to feed her anxiety. Dropping little breadcrumbs here and there, about how much *Jesus* adores me.

Her anxiety is causing her to be careless. She's left the bathroom window uncovered several times. It's a small thing, but it's helped orient me to day and night, and planted an idea. The swamp is located directly under the double casement window—four stories down. My plan is to persuade her to let me jump into the murky water. My survival is dependent on the depth of the water, what lies beneath the surface, and whether she's willing to free my hands.

The lock clicks, and the door opens. *Today is the day.* The Feast of St. Magdalene is approaching—it has to be. I'm not sure what significance it holds for me, but I've caught enough to know my fate is tied up in it.

"I need to bathe you," Virginia says, putting down a small tray by the bed. "Eat quickly."

"I'm not hungry right now. I'll try after my shower." Even though I'm bathed daily, I smell wretched. My ankles and wrists are cuffed continuously, and the skin underneath stays wet after I bathe. It's become infected, emitting a foul yeasty smell. Not to mention something she feeds me causes me to vomit frequently.

Virginia adjusts the chains so that they reach the bathroom, where she shortens them again, with my wrists securely fastened behind my back. "Can we remove the chains just while I'm in the shower?"

"No. I'll get into trouble."

"I can help you," I say softly.

"I don't need help."

"I know you love Jesus. He's planning to keep me as his bride. He told me that. What will happen to you then?" When she stiffens and the tears begin to pool, I know I've plucked the right nerve.

"We don't know who he's going to choose to be his bride," she admonishes, brusquely.

"We do. He told me," I whisper. "I'm not supposed to say anything to you."

"I don't believe you." She lays out a wide tooth comb on the sink for after the shower. "He's loved me for a long time," she says.

"Then why hasn't he made you his bride yet?"

She stills, staring into the shadows. It's the haunting stare of a petrified woman. "Unchain me," I say softly. "Let me jump out the window."

"You'll die." *Probably. But it couldn't possibly be worse than what's to come.*

"I know. I've prepared myself for death." She rushes around the small room, gathering shower supplies. "You won't need to worry about me anymore, Virginia. You'll be able to live with your Master and play kitty, like you've always done. Think of Petey. He needs you."

She freezes for a moment, before going to the window. "It's a big drop to the swamp," she murmurs, peeking over the ledge. "Even if you survive the fall, there are creatures in the water." *There are far worse creatures here.* "No one could survive the fall," she mumbles to herself.

"You can unchain my ankles. Undo the restraints on my wrists. Tell Jesus I overpowered you and jumped."

"Okay," she acquiesces finally, in the little girl voice she normally reserves for her Master. "But only your legs. Not your arms."

I draw a large breath and fill my lungs with air that I'm going to desperately need—but it can't be reserved. That's not how it works.

I wanted this moment, and I'm not fearful of heights or of water. But still, the sheer gravity of a dive into the unknown with my hands bound threatens to consume me. I've reached the hour.

"Okay," I agree quietly. It probably wouldn't matter if my hands were free, anyway.

She opens both panes. Just as she begins to unhook the chain from my cuffed ankle, the wind howls, blowing one side of the window shut. The bang is so loud, it startles us both, leaving

Virginia pale and shaken. "No," she says, "you need to get into the shower. It's your birthday tomorrow."

"That's correct, Gigi," the priest says from the bathroom doorway. We both freeze at the icy voice. "Her cleansing will wait for now. Bring Magdalene out here."

"Yes, Master."

Without another word, we follow him out. *How much did he hear?* "Sit her there," he instructs, positioning a chair a few feet from the bed. "Prepare yourself," he tells her. By now I know that means use the toilet and undress.

He adjusts the restraints, without a word, so that I can't move. When he's finished, he stands back, apprising my naked body until my skin crawls.

When Virginia returns, he drags her to the wall by her hair. She whimpers while he shackles her wrists to the rings fixed to the stone. Her back is facing me, but I hear the muted sobs. "You were going to let her go. I am so angry with you, Gigi. So disappointed," he says, unfastening his belt, and pulling it through the loops.

He's going to beat her. "It was my fault," I plead. "Don't hurt her."

He turns to me and smiles, before the belt flies through the air and catches her skin, landing where her buttocks and thighs meet. Her scream is blood-curdling.

"Gigi is pure," he says. "She didn't know she sinned, unlike you. You offered your body to Sinclair. Do you know how much pain it caused me every time you let him soil you? I watched as you sullied yourself with the devil. I needed you pure."

He lets the belt fly again, and Virginia screams when it lands on her back.

"Beat me, instead. She didn't do anything."

"I tried to warn you, but even a dead cat wouldn't stop your whoring. Do you know how much trouble it was to find that cat for you?" *He killed Fenny.* "Do you?" he asks, his eyes burning. He turns the belt on Virginia when I don't answer.

"No," I say quickly.

"You were an ungrateful whore. Each time I got a little closer, you would run to Sinclair." He lashes Virginia's thighs. Her screams echo in my veins.

"Then the picture of the Wilder girl, the president's granddaughter, showed up in your files. Instead of turning you away from him, I turned him away from you. Don't look so surprised. You didn't really think I was a fool who didn't understand technology, did you?"

He stands over me, belt in hand. His arousal evident. "I spent hours gaming at my grandmother's, then later, I learned to hack into secure files. It gave me such great pleasure all alone in my room. It was the kind of pleasure you derived from the pink vibrator you fucked yourself with when Sinclair wasn't around." I cringe when he mentions my vibrator. *It is pink.*

"I watched you hold it against your cunt, before sliding it inside the wet swollen flesh. The more aroused you became, the more you writhed all over the bed, your face red and sweaty. Do you know that your hips buck erratically right before you come?"

He takes a drooping curl between his fingers. I flinch at the touch. "You were beautiful when you were alone, curled up on your bed, sated. You were a Madonna. But when Sinclair was there, you were nothing more than a filthy whore for him."

I feel faint and shut my eyes. It's only seconds before the belt slithers across my thighs, and I jump.

"Your penance is to watch and listen to Gigi's screams."

He lashes her again and again. Her agony bounces off the walls. When he's done, he unshackles her.

"Isn't this lovely, Magdalene?" he asks, showing me the angry welts on her skin. I can barely stand to look at them.

"Bring me your brush," he instructs Virginia.

She obeys immediately, scurrying on all fours to retrieve the brush. She carries it to him in her mouth. He pats her head and sits on a chair across from me. Without a word spoken between them, she lays her tearstained cheek on his lap. Her welted buttocks in the air, as he caresses her gently and brushes her hair.

After a little while, he murmurs something to her that I can't hear. Her fingers go to his pants zipper, and from her knees, she releases his swollen cock, tonguing the stretched skin. Eventually he peers over at me.

"She's very skilled, Magdalene. I watched you with Sinclair. You're skilled, too. Would you like to be my pet?" Virginia continues to suck him while he speaks to me.

When he wants more, he holds her head between his hands, and roughly fucks her mouth. He stares longingly at me while she gags on his cock, the drool dripping from her mouth. It goes on and on, but I don't dare look away.

Finally, with a grunt, the priest finishes inside her throat, his gaze still on me.

Virginia averts her eyes, gasping for air.

"My good little slave," he coos. "Choose a toy from the chest."

She crawls to the chest and returns with a wand.

He smiles. "You plan on being well-satisfied, don't you little slave? Has worshiping your Master in front of company made you especially aroused?"

She nods, lowering her eyes demurely. "Let me see," he says. She parts her legs, and he sweeps his hand between them, then holds his glistening fingers in the air so I can see the prize. He smiles, a sadistic curl, and brings them to her mouth so she can lick them clean.

"Sit at my feet, Gigi, and spread your legs wide," he commands. "Turn the wand on high and place it on your cunt." When she does, her mouth falls open with a gasp.

I shut my eyes. "Magdalene, if you don't keep your eyes open, and on Gigi, I will shackle her to the wall and beat her again. It's your choice."

I force myself to watch as she leans back on her elbows, her cunt fully exposed to us. She adjusts the wand on her folds, and he lowers the sole of his shoe over it, grinding the vibrating head into her flesh.

"Do not come without permission, or I will put welts on your skin that will be raised for a month. And there will be no pleasure for you, until the days grow short again."

"Master, please," she begs in a breathy, tortured voice.

"Stop squirming, or we're done." But she doesn't stop.

He yanks his foot away, and the wand clanks to the floor. "Leave it," he instructs cruelly.

Eventually, he lets her pick it up and they begin again. But she doesn't please him, and he takes his foot away and the vibrator falls on the stone floor. She's a shaking sweaty mess, but it happens three more times before he finally lets her come.

It's abusive and awful, but God forgive me, my body is behaving as though it's aroused. Even though I'm not. Even though I don't want to be. Even though I'm disgusted by all of it, and terrified, not of death, but of rape.

Still, my nipples furl and tingle, and the dull ache of arousal lurks low in my belly. A piece of my soul withers and dies as my body betrays me in this unimaginable way.

45

SMITH

I use the key Lucinda gave me to get into Kate's house. When I step inside, it's as though a huge crater swallows me.

The place smells like it's been closed up with the air conditioner turned up high, just cool enough so mold doesn't grow. But Kate is everywhere. Calling to me from every corner.

Lucinda was right, it doesn't look like anything has been disturbed. Her new laptop isn't here, but she probably took it with her. The backup is still on the dresser, and that ugly rug is here, too.

I scour the usual places with the blacklight and another instrument, looking for blood, or bleach, or solvents used to clean up blood and other bodily fluids. It's normally tedious work, but today it's heart-wrenching. Every inch I cover where there is no evidence of Kate's blood feels like a major victory.

Josh comes in while I'm working. "Let me do that," he says gruffly, taking the instrument out of my hands. "There must be something else you can do."

The door creaks again. It's Chase. "Anything?" he asks.

"Not yet." It's a double-edged sword. If we find something, it's not likely to be good news. But if we find nothing, it doesn't get us any closer to discovering what happened to her.

Chase sets up his equipment on the kitchen table, then methodically sweeps each room for listening devices and cameras. When he gets to the bedroom, he stops short in front of the television. After a few seconds, he heads to a utility closet off the kitchen where the fuse box is located.

"What did you find?" He meets my eyes, shaking his head, and motions for me to follow him back into the bedroom. When we're there, he unplugs the television from the wall.

"This is a smart TV," he says. "It can be hacked into and used as a spy tool. They watch you right here, through the camera. The microphone carries back, too. A hacker can get into the system and access bank accounts, anything, really."

It was right in front of my goddamn eyes the entire time, and I didn't see it. "How did I not know this?"

He shrugs. "There's been chatter since the TVs first came out. But the FBI just started talking publicly about it sometime around Thanksgiving."

"That was eight months ago."

He shrugs. "You're not a tech guy, so you don't think like us. You've become a big picture guy, but basically, you're a grunt with mad skills."

"The priest. The fucking priest."

"What priest?" he asks, looking at me like I've lost my mind.

"This weird priest gave her the TV."

"All priests are weird, if you ask me. But don't jump to conclusions. Usually hackers get in using the serial numbers and passwords that come with the system. People don't understand the importance of changing passwords on their computers, let alone on a TV. You don't need high-level skills. It's not like infiltrating the president's calendar, but you have to have some idea of what you're doing."

I know that fucking priest is involved. First the cat, and now the TV. Both *gifts* from him.

I don't buy it's a coincidence. *But what now?* Should I go over to the church and lean on his carotid artery until he talks, or do I sit on the information until we have a timeline?

Even if he's involved, he's probably not the ringleader. But whoever is pulling the strings is not playing. If I show up at the church, I'm likely to tip someone off. I'm not ready to do that yet. I'm going to have to trust Delilah.

"I turned off the Wi-Fi," Chase says. "This way we don't need to worry that someone is watching us. Did you ever log onto any of your devices using her Wi-Fi?"

"No. I never use someone else's internet." I'm stupid, but not that stupid.

"I'm going to stay here for a little while," Chase says, "see what I can find."

"Josh will stay here with you. Meet me back at the security office when you're done. Don't forget about her phone and car. Those might be our best clues."

———

By the time Chase and Josh get back to the security office, we've put together a timeline, but it has holes. Huge gaping holes. My guys are working on piecing together her movements using footage from cameras across the city, but that takes time. *Too damn much time.*

"She didn't send the photo to the paper," is the first thing Chase says, entering the conference room. His eyes dart from Lucinda McCrae to me.

I nod at him. "Say what you gotta say."

"Someone was using the TV to spy on her. They hacked into the system and got into her Wi-Fi, including everything she had stored in the cloud. They had access to it all. Her bank accounts, everything. I was able to do some forensics using her backup device. They did leave prints everywhere, but they weren't readily traceable. It was somebody who knew what they were doing. It's going to take some time." The one thing we don't have.

"Tell me more about the gardener," I say to Delilah, who has already confirmed she got a hinky feeling from both the priest and Virginia.

"His name is Silas Drury. He has a record. Spent ten years in jail for rape. It appears he's stayed out of trouble since. But I'm not done looking at him."

"Don't go too far down the rabbit hole. It was statutory rape," JD says. "Underage girlfriend. Rumor has it that it was consensual."

"The youngest Beaufort girl," Lucinda pipes in. "There was only three years between the two. Her daddy hated him. Their families traveled in different circles. But no matter what he did to keep them apart, they always managed to be together. The day Silas turned eighteen, they were caught in the act and her daddy had him arrested. There was a set-up, a quick trial, an inexperienced court-appointed lawyer, and a judge who belonged to the same society as the Beauforts."

"Where does he live?" I ask.

"North Charleston with his girlfriend," Lucinda answers. "I think his official residence is on Albert's Island, but he stays with his girlfriend."

"Get an address," I instruct Delilah. "Miss McCrae, how do you know this?"

"There is very little that I don't know about Charleston. Lived here all my life. I volunteer where I can, and work at the library," she adds, like the library is the font for all information. What she failed to say is she's a busybody.

"What about Father Jesse Creighton?" I ask. "What do you know about him?"

She purses her lips. "Albert's Island isn't *exactly* Charleston.

But he's been here about ten years. Comes into the library with cards for us to give to the homeless women. His secretary has a boy who was born with some mental limitations." She shrugs. "That's all I know. I don't get too close to preachers."

"Got the address. The house belongs to Melinda Beaufort," Delilah says. "Does that sound right, Miss McCrae?"

Lucinda nods. "That's right. Let that be a lesson to all you daddies." She doesn't spare JD a glance, but that comment was aimed at him.

I nod at Delilah. "Meet me in the Jeep."

"Chase, reconnect the Wi-Fi and the TV at Kate's. Take two of my guys with you. Give whoever might be watching a show, so they think we're looking for her because of something related to the photo—make it up—let them believe we're giving up our search, because it appears she's left town, and it's not worth our time to chase her."

Before I leave, I pull JD into my office. "What do you need?" he asks before I can say anything.

"Another favor you're not going to like."

"Name it."

"I trust Lucinda McCrae—to an extent. Make sure she doesn't leave Sweetgrass or use the phone. Delilah took her cell phone to be on the safe side."

"Does Lucinda know Delilah has it?"

"No." JD's lips twitch.

"We'll take her over to the main house. That'll keep her busy. Don't give her a second thought."

This is the way it's always been with JD and me. We rarely apologize with words. We apologize by standing up when the other needs something. Doesn't matter how big or small.

"You're going to find her," he says, with a hand on my shoulder.

"You bet your ass. And when I do, I'm bringing her here."

"Wouldn't expect anything different."

When we get to Silas's house, before I break in the front door, Delilah gives me a stern warning. "We need Silas alive until we find her. You can kill him later," she calls over her shoulder, heading to the back of the house, where she grabs him by the throat when he opens the backdoor to sneak out. While he begs for his life, she drags him inside with a gun barrel against his head.

Prison breeds two kinds of men. Those who assimilate, thrive in the structure, and don't mind going back. And those who will do anything in their power to never go back. My bet is that Silas falls into the latter camp.

We've got to make him believe the alternative to telling us the truth is far worse than any prison.

"Have you ever seen this woman?" I ask, holding up an image of Kate from my phone. My foot is on his chest in an encouraging gesture.

"No."

Delilah reaches over and grabs his testicles. "I'm going cut off your balls one at time and shove them down your throat, before I scatter your itty-bitty brains all over this pretty rug." The stench of his bowels emptying tells me he doesn't want to die.

"Y-Yes," he stutters, sweat dripping off his face.

"Where?"

"The rectory. St. Maggie's."

"When was the last time you saw her?"

He doesn't say anything. "When?" I bark my heel grinding into his chest.

"Last week."

Delilah pulls out a knife and runs the point over his crotch. "We don't have time for starts and fits. Tell us everything you know, and be quick about it," she says, scraping the blade over his balls.

"They have her. Not sure where they keep them when they're alive."

"Who is them?" I interrupt.

"The women. Buried in the back in the old well after St. Magdalene's Feast."

You have got to be fucking kidding me. "When is that?"

"Tomorrow."

"Who kidnaps and kills women?"

"Not sure," he coughs, and I grind into his chest harder. "I think just—the priest and Virginia. I don't know anything about it."

"Any weapons at the church?"

"Never seen any," he grunts.

"Have you ever talked to the police about the dead women?"

He looks up at me. "Who would believe me? An ex-con. They'd blame it all on me. I never saw them do it."

I reach down and compress the artery in his throat. "Not yet," Delilah warns. "We might still need him." I don't kill him, but I squeeze while he teeters on consciousness.

"Call Ty," I tell her. "Get him over here and have him bring another guy with him." I stand up and shove my boot into Silas' ribs. "When they get here, you will give them any information you have about the layout of the church."

"Let's tie up this bastard so we can get out of here."

While we conducted the interrogation, I was in full commando mode. Not one emotion interfered with the mission. But in the car on the way back to the office, I'm struggling mightily.

She might be dead before we get to her. And if she's not, she will be soon. My mind goes to all the awful places. The things they could do to her until all I see is her face—contorted in pain.

"Don't," Delilah admonishes, without a trace of empathy. "Wherever your head is, get it the hell out. There's no time for licking your wounds. She's just another hostage. We have a rescue to plan, soldier, and no time for dicking around. Man the fuck up."

Her words are jarring. The years of training, of developing mental toughness and laser focus, flood in with a force that won't let up until I tell it to stand down. And I won't do that until the rescue is complete.

46

SMITH

When Delilah and I get back to office, the Wilder brothers are all there, along with my entire security team not on duty elsewhere. Even those who are off. The show of support almost dredges up emotion I can't afford.

"Where's Lucinda?" I ask JD.

"With Gabrielle and Lally. They know the score." *God help her if she steps out of line.* "She's staying the night," he continues. "They have her so busy, she hasn't looked for her phone."

"Did someone contact the police?" Gray asks.

"No," I say pointedly. "We have no idea what involvement, if any, the police have in this. Judge King has always been a law and order guy. The cops love him." They sat on the missing person's report. They don't get any more chances.

"Delilah." She looks up from her laptop. "Vests, night-vision goggles, a scope—"

"I know what we need," she says, out the door before I finish.

"You're going in tonight?" Gray asks.

I don't have time for twenty questions from someone who is as useless as tits on a boar hog. But I'm sure he means well.

"No choice. This might be connected to the Feast of St. Magdalene, which is tomorrow."

"Connected how?"

Why can't he just shut his damn trap? "No fucking clue."

"I made a few good friends at the FBI while DW was president," Gray says, watching me carefully. "We've stayed in touch. I can call in a favor."

"Not yet. I'm not sure how far up the food chain this goes. I want to be on the scene before any cowboy gets there."

"All set," Delilah says, coming back into the office.

"Chase, I need you to draw a perimeter and text me the coordinates. Have one of my guys help you. And see if there's any way to get a visual inside the church or the rectory. Ty is with the gardener, if you need additional information on the layout."

"Anything else?" Chase asks, his nose already in the computer.

"One more thing. We need to go in through the main road—it's our best bet tonight. I want to know how close we can get the vehicle without being seen. We'll hike the rest."

"Who you taking with you?"

"Small team. We'll secure the perimeter, and Josh will man it unless you tell me it's too big for one guy. There's water on three sides, so I don't see containment as an issue. Delilah will go in with me."

"No."

Delilah whips her head around, following Gray's booming voice in the corner.

"You have no idea what you're going to find when you get inside," Gray says through gritted teeth. "You're working off thin information. It's too risky. Not to mention it's a fucking church, Smith. She can't afford another scandal."

"No?" Delilah repeats incredulously, walking straight up to him. "You haven't earned the right to tell me no, pretty boy." She might have a sweet voice, but she's not using it now. The room is deadly quiet, mouths hanging open, eyes trained on the pair.

"Hey, asshole," I bark at Gray. "I need her with her head on tight. When this is all over, you two can rip off your clothes and have at it. But not until Kate's back." I turn to Delilah, "Are you in or not?"

"I'm in," she snaps. "Don't ask again."

"Hey." JD steps closer, so only I can hear. "I know my way around a gun."

"I'm well aware, and I appreciate it. But I need you here." He nods. "I also appreciate that you went behind my back and paid extra for those goggles and the heat-seeking devices. We'll need them tonight."

"Call if you run into anything unexpected," he says, ignoring the last part of what I just told him. "Antoine is keeping me company until we hear something." Antoine is a former Marine and JD's driver. He's a good person to have on the premises tonight in the event of trouble.

I glance at Gray on the way out. "Give us a thirty-minute lead, then make the call."

47

KATE

Virginia spent the afternoon *purifying* me. She scrubbed my skin raw, administered a douche and an enema. The degradation was unspeakable, but I didn't say a single word while she worked. All I could think about was the beating she endured earlier because of me.

I'm given salty broth for dinner. I suspect it's laced with something sinister, but I am so dehydrated from all the cleansing, I drink most of it anyway.

There's something afoot. I felt it all day, but when the priest and Virginia come for me, I know my instincts were right.

Virginia takes my nightgown, and dresses me in a hooded cloak that reaches mid-calf. I am leashed by one ankle, my hands restrained behind my back. Otherwise, the chains are gone.

"Where are we going?" I ask, although I'm not sure I want to know.

"It's the eve of your birthday, Magdalene," Father Jesse responds from the doorway. He gives me a ghastly smile. "We have rituals to perform and the altar to prepare."

They lead me down the turret stairs, out through the back of the rectory, and into the church through the sacristy. In the sacristy, the leash is attached to a wardrobe door while Father Jesse puts on white vestments. Virginia takes the cape from my shoulders and hangs it in the closet.

When the priest is done dressing, he turns his attention to me. His eyes slither over every inch of my skin while he oohs and ahhs. It's vile and degrading, and my mind begins to turn itself off. A trick it's learned since I've been here.

"Magdalene, you're not like the other women. You're heavenly with your creamy pale skin and red hair. The others were imposters meant to tempt me, but you are a gift from my Father. I will not sacrifice you."

"You must," Virginia cries frantically.

"Gigi," he tips her chin so that she looks at him. "Jealousy is a grave sin, punishable by God."

"I'm sorry, Master. I want to be your special kitten forever."

"Jesus," he admonishes. "We're in the sacristy."

"Jesus," she repeats. The back and forth is too much for my brain to process. The drugs must be taking effect.

"You'll always be my pet. But Magdalene will be my bride." He steps away from her. "Let's begin the ritual."

I am taken, naked, into the sanctuary. I glance up at the cross. The bitterness of betrayal fills my soul as I stare into Christ's face.

"Light the censer," the priest instructs Virginia, "and bring it to me."

I stand idly, my mind refusing to rouse itself.

Father Jesse takes the censer, shaking it while he walks around the altar, chanting a Latin prayer. The frankincense and myrrh curl around us. It's trancelike and strangely calming.

My leg is tethered to the foot of the massive altar, but my hands are freed. I watch my fingers wiggle slowly. They seem to belong to someone else.

My hands have not been free since—since I was taken captive. But I'm not elated, as I would expect to be. It's as though my emotions—my reactions—have been muted.

Virginia and I follow Jesus's commands carefully. We prepare the altar with fresh cloths and add three long leather straps, which are hidden underneath.

"You will be strapped to the altar tomorrow, while I anoint you with my seed." My brain is slogging. The thoughts are disconnected and floating in slow motion.

Father Jesse sits on the high-backed, cushioned seat reserved for priests during Mass. There is a basin of water and a Purificator—the white linen cloth used to wipe the chalice, near his feet. "Kneel before your Lord and Master, Magdalene."

I kneel immediately. "Remove my shoes, and wash my feet." My hands move to do as he asks. But it's as though they are disconnected from the rest of my body. "Now dry them."

When I'm through, I sit back, still on my knees. "Bring Magdalene the nard, Gigi."

She gingerly places the alabaster jar with the perfumed oil into my hands. "You will anoint my fingers," he says. "For tomorrow, I will use these fingers in sacrifice. I will probe your body and satisfy myself with your flesh. It is my reward before I die for mankind. You love your Lord, don't you, Magdalene?"

"Yes," I murmur.

Jesus smiles. "Now my feet," he instructs. "Then wipe them with your hair, as written in the scripture."

It wasn't Mary Magdalene, Jesus. It was Mary of Bethany who wiped your feet with her hair. Don't you remember? I want to remind him, but I don't. Instead, I rub the earthy oil into his feet and lower my head to wipe away the excess with a handful of my hair.

"Get the hell away from her, you animal," a familiar voice booms from the nave.

While I'm still on my knees, Jesus stands so abruptly, I fall back.

"How did you get in here?" Jesus demands.

The man approaches. I know him. But I'm not sure. "Get away

from her," he says in an outraged voice, "or I'll kill you on the altar where you pray in blasphemy."

"Magdalene," Jesus says calmly, holding me in front of him. "The devil has come to wrest you from your Savior."

"Her name is Kate," the devil says.

Kate. Her name is Kate. Why is that so familiar?

I freeze in place. Kate. My name is Kate. Smith. Is he really here, or am I dreaming? How would he know where to find me? *My name is Kate.* I step away from the priest. The man steps closer. He looks like Smith. I hug myself. But what if he is the devil? "No! Get away!" I shout at him, hurrying back to Jesus. The big man stops.

"You are a saint, Magdalene," Jesus murmurs. "He is the devil. Stay with Jesus. I'll protect you."

"Kate," the man says gently. "I talked to Fiona this morning, she needs you in Boston."

"Don't listen to him," Jesus says. "The devil is full of trickery."

The big man is getting closer, and Jesus is stepping back from me.

"Kate," he says, handing his gun to me. "You can save yourself."

I snatch the gun from him with a trembling hand and take several steps away from them both. I wave the gun between them. Jesus and the devil.

"Give me the gun," Jesus says. "So I can protect you from the devil, Magdalene."

"I trust you, Kate," the devil says.

"Gigi, go get the gun from Magdalene." She doesn't move. "Go," he says harshly." She begins to walk toward me, but in just three steps she falls to the ground with a thud, screaming and gripping her ankle. It's bleeding.

It's as though she's been shot. But I didn't hear anything, and I don't see anyone. I'm the only person with a gun. It's the devil's trickery.

"He's going to hurt you, Magdalene. Just like he hurt Gigi. They've come for me. I'm not ready to go. My work on Earth isn't done. Don't let them take me. Shoot him. Shoot the devil."

I turn toward the devil. "It's going to be okay, Kate. I've got you," he murmurs.

In a heartbeat—I swivel, cock the gun, and take the shot. The boom reverberates throughout the church. The recoil takes me to my knees, and instantly, Smith is behind me, stripping the gun from my trembling hands. We watch the priest writhe, and gurgle his last breath on Earth.

"You killed him," Virginia shrieks, draping her body over his. "You murdered Christ."

I collapse into Smith's arms.

48

SMITH

Delilah drags me out of Kate's room when the Sexual Assault Nurse Examiner arrives to collect evidence for the rape kit. "If she wants you to know what happened," Delilah says, "she'll tell you. In her time."

"She can't be alone in there."

"I'll stay with her until Fiona gets here. We can call Gabby, if she prefers, or if you think it would be better. It's her story to tell, Smith. You don't get to learn the details by overhearing them. Not if you ever expect to be the man in her life."

"Fine," I snap. "Go. But give me your weapon. It was fired."

"I didn't take a single shot," she says. "Although I considered shooting you when you gave her your gun."

I ignore the last remark. "Who shot Virginia?"

"I'm not sure. It came from up top. I didn't detect any movement. But I couldn't leave my position. You gave a delirious woman your weapon. What the fuck, Smith?"

"You never saw anyone?" I ask.

"No. I went right over there when that bastard excuse for a priest was laying on the ground. But whoever took the shot was long gone. I checked with Josh. He didn't come into the building until later. The FBI showed up not long after. That team was assembled quickly, maybe someone came inside before the rest got there and didn't want to be caught violating protocol."

I nod. "Maybe. Go be with Kate."

"I'll take good care of her. No one's going to hurt her without getting through me."

Not a soul leaves Kate's room for two hours, except for the nurse in search of a warm blanket. It's Charleston, at the end of July. The only explanation for a warm blanket is—the fuck if I know. The nurse assures me she's holding up well. But that's all she's willing to say.

Soldiers are good at waiting. That's mostly what we do. But I'm climbing the walls right now. Blaming myself at every turn. I knew there was something wrong with that priest. I knew it from the first moment I laid eyes on him with Kate. But I let it happen. I glance at the door hoping Delilah's nurturing skills are cutting it—and wonder if I should call Gabby. But I decide against it.

There's someone else who might be better to help Kate. Someone who has had decades of experience comforting young women who lost everything.

"Smith," a groggy voice says when she answers the phone. I didn't even give the late hour a second thought. "Is everything okay?"

"I'm fine, Mom. Sorry to call at this hour and scare you."

"You don't sound fine."

"A friend of mine was captured and held hostage for almost a week. We're at the ER now. She's got friends, but her mother died when she was a baby. It seems that if a woman ever needed her mother, it would be now. I'm wondering if you can come to Charleston. She could use your help."

"How is she?"

"Physically she appears to be okay. But—a week in captivity is a long time."

"She must be a very special friend."

"Yeah. But I managed to be one of the bad guys in this mess."

"When do you want me?"

"Give us a couple of days. I'm sorry, again, for waking you up."

"I'm glad you did. Sometimes a sincere promise to do better," she says softly, "with some real effort behind it, goes a long way to mending fences. Especially when it's accompanied by a big man groveling."

Although I can't picture it, I suspect my father has done a fair share of groveling over the years. "I'm not sure this is salvageable."

---

*B*efore the first light peeks over the horizon, Gabby and JD are at the hospital, along with Lucinda and all my people. Fiona is here, too. JD had his plane waiting in Boston so we could get her here as soon as we had Kate.

Her father refused to come. With all his law enforcement connections, he never lifted a finger to find Kate. I wanted to give him a piece of my mind, and drag his sorry ass here, but he's still drunk and cursing his daughter. He's on my list of people to deal with later.

The FBI and the Charleston police questioned me extensively, wanting to know how Kate got my gun. They stopped when I vowed to take out a billboard and sue their asses for every dead woman buried on the church property.

I never use my father's connections—not for myself. *Never*. But I remind every one of those bastards that he was head of the Joint Chiefs of Staff, and there will be hell to pay for every sonofabitch who knew something that might have stopped the carnage. That pretty much shut them all the fuck up, especially the police.

By the time I'm allowed to see Kate, she's sitting on the edge of the bed, ready to be discharged. She's dressed in clothes that don't match, but they're hers. I am overwhelmed with emotion. I don't remember ever feeling this way. We almost got there too late. But somehow—somehow—she managed to survive a week. Physically, anyway.

"Hi," I say, gently, taking a seat next to her on the bed. "Someone brought you clothes."

"Josh. Delilah sent him over to my house. Thank you for rescuing me," she says so softly, it's almost a whisper.

"You rescued yourself."

"I'm sorry—"

"No, Kate. You're done apologizing to me—to your family—to the entire damn world. But I have plenty of apologizing to do. Not now—but when you're up to hearing it. I have a lot to say."

"Why did you give me your gun? I could have killed you. I haven't stopped thinking about it the entire time I've been here."

"I wanted you to know that we're a team. That I trust you. And I wanted you to know you could save yourself."

"What if I had killed you? I was drugged. I didn't know for sure if you were real, or part of a dream, or a delusion, or—I could have never lived with myself."

"I didn't think about the last part—at all. Maybe that was wrong. I just wanted you to know—"

The door opens and a doctor comes in. I get up and offer to step outside. Not because I want to, but because Delilah is right. This is Kate's story to tell, when she's ready.

"Stay," she says. "Please." *Stay*. Such a small word, but it fills me with hope.

"You're dehydrated," the doctor says, "but the fluids we gave you will help. Your skin already looks better. Just as the preliminary bloodwork showed, you had drugs in your system when you arrived. I expect you were also given things that we can no longer detect." My chest is closing in and I want to go find that priest and kill him again.

"The CAT scan's negative," he continues. "If you don't have

someplace safe to stay tonight, I can admit you. Offer's still open. Otherwise, you're good to go. Follow up with a primary care doctor in a couple days—we found you one, and I would highly recommend mental health services. You've been through a lot."

"I'd like to go home," she says. "I have a friend staying with me for a few days, but thank you."

"You bet. I'm going to finish up the paperwork, and we'll have you out of here in no time."

When the doctor leaves, I sit back down next to her on the bed. "Can I hold your hand?" I ask.

She looks at me with gut-wrenching sadness, and nods. I cradle her hand gently in mine. I want to squeeze, but I don't. "We're not sure if there was anyone else involved. It's not safe for you and Fiona to be at your house until we finish putting the pieces together."

"King," she says. "It sounds far-fetched. But the priest called Virginia 'Gigi.' Do you remember what Judge Sorlin said about Gigi?"

I nod. "They've questioned her. Petey is King's son. He had sex with her when she was underage. There was some kind of botched abortion attempt, and the baby was born prematurely. Sorlin was a member of St. Magdalene's at the time. The priest took her in, and she's been there ever since."

"Father Jesse has only been there for ten years."

"Priest before him who retired. He wasn't a psychopath, just an asshole. Creighton had some trouble in the seminary, and in his first parish. They thought putting him at St. Maggie's—a dying parish, would keep him out of trouble. He kept King's secret."

"I'm so numb and exhausted," Kate says, hanging her head. "I don't have the energy to summon any anger, but I'm sure I'll get there."

"Everything in time."

She gazes up at me. "Did they kill Fenny?"

I suck in a breath. "Yes, according to Virginia. There are so many layers. Some of which are still being unearthed. We don't have to do it all today."

She sighs, taking back her hand and placing it on her lap. "I'm not up to any more right now."

"I want you and Fiona to stay at my place. I'll stay next door at the security office. There are beds there—we're set up for overnights."

"I don't think I should go back to Sweetgrass."

I ignore that comment. "Gabby wants you to stay in the main house. It's definitely more comfortable, but I thought you might like some space."

She twists her fingers nervously.

"I can set you up, and Fiona if she wants, upstairs at my place. Or she can take one of the bedrooms downstairs." Even though I mean every word, I grapple with the next part. "You don't need to be in my bed tonight, or tomorrow, or ever, if that's not what you want. The invitation to stay at my place isn't contingent on anything."

She's quiet, struggling with her thoughts. "I'll stay upstairs with Fi," she says after a little while. "We're used to sharing a room. You don't mind staying downstairs?" There's a knock on the door, and Fiona pokes her head in.

"Just checking," she says, coming into the room. Kate smiles at her. It's a weak little smile, but it's promising. Apparently, she hasn't said much to Fiona about what happened, but just having her around is comforting for Kate. I can see it.

"I'll leave you two alone," I say to Kate. "Do you need anything before I go?" She shakes her head.

"Smith," Kate calls. I turn. The concern in her voice seeps into my chest. "Please don't go too far."

"I'm not going anywhere. I'll be right outside the door if you need me."

49

KATE

Fiona went back to Boston this morning. We clung to each other and cried when she left.

I'm sure she was disappointed I didn't confide in her more while she was here. I couldn't find the words. She didn't push, and Smith hasn't, either. Although we really haven't had much time alone, and we won't for another few days because his parents are visiting.

I hear his mother in the kitchen making dinner. I should go down and see if she needs help, but I'd rather hide up here.

Neither of Smith's parents have said a word to me, but I'm sure they know all about what happened. It's awkward. Although, it's not just that. My relationships with older women have always been strained, with well-meaning souls trying to make up for the mothering I missed, or maybe they were just trying to curry favor with my dad. Either way, I've learned to shy away from them. Lucinda is one of the few exceptions. She's content with friendship.

As the clattering of pots becomes louder and more frequent, I decide staying up here isn't an option.

"Hi," I say when I get to kitchen. "Do you need some help?"

"I'd love some help." She glances at me with a quick smile before going back to pounding chicken cutlets. "Thank you for letting me use your kitchen. I'm not much of a woman of leisure, and as pretty as it is here, I like to be useful. I was planning on breaded cutlets and a big salad for supper. It'll be light enough to have blueberry crisp for dessert."

"It's not my kitchen, but I know it pretty well. Do you have everything you need?"

"I went to the grocery store this morning but forgot the ice cream. On purpose." She waggles her brows at me. Her eyes are light brown with gold. Same as Smith's. "Figured it would give my husband something to do this afternoon. He likes being idle less than I do."

She washes her hands and brings me a bag of green beans and a colander. "You sit right there and keep me company."

I start to trim the beans with a paring knife from the counter and notice her side-eying me. "Kate, don't feel you need to trim those beans fancy because I'm here."

Fancy? "This is how I normally trim them. Is there another way?"

She takes a bean and snaps off the top. "They're not as pretty or even this way, but they taste the same, and there's something satisfying about snapping the damn things."

She goes back to mixing breadcrumbs and spices, and I give her way a try. She's right. There is something satisfying about snapping the heads off.

"I'm sorry you're staying at the main house. I'm sure you would have liked to stay here with Smith."

"Don't be sorry," she says in a stage whisper, with the gleam of fun all over her face. "It's so much nicer over there. It's like staying at an exquisite bed and breakfast run by people you adore. And it gives me a chance to cuddle with Gracie. My children are scattered everywhere, and we don't like to visit too often. They're entitled to their own lives, but I miss my granddaughters when I don't see them. They grow so fast. Do you have siblings?"

"I have three brothers. *Had* three brothers. The youngest died in Iraq. No sisters."

"What was your brother's name?"

"Liam."

"I'm sorry about Liam. War is a terrible thing. Not just for those deployed, but for those who are left behind to carry on, and to worry." She's wistful. "You made quick work of those snap beans. You ready for the blueberries?"

"I think I'm up for the challenge. Any tricks?"

"Afraid not." She replaces the beans with two quarts of blueberries. "It's tedious."

"This is a lot of berries."

"I'm making a big crisp. Smith likes to eat it for breakfast. He never asks for much, so I like to spoil him when I can."

It's true. I smile to myself. After his run and a protein shake, he scrounges for leftovers before he leaves for work.

"My mom died when I was thirty-five," she says, with a touch of melancholy. "I was married with children, but it was still awful."

Here it comes. I'm not sure what exactly, but—

"My dad remarried a few years later," she continues, wiping up the counters as she talks. "To a woman named Alice. It was uncomfortable when he started bringing her around, but he had loved my mother deeply, and he was lonely. My sisters and I decided we were going to suck it up—to use a phrase my children are partial to." She smiles. "What I love most about Alice is that she never tried to replace my mother. She let my sisters and me dictate the boundaries to a large extent, and we each have a wonderful relationship with her—but all different. She was wise from the start. Mother's aren't like trading cards. You don't swap them out." She sighs, drying her hands. "How do those berries look?"

She just sent a message, in her own roundabout way, which is interesting because her interactions with Smith and her husband are very direct. But I appreciate it, because I don't have a heart-to-heart in me right now, or the fortitude to deal with direct. "The berries are plump and juicy," I respond with a grateful smile. "They're almost destemmed."

"Give them a quick rinse when you're done."

She looks out the kitchen window. "He's already back with the ice cream. That didn't take long. I hope you've got some errands to keep him busy. I don't care how many presidents he's advised, when he's sitting around with nothing to do, he's a pain in the ass."

I laugh. There might be plenty of people who have taken orders from General Sinclair over the years, but I suspect this woman, standing right here, isn't one of them.

"I don't. But maybe Smith has something to keep him busy."

"Now that would be interesting," she says.

50

KATE

I go down to the kitchen to find Smith's dad sipping coffee. "Good morning," I say, glancing at the toolbox at his feet.

"Good morning."

"Smith out for a run?"

He nods. "I noticed last night that this faucet leaks. I didn't mean to interrupt your solitude."

"My guess is I interrupted yours." The corner of his mouth twitches as he takes another sip. "Can I make you some breakfast?"

"I've already had breakfast, but how about if I get you something? I make a mean omelet."

He says it with such zeal that I laugh. "No, thank you. Just coffee for me."

It's quiet while I pour cream into my coffee. Almost too quiet. "What are your plans for today?" I ask, as he organizes some tools at the base of the sink.

He doesn't say anything for a moment, and the quiet vibrates in the room.

"Kate, bring your coffee and keep me company for a minute," he says on his way to the kitchen table.

I don't want to keep him company, but I follow his directions, because he didn't mean, *if you feel like it*. He meant, *get over here and sit your ass down*.

Smith might have his mother's eyes, but he has his father's strong jaw and his build.

"I'm not what you call a big sharer," he begins. "I mean, I'd share my last drop of water with a thirsty man or my last bite of food. Unless it was chocolate cake, then all bets are off." He smiles, and I smile back—his is wistful and mine is nerves.

"But I don't share my feelings. I'm a private man. Especially about things that happened while in combat."

I glance at him. He's clutching the coffee mug between his hands. "But there's something that happened to me when I was a young soldier that I think you need to hear."

His tone is serious, and although I don't know exactly what to expect, I suspect it's not a heart-warming story about teaching Iraqi children how to play soccer in an empty field.

"When I was a young captain, a mission I was on went bad. I was captured. Held for a month before they found me, and longer before I could be extricated safely." He peers into my eyes, seeing more than I want to show him.

"During that time," he continues, "I was beaten, waterboarded, starved, left naked in a room with rats who fed off my open sores. I didn't know day from night, and I was penetrated with objects by men who believed they were doing God's work."

Despite my numbness, I feel the trickle of a lone tear slide off my chin.

"I had a new bride, and a war to win, and a lifetime of shit to get done. Just like you. There's nothing that you can tell me that I haven't personally experienced, or that I haven't heard before."

We sit in silence for what feels like an eternity. "When you're ready," he says gently, sliding me a card with his contact information. "I'm a good listener." He stands and starts toward the sink.

"I don't remember everything," I say with a wobbly voice. "Sometimes I think I don't remember the details because they're too painful—physically painful—to recall."

General Sinclair comes back to the table and sits down quietly.

"I woke up chained to a bed in a cold room." The story, everything I know, begins to pour out. It starts dispassionate, a bubbling brook, but the storm surges, until the flood of emotion breaches the barrier and the memories spill out.

The general sits calmly across from me. He offers a pressed handkerchief but doesn't say a single word until I've gotten it all out.

"You did great, young lady," he says after I've quieted. "You had one objective, and that was to stay alive. You did it, and the enemy has been defeated. You deserve not only a medal, but a promotion."

"What if I had killed Smith? Why did he take that chance with his life?"

"Because he's a good soldier. A natural leader. He was born with instincts some men never learn."

I still don't understand. *What if I had shot him?* It haunts my dreams.

"He could have taken out the enemy, but that would have left you always looking over your shoulder. Always wondering if you could take care of yourself. You must be pretty important to him."

I sniffle.

"Can I touch you?" he asks, before taking my hand, just the way his son did. It's clearly something they were taught about trauma victims. Only from him, it's not so hard to hear.

I nod.

"Smith is up to this, Kate. He's been in some bad places with some bad people. What you have to say to him will surely feel like a dagger through the heart, but it's not the first time he'll have heard it, or something damn close."

"I don't know how we can go on from this."

"Because you're broken? Dirty? Ashamed? I felt that way for a long time. There's something about being sexually violated—and you were, even if you weren't raped. You were forced to watch what he did to that woman and made to believe your turn was coming. You felt as close to death as you've ever been." He grips my hand tighter.

"But not getting through it. That's bullshit, Kate. I can't tell you how, because it's different for everyone, only that you can. I'm sure of it."

"I'm not," I whisper.

"You gotta want it bad enough. My biggest regret was that it took me a decade to tell my wife what happened. I held the shame close. Took it everywhere, even into our bed at night. It didn't make me a better man, or a better husband, or even a better soldier. Don't make the same mistake."

I'm wiping away tears when the kitchen door slams shut. "What the fuck did you say to her?"

General Sinclair stands, with his shoulders squared and his head high.

"Smith, stop!" I jump up. "Please, stop. He didn't do anything."

"I don't need you to defend me, Kate," he says, before turning to his son whose hands are fisted at his side. "I told her some things she needed to hear. I don't need your permission, son, to talk to anyone. And if I were you, I would learn to use my words more judiciously. This might be your home, but I still outrank you in every way that counts."

He lays a comforting hand on my shoulder. "I know it doesn't seem like it, but everything I said earlier about him, it was all true."

I turn and wrap my arms around him, clinging tightly as he embraces me. He's a four-star general, the former head of the

Joint Chiefs. I'm not under his command or his responsibility. He doesn't even know me, but he threw me a rope, one human being to another, and secured it to an anchor. He recognized that I needed to talk but didn't know how. He trusted me with, perhaps, his darkest secret, *even though I'm a reporter.*

"Thank you," I say quietly. It hardly seems like enough.

"Hang onto that card," he tells me, before giving Smith a stern look, and walking out the door.

"What happened with my father?"

I'm not sure what to say. "He told me about an experience he had as a young soldier."

"When he was captured?"

"If you want the details, you'll have to ask him."

Smith nods. "You sure you're okay?" I expect him to pull me in, but he's still careful about my personal space, and he doesn't. It's another one of the many things that's changed between us.

"I'm fine."

"Why are his damn tools all over my kitchen?" he asks, in an obvious pivot. I'm sure the changes eat at him, too.

51

SMITH

My father is fixing a leaky faucet that I keep forgetting about. Something about seeing him taking care of it makes me feel inadequate. Like I'm not man enough to take care of my own business.

"You don't have to do that," I say more gruffly than I intend. "I'm capable of putting in a new washer."

"It's the gasket, and you've got a lot on your hands. I've got nothing but time on mine. Retirement is horseshit."

My mother has stronger words for it. I'm sure he's insufferable hanging around the house without wars to plan, or troops to inspect, or presidents to confer with. I owe him an apology, and this seems like as good a time as any to grovel.

"I don't know what you told Kate, but she seemed to appreciate it. I'm sorry—I was disrespectful earlier—but she's been through a lot, and sometimes you're heavy-handed."

He chuckles. "I have a wife, three daughters, and five granddaughters. All of them handfuls—especially the wife. I have plenty of experience talking to women. Hand me that socket wrench, will you?"

"I can fix the leak later."

He ignores me. "She's going to need some time, and someone to listen without judgment, and without flying off the handle when they hear the story. I told her you're up to the job." He grunts as he pulls off the washer. "Why didn't you call me when you knew they had her—before you went in?"

"I knew I could take care of it."

"Men don't go in alone."

"I wasn't alone."

He hands me the wrench. "You took a risk handing her the gun. She was disoriented."

The image of Kate in that church is something I'll never get out of my mind. "It was important."

"I told her that, too."

"I didn't call because it was a simple extrication that any rookie could have successfully completed."

"Extrications are never as simple as they look from the outside. You can't plan for all the contingencies. That one certainly wasn't simple. The thing that made it complicated was how much you care about the hostage. It would have been prudent to run the plan by someone."

"I'm sorry I disappointed you."

"I'm not disappointed, although the plan was ill-advised. But do you know how many times I've headed into danger with an ill-advised plan?"

I shake my head. "Not about the rescue. I'm sorry I left the Army—that I didn't make it a career. I don't regret the decision, but I'm sure it was hard for you to swallow."

"You'd have never been satisfied with their plan for you. Not at your age."

"I volunteered to give up a piece of my liver—it was an excuse for getting out. I'd had enough of the politics. That doesn't make me a very good soldier."

"You are the best kind of soldier. You served with honor."

"I didn't want to follow orders anymore."

"So you left. That's what good soldiers do. What they don't do is stay in, and then do whatever the fuck they want. You served honorably right up until the moment you were discharged. You have never disappointed me. Was I disappointed by your decision? Not going to lie—you're the kind of man that men like me dream of having under our command. It's a loss to the United States military and to the country. So yes, I was disappointed in the way it worked out, but never in you, son. Never in you."

He looks up at me. "But when I hear you talk like this—I'm disappointed in myself that I didn't speak up. That I didn't tell you how proud I am, and have always been, to be your father. I'm sorry I pushed you into the military."

"You didn't push me. From as far back as I can remember, I wanted to be a soldier—like you. It was an honor to serve … until it wasn't."

"You didn't go to West Point because your mother believed you should have a choice. She understood that you had a rebellious streak in you that would make following orders that didn't comport with your worldview difficult. I thought it made you a badass. I should have bent over backwards to make sure you looked carefully at all the choices."

"I don't regret one second of it," I say firmly. It's the truth. "It's just the politics became too complicated, and it was showing up in all sorts of ways that made it hard for me to sleep at night."

"I respect that. More than you can imagine. And what you're doing—what you're planning to do—I respect that too. Not everyone who serves wears a uniform."

"What I'm planning requires a good deal of expertise and sound judgment. JD is helping me get the business aspect off the ground. But there's the planning and execution—I could use some advice with that part."

"You want me to work for you?"

I laugh because he asks it in a way that screams, "You have to be fucking kidding me, kid."

"Yeah."

"It would be an honor, soldier. But I promised my wife I'd retire, so it will have to be strictly on a consultant basis. She probably doesn't need to know the details. And I still outrank you, of course."

"I could have fixed that faucet about three times by now. I think you've been polishing the brass for too long."

He hands me the wrench. "Have at it."

52

KATE

I'm alone for the first time since I've been back. Smith's parents left early this morning, and he's at work. I assured him I would be fine, but a panic threatens to derail me when the doorbell rings. I force myself to take several calming breaths. It's impossible to get onto the property. At least that's what I tell myself.

When I get the courage, I peek through the peephole. *JD.* What could he possibly want at this hour? I grip the wooden frame, opening the door.

"Good morning," he says, in a non-threatening way that helps me relax a bit.

"Smith already left for work. He's probably next door."

"I came to see you," he says pointedly, in that clipped tone he uses.

Immediately, I want to say, *I'm sorry I'm still here. I know you don't want me here, but I'll leave as soon as I can*—but I don't say anything resembling that. I'm through apologizing to every goddamn person just for breathing.

"What can I help you with?" I ask in a voice that's not aggressive, but not particularly friendly, either. It's déjà vu, I realize, only this time, he's the unwelcome guest.

"May I come in?"

I step aside. "It is your house."

"It's Smith's place," he answers curtly, on his way in.

"But you own it."

He doesn't respond to my churlishness. "I came to apologize."

My jaw falls open. He's caught me off guard and I don't know what to say.

"I'm surprised too," he quips. "I'm not big into apologies."

"Did Smith ask you to come?" Why else would he be here?

"Smith doesn't know I'm here."

"Gabby?"

"No, Kate," he says impatiently. "Despite what everyone seems to believe, I'm quite capable of conducting my own affairs without input from my wife. Although if she learns about this, it's likely to buy me a lot of goodwill."

I almost smile, because he's right.

"Gabrielle likes you," he continues. "And Smith liked you from the minute he set eyes on you. I did everything I could to discourage it. That was wrong," he says, sincerely. "You're Smith's person, and that should have been enough for me. More than enough."

He seems so contrite, so earnest, I almost feel bad for him.

"I know you've dealt with a lot of press in your life, and I'm sure that it's often been unpleasant," I say. He raises his brow, leading me to believe that unpleasant is not the word he would ascribe to the encounters.

"That's part of it. No doubt. But this was more personal than that. When you came around last year to do a story on my brother Zack, you ensured a top spot on my enemies list."

He takes no prisoners. I should have known his feelings for me were rooted there.

"I won't make any excuses or offer any apologies for that." I tip my chin up. "Your father sought me out. He encouraged me to write the article. He was the president-elect. I had no way of knowing what was happening behind the scenes."

"I know. But I protect everyone I love—especially those who can't protect themselves. That's my most important job in life." The man is intense. But what he misses in style, he more than makes up for in substance. I have to give it to him.

"That includes Smith," he adds. "Although the big lug can take care of himself pretty well."

As much as I want to, it's hard to stay angry at JD for protecting his brother, or Gracie, or Smith.

"You need to be good to him," he warns. "If it gets to the point where you've had enough of his shit, let him down easy. Otherwise, he'll be crying on my shoulder for months. He's a pussy."

JD and Smith are actually a lot alike at their core. For the first time, I see what they have in common. I try not to smile. "Delilah already warned me that I'd have to answer to her if I hurt Smith."

He lifts his hands. "That's a threat I would take seriously. That woman looks like she descended directly from the angels, but she is one scary motherfucker. Don't get on her bad side."

"You should tell Smith."

"He knows all about Delilah. He hired her."

"Not about Delilah. About how you were wrong not to trust him."

"Smith knows. But I'll remind him. I wanted to talk to you first. I might not be much for apologies, but I am big on putting things right. I am who I am, Kate. It's rarely pretty, but you'll never wonder where you stand with me."

53

KATE

Smith and I are eating dinner at the kitchen table, making small talk to avoid the elephant in the room. We're alone together in the house for the first time since ... I'm still not sure what to call it. *An abduction? Assault? Kidnapping? Imprisonment?* I don't know, but I suppose I'll eventually find the right word.

"Heard you had a visitor this morning," he says, side-eyeing me for a reaction.

"I almost didn't let him in, but then I remembered he owned the place."

Smith rests his fork and knife on the plate, giving me his full attention. "We can find somewhere else to live. It's about time I bought something, anyway."

"If you want to buy a place, that's fine. Don't do it on my account."

"Why not?"

Why not? Because I'm not staying. Because I can't bear to watch the fractures in our relationship widen until it splinters apart. Because I don't have the energy to repair it, to fight for it, or even for you. I'm exhausted, and broken, and trudging through emotion so dense, it seems impenetrable. I might never get through it, even if I live for another fifty years. But I don't burden him with any of that.

"I like it here," I say quietly. "It's comfortable and safe. Someone's always right next door."

He picks up the fork, pushing Lally's brisket around his plate without a bite. "How did you leave things with JD?"

"He didn't tell you?" That's hard to believe. Those two tell each other everything—or at least they did.

"He did. But I want to hear it from you."

He wants to hear it *from me*. The implication of those simple words is not lost on me. There was a time, in the last month, when JD's word was enough. It still stings.

"We talked," I say matter-of-factly. "He apologized for the way he behaved—toward both of us. Promised it would be different—*even though I'm a reporter, which still gives him heartburn*. Basically, he called a truce—more than that really—he gave us his blessing."

"What he thinks isn't important." Smith is dismissive. Too dismissive, and I don't buy it for one second. They've been thick as thieves for too long.

"If his opinion isn't important, then why did you keep pushing me away? Why were you so conflicted about dating a reporter?" Then I ask the question that burned a hole in my heart after he kicked me out. It's still raw, but there's so much pain now, it's a dull ache in comparison. "Why did you immediately take JD's side when Grace's picture was published?"

He throws his head back with a grunt. "My new business. I can't afford to have stories showing up in the news. My loyalty to the Wilders—to JD—played a big part, too. I don't deny it. And on top of it all, I'm an idiot." He hasn't looked at me or apologized, but I feel his turmoil from a few feet away.

"What's changed?"

"I'm still an idiot—and I am so sorry." There's distress in each syllable of the apology. "If I hadn't—" He pauses, for long awkward moments, with his eyes trained on the plate. The silence is so extended, so sober, I begin to think he's searching for an end.

"I want to build a life with you," he says tentatively, testing the words the way a newborn giraffe tests its legs. "I didn't want to admit it to myself for a long time—I wasn't ready. But when you almost slipped out of my hands forever, it brought it home pretty quick." He was searching, not for the end, but for a beginning. Wrestling with the emotions, molding them into words. "We can live wherever you want. Boston—it doesn't need to be Charleston."

My heart pounds with the blood rushing in my ears, so hard, I almost miss the last part. Build a life together—*I wish it was possible.*

"I'm broken," I confess, before I get too caught up in happy endings that will never happen. "I was probably already a little broken, but now—I'm shattered inside. The kind of shattered you can't fix." It's heart-wrenching to admit, even to him. "My emotions are erratic. They move at warp speed at times, until the build-up is so great that I might explode, and at other times, they stand perfectly still inside my numb body."

Although I don't have the courage to look at him, I hear every strangled breath. "I'd like to stay here for another week or two until I figure out what's next. If that's okay."

"Of course, it's okay. But two weeks isn't enough. I want more, Kate."

"I'm not ready for a relationship. And I might never be." I force myself to speak the words through the agonizing pain of a twisting knife.

He drags his chair against the wooden floor, until his knees are almost touching my thighs. "Look at me," he says, tucking the hair off my face. "You've been through hell." Hell? *Hell* sounds about right. "It's been less than a week. You're going to feel dozens of emotions while you heal. Sometimes all in the same moment.

There will be good and bad days. There's no linear path to recovery. That's not how it works. But you will heal. Until then, you're not going to be in any condition to make a decision about relationships. I have some work of my own to do, too." He squeezes my fingers. "The only thing I know for sure is that if you go your own way to heal, and I go mine, we'll drift apart."

"I killed a man, and I'm not sorry." I gaze at him as the words tumble from the depths of my soul. "I feel no remorse. Not a twinge of conscience. What does that make me?"

"Human," he says flatly. "I've killed more than my share of men in battle—"

"I didn't kill him on the battlefield."

"Yes, you did. You absolutely did." He cradles both my hands in his. "There are three kinds of killings that happen in war. Your conscience should be restless at two. The killing of young enemy soldiers, duty bound, not always there of their own volition, and the innocent casualties. People who are in the wrong place at the wrong time." He's pensive, bringing my hands to his mouth and pressing a kiss onto the them before continuing.

"The third type, is the elimination of evil motherfuckers who need to die. That priest was one of them. You're right to feel no remorse. He was a monster and his reign of terror would only end with his death."

I get up and begin to clear the dishes, because this is too much and I need to do something to deflect the angst that's building inside me.

"Don't, Kate. Don't walk away from this conversation. It's hard because it's important."

I freeze, my hands clutching the edge of a ceramic plate.

What we have—our relationship—isn't built for the long run. It might have been at one time, but fate intervened, creating a chasm between us that will only grow larger. I'm certain. Just like I'm certain that I can't face any more loss. But I sit down and have the discussion, anyway. Because it is important.

"The climb is too steep," I say softly, the dishes still in my hands.

"Steep? Yes. But *too* steep? I don't buy it." He brushes his palm along his jaw. "I'm not an expert on relationships, but I've watched my parents, my sisters with their husbands, even Gabby and JD. The struggle is what makes the foundation airtight."

The foundation already had holes. We patched them, but it's not even clear they were sealed—and then *hell* happened.

"I don't think I was raped," I say with a wobbly voice. He takes my hand, weaving his fingers through mine in unshakeable solidarity, and I continue before I begin to cry. "But I was drugged for a lot of it, so I'm not certain. But I witnessed—I watched him do things with Virginia that were a lot like some of the things we did—like some of the things, that maybe, you were hoping we'd do."

"What you witnessed, was it really like the things we did? Was it consensual and about mutual pleasure—and safe?" His voice is gentle as he ticks off the differences. "Did he respect her? Did he check in with her to make sure she was okay, and her needs were met? Or was it some bastardized form of sex? Of kink?" He lowers his head, his forehead touching mine. "Because I like to think what we did was pure—that it was something we both enjoyed. Not just a huge mind fuck, one animal preying on another."

It doesn't matter. I still see them vividly. I smell their filth everywhere. Their voices, the sounds of pleasure and punishment shriek inside my head when I lie quietly in bed at night.

"At the time, even now, it feels similar," I whisper, knowing I'm causing him pain.

When he pulls away, his features are flat. "We don't need to go there any time soon—or ever," he adds. "I'm totally okay with that."

I gaze up at him. "Now I know why you don't deal. You're giving too much away in the negotiation, Smith. Kink is important to you—you said so yourself."

"It's not—not in the grand scheme." I'm not sure if he's trying to convince himself, or me.

"Don't do this. Please don't do this." I sigh, tortured, but staunch. "You're not being honest with me—or with yourself. It's the sense of duty and honor imprinted on your DNA talking. You blame yourself for what happened, and now you're bound by a sense of responsibility to me. That's not a relationship that either of us should want."

"I do feel responsible." His head bobs slowly. "And I am. But that has nothing to do with why I'm here begging for another chance. Sex is one aspect of a relationship. It's not any more important than any other part."

Oh, Smith. "Sex is an important aspect of a relationship between two people who are as young as we are—let's not kid ourselves. One day, you'll wake up, and it won't be enough, or you'll spend your whole life compromising on something you said you'd never compromise on." He buries his face in his hands and I want to comfort him, but it would weaken the fortress I'm constructing around my heart. "You know I'm right."

When he lifts his head, he looks beaten. "Let's take it one day at a time. That's all I'm asking."

He's not making this easy, but I'm determined to save us both from any more sorrow down the road.

"I'm not sure I can. The feelings I have for you are already so intense. I can't get any more involved. It's not just the kink—I'm a shell, Smith. I have nothing to give. I don't want you to live half a life." I pause to catch the breath that the ugly cry has stolen and blow my nose on a paper napkin. "You deserve to have everything. I want that for you."

Smith pulls me onto his lap, smoothing my hair with his lips. We sit quietly for long minutes. The warmth of his body and the strength he projects is soothing. Eventually I stop sobbing and gasping for air.

"We're all a little broken," he murmurs. "Love is about finding someone who has the right glue to hold your pieces together. You're my glue. I've always known it—even when I didn't. But the fact that you care enough about me to let me go, even though you love me—and I know you do—it's more than I deserve," he chokes out, in a voice teeming with emotion. "Life is full of challenges—we were tested early, that's all." He pulls me closer. "Don't give up on us yet."

I feel the prickle of his unshaven beard against my scalp. He's been through hell, too. I do love him. I don't want to give up on us. Maybe I don't need to decide today, or even tomorrow.

"I love you, Kate," he whispers into my hair. "I'm not letting you go."

54

8 MONTHS LATER

Smith

Today is my birthday, and I'm on my way to Miss Macy's to meet Kate. She has something up her sleeve. First, she wanted to drive tonight. Then, she wouldn't tell me where we were going. Imagine how twitchy that made me. I finally managed to convince her we should get a driver for the evening. But other than supper at Miss Macy's, I still have no clue what we're doing.

It's been a busy eight months since I found Kate in that church. My business is off the ground and I have more work than we can handle. Things between Kate and me are rock-solid. In many ways, she's stronger than before the abduction. In others, she's more vulnerable. According to her therapist, it's a normal part of recovery.

Her therapist has been great. She's even helped us with the physical part of our relationship. Not gonna lie, having a weekly *prescription* for sex—that's what it's called—left me feeling more inadequate than I've ever felt. I wanted to be the man who fixed it for her, and no matter how many times I told myself it was beyond my ability, it was still tough.

It was also unnatural. I've never been the guy who got enjoyment from planning a scene. I like to keep a well-stocked playroom, get naked, and see where it takes us. Prescriptive sex was a slow process, consisting of multiple baby steps. First week we cuddled, second week was massage, third week was kissing, which turned into a make-out session where we incorporated massage. What happened next wasn't my fault.

Kate was giving me a massage. My eyes were closed while I tried to focus on something besides my aching dick. All of a sudden, I felt her lap a bead from the swollen tip, and before I could stop her, she was climbing on my cock. That's the story I'm sticking with.

Truth is, I've been more hesitant than Kate. I'm in this for the long haul, and I don't want to do anything stupid that could fuck up what we have now, or what we might have in the future. Soldiers understand the benefit of patience.

One of my birthday presents to Kate—the one she's never going to hear about—is that I didn't snap Ryan Donovan's neck.

I hunted down all four bastards from the night in the frat house. Two of the guys appear to have become decent men, with that night being more of an anomaly than a way of life. The third is a weasel lawyer, but the worst thing I could find was that he cheats on his taxes. He has a young son and a mother who he supports. As much as I believe they need to be punished, I left them all alone.

Ryan Donovan, the ringleader, and the one who took Kate's virginity when he was a man and she was still too young—the one who set her up that night—he's still a scumbag. No surprise there. He amassed a small fortune doing dirty deals, and until he got caught, cheating on his wife was a way of life.

I would have enjoyed watching him take his last breath—but

it was a present for Kate, not for me. After Silas Drury hung himself the night before his trial was scheduled to begin, she fell apart. He had been charged as an accessory after the fact in the murders of ten women. The state had a strong case against him. I was right about Silas. There was no way he was going back to jail.

Kate doesn't want any more death in her name—and I will respect that as long as no one comes near her again. But that sonofabitch Donovan wasn't getting off scot-free.

Chase and I collected every bit of information we could find about Donovan's whoring, and traced the assets he was hiding overseas. On Kate's birthday, right before we boarded a flight to have dinner with Fiona and Brett in Boston, I sent the entire folder to his estranged wife's lawyer. It was almost as satisfying as snapping his neck. *Almost.*

I see Kate's new car parked on the street across from the restaurant. Her old car had been found in the ocean, submerged off of Albert's Island. It had been pushed off the dock.

---

*K*ate and I have finished all the shrimp and grits we can stuff into our bellies, and she's still hiding something. She's the worst liar—and poker player. I laugh every time she tries to bluff. We'd be piss poor if she ever had to earn a living playing cards.

Jasper and Jolene, and the entire waitstaff, come over to the table and sing "Happy Birthday." I throw Kate a look, and she grins. I'm willing to play along with the nonsense for the big slice of chess pie and the bowl of chocolate ice cream they brought with them.

Kate is glowing tonight. It makes my heart swell to see her like this. I often watch her while she sleeps, or when she's busy and doesn't notice me. I came so close to losing her. I'll have nightmares about it, forever.

After Jasper gives me shit about being an old man, they leave us. "Where's your dessert?" I ask, dipping a fork into the pie. "Didn't want any?"

She laughs. "I thought we'd share," she says, bringing her fork to my plate.

I swat her away. "Forget about it."

As I take another bite of pie, she reaches over, dips her finger into the ice cream and brings it to my lips. "Midnight cookies and cream," she murmurs, while I suck it off her finger. It's so damn sexy, for a minute I forget that it's how I first described kink to her.

"Finish your dessert," she says in a husky voice. "The evening's just beginning."

"I'm good." Without another bite, I grab her arm and haul her out of the restaurant. "Put it on my tab," I call to Jasper on our way out.

Someone will pick up our cars later. Antoine is driving tonight, and from the look of Kate, I'm damn happy I made that decision, instead of having one of my guys drive. "Where we goin'?" I ask, leaning in for a kiss.

"You'll see." She speaks to Antoine in a hushed voice, and slides in beside me for the short drive to Tallulah's.

When we get to the bar, it's standing room only, and the music is slow and easy. "You want to play a game of pool?" I ask, after the waitress takes our order.

"I want to dance," she says, brushing her hand over my chest.

"Dance? What kind of birthday present is that?" I groan and complain as she pulls me onto the crowded dance floor, but I don't mean it, and she damn well knows it.

The lights are low, and I'm not shy about pulling her against me until my cock is pushing into her belly. "*Mmmm*," she murmurs, pressing into the thickening shaft.

"You are the best birthday present." I palm her ass, pinning her against me, while my lips find hers in a lazy kiss that goes on forever.

When I pull my mouth away, her eyes are dark, and she's gasping softly. She's gorgeous. I want her, here and now. It's only my more evolved ego that stops me.

"Do you remember the song that was playing the first time we were on this dance floor?" she asks, nuzzling my neck.

"*Mmhm*. There was more than one song, but I'm pretty sure you're talkin' about the one by Lady Antebellum."

She nods. "I like that song. It's a shame Beau banned it from being played in the bar." She's trying to keep a straight face, but when I grin, she loses it.

"Delilah is a snitch."

"You best remember that," she warns, still smiling. "Do you remember the secret I told you about the bathtub?"

She has that look about her that she gets. Part coy, part sass. The one that says, *you can fuck me, but you'll have to catch me first*.

"I'll never forget it. You still get off in the bathtub thinking about me?"

"Shower. The nozzle in there is *amazing*."

My dick can't take too much more of this teasing. And she's well aware, because she keeps rocking her hips into it.

"What do you think about when you're letting the spray beat on your pussy?"

She tips her chin up and meets my eyes. "The saddle."

I swallow hard. She smiles at me, angelically. And I swallow again. "I climb onto the saddle—it's already prepared. You caress my breasts and whisper how much you want to fuck my ass. Your voice is rough and sexy. Then you wrap both arms around me and slide inside, 'til both my holes are full." She says all that with her sweet mouth.

My jaw is on the floor, and I'm sucking air, trying to breathe. But I play along. "You wanted me to know."

"I did. What are you going to do about it?"

Fuck you right here on this dance floor right now, doesn't seem to be the appropriate response. While I'm searching for it, she continues to stoke the fire. "I think about it all the time. Is the saddle still in the apartment?"

"Not sure," I answer gruffly. "Haven't been there in ages."

"We should go check."

It's less than thirty minutes from Tallulah's to the Wildflower apartment. Have I mentioned I'm so damn happy Antoine is driving?

The privacy screen is all the way up and Kate is straddling me, rubbing her bare pussy all over my cock. My pants are on, but she lost her underwear somewhere along the way.

"Are you sure?" I ask, with my lips on her throat.

"Never been more sure."

I force my mouth away from her soft skin and tip her chin until we're eye to eye. "You don't have to do this."

"Don't be a chicken," she says.

"Kate." I don't want this to be some ill-conceived birthday present from her. One she's not ready to give. "Don't rush it, for me."

"Are you rusty?" She tilts her pretty head to the side, and her hair grazes my arm. "Have you forgotten how? I can show you how to use it."

"Wench." I sink my teeth into her neck until she moans. "I would show you, right now, how out of touch I am, but I want you needy and begging when we get there." I feel her lips curl against my skin.

When we arrive, Antoine drives through the crowded parking lot into the garage. A year ago Kate would have been thrilled to be here. I gaze at her. She's still pretty damn happy, but this time it's because of me.

We take the elevator up, and I drag her down the hall and into the apartment. We shed our clothes on the way to the bedroom. But I stop before heading into the playroom. I glance at her, and begin to have second thoughts.

"Don't you dare," she says, walking her fine naked ass into the room with the toys.

"It's here," she squeals. I follow her in, and pull her luscious body toward me, lifting her off the floor. She snakes her legs around my waist, rubbing herself on my steely cock.

"Let's start here." I lower her carefully onto a chest. "I want to lick your pussy until you're begging for it." Her eyes shimmer as she leans back on her hands and spreads her legs for me.

I growl as my tongue connects with the sweet pink flesh. My mouth takes her to the edge, but I don't let her come. It'll be better for her first time with the saddle if we don't take the edge off.

She's breathing heavily when I pull away. "More. I need more."

"There's more. Come with me." I take her by the hand, to the drawer with the silicone phalluses, wrapped in plastic. "Pick one." Her hand reaches for a long fat one. "No. It's too big."

"I like big," she says, her eyes on my throbbing dick.

"You're going to have big, princess." I bring her hand to my cock. "But they don't both need to be big." I kiss her, roughly, because I'm all out of gentle.

"Isn't there another attachment?"

"You are a greedy little princess." I brush my nose against hers. "There is, but I'll choose that one for you."

She's intently focused on my hands, as I attach the silicone pieces. "Are you going to watch or—play?" she asks.

I touch her cheek. "It's your fantasy. I'm just along for the ride."

She brushes her fingers over mine. Her skin is soft and warm. "Can't it be both our fantasies?"

I nod. "Why not?"

"I want you to play," she says, in a breathy voice, her rosy nipples furled tight.

"Then let's play." I lower the mount and help her straddle it. "Put your feet on the footrests for leverage. I can help, but it might be better if you insert it yourself."

She nods carefully and lowers herself onto the silicone cock. I don't take my hands off her. I'm so hard, my dick is leaking. "How does it feel?"

"Like a vibrator. Before it's turned on." I pull up a padded leather-covered board that's tucked underneath, and angle it so she can rest her chest on it when she leans forward. "This will prevent you from falling off. You can wrap your arms around it or hold it any way you like."

She's flushed, and her eyes are hooded. She leans forward, gasping when her clit makes contact with the ridged wedge. "*Ohh*. It vibrates," she murmurs, squirming against it, before pulling back.

"Feel good?"

"So good," she moans, forcing her body forward again. Both her arms are wrapped around the leather pad. She's angled, cheeks spread wide, and all I can think about is sliding into the tight little rosebud.

"You can move," I tell her, sweeping my hands up and down her back, and across her shoulders. "Ride it just like you ride me."

Her hips rock back and forth, tentatively at first, and then they sway from side to side. I watch her blissful expression in the mirror. She needs no more instruction.

"Smith," she gasps. "I want you, too."

"Anything you want, princess." I lube my finger and spread it over her pleated hole, before sliding it through the tight muscle. She moans as I press into her.

I feel the plastic cock through her walls. It sends a prickle into the base of my spine.

I add another finger, with my tongue in the hollow of her back, licking my way up, and kissing my way down, all while working her good, so she can take me.

When she's ready, I'm long past that. "Kate. Open your eyes. Look in the mirror." I lube her well and coat my cock with the thick liquid. I pause at the entrance. "Open your eyes." When she does, I slide in, an inch at a time. Carefully breaching each ring of muscle. "You're so tight with that fake cock in your pussy." I enter her hot body, slowly. It's sweet agony.

"Relax. Breathe. Push out." I remind her when I can form words. She always forgets.

Her face is sweaty in the mirror, her red hair matted against her creamy skin.

I'm nearing the end of any control I had.

When she begins to move, riding the silicone cock and grinding her clit against the ridged rubber. I begin to move, too. Deeper and faster.

Palming her breasts in my hands, I kiss her neck, and slide my teeth over her flesh.

"Look at you, princess." I wind her hair around my hand. It's soft and silky around my fingers. When I tug her head back she gasps. I feel it in my groin.

"You're so tight, Kate," I murmur near her ear. "I'm going to come so hard inside you." I push her forward with my hips, pinning her clit against the vibrating wedge. Her entire body tightens and she bucks wildly. The orgasm consumes her, milking my cock until I can barely see. I wrap my arms around her torso tightly, fucking her right through the waves of pleasure.

We gaze at each other in the mirror, while I thrust with abandonment. I feel her climbing again and force myself to find a sliver of control. When she trembles, with my name twisting its way free from her lips, a roar escapes from somewhere deep and primitive, and I empty myself inside her.

My legs are still jelly when I find the strength to separate. I lift her off the saddle, and sweep back her hair so I can see her face. Her eyes are closed, but she smiles at me. The groggy contented smile of a woman who has been thoroughly fucked by a man who loves her.

EPILOGUE

Two years later
Kate

In the end, I didn't want to go back to Boston. Not because I don't love Boston, and Fi, and even my family, but because I love Smith more, and the life we've built is in Charleston.

For months after *hell*, I lost entire days fitting the pieces together, large and small, until the puzzle was complete. There were some days that I only got through because Smith was beside me, and his rock-solid strength was enough for both of us.

With the help of Dr. Long we were able to track Fenny's original owners. Although I didn't know it at the time, Smith contacted her the night Fenny was killed. Fortunately, she had the presence of mind to remove the microchip before the guys buried what was left of the poor cat. The serial number on the chip helped us locate the original owners, Jessica Daniels and Rory Lister, graduate students in town. Rory was odd on the phone, but it was a strange call to receive, I'm sure. We agreed to meet at their home the next evening.

I spent the following day assembling a small scrapbook for them, with two dozen of the best photos I took of Fenny while she lived with me. When we got to the house, it reeked of weed. Smith coughed several times in what was a gross exaggeration, and within five minutes I could tell he was done with those two.

They hadn't known *Disco* was pregnant—that was her real name, and although they missed *the little bugger*, they never bothered to look for her, either. They couldn't explain it—she just never came home again. By the time we left, I decided to keep my photos. While Fenny's end was tragic, her last month spent with me was probably the best of her life. "Those two morons should *never* reproduce. The world can't take it," Smith said loud enough to be heard on our way out.

Virginia is serving a life sentence in prison for her part in the murder of ten homeless women, who nobody ever reported missing. *Don't get me started.* I spoke at her sentencing hearing in favor of leniency, because I believe she is also a victim of Father Creighton and Warren King, and all the others who covered up the abuse of a young girl.

It's been difficult for Petey, who doesn't understand why his mother can't come home. But his father has deep pockets and that's made it a little easier on the boy. It took sworn testimony, court orders, blood tests, and a threat to send the Federal Marshals to his doorstep, but Warren King is officially Petey's father.

Judge King never made it to the Supreme Court, but he remains on the federal bench. There were not enough votes to impeach in the House. At the time, I was speechless, but perhaps it's for the best. If he had been impeached and convicted in a Senate trial, he would have slithered away from the public eye. But now, whenever a case comes up involving— well almost anything, the attorneys ask for his recusal. Each time it happens, it makes the news, reminding everyone that he impregnated an underage girl and tried to abort the fetus without her consent. Even for a scoundrel, it must be embarrassing.

Smith and I were married at St. Claire's by Father Tierney, who had been such a big part of my life growing up. When he first proposed, we thought a civil ceremony made the most sense. I still wasn't sure about priests or churches, or even God some days, and Smith didn't have an opinion. He just wanted it to be legal so I couldn't get rid of him easily, as if I would ever.

But as the prospect of marriage sank in, I began to have second thoughts about being married by a layperson, even if he was the governor. The Catholic church had played an important role in my life, and in my family's history. Ultimately, I decided a psychopath, masquerading as a priest, wouldn't destroy my faith.

The only hiccup happened on the day of the rehearsal. There had been a funeral Mass that morning at St. Claire's and traces of frankincense and myrrh hung in the air, clinging to surfaces as incense is wont to do. It started with an unease and the bitter taste of adrenaline. Then my chest tightened, as the airways closed in.

I blamed the lightheadedness on pre-wedding jitters and not eating lunch, but it didn't fool Smith, or Fiona, or Gabby, or maybe anyone for that matter. It was a panic attack.

When I came clean, Gabby had the solution: have the entire church scrubbed by fire restoration experts. "With an experienced company," she assured me, "you won't be able to detect the smell."

When you have unlimited resources and are a former presidential family, like the Wilders, you can make things happen that seem like miracles to everyone else. The church was thoroughly scrubbed before morning Mass the next day.

I slept in my childhood bedroom the night before the wedding. With Joyce out of the picture, the room has been restored to my liking.

For weeks, I had been torn about my father walking me down

the aisle. He had a way of sneaking in little digs when I least expected them, and I didn't want anything to spoil the day. But I didn't want to be vindictive, either, because that would ruin my happiness too.

After watching me wring my hands about it for too long, Smith gave me the answer. "He doesn't deserve the honor, if you ask me. But if that's what you want, talk to him. Tell him straight up there will be no bullshit that day. If you want, I'm happy to have the discussion with him."

And that's what I did. Not Smith, but me. I should have done it long ago. When we were finished, my dad and I were both in tears. I was under no illusion he would stop overnight, but I was done tolerating the bad behavior, and we both knew it. My brothers were another matter.

My brother Tommy couldn't get any of the wedding weekend off—probably because he didn't try. I didn't miss him. Liam, however, I missed terribly.

Sean was deployed at the time, but he sent me his good wishes and a package containing my mother's rosary that he keeps with him. I hung it out my bedroom window the night before the wedding, because that's how Catholic girls from Boston ward off the rain before they get married. I held the rosary close during the ceremony, and then sent it back to Sean on my way to the reception. He's far away from home, in his own hell, and although I know my mother is with him, just as she was with me, I also know it brings him great comfort to have her rosary.

"*What?*" my new husband asked incredulously. "You want to make a stop at the post office, in your wedding dress? Today? What about the reception?" But when I explained, he gave my fingers a quick squeeze. "It's just a small detour," he murmured. "The guests can wait a few extra minutes."

During the ceremony, Father Tierney reminisced about my childhood, recalling my love of reading and of chocolate cupcakes with white frosting from Rita's Bakery. He never actually admitted to it, *but it was him*. He sent the cupcakes to school on my birthday. My smile reached from ear to ear. Smith kept glancing at me while I grinned like a fool, which made me grin longer and harder. I half expected him to lean over and say something lewd about my smile and the wedding night, or to pinch my ass. Thankfully, he did neither.

I felt my mother's presence strongly the entire weekend, just as I did while chained in the tower. She protected me until Smith got there. The gust of wind that prevented my dive out the turret window was her. I know it was, just like I know the nagging feeling that brought me to Charleston and kept me there until Smith and I could work things out was her.

I never did win the Pulitzer Prize for my mother and I never will, because I'm no longer a journalist. With Smith's support, I've forged my own path doing something I truly love instead of living my life in service to my mother. I'm quite certain she wouldn't have wanted that for me.

I write books now, telling stories of heroes and villains. They are everywhere, in all walks of life, sometimes existing side by side within the same person.

After I was able to remember the events of *hell* without reliving them, I wrote a book. There are both heroes and villains in the story, and plenty of heroines. I'm proud of the accomplishment. My mother would be proud, too. If my story saves even one woman, I will have honored her sacrifice.

Writing a book forced me to unearth painful memories and examine them closely. I didn't always like what I found, but in the end, the exercise made me stronger. It was cathartic not only for me, but for Smith too, because I didn't write it alone, of course. I relied on chunks of my husband's memory to round out the edges. To give life to the moments I wasn't privy to. I did my very best to convey a true and honest portrayal of the events as we lived them.

Bound is many things, but at its very core, it's the story of two people constrained by duty and loyalty to others, tethered with a hefty dose of guilt. It's about a hard-fought journey to love. Mine and Smiths. I hope you enjoyed our story.

---

*T*hank you for reading Bound! Find out what happens with Gray and Delilah in **DECADENT HERE!**

*F*OR SNEAK PEEKS and treats sign-up for my newsletter **HERE**

JOIN me in my FB group, JD'S CLOSET for all sorts of shenanigans **HERE**

*I*f you enjoyed Bound, please consider leaving a short review so that others can find it, too!

AFTER THOUGHTS FROM EVA

Thank you so much for reading my sordid little tale! I hope you enjoyed reading Kate and Smith's story as much as I enjoyed writing it.

What inspired me to write a book about a priest? Who is Sister Jackie? The answer to the second question informs the first, so let's begin there.

Many years ago, I was the director of social services at a small agency outside of Boston that served Portuguese-speaking clients. Sister Jackie came to work at the agency before moving to South America where she would minister to Portuguese-speaking families. She wanted to better understand the culture and practice the language. As ridiculous as it seems, I was her supervisor.

On the outside, Jackie and I appeared quite different. While we were both petite women, she was in her forties, reed thin, with short, straight sandy hair, and I was twenty-something, with hips meant for birthing babies, and long, dark wavy hair. She was modest and chaste, and, well, I was neither. But we were both passionate about social justice. Her passion was quiet and reserved, mine involved waving my hands wildly while I spoke.

Despite our differences, we learned a lot from each other. Mostly I learned from her.

Jackie was the first nun I had ever met who didn't wear a habit or expect me to refer to her as *Sister*. She taught me not to take more than I needed, and to this day, I still take only one napkin from the dispenser because of her example. She also taught me that nuns do not follow the orders of priests, nor do they take vows to serve them. Something the Sisters of the Sacred Heart and the Jesuits failed to mention during all the years I spent with them. She also told me all about her enlightened mother superior, who I never met, but so wish that I had.

Perhaps the most startling thing Jackie taught me, in hushed whispers over lunch, is while we often hear tragic stories of children, the abuse of women by clergy—of nuns in particular—is far more rampant. She was headed to the outer-reaches of Brazil to stymie some of that abuse.

I was surprised by the revelation. Growing up, there were whispers of priests and altar boys, but I had never heard anything about the abuse of women, and certainly not of nuns. Although much later, my mother told a story about how uncomfortable a priest had made her during confession, coaxing her to answer explicit questions about her sex life. She was a young bride at the time, and after the incident, it was decades before she went back to confession. Unlike her daughter, my mother was extremely modest, and the experience left her rattled and ashamed.

After about six months with the agency, Jackie moved to Brazil, and shortly later, I married, moved to Washington DC, and went to law school. Our paths never crossed again. About two years ago, right before Pope Francis denounced the sex abuse and sex slavery within the church, I came across an article in the glossy Vatican publication, Women Church World, written by Lucetta Scaraffia. It confirmed everything Jackie had confided in me years earlier, and much more.

Bound is a work of fiction. But as I've said many times, while I write to entertain, I can't seem to help myself from sneaking an actual fact or two into the story, or flashing a light, however brief, into a dark corner. This book is no exception.

If the story offended, I am truly sorry. It was not my intention. But if it gave you pause, food for thought, or if you learned something you didn't know, say a small prayer of thanks for Jackie. Above all, I hope that Bound brought you great pleasure and a small escape.

xoxo
Eva

ACKNOWLEDGMENTS

A psychopathic priest, a woman with Stockholm syndrome, an abduction, Mary Magdalene, a supreme court nominee who impregnates a teenager, and a love story—Yikes! What was I thinking? Of course, there is no way I could have woven all the threads together, without the help and generosity of so many kind souls.

Veronica, I thank you first, always, because this series would not exist without you. Neither would Eva Charles, the author. The debt of gratitude I owe you, not just for your professionalism, but for your friendship, is ever growing. Although you left me in the very capable hands of Heather Roberts, and for that I'm grateful, there will be no more babies in your future. One and done. I'm kidding, of course—mostly.

Catherine Anderson, thank you for being the blessing you are, swooping in and carrying this release to the end without batting an eyelash. You are truly a lovely human being, and a consummate professional, with mad organizational skills. Your gracious demeanor aside, you know how to get stuff done.

Dawn Alexander, there is not enough space in the back of any book for the thanks I owe you. Your patience and ability to cut through skeleton thoughts and barely formed ideas is unparalleled—as is your patience. I am so fortunate to have you in my corner! Thank you for your generous support, clear-thinking mind, and friendship. Sexy Sinner is next, and then back to Charleston! #teamsmith

Nancy Smay, I'm quite sure I'll never read or hear the words cock ring without picturing your highly descriptive definition. Even full-strength bleach can't wipe away that image. Thank you for your vast expertise on all matters, and for your unending patience with my love of commas. You're the best!

Virginia Tesi Carey, I nearly had a heart-attack when I first heard your February schedule. Thank you for finding a spot for me. At this point it's become almost superstition, but the thought of releasing a book without your eagle eye on the manuscript, pains me. Thank you for your ongoing support, friendship, and your generous spirit.

Stephanie Taylor, you were a new, and valuable member of the team on this project. I so appreciate your flexibility, good nature, and careful attention to detail. The book is better because of your efforts.

Tami Thomason, thank you for reading the unedited manuscript with an eye on the highly-complex timeline, for your unflagging support, and your wonderful sense of humor. Tom Hardy doesn't know what he's missing! Oh, and that sex scene against the window? It will definitely be an extra.

Danielle Rairigh, you are an amazing woman with a big heart, and a plethora of gifts. I'm still amazed by your close attention to storyline and plot. Thank you for your friendship and support, and for the positivity you bring to the world.

A very big thank you to Alessandra Torre, who when I was struggling with Bound, took the time to turn me around and point me toward the light. Every time I glance at the white board with multi-colored sticky-notes in my office, I think of your kindness.

Thank you to Letitia Hasser of RBA Designs who created the original cover. Lovely, talented, and generous. There aren't enough positive adjectives in any language to describe her.

Thank you to L. Woods PR, Enticing Journey, and Give Me Books. As always, you were highly organized, wonderful to work with, and just plain amazing.

To the bloggers, bookstagrammers, and bookTubers, there is no way to fully thank you for all that you do to promote authors, myself included. There are few professions where people spend hours of their time for the benefit of others, out of kindness, and not for the rewards. Thank you for your tireless energy and generosity in promoting Bound, and the entire Devil's Due series. I am eternally grateful to you.

To the readers, THANK YOU for embracing my Charleston series, and for all your love and support! Your generosity, kind words, and willingness to share the stories with others have given the Wilders and their friends tremendous life. What was originally meant to be a duet, is now a series. I am still blown away by all the love you've shown the characters, and me.

To the members of JD's Closet, I love, love, love you all so hard! You are my happy place. Your support, encouragement, naughty sense of humor, and friendship make every day brighter. I hope you find as much love, fun, and support in the group as I do. I also hope Smith lives up to your high expectations! #teamsmith or #teamjd?

Andy, there really are no words to describe how much I love you. There is so much of you in Smith—honor, character, loyalty, a sense of humor, and that take no prisoners attitude that emerges every now and again. Don't worry, I won't embarrass you by mentioning the sexy times. Not that you'd be embarrassed.

ABOUT THE AUTHOR

After being a confirmed city-girl for much of her life, Eva moved to beautiful Western Massachusetts in 2014. There, she found herself living in the woods with no job, no friends (unless you count the turkey, deer, and coyote roaming the backyard), and no children underfoot, wondering what on earth she'd been thinking. But as it turned out, it was the perfect setting to take all those yarns spinning in her head and weave them into sexy stories.

When she's not writing, trying to squeeze information out of her tight-lipped sons, or playing with the two cutest dogs you've ever seen, Eva's creating chapters in her own love story.

Let's keep in touch!!

Sign-up for my monthly newsletter for special treats and all the Eva news! **VIP Reader Newsletter**

I'd love to hear from you!!
eva@evacharles.com
Check out my website!
evacharles.com

MORE STEAMY ROMANTIC SUSPENSE BY EVA CHARLES

THE DEVIL'S DUE SERIES

Depraved

Delivered

Bound

Decadent

A SINFUL EMPIRE TRILOGY

A Sinful Empire (A Prologue Novella)

Greed

Lust

Envy

CONTEMPORARY ROMANCE

THE NEW AMERICAN ROYALS

Sheltered Heart

Noble Pursuit

Double Play

Unforgettable

Loyal Subjects

Sexy Sinner

Printed in Great Britain
by Amazon